THE SECRETS UNDERNEATH

... a powerful story about how the secrets and lies layered into our family history can affect generations emotionally, spiritually, and even physically. It grabbed me from the first-page and then built to powerful conclusions: our family secrets known or buried deep can confine us; and the truth, no matter how shocking, can release us from our pain and lead to freedom, forgiveness, and healing. It's a beautifully written book filled with hope, empathy and a compassion that is tangible and moving. I couldn't hold back the tears...This is by far the best book I've read this year.

— *Sean K. Fay, Lifestyle Entrepreneur & TV Producer, CEO of Envision Response, Seattle, Washington*

This book was incredibly wonderful, so engrossing I couldn't put it down... I read the book looking for the answers to many...questions... and found insight into my own defenses and walls. I feel a little undone, but grateful for the window into Love!

— *Catherine Kehoe Fallon, MA (counseling psychology), LMHC, Seattle, Washington*

The story grips you by page 3 and keeps you engaged until the end, and like all good books, it leaves you wanting more. This book is a journey to forgiveness and the power of healing. Lessons for us all.

—*Meg O'Connell, CEO & Founder, Global Disability Inclusion, St. Augustine Beach, Florida*

[This] book...brought me to tears more than once... the story was just lovely and poignant and raw and mystical and so many other things...I couldn't put it down!

— *Sabrina Jones Schroeder, J.D., Spokane, Washington*

I love this book!!! OMG it is an amazing story! I read it all yesterday...I couldn't put it down!"

— *Connie Whitman, host of Enlightenment of Change radio show, Middletown, New Jersey*

[This] novel highlights the danger in keeping secrets…[The story] presents characters in the aftermath of destruction brought about by concealing the truth, while also celebrating synchronicity, faith, and love in its ultimate revelation. As readers, we come to appreciate that the enemy is not death or grief. The enemy is refusing to live one's life, even amidst the carnage.
— *Nancy Miller, Co-author of Griefland: An Intimate Portrait of Love, Loss, and Unlikely Friendship, Olympia, Washington*

A great soulful piece—anyone can relate to this novel! The way [the story] weaves through space and time while developing characters…is marvelous! The subtle magic of each page made me unable to put the books down and even brought sweet tears to my eyes. I highly recommend this great read!
— *Amanda M., Therapist and avid reader, Seattle, Washington*

This weekend, I truly escaped with your book. I was so vested in Sean and his journey for the truth…I loved how each character was revealed in perspective for a 360 look into this broken family. And when I say escaped, picture…me lifting my head after midnight only to see that everyone was asleep and I had completely lost hours in your book. I haven't done that in years.
— *Nicole Martin, CEO at HR Boost; Author, Speaker, Futurist, Culture Coach, Chicago, Illinois*

… As a landscape architect I couldn't help but be drawn into Barbara's attention to environmental and psychological detail in the development of the people and place. Much like Margret Attwood's **Surfacing**, Barbara's use of horizontal and vertical placement of her characters, reflective retrieval of fresh and not always pleasant memories drew me through to the narrative's not-quite-expected conclusion.
— *Bob Scarfo, PhD, Spokane, Washington*

THE
SECRETS
UNDERNEATH

BARBARA MULVEY LITTLE

Better Life Press • Spokane, Washington

Published by *Better Life Press*
Spokane, Washington
BetterLifePress.com
BMLbooks.com

BarbaraMulveyLittle.com; Barbara@BMLbooks.com

Cover photos: © Mark Groves
Author photo: Maureen O'Brien, www.bench14.com
Book design: Russel Davis, Gray Dog Press, www.GrayDogPress.com

Print ISBN: 978-1-945843-91-4
ePub ISBN: 978-1-945843-00-6
Kindle ISBN: 978-1-945843-92-1

Meta: 1. Magical Realism: Fiction, 2. Medical mysteries, 3. Death, grief, loss, 4. Alcohol abuse and family violence, 5. Love and forgiveness, 6. Healing, 7. Seattle and Spokane

DEDICATION

To Keene.
My greatest supporter; my biggest fan; my forever love.

CONTENTS

PART 2

Prologue

Spokane Then

Spokane Chronicle: Front Page Headline Story
Thursday, January 16, 1986
Afternoon Edition

COP UNDER INVESTIGATION FOR MISSING DRUGS KILLS FAMILY, THEN SELF

YESTERDAY SPOKANE POLICE CHIEF STEVEN HOOPER confirmed that Detective John (Jack) Gallagher shot his family before killing himself Wednesday. Gallagher was one of two officers who were the subjects of a recently completed investigation by the Spokane police department's Internal Affairs Division (IAD). Following the results of that investigation, Spokane County Prosecutor Andrea Warner announced late last week that a grand jury would hear testimony about the case.

Chief Hooper was surprised by Detective Gallagher's deadly assault. "He showed no indication of this kind of violence," Hooper said. He added that Gallagher was placed on paid administrative leave in late November pending the resolution of the IAD investigation which began last October.

When asked about the allegations contained in the investigation Hooper declined to comment. However confidential sources inside the department said Gallagher came under suspicion following the disappearance of a kilo of heroin which went missing from the evidence locker last spring. The missing drugs subsequently forced a mistrial of an alleged drug dealer when defense lawyers claimed the prosecution had no evidence of a crime committed by their client. Gallagher was the lead detective on the case in which the drugs were seized.

Gallagher's partner, Detective James Bowen, who was also placed on administrative leave, denies any wrong doing by both detectives. Bowen insists that neither he nor Gallagher were dirty cops. He also noted that Gallagher earned six commendations for his work with the vice squad. "Jack was a good man," Bowen said. "He just snapped under all the pressure from this ridiculous investigation."

This is a tragic end for a man who was a local hero for decades. Gallagher was a high school and college football star, then a decorated Marine before he joined the FBI. During an undercover operation in 1979, Gallagher was held hostage and then shot during a daring escape. He survived alone in the Idaho wilderness for three days before being rescued. His injuries forced him to take a disability retirement from the FBI in January of 1980. A source close to the family speculated that the anniversary of Gallagher's forced retirement may have played a role in the timing of the tragedy.

A police informant has also surfaced saying that for the past two years Gallagher has paid him with cash and preferential treatment to keep Gallagher in a steady supply of narcotics and amphetamines. If these allegations of drug use are confirmed by the medical examiner's autopsy report due at the end of the month, they could possibly explain Gallagher's actions.

Funeral services for Gallagher's wife, Quinn Kelly Gallagher, 40, and two of their children Daniel, 16, and Colleen, 13, are pending. No date was given and spokesperson for the family, Brendan Gallagher, refused to comment except to say the services will be private.

A spokesperson for Spokane Prep High school confirmed that Quinn Kelly Gallagher had once been a teacher there and that two Gallagher children were current students. Daniel was a junior and three-year veteran of the varsity soccer team and Colleen was a freshman starter on the girls varsity soccer team. Grief counselors are at the school to assist classmates and faculty in dealing with this tragedy. Plans for a memorial service at the school to honor the slain students will be forthcoming.

The only survivor and youngest member of the family, five-year-old Sean-Patrick, was airlifted by Mercy Flight to Seattle Regional Medical Center where he remains in critical condition. His aunt and guardian, attorney Regan Kelly, refused to comment on the extent of the boy's injuries.

PART 1

SINS OF THE FATHERS

The past is never dead. It's not even past.
—William Faulkner

CHAPTER 1

SEATTLE NOW | 2013

THE WHIR AND CLICKS of the espresso machine mask the distant blare of a horn piercing the predawn mist. It will be hours before the sun burns off the cool grey November fog that perpetually makes Sean Thomas want to sleep in. He exits *The Buzz Stop* sipping his usual Grande Americano with an extra shot and walks south towards the hospital. The heat from the cup warms his fingertips while the coffee's aroma tickles awake the remainder of his sleepy brain cells. Coffee is a multisensory nirvana, he muses, custom-made for Seattle weather. It's no wonder everyone here craves it.

Wind from the Puget Sound bites Sean's skin and muffles his hearing as he moves toward Pike Street. With his free hand he deftly zips his hooded jacket close against his neck and adjusts his scarf to cover up any leaks in a well-practiced routine for a man who walks to work every morning in any weather. As he waits for the light to change, he notices how the red halo around the traffic light facing him bleeds into the green halo of the light controlling the mostly non-existent traffic on Boren. The colors switch and a ghostly white-walking-man invites him to cross. In the middle of the crosswalk, the sudden squeal of tires startles him, sending hot liquid over his knuckles.

"Shit," he says looking once more up the hill. Headlights bear down on him. It takes a moment to register that he is directly in the path of a speeding SUV. At the last instant, Sean jumps clear. Stunned, he hears the engine's pitch rise after the SUV bottoms out on the flat pavement of the intersection and rocks front to back while the driver seems to struggle to regain control. The speeding monster then veers left, hurtles past the large colonnades that festoon a small triangle of urban parkland, plows through

3

bushes and careens onto a small chain link fence. The fence bends under the truck's weight as speed and momentum propel it into a deadly cart-wheeling roll. Then, with the appearance of a perfectly executed Hollywood stunt, Sean watches as the white SUV cartwheels over a second fence further down the hill and plummets over a retaining wall. A moment of eerie quiet—like waiting for thunder after seeing lightning—is followed by what sounds like a cannon blast as the SUV hits Interstate-5 forty feet below. The sound sends a searing bolt of pain through Sean's head but his feet move him toward the guaranteed carnage as he hears sounds of squealing tires and the smaller aftershocks of lesser collisions echoing below.

With the agility of a natural athlete, he jumps the fence and struggles down long vines of English ivy meant to soften the appearance of I-5's man-made cliffs that hold back the steep hills for this subterranean section of highway. Grabbing fists full of ivy and praying they will support his weight, Sean skids down the vines then jumps the final fifteen feet to the highway, rolling as he hits the ground.

A dozen mangled cars have settled helter-skelter across the highway having met with varied success avoiding the median and overpass support columns. The wrecked cars create a barrier halting oncoming traffic. The sickly-sweet smell of gasoline hangs ominously in the air as cries for help bleat through the concrete canyon.

One particularly unlucky commuter took a direct hit from the SUV, which tumbled off a blue car and came to rest in an upright position next to it. Years of triage experience kick in as Sean surveys the scene. The body in the crushed blue car shows no signs of life. Odds don't look good for the driver and front passenger in the crumpled white mess of the SUV either. The upper half of a woman, who apparently had not been wearing a seat belt, shot through the shattered front passenger window. Her broken body is folded over the door, her head dangling like an unstrung marionette. She is covered in blood. The driver, a man, is hugging the steering wheel, green-glass diamonds blanketing his head and shoulders; his face is turned to the side, eyes open and vacant. The partially crushed roof holds him in its vise-like grip.

Quick, methodical checks confirm no pulses.

Three dead.

Sean turns his attention to the back seat. The rolling crash broke all the windows and sealed the doors shut which would have made a rescue of back seat passengers next to impossible. Nothing. He sighs in relief.

A quick scan of the cargo area makes Sean's heart sink. Inside is a girl tightly wedged between duffle bags and other gear. Her right arm and leg are straddling what looks like a pillow; her head is folded against the backseat, resting on her outstretched left arm. Her face is tilted slightly up almost as if she is looking out the window. Sean notices that she has the awkward beauty of a pretty child on the verge of becoming a stunning woman. Thick golden-brown hair still streaked with summer highlights cascades midway down her back. She is motionless and unmarked. He would almost guess she was sleeping except for the odd, unnatural angle of her neck. Sean moves quickly to reach her through the back hatch. He climbs carefully through the broken glass into the space narrowed by the partially collapsed roof. He gently pushes aside the girl's hair touching her neck hoping to find even a trickle of life. He feels nothing.

He shifts his weight back onto his legs in the posture of a supplicant at prayer settling momentarily in defeat when he hears a tiny moan. For a moment he is unsure that he's heard anything more than his own hope. He presses again on the girl's neck. Definitely no life. Sirens begin to echo off buildings above and he is about to leave the SUV to check the injured in other cars when he hears it again. He raises the girl's lifeless arm. Beneath her protective embrace, wrapped in a blanket, is a young boy with the same thick golden-brown hair. The boy, about six years old Sean guesses, is unconscious with shallow breaths and a thready pulse.

"Stay with me kid," he says as he does a quick check for obvious injuries. He would prefer not to move the boy without first bracing his neck, but the kid's pulse is so weak he may not last long enough to worry about neck injuries.

Sirens now blare off the concrete canyon walls. Sean curses when he realizes the rescuers are not on I-5. The first 911 calls must have come from the apartments on Pike. The fire trucks and ambulances are lining up on the overpass but the victims are on the highway below. Entrances onto this subterranean portion of the highway are few and far between;

the rescuers will have to double back to the Madison Street entrance ramp and struggle through the parking lot the accident created. After what seems like an eternity, Sean hears the sirens whoop and wail in the tunnel under Freeway Park as they try to open a path to him.

But they are not quick enough. The boy's heart stops and his life ebbs away. Refusing to let the boy die, Sean gently places the girl in the back seat and throws the gear out the windows to make room. He lays the boy flat in the center of the cargo area, blows two quick breaths in the boy's mouth and begins chest compressions. This must be the only positive use for an SUV he thinks as he counts, one . . . two . . . three . . . four . . .

"Here!" Sean yells as he continues the rhythmic compressions hoping that one of the firefighters will get close enough to hear him. He can see them checking the injured in other cars and is frustrated by the noisy chaos around and above him. The whop-whop-whop of news helicopter's rotor blades drown out his voice.

Two more breaths again, then, one . . . two . . . three . . . With each compression he huffs, "Come on, little man . . . you can do it . . . come back to me . . ." Sean believes the young girl tried to save this little boy. He can't let her selfless act be in vain.

He will not let her down.

| FRIDAY | NOVEMBER 22 | 7:13 AM | SEAN |

"Dr. Thomas . . . Sean," Rose said as she lightly touched his shoulder trying to wake him. Sean's arms flail outward despite Rose's gentle touch. Realizing he almost hit her Sean mumbles, "Sorry."

Rubbing his eyes, he asks, "How's the boy?" and then launches into a second question before Rose can answer the first, "I slept through shift change?" Swinging his feet to the ground he notices that he didn't take off his shoes. Exhaustion had overtaken him sometime after 4 AM when he went to the doctor's lounge to stretch out on a couch whose days of comfort ended at least a decade ago.

"He is still unconscious, but stable. There wasn't any reason to wake you until now," Rose said. "There are reporters outside who want to speak to you. They're calling you a hero," she said dropping onto the couch the *Seattle Times* she'd grabbed from a newsstand.

"I'm no hero," he said. He tore off the front page, crumpled it and tossed it to the garbage can.

"Throwing that away won't make that photo disappear," Rose said. She smiled when Sean reflexively raised a two-finger salute as the paper hit its mark. "A friend in admin told me that the guys upstairs are planning a news conference soon and they're going to want you there. Stuff like this is great for the hospital's image."

"Almost getting run over by a speeding SUV does not make me a hero and I could give a rat's ass about image right now."

"You saved a boy's life."

"*We* saved a boy's life and besides it's my job. I'm a doctor. It's what doctors do every day," Sean said.

Sean had wanted to be a doctor for as long as he could remember. He wanted to save lives like Dr. Kovac once saved his. If anyone he knew deserved hero status it was Kovac. He not only fixed Sean's body, he nurtured him during his long recuperation and continued to care about Sean long after he was discharged. It was Dr. Kovac who'd suggested volunteering at the hospital when Sean was in high school to see if he really wanted to be a doctor. It was also Dr. Kovac who Sean turned to when he needed a letter of recommendation for college and medical school applications. Dr. Kovac couldn't fix Sean's life at home, but he was a beacon of hope for a better future. After med school, when Sean competed for the hard-to-get emergency residency, he's sure it was Kovac who put in a good word for him.

"Most doctors wait until the patient shows up here. They don't chase after speeding cars to get them," Rose said smiling.

Sean knew he wasn't like most doctors. Then again, he knew his whole life was a bit unconventional. Unlike so many of his colleagues, Sean was not a maverick and he knew he couldn't do what he needed to do on his own. Plus, the team approach he cultivated had the added bonus of helping him fill the void where family should have been.

One reason his team worked so well was his deep respect for nurses, especially ones like Rose. Rose was already a great nurse when Sean was in diapers and he relied on her experience and wisdom more times than he could count. In his estimation, she was the very best of the best. And she was also a friend, something that he was especially grateful for at this moment.

"Did you sleep long?" she asked in a motherly tone.

"Maybe three hours. Dreams," he said fingering the scar that bisected his head from his left ear to the back of his head. Rose had befriended Sean when he was a newly minted doctor and first year resident. She treated him almost like a son and he had confided in her about his bouts with nightmares that made a decent night's sleep impossible. She had convinced him to go to a sleep clinic once but the nightmares continued to torment him.

"I'd tell you to head home for a few hours, but that detective is back and asking to speak to you again. I hear the report on the victims is kind of odd. The detective thinks maybe you can shed some light on it."

"They died when the man tried to fly in a car," he said. "My guess is blunt force trauma to the head and body. Nothing odd about that. It's exactly what I'd expect."

"Well, yes but most crash victims don't have stab wounds too and the woman's throat was slashed. She probably bled out long before the crash. Looks like this one may be domestic violence of the worst sort."

Sean remembered the copious amounts of blood on the woman. He just assumed all her injuries were from the accident. He took a deep breath and shook his head. "I didn't imagine it then."

"Imagine what?"

"I could have sworn that right before the SUV went over the embankment, the driver deliberately turned toward it like he wanted to die."

"Well, the detective wants to talk to you about it," she said. "He's with the grandparents now."

"Grandparents? Someone's claimed the boy?"

"A couple from Spokane heard about the crash on the news last night. They called police and said they thought it might be their daughter and her family. The grandparents arrived about 5:30. The detective arrived about 6:00. They're all waiting for you in Michael's room. That's the boy's name. Michael Brennan."

"Crap. Another kid with a perverted kind of Irish luck," he sighed.

"Excuse me?"

"Nothing," he said as a quick burst of headache flashed behind his eyes. "Please tell the detective I'll be right there."

He stood, sniffed at the coffee in the coffeemaker and said, "Wait, Rose! Do me a favor please? Grab me a cup of real coffee from the espresso stand when you get a chance." She smiled at him when he handed her a five before she walked out. "I think I'm going to need it."

With no palatable coffee in reach, he splashed water on his face to help him wake up, then finger combed his hair. He pulled a set of clean scrubs from the stack of linens. As he put them on, he realized that yesterday was such a blur he couldn't quite remember when he put on the set he was wearing. It must have been some time after arriving in the ambulance with the boy. He had kept up CPR until EMTs noticed him in the back of the SUV. It was quite a dance getting the boy into the ambulance as Sean kept up the rhythm of the compressions—a moment that was now flashed on the front page of the newspaper. One EMT offered to take over but Sean wouldn't relinquish what by then had become a sacred duty to him. He couldn't quite figure out why he felt so connected to this boy, but he knew he had to see this case through himself. Without even knowing the extent of the boy's injuries, Sean vowed he would keep him alive after seeing how the girl had tried to protect him.

But there was something more to it than that. Michael reminded Sean of himself. Seeing Michael in the ICU yesterday, Sean realized how small, how vulnerable he had once been. Walking down the hall to Michael's room now, Sean again fingered the scar by his ear trying to catch memories that refused to materialize.

He both hated and loved that scar. He hated the headaches that plagued him since childhood that seemed to originate at the back of his head where the scar began. But it remained the only connection to his life before—when he had a mother and father who loved him. He was not quite six when his parents died. He was the only survivor of a car accident that created the scar. He woke up terrified and alone in this same hospital. Afterwards his mother's sister, Regan, raised him. She gave him food and shelter but not much more. Nurturing, something lawyers are not known for, was well beyond his aunt's talents. Her professional skills did help her obfuscate when he asked about the accident or his parents. Her well-perfected icy stare accompanied outright refusals to discuss his memories; and snarky condescension greeted him when he tried to explain his dreams or nightmares. He lived a lonely existence with a woman who clearly didn't want him, whose eyes never hid her resentment for him, and whose arms never comforted him—not even as a little boy when he would wake up sobbing for his mother. He often wondered if she refused to hug him because she was afraid he'd break, or that she would.

For years, he could only imagine what life might have been like if he had a real family to belong to. As he pushed open the door to Michael's room, he prayed that Michael would awaken to someone who loved and wanted him. Then, as an afterthought, he prayed the same thing for himself.

CHAPTER 2

SEATTLE NOW | 2013

FRIDAY   NOVEMBER 22   7:30 AM   SEAN

As HE ENTERED MICHAEL'S ROOM the curtains were still drawn; the muted television cast a flickering white glow in the darkness. The room's quiet was broken by beeping monitors and the squish of air from an accordion bladder attached to a tube forcing air into the boy's lungs.

A man with a great shock of white hair sat in a chair facing the television with his elbows on his knees holding his head in his hands, speaking in hushed whispers to the detective Sean met yesterday. An elegant woman was leaning over Michael's bed with her back to the men. Sean guessed she was in her sixties if she was to match the man's age but she looked much younger. She was stroking Michael's hair with her face close to the boy's. She was softly humming, the tune soothing. Perhaps it was a song meant to call the boy back to the nightmare of his life.

Everyone turned to look at Sean as light and noise from the hallway invaded the quiet darkness of Michael's room. Detective Santini stood quickly and took command, speaking first.

"Judge and Mrs. Powell, this is Dr. Thomas, the man who saved your grandson's life. Dr. Thomas, this is Judge James Powell and his wife, Anna. Michael Brennan's grandparents," he said. Before anyone else could speak Anna Powell rushed to Sean, her eyes pleading for any good news. She had that familiar expression of exhaustion and despair mixed with hope that only the grief of a bedside vigil can create. Her eyes locked on his as she asked, "Is Michael going to be all right?"

The one thing Sean hated about his job was giving bad news. Of course, Michael's grandparents had already gotten the worst news possible—their daughter and granddaughter were dead. At least Michael was alive and, for now, he was stable. Looking over the boy's chart, he noted there was swelling on the boy's brain. And, of course, he was comatose. There was no telling how long that would last.

"Michael suffered a lot of trauma, Mrs. Powell," Sean replied, "but he made it through the night. That's a good sign. We aren't sure of the extent of his head injuries so I can't promise there won't be some lasting brain damage, but he's so young. Kids can do amazing things. We just have to wait and see. His condition is critical but he's also stable now and that is a good sign too."

Tears began to well in Anna Powell's eyes. The veneer of composure that she had maintained began to crack. Sean was sure he hadn't answered all her questions or prayers. But at least he might have answered some of them. In a voice just above a whisper she said, "Thank you, thank you" as she stepped back to the bed, kissed Michael's forehead, then continued to stroke his hair. Judge Powell stepped up to Sean once his wife turned away.

"Dr. Thomas, I understand from the detective that you were first on the scene after that madman tried to run you down. You saved my grandson's life. I am indebted to you," he said as he firmly gripped Sean's hand. Then, with the tone of a man used to having his demands answered quickly he asked, "Please tell me everything you remember."

"Sir, let me finish checking on Michael. Then we can step outside and I can answer your questions and the detective's." Sean did not want to talk about the crash near the boy because he knew that comatose patients have been known to recount conversations that occurred within their hearing after they awaken. If Michael had any hope of getting well, he needed peace.

Sean went to Michael's bed, took out his pen-sized flashlight to check the pupils of eyes resting under lids as delicate as butterfly wings. No matter how often he tended patients this young, Sean was always amazed at how small and fragile they looked with all the equipment around them. He methodically went through all the vitals though he had just read through them in the chart. No setbacks. At this point, that was as much as anyone could hope for. He also checked the ventilator; its whoosh and click creating a steady cadence of life. Finishing his once-over of the monitors, Anna Powell's eyes met his. He knew she was silently asking for more reassurance.

"Everything is as we would expect, Mrs. Powell. His little body just needs time to heal," he said as he thought to himself, lots of time.

Sean and the Judge joined the detective who waited at the door. As they left the room, the detective asked if there was somewhere they could have a private conversation. Sean led them to the doctor's lounge. Detective Santini asked, "Dr. Thomas, tell me again what you saw yesterday just before the crash," mispronouncing his name again, accenting the last syllable with an Italian flair.

Sean was too tired to tell the detective his name was pronounced just like a guy's first name. He simply motioned for everyone to sit.

"The guy was driving at an insane speed down that steep hill on Boren. I was waiting to cross at the Boren-Pike intersection. When I got the green, I looked uphill just before walking into the intersection. I saw no one. I wasn't even halfway across when I heard the SUV bottom out on the intersection just above me. Before I could think, he was less than a half a block away. I dove for safety; he nearly ran me over. That hill is so steep most people brake all the way down but that guy was driving like he was in a race car. At Pike he bottomed out again and lost control again but he got it back and I thought they might actually make it. Then it sounded like he gunned it. I think he intentionally swerved left to head for the fences in Pilgrim Park. It really looked like he had gotten the car under control. If he hadn't gunned it, I'm sure he could have saved it."

"Did you notice anything about the front passenger?" Santini asked.

"No, it all happened so fast. Then when I was checking after the crash, I was moving so fast looking for survivors that I didn't notice much more than that she was dead," Sean said cautiously not wanting to reveal what Rose had told him.

"Thank you, Dr. Thomas," the detective said. Sean was about to correct him this time, but the Judge spoke first.

"I knew he would do it. I knew he would kill them," Judge Powell growled.

"How did you know?" asked the detective

"He was a drunk. A violent one. I can't understand what she saw in him. She was a smart, beautiful girl. A Vassar graduate for God's sake.

She could have had her pick from dozens of suitors. But she chose that controlling, lying, possessive, drunken bully. Why she couldn't see that I'll never know."

"Had he been violent with her before?"

"Hell yes. She left him twice before, but she kept going back. He'd beg her, he'd tell her he changed. She would believe him. But animals like him don't change. I've seen plenty of them in my courtroom. He was a loser and each time he failed, he blamed her. When he moved them over here from Spokane to get away from us, she told us not to worry. He had a good job lined up and things were going to work out great she said. But he started drinking again and then lost his job again. By then he controlled her every move. He controlled the bank accounts and credit cards, nothing was in her name. That fucker even used her money to drink. We sent a cell phone when he canceled their long-distance service but he found it. He called us and said we were interfering in his family. We had no right he said. Then he smashed the phone and sent me the pieces. That was six months ago. Lexi called her sister from work last week saying she was planning to go to a shelter and she would call us when she was safe. We never got that call."

As the Judge spoke, Sean's scar began to throb. He reached up to massage the back of his neck and the room began to swim. His vision began turning grey at the edges as buzzing in his ears overtook the sounds in the room. He leaned forward to put his head in his hands and his elbows on his knees.

Somewhere in the distance, Sean heard the detective ask, "Dr. Thomas, are you OK?" Then everything went black.

∞

"Dr. Sean?"

Sean jumped, startled by the little girl's voice. He had no idea where he was and he couldn't see anything in the blackness. He turned toward the sound and the partial form of a young girl began to appear. He could only make out her face, which seemed to be glowing with a light coming from within her. The rest of her body was hidden in the darkness that enveloped them both.

"I'm sorry, I didn't mean to startle you," the girl said.

"Who are you?" Sean asked. "Where are we?"

"My name is Faith," she said ignoring his second question. "Thank you for trying to save me."

Sean recognized her now. She was the other child in the car with Michael, the one who died. If she's dead, how can she be talking to him? He looked left and then right but he couldn't see anything other than the girl. He could see her shoulder now along with her face, but they were like a hologram. This is crazy, he thought. Where the hell am I? When the girl spoke again he didn't know if he'd actually spoken his questions or if she could read his mind.

"Don't worry. You're not crazy and you actually can see me," Faith said. "You're kind of asleep. You were talking to the detective and my Granddad when you, ah, well, you know."

But Sean didn't know and he was none too happy about that.

Faith continued, "I came to thank you for what you're doing for Michael. He would come too, I think, but he's scared. He's not ready to talk yet." She paused as if she were thinking. "I don't know if he can talk to you like I am since he's not all the way dead yet. There's so much I still have to learn."

"Learn? How can you learn? You're dead, right?" Sean asked. "You're dead," he said again with conviction. She was dead. It was a fact. "What the hell is going on?"

"Well, my body is dead," Faith said. "But it's OK. It's nice here from what I can tell so far. My mom is smiling all the time now and she is really happy. She said it was OK if I came to tell you what happened. She thinks it will help you somehow."

"What do you mean, tell me what happened?"

"You know, what Daddy did to Michael and me and mom before we died."

"Is Michael with you?"

"Sometimes. He can go back and forth but he's not dead. Not yet anyway. Momma keeps telling him to stay alive. She says he can have a good life. But he cries and says he wants to stay with us. I think he should stay alive too. Nana and Granddad need him. He likes listening to Nana sing and he likes it when she strokes his head but he doesn't like it when Granddad gets angry," Faith said as she came closer. Sean could almost touch her. In the light she cast he could see her face clearly now and he could see her arms and most of her torso but everything else was still blackness. He reached his hand out toward her and noticed that his arm was shaking back and forth. Faith noticed it too.

"Uh oh. I think they're waking you up. I'll come back to see you later. Thanks again," Faith said. Then she was gone.

∞

When Sean opened his eyes, he was on the floor of the doctor's lounge. Detective Santini and Judge Powell were staring at him as a nurse was squeezing a blood pressure cuff on his arm—the same arm that was shaking when he reached out for Faith. He unlatched the cuff, told the nurse he was fine and slowly sat up, resting his back against the couch. The nurse wanted him to stay prone but he ignored her pleas even though the room began to swim. He closed his eyes tightly and rubbed them before setting his hands on the floor hoping to steady the room. The nurse tried again to check his blood pressure, but he shooed her away saying he was fine. The nurse said he needed to be evaluated immediately. When Sean put her off again with another *I'm fine,* she left the room saying she'd be right back.

"You gave us quite a scare when you fell off the couch doc," Santini said. "Are you sure you're all right?"

Sean looked at the men but didn't quite register the question. He heard it but his mind felt fuzzy like it did when he awoke from some of his nightmares. He knew who the men were and he knew he had been talking with them before he was talking with the girl . . . the girl . . . did that really happen? Was he talking with Michael's sister?

"Sir," Sean said, looking at Judge Powell, "What is . . . I mean was . . . what was your granddaughter's name?"

"Faith. Her name was Faith."

True to her word, the nurse returned with a very large orderly pushing a wheelchair. Sean guessed she hadn't taken kindly to his previous lack of cooperation.

"Dr. Thomas, you're going to emergency," the nurse said. "You fainted. You need to be evaluated. Matt will help you into this chair." It was not a request.

Sean knew the policy so he decided not to argue. The sooner he was evaluated the sooner he could get back to work. Matt moved toward him reaching for his arm to help him stand.

"I can stand on my own, thanks Matt," Sean said as he got to his feet trying not to reveal that the room began to spin again. He really did need Matt's help and he hated that feeling. Sean didn't object when Matt ignored his words and used pro-wrestler-sized arms to guide Sean into the wheelchair. As Matt turned the chair toward the door, Sean looked at the detective and Judge Powell and said, "Gentlemen, it appears I'll be a bit indisposed for a little while. When I'm cut loose, I'll be back to finish this conversation."

"Don't worry," Santini said. "I have what I need for now. I'll be in touch if I need anything else. You take good care doc."

With that, Matt wheeled Sean out of the doctor's lounge with the nurse in tow. Once in the hallway, the overhead lights felt bright enough to scorch his retinas but closing his eyes made his stomach lurch so he compromised by squinting. With the slightest concern about his symptoms, he convinced himself that all he really needed was a few more hours sleep. After that, he was sure he'd be fine. But sleep was not in the cards for a while if everything went as he guessed it would. First, he would see the resident in emergency who would no doubt call for a neuro consult (just to cover his or her ass), and then the neuro doc would probably want a *c-y-a* MRI. If Sean was lucky, the neuro doc would be someone he knew well and Sean could convince him to forgo the MRI so that he could just go home and sleep in his own bed because right now he felt absolutely exhausted.

The evaluation by the third-year resident was competent, even if she was a little nervous. Nothing like feeling your every move is being watched by your boss. He tried to be a good patient and be just a patient, not a doctor, but it was more or less impossible. Sean couldn't help but suggest the neuro consult while the resident was finishing her notes. Not because he felt like he needed one and certainly not because he wanted one, but because he wanted his residents to think of everything when they were examining any patient.

"Yes, sir," she said. "I was just about to tell you I was ordering it."

"Do you know who is on call today?"

"No sir, but I'll find out and let you know right away." With that, the resident left him sitting on the exam table. He looked around and realized that from a patient's perspective the tiny windowless room was a bit claustrophobic. It was also sterile—nothing the least bit interesting to look at. And cold. Damn, he was cold. Just another sign of how tired he was. They did keep the rooms a bit cooler here in emergency since everyone was moving so much and those lab coats were much warmer than they looked. But geez, as a patient you just about froze your ass off. He made some mental notes about adding some small touches that would make the room less intimidating and talking to maintenance about raising the temperature in exam rooms to somewhere north of ice box.

The nervous third-year poked her head in the door saying Dr. Kenji Takano was on call today and he'd be down in about ten minutes. She asked if she could get him anything and he remembered that cup of coffee Rose was going to get him. He asked if she'd send someone to track down Rose for his coffee. He could really use that boost of caffeine now. He hadn't had any coffee at all yet and since the day wasn't getting any better on its own, he really could use some. And he asked for a blanket.

After she left, Sean asked himself what that resident's name was. He should know it. He tried to make a habit of introducing himself to all the new residents as they came on board for their rotation. But no matter how he tried, he couldn't recall her name. And he was so busy trying not to be a pain-in-the-ass patient that he didn't remember what she said when she introduced herself. Then again, did she miss doing that? Another mental note to self about training protocols. But first, he laid back and closed his eyes because ten minutes could last forever in a hospital.

When his old roommate, Kenji Takano, and Rose walked in his room at the same time he spoke to Rose first. "Ah, Rose, you are a sight for sore eyes."

"I wondered where you'd gone. I was wandering around the nurse's station down here when a very nervous resident asked if I knew who Rose was. Given that there aren't many Roses who work here, I figured she meant me. Then I knew she did when she said you were looking for your coffee," Rose said as she smiled and handed it to him. "You know I don't do this for any other doctor."

"Aww, not even me Rose," Kenji chimed in.

"Especially not you Ken," Rose said with a smile. Had Sean been a normal patient Rose would have used Dr. Takano, but not now. When Kenji had his emergency rotation during medical school, Rose had been his savior, too, more than a few times. Alone here they were all friends, not just colleagues. Sean took a big swig of his lukewarm coffee and said, "Nectar of the gods. Thanks Rose." He started to get off the exam table saying, "I feel well enough to go home now."

"Hold up there, buddy. That cute little resident didn't find anything wrong with you but that doesn't mean I won't."

"Kenji!" Rose objected.

"Sorry Rose. I meant no disrespect." Sean knew that was true. Kenji might be a bit of a jock and a big mouth but he was happily married to an amazing lawyer and had three little girls. He was a champion of equality for women. And he truly valued the different way women approached medicine. In fact, he had an absolute professional crush on a researcher who was making huge strides in her research on the workings of the brain. He couldn't stop talking about the breakthroughs she was making. If she'd been a celebrity, he would have started her fan club.

"So SPT, what's the problem?" Ken asked. Kenji Takano was incapable of calling anyone by their given name. Everyone had a nickname, except Rose (not that she would have minded but Ken respected her wisdom and experience too much for that kind of teasing).

"Honestly, Ken, I think I'm just tired. I had a hell of a day yesterday followed by a mostly sleepless night on the couch in the doctor's lounge up on four. It's been a while since we were residents and had to survive that way. I just need a good night's sleep."

Sean knew that wasn't quite true but he also knew that if he mentioned that he'd met the dead sister of the kid he rescued when he blacked out, he wouldn't only be having a neuro consult. Sean was pretty certain this episode wasn't all that different from the headaches he'd tolerated in the past. Since there was no organic cause for them, there wasn't any reason to believe there was for this one either.

"Stand up," Ken said.

"What?"

"Stand up. Let me see how you walk across the room."

Sean did as he was told. He was glad for the latte Rose had brought because the combination of caffeine, fat, and sugar did make him feel better. He walked across the room with no problem.

"Close your eyes," Ken demanded next, "And lift one foot."

"What is this, a sobriety test?" Sean replied.

"No, just checking your balance. I'm not saying I wouldn't believe you if I asked if you were dizzy, it's just that doctors are notoriously bad patients so we have to be clever to get at the truth, the whole truth, and nothing but the unvarnished truth, as my better half would say," Ken said as he grinned.

"Are you going to read me my rights next?" Sean said as he finished his latte and complied with Ken's orders. "See? Fine. Can I go home and sleep now?"

"Well, I'm thinking an MRI would be a good idea," Ken said.

"Ken, I don't need an MRI, I need rest. You know that if you call for one, I'll be here all day and won't get any rest. Just let me go home and sleep," Sean pleaded.

"Tell you what. It's Friday morning so I'll cut you loose without an MRI on one condition. You have to take the weekend to do nothing but rest. If you're simply tired from being such a hero, the weekend should be enough to set it right for an old man like you. Come see me first thing Monday morning. I'll check you over. If all is good, we'll chalk this one up to the stress and the exhaustion of being Superman and I'll sign the papers that let you get back to work because as of this moment, you my friend, are on medical leave." Kenji put his hand up to his mouth in a stage whisper and said, "It just doesn't look good to have the doctors dropping to the floor when the patients come in."

"Deal," Sean said. But what choice did he have really?

"One more thing, buddy-boy," Ken continued, "Go straight home, don't pass go, don't collect $100, don't flirt with any pretty girls in your favorite coffee shop. Home. Bed. Rest." Ken grabbed the door, tipped a non-existent hat and said, "Monday" as he walked out.

"Do you want me to call you a cab?" Rose asked.

"Thanks, but no. I'll get changed and walk home. Hopefully the fresh air will do me good. Thanks again for that coffee. It really saved me just now."

Rose walked with Sean back to the doctor's lounge to get his street clothes. Before leaving she told him she'd see him later in the afternoon to drop off some hearty soup on her way home. He was to look for it outside his door in case he was asleep when she dropped it off.

Rose was such a deeply compassionate person. Sean often wondered if things would have turned out differently for him if his Aunt Regan had even a speck of the caring ways Rose had. He'd met her kids. They were right around his age, two were older and one younger than he was; all three happily ensconced in relationships. Some even had given Rose grandchildren already so she only worked three days a week now so she could spend time with them. For her, nothing mattered more than family. Regan had never even worked part-time in that first year they were together. Never chose him first. Hey, but at least now he had Rose to look out for him when he really needed it. It was good to know someone cared, especially after Savannah left.

Sean had every intention of following doctor's orders but once he got changed, he decided to check on Michael just one more time before he left telling himself he'd relax and sleep much better if he knew Michael was still stable. It would only take five extra minutes and then he promised himself he would follow Kenji's orders to the letter.

On the way to Michael's room, Sean thought about Savannah. In fact, he had been thinking about her almost every day for weeks now. It was almost as if he could feel her presence again. God, even five years out, he still missed her as much as the day she left him. He hadn't had a serious relationship since then. What was the point?

He entered Michael's room quietly. The curtains were still drawn and the only light was the glow from that silent TV. The Judge greeted him with a hearty handshake, saying he was glad to see him up and about.

"I wanted to stop in once more before heading home. My doctor wants me to take the weekend off. He thinks the fainting is likely from exhaustion," Sean explained before noticing the woman with Anna next to Michael's bed. "Oh, excuse me. I didn't mean to interrupt," Sean began to turn toward the door when Anna stopped him.

"No, wait Dr. Thomas," Anna said, "I want to introduce you to our chaplain." The woman stood, turned to face him, and said, "Hello, Sean. I mean Dr. Thomas."

"Savannah!"

Chapter 3

Spokane Then | 1969

No one was surprised when Jack asked Brendan, his only brother, to be his best man and Quinn asked Regan, her only sister, to be her maid of honor.

The community room below the church was turned into a dressing area for the women. Jack's sisters planned an event around getting Quinn and the flower girls dressed. Regan told Brendan she thought it was all a little over the top, but Quinn wanted the Gallagher women to have their fun. Regan and Brendan were the only adults. The rest of the bridal party consisted of five flower girls, the eldest of Jack's many nieces.

All the women, including the mothers of the bride and groom, the nieces, Jack's six sisters, and Quinn and Regan, arrived four hours before the service with a stylist, manicurist, make-up artists, and brunch. A party before the party. For women only.

Fifteen minutes before the service was scheduled to begin, there was a knock at the door to the women's room. Regan peeked through, shielding the view inside the room. "Brendan, what are you doing here? It's almost time to begin," Regan said with a hint of impatience. Brendan sighed and lowered his head. She could see a flush growing from his cheeks to his ears. Sweat formed at his hairline.

"I can't find the rings. Jack gave them to me when we were putting on our tuxes, but now I can't find them."

"Who is it?" Quinn called from inside.

"It's nothing. I'll take care of it. I'll be right back," Regan said as she stepped outside closing the door behind her. She began her interrogation as Brendan paced in circles. "Tell me everything you did after Jack gave you the rings."

23

"That's just it, Regan. I didn't do anything. We were getting dressed, Jack handed me the rings, I put them in my pants pocket and now they're not there. End of story. Jack's going to hate me. He'll say I did this to get back at him."

"For what?"

"Shit . . . Nothing, for nothing," Brendan said refusing to meet Regan's gaze.

Regan stared at Brendan as he inspected the floor, apparently willing the ring to appear on it. She sighed. He still didn't look up. "Let's go over it step by step from when you got dressed," she said.

"I already told you everything."

"Don't snap at me. You're the one who came looking for help and that's what I'm trying to do. Are you sure you checked all your pockets?"

"Of course I did."

"Do it once more."

"Regan . . ."

"Just humor me."

Brendan fished into the side and back pockets of his pants. He wiggled his index finger inside the outer jacket pockets which had been stitched closed in the center. He did the same with the pockets of his vest. He patted his hands over all the pockets once more just to prove there was nothing in them. When he finished, Regan pointed to the handkerchief pocket on his jacket.

"I wouldn't put them . . ."

"Just check," Regan ordered cutting him off.

Brendan pulled out the pleated handkerchief and the rings fell to the floor. "I swear, I didn't put them there," he protested as the color rose up from his neck this time, turning his ears bright red and splotching his cheeks. Regan smiled at his embarrassment and kissed him on the cheek, then wiped away her lipstick with her thumb.

"You better get upstairs before they notice you're missing. See you in a few."

As he took the steps two at a time, Regan watched him disappear wondering if there was really anything between them. They had been dating for months now. When Quinn introduced her to the Gallagher brothers, she was immediately attracted to Jack but she knew he would never look at her the way he looked at Quinn. Quinn was the one who could steal any friend of hers, boy or girl, just by walking into the room. Regan knew the thefts were unintentional; it was just a fact of life. She spent years trying to figure out what was so different about her that caused every one, even their parents, to prefer Quinn.

With her father, she wondered if his preference was as simple as being disappointed because Regan wasn't the son he expected. Or was it just that he was a pompous-ass jerk? After all, who names a daughter after himself because he wanted a boy? Regan could never be the son their father wanted no matter how much she followed in his footsteps. Did Quinn catch a break simply because she came after Regan? That might explain it for him, but what was it with everyone else?

Regan really wanted to hate Quinn sometimes but even she was taken in by Quinn's charms. And sweet, charming, clueless Quinn wanted Regan to be in love, just like she was with Jack. She hoped Regan would be interested in Brendan. She said they had so much in common. Quinn, though, neglected to mention that she first dated Brendan but immediately lost interest when Brendan brought her home for Sunday dinner where she met Jack.

The only thing Brendan and Regan had in common was being the dimmer-planet older sibling in the orbit of the youngest shining star. Brendan was a pleasant enough guy, fun to be around, a little on the serious side so not usually the life of the party. But he had a dry sense of humor. He was dependable. And he was a genuinely nice guy. He worked as a high school teacher (calling it his vocation) and soccer coach (a thinking man's game he said). Jack was an ex-Marine turned FBI agent and wore the cache of his work like a super hero's cape. Brendan looked similar to Jack except Brendan had black hair to Jack's auburn. Brendan was smaller by a few inches and not quite as rugged as his baby brother but he was attractive in his own right. Brendan was normal, ordinary, comfortable, and safe while Jack was . . . well, Jack.

Jack was the guy who quarterbacked his team to the state football championship in high school and played some college ball on scholarship before volunteering for the Marines and Vietnam. He then joined the FBI after returning home a decorated hero for saving the men in his platoon during the Tet offensive. Jack thought the war protestors were traitors.

There was one way Brendan was just a little dangerous, a little out of the ordinary. Brendan was a conscientious objector. He opposed the war on geo-political grounds and he disagreed with it on moral ones too. After years of Jesuit education in high school and college, his heroes were the Berrigan brothers, not his own sibling soldier. He thought the war was unjust and that his younger brother was a pawn in a power struggle among men who hadn't earned the right to lead.

Two brothers could not have been more different in temperament and personality but they shared one feature that all the Gallagher siblings shared; crystal blue eyes that sparkled as they laughed, which was often. The whole clan laughed easily. That was so different from how Regan and Quinn grew up. Laughter rarely happened when their father was home from deployment. Their house was orderly and their father was regimented, even after he retired from the service. Regan could only imagine the blow-up Brendan would ignite if her father ever heard his political or religious views. Luckily, they didn't spend much time with her parents. In fact, Regan would regularly meet her mother for lunch just to avoid having to go to dinner at the family home. She'd make any excuse. Work, school, whatever. The less time Regan spent with her father, the more peace reigned in the family.

Regan liked being at the Gallagher house. There was always something interesting going on with one of the sisters (if only she could keep all their names straight), their husbands, or kids. Even though Regan did not want to be saddled with a passel of kids herself, there was something endearing about this huge Irish-Catholic family that wore their emotions on their sleeves and adored their "wee ones." Regan and Quinn were Catholic too, sort of. They lost their religious connection about an hour after Quinn's baptism, one of the few times their Catholic mom won an argument with their Protestant dad. Seamus Regan Kelly, despite his name, descended from Northern Irish stock and he didn't go in for what he called "that Catholic Pope nonsense." For a man so regimented and enamored with chain-of-command, he resented all the rules that came with being Catholic.

The Kelly girls were baptized but that was where their involvement ended until Quinn started taking lessons with a priest after she and Jack became engaged. Because she was nominally Catholic, they would have no problem getting married in a big church wedding, but she didn't want to be the only one who didn't know when to stand or when to kneel. And the more Quinn learned, the more she loved being Catholic. Regan surmised that, for Quinn, the absoluteness of the church was a good counterbalance to the cultural, social, and political craziness of the 1960s.

Regan didn't particularly feel a need for God and she certainly could not stand the authoritarian nature of the Church. It reminded her too much of her father. Regan also embraced the wildness of the 60s and questioned authority every chance she got. If she couldn't confront her father head-on, questioning any other authority seemed to help.

When Regan headed East for college, she had no intention of ever living near her parents again but then law school happened. She was accepted at only a few law schools (many didn't want women). But she chose the one in Spokane, the town where her father retired and where Quinn lived too, because they actively recruited her with a bit of scholarship money.

After so many years away and so much change sweeping the whole country, Regan felt she'd grown up enough to handle her father. She also fantasized that he would be so impressed with her accomplishments that they would have grand conversations over dinner during her law school years. The Colonel, she thought, would finally see that she was just as smart, sweet, and interesting as his darling Quinn. But dinner with her dad remained a sullen affair; if he wasn't bragging about his own exploits, he was focused on Quinn's. She wondered how her mother could stomach him all these years. Her disappointment that her fantasy never came to fruition made her even more driven to succeed and she planned on doing that anywhere but Spokane, a town that seemed to have completely missed the counter-culture revolution.

The year Quinn became engaged, Regan was in her final year of law school and she planned to pack up and leave for good when it was over. She told Quinn of her plans but Quinn had other ideas. She liked having her sister close by so she was determined to change her mind. Quinn knew

Regan needed a good reason to stay so she invited her to a Gallagher Sunday dinner. Regan knew her sister's motives but, she thought, what could be the harm? Quinn said the food was good and food made by anyone else was great for a third-year law student. And it turned out that hanging out with the Gallagher clan, and with Brendan specifically, was a welcomed respite from the constant competition for grades, internships, and standing. She even had some of those conversations she'd fantasied about having with her dad with Tim Gallagher (the patriarch) and although it wasn't her dad, the attention was nice. Besides, Tim had valuable connections all over the state and those connections would be useful when Regan graduated.

Regan became a fixture at the Gallagher Sunday dinner weeks before Brendan asked her out for a real date, just the two of them. It was awkward at first. It seemed as if they had both forgotten how to make conversation but eventually they relaxed and realized that with only two people present the conversation could include multiple sentences strung together without interruption. Regan continued to come to Sunday dinners, but now she and Brendan would get together alone once or twice a week too. They developed an easy friendship and, maybe, even a budding romance with few demands on each other.

Regan would have liked a little more passion, but it wasn't like she was turning down dates with other guys to see Brendan. He would be a pleasant distraction until law school was done and then she'd high-tail it back East, or to Seattle, or anywhere a high paying job might land her. She doubted the relationship would survive that. Brendan had never been east of Missoula, Montana—which was as far east as he ever intended to go he said, and that was only to go hunting or fishing. And he hated Seattle. Too many cars. Too many people. Not enough snow. And not a single Gallagher within walking distance. No, Brendan would not move away from his family and Regan could understand that. It was a great family. But the last place she wanted to be trapped was in Spokane near her dad. She loved her sister but she was a big-city girl who not only had the guts and ambition to make it in Seattle or San Francisco or New York or Chicago, but she had the talent too. She had already proven that with her pharmaceutical sales career. Top producer in under a year, right out of college. Now with a law degree, she'd be unstoppable.

Over the last six months as Quinn and Jack's wedding approached, Brendan's sisters would hint that it was time for him to settle down. Last sibling to find "the one" and get married. Tim Gallagher (Pops to his harem of granddaughters) was getting anxious for a grandson—a baseball player, a boy to take fishing and hunting, another star on the Spokane Prep football team. Pops complained good-heartedly about his overabundance of granddaughters saying that he was counting on his sons to bring some balance. "No foreign male seed could grow in such an estrogen rich environment" he would joke about his daughters' homes. What was needed, according to Pops, was for Gallagher men to begin making the boy babies he craved. All those "outlaws," as he called his six sons-in-law, were powerless in the face of Gallagher women and had produced nothing but granddaughters. When his sons-in-law noted that he himself had produced six daughters, he reminded them that he persevered until he got sons. None of his daughters were willing to roll the dice that many times just to satisfy a silly male bias. Pops was not biased he insisted, just lonesome for a little male company.

The ceremony went off without a hitch. Everyone oohed and aaahhed at how beautiful Quinn and Jack looked and more than one person commented about how their babies were destined to be gorgeous with some combination of Quinn's strawberry blonde curls and Jack's thick auburn tresses, which he still kept shorn in nearly a military style.

An open bar, hors d'oeuvres, and music got the party started the moment the guests arrived at the reception. Regan noticed that Brendan imbibed enough booze in the first hour to transform him into Elvis Presley. He seemed like someone else entirely on the dance floor. After dinner and the traditional dances between father and daughter and mother and son, Quinn beamed in Jack's embrace as they cut the cake with Jack's hand enveloping hers before daintily feeding each other with the photographer catching every perfect moment. Regan could tell her father relished his role as father of the bride. He began clinking his glass with his knife to get everyone's attention as the cake was served.

"I know it is traditional for the best man to begin the toasts, but I hope y'all will forgive me if I ignore that protocol," Colonel Kelly began. Regan rolled her eyes, especially at the "y'all" part. They hadn't been in Texas since she was a baby when her father was in flight training for the Air Force but he refused to let go of his Texas drawl.

"I always thought we would have returned to my great home state of Texas to find my girls some proper men to marry . . ."

"In your dreams," Regan said louder than she intended; drink no doubt had loosened her tongue.

Glaring at her before ignoring her outburst, the Colonel continued, "But a man who chooses to serve his country in the way Jack Gallagher does earns his stripes in my book and is almost, I say almost, as good as any Texas Ranger."

"Oh, Daddy," Quinn giggled. Regan remembered the stories their father would tell of their great-grandfather who was a Texas Ranger. It was one of his highest compliments for Jack so far.

"John Andrew Gallagher, I do not care how many guns you tote or how many bad guys you put away, don't let me ever get wind that my baby girl, my pride and joy, my angel from heaven who is more beautiful than the finest Texas rose, has one moment of heartache from you or you'll answer to me, son."

"Yes sir," Jack said as he jumped to attention and saluted the Colonel who, though retired, was in his dress blues, sporting a chest full of medals earned as a pilot before he moved into the JAG corps to finish his years of service as a military lawyer.

"To the happy couple," the Colonel said as he raised his glass in the air. Regan was halfway out the door as she heard the tinkling glasses and shouts of "here, here."

In the lady's room, she splashed water on her face and studied her reflection. Why did she let him get to her? And why couldn't she tell everyone what a sham the dear old Colonel was? He was no Southern gentleman. He was a tyrant who cared more about appearances than just about anything else. At home, he ordered Regan and her mother around like they were his lackeys. He so confined her mother's every decision that Regan was sure her mother wouldn't recognize a desire that was uniquely hers if it slapped her in the face. And if control of poor, plain Jane wasn't bad enough, their dear-old-dad ignored every one of Regan's many accomplishments while Quinn practically walked on water. Regan wondered if there was anything she could ever do to hear similar words of affection from her father.

She was the oldest child. *She* was supposed to be his pride and joy, his daddy's girl. It wasn't her fault she was a girl. She was as ambitious and as smart as Colonel Kelly; she had just graduated law school with honors. She had been a top producer in her career in pharmaceutical sales, a game where few women were allowed entry other than as secretaries (having a man's name didn't hurt there). She was attractive enough, though she had to admit that she was not stunning like Quinn. But none of that was good enough. Daddy dearest hardly ever even noticed her.

She studied her face in the mirror for a long time but she could not see what was missing that made her so invisible when Quinn was around. As hard as she looked, she couldn't pinpoint it. Fine then, she thought. She'd had about as much as she could take. Since she was so invisible, no one would miss her if she left the wedding reception now.

As Regan opened the door on her way out, she nearly tripped over Kit—Gallagher sister number three, Mary Katherine—and her husband Bill. Each had one of Brendan's arms slung over their shoulders, practically dragging Brendan.

"Regan, thank God we found you. Brendan's begun to make a fool of himself."

"Him too?"

"What?" Kit asked, confused.

"Never mind."

"Anyway, I hate to ask you to leave before the bouquet toss since we'd all love another Kelly/Gallagher wedding, but would you be willing to get Brendan home? He's had about ten too many and I think my dad may throttle him if he gets his hands on him."

"What happened?"

"Nothing, really. Just a stupid, really stupid, toast. Sibling jealousy no doubt. Brendan won't even remember it in the morning. But it would be

31

best if he is on his way now and since he's in no condition to drive, we were hoping you could just take over from here."

"No problem. I was planning to leave now anyway."

Bill poured Brendan into Regan's BMW (a prize from her sales days), saying, "Drive slow so you can throw his ass, excuse my French, out the door if he tries to vomit on these nice leather seats."

Regan laughed, "I can handle a drunken Gallagher, don't worry."

They hadn't driven ten blocks before Brendan cried out, "Stop the car!" He opened the door before the car came to a stop, jumped out and threw up like a high-schooler. Sheepishly, he approached the car and said, "Regan. I. Am. Drunk."

"Yep."

"I'm sorry you had to leave early."

"Don't be, I was on my way out anyway."

Brendan climbed back in the car, leaned the seat way back and asked, "Did they teach you any special tricks in law school to sober up a client?"

Regan chuckled. "Everything I know about sobering up comes from college. If I remember correctly, greasy food and lots of it seems to do the trick. You up for Sal's Diner?"

"Will it make the stars stop spinning?"

"Been known to happen."

Brendan raised a finger saying, "Momento," before jumping out of the car once again to wretch. He coughed a few times, wiped his mouth with the back of his hand then pulled himself together and gently settled back into the passenger seat keeping his head as still as possible. "Sal's Diner awaits us, ma'am," he slurred.

Regan kept quiet on the drive to the diner. She also left her window open forcing cold, fresh air into Brendan's lungs. The day had been stunningly bright and even warm but the nights were still frigid once the sun went down. When she parked the car she was not surprised to find Brendan asleep.

Since the diner would be open for a few hours still, Regan decided to go for a drive, letting Brendan sleep it off. She wasn't much in the mood for conversation anyway. Without a plan, she put the car in gear and headed north.

Chapter 4

North Idaho Then | 1969

Sunday   June 1   North Idaho   Regan

Brendan's snort startled Regan awake. Her back ached and her face was cold against the window. She wiped a bit of crusted saliva from the corner of her mouth as she tried to wet the insides. She hated sleeping with her mouth open.

The air was cold and it was dark still. For a moment, she was unsure where she was. Her dress and a drunken tuxedoed Brendan in the passenger seat brought it all back.

She had driven a few hours before pulling over. While driving, her thoughts hop-scotched over anger, disappointment, resentment, and sadness. She wanted to be happy for Quinn, she really did. But Quinn never needed her encouragement; Quinn always had their father's (and it seemed like everyone else's) rapt attention. Quinn the favored daughter. Quinn the beauty queen. Quinn the accomplished teacher. Quinn, the one who would never read *The Feminine Mystique,* never mind agree with even one concept in it. Quinn, the one who never participated in a sit-in to protest the war. Quinn, the one who so perfectly does everything she is supposed to do. And now Quinn, the new wife of Jack, the war hero turned FBI agent.

Regan hadn't been watching the signs while she drove and now had no idea where they were. She dozed longer than she'd intended following a close call with a small but startling ditch that warned her she was beginning to fall asleep at the wheel. She'd pulled over in the first reasonable turnoff and planned to close her eyes for just a moment but that moment must have turned into many given how her back ached.

The car smelled of stale whisky but cold air bit her skin when she opened the window to get fresh air. She had to choose between warmth and stink.

Warmth won. Even so, she cracked open the window a tiny bit and then grabbed the blanket she always kept in the back seat. She wrapped it around her shoulders and peered into the blackness.

She had no idea of the time but she could see the faintest light in the far eastern sky. When she looked directly above her, she could see thousands of stars. She had never seen so many stars before. They must be in the middle of nowhere. How typical. She's sleeping in a car with a drunk by her side in God-knows-where while Quinn is in some honeymoon suite probably bathing in champagne and eating strawberries. As usual, Quinn grabs the golden ring while she goes home with the booby prize.

A knock on her window made her jump. The warmth from the blanket had lulled her back to sleep and it was now fully daylight. A guy dressed like Smokey the Bear was calling to her, rapping on the window she'd used for a pillow. The full morning sun was glinting off a lake in front of her. She saw frost on the tips of grass and wondered again how far she'd driven the night before.

"You OK, ma'am?" Smokey Bear said as he knocked the glass again.

"Oh, god," she murmured as she keyed the ignition so she could lower the window enough to talk to him.

"Morning ma'am," he said in an accent thick with country. "Is there a problem here?"

"No sir. No problem. I just got tired driving last night and thought it best to stop and rest. I must have fallen asleep."

"Well, ma'am, we may not be a big city here but we do have motels and even a few fancy resorts in these parts for that sort of thing," he said as he eyed their wrinkled, expensive-looking formal attire. She wondered if he could smell the whiskey. "You and your husband look like you were at a big to-do last night. I guess your suitcases are in the trunk." She didn't contradict the trooper about the husband/wife thing and she hoped he didn't ask for licenses from them both. Regan played along knowing that Smokey had seen the Washington plates on her car and because she knew she'd better be married if she was spending the night—even in the car— with a man.

"Yes, they're in the trunk. We didn't have time to change last night after the wedding because I was hoping to find our lodgings but I got lost and tired. I'm sure you understand."

Brendan started stirring when she was in middle of her wedding explanation. He pried his eyes open and immediately raised his hand like a visor and squinted against the morning light. All she could think of was that she needed to pee so bad that if this cop didn't shut up soon, she'd wet herself. She had no idea what he'd been saying to her before he finally said, "Well, there's a little place to eat along the lake just down the road a piece and then Elkin's Lodge is not far from it. I'm sure that's where you were headed, right? Just continue on down this road a few miles and you'll see it all."

"Absolutely, sir," Regan said having no idea what Elkin's Lodge was but relieved to finally be on her way to someplace with a bathroom. She thanked the trooper, started the ignition and closed the window while Smokey was in the middle of his "You have a pleasant day now." She saw his shrug and head-shake at her rudeness. Pebbles spun from her tires as she gunned it more than intended. She was relieved when Smokey didn't follow her.

Brendan rubbed his eyes, then finger-combed his hair before asking, "Where the hell are we?"

"That is the question of the morning Mr. Gallagher," Regan snapped, "and as soon as I find out, I will let you know."

"Morning's not your best time of day, huh?"

"I do much better when I've slept in a bed rather than a car."

"Did I hear that cop call us husband and wife?"

"Trooper."

"What?"

"Trooper. Good ole Smokey Bear was a state trooper not a cop. And yes, he thought we were married. Given the circumstances, I figured it was best not to overshare. Where the hell is that diner? If I don't find a place to pee soon I'm going to explode."

"Want me to drive?"

"You kidding? After what you drank last night, you won't be able to drive for a week." She was about to ask him if he remembered anything when she spotted the diner. She didn't wait for Brendan to get out of the

35

car before rushing in to find the bathroom. He was at a table with two cups of coffee when she came out. More than one customer stared at them. It's not every day someone shows up for breakfast in a tuxedo or gown. Fuck 'em she thought, because now that her bladder was empty she realized her stomach was too.

After ordering, Brendan continued to read the restaurant's history on the back cover of the menu. There was also a little bit about the town, and photos that showed the owners twenty years ago. Now at least she knew where they were so all they had to do was figure out how to get back home. But first things first. A short stack of pancakes, two orders of eggs with hash brown potatoes, sides of bacon and sausages plus biscuits and gravy, orange juice, and endless coffee were on the agenda. Breakfast at its best. She might even order huckleberry pie for dessert.

Brendan ate steadily but not hurriedly. She watched him chew slowly and then alternate sips of coffee with sips of fresh squeezed orange juice. When his food was almost gone he said, "Let's stay."

"What?"

"Let's stay here a couple of days. There's no need to rush back and I haven't been to Priest Lake since I was a kid. Let's stay."

"You're nuts," Regan said.

"Look, I bet neither one of us had much fun at that wedding yesterday. Hell, I can't even remember what happened other than I drank too much. I could use a little fun today. Let's stay and have some fun."

"We can't stay. We have nothing to wear. Besides, no one knows where we are. I was supposed to get you home last night, not kidnap you."

"Aw, come on, Regan. We've always been so responsible doing what's been expected of us. Wouldn't you like life to have a few surprises? I had a shit day yesterday but I can have a good day today. Let's let loose some. Let's take a risk and do the unexpected."

It was the huckleberry pie that did it. Regan agreed to stay one more day just so she could have another piece. The next thing she knew, they were parked in front of the check-in for Elkin's Lodge and Brendan was inside trying to get them a cabin. They'd concocted a story that they just got married and were going to honeymoon in Hawaii but when they got to the airport, Regan couldn't get on the plane because she was afraid of flying. They got in the car and started driving ending up here.

Brendan jumped back in the car smiling broadly and holding keys up in the air like a cookie he'd just stolen from the cookie jar. "Success *Mrs. Gallagher!* Your cabin awaits. The desk clerk bought the whole sob story and we got one of the nicest cabins in the place. Some big party cancelled, so they had a few cabins free. He even gave me a deal since '*we lost our shirts*' on the trip to Hawaii," Brendan said laughing. "Turn left and go almost all the way to the end. We're right on the lake."

She laughed. She couldn't remember the last time she did anything this naughty. Probably because she never did anything this naughty. Her roommate would laugh with her but her father would shit a brick when he found out. She could hear the cut-off speech already. Quinn would never think to bring such scandal on the family, her father would tell her.

"Brendan, does this cabin have a phone? We'd better call someone and let them know we're okay before they put out missing persons bulletins." She could just imagine the rage her father would be in when he found out she took off with Brendan. She could only hope that if he knew she was safe at least the police wouldn't be looking for her car.

"No phones. We're on our honeymoon, remember? But I thought of that too and already took care of it when I was inside. I called my folks and they'll call yours."

"Careful with that honeymoon crap," she chided. "Oh my God, what did your parents say?"

"They hadn't even noticed I was missing and probably wouldn't have until dinner tonight. They figured I was at my place but I had to call them since they would have expected me for dinner. I didn't know your folks number but I knew your father would be looking for you today."

"Did they ask where we were or why we were gone together?"

"I didn't give them a chance," Brendan said. "I let them know we were going to be gone for a while."

"Brendan, I just need to get some sleep and maybe another piece of that huckleberry pie. Then we're heading back. I don't have anything else to wear and can't keep wearing this dress."

"One day at a time, my love," he said with a chuckle. "Hey, I kind of like the sound of that."

"Careful, buster. Don't start believing your own lies."

"It's not a lie. We've been dating for months now. I have feelings for you. I know this isn't a honeymoon for real, but let's relax into it. We deserve it."

They pulled in front of a small cabin at the end of a long driveway. The cabin had a deck running its whole width that faced the lake; the view was incredible. Inside there was a cozy room with a fireplace, to the right was a small kitchenette, and to the left was the bedroom. The bathroom was small but had all the necessities, like the bathtub Regan planned to use right away. It would have been a nice place for a honeymoon if they were really on one.

"What have we here?" Brendan said seeing the large basket on the coffee table in front of the couch. "Looks like that cancellation was a real honeymoon couple. This basket is full of goodies 'for the bride and groom.' No wonder that guy was willing to give me a deal. This room was already paid for. I wonder what happened to the couple who was supposed to be here?"

Regan heard him but had shifted her focus. She'd gone through the bedroom, into the bathroom and was already filling the tub. When she came out after the bath water turned cold, wrapped only in a towel, she found a fire blazing in the fireplace and the cabin empty. Brendan left a note on the coffee table near the goody basket. It said, "Regan: I've gone out to wander since I had some sleep and you need your privacy. I'll be back in a few hours. Sleep well, my love." He'd drawn a heart at the very bottom.

The clock said 4:30. She smelled coffee. On the bedside table she saw a sweatshirt with an Elkins Resort logo, a button-down shirt also with a logo, and a pair of shorts. On the floor next to her she found flip-flops in her size. The bathroom now held a hairbrush, a toothbrush, and toothpaste which she happily used. When she went into the main room, the fire was still burning and she saw her undies drying on the hearth.

"Ah, m'lady. You're awake and the picture of resort wear. Want some coffee?"

"Please," she said noticing that Brendan also sported similar clothing and flip-flops. "You've been busy."

"Yes I have," he said handing her a cup of coffee as she sat on the couch. "Sorry, I hope you don't mind," Brendan said seeing her eye the panties that he found on the bathroom floor and washed in the sink. "I had six sisters. Girls underpants are nothing special. I thought you'd want clean ones and they didn't sell those at the gift shop. It's the only thing open around here on Sundays. We do what we must. Tomorrow we can find a store to get a few things."

"Thanks. But Brendan, we won't need more clothes. We can't stay."

"Aw, come on Regan. You know you've got nothing pressing to get back to. Graduation was weeks ago and I can get a substitute to cover a few sick days. Let's just stay. I can sleep on the couch and you can have the bed. It'll be fun. I already picked up a few things to eat—that gift shop has everything. Plus, I already paid for the whole week."

"But . . ."

"But nothing. We've always followed all the rules and look where it's gotten us? We do everything right but no one ever notices because everyone's attention is always on our oh-so perfect, oh-so beautiful, oh-so accomplished baby brother and sister who somehow do everything so much better. So screw them all. Let's do something they can't help but notice. Let's just stay here for the week. We'll relax. We'll have some fun. We'll generate a little gossip."

"We'll generate a LOT of gossip. Brendan this is crazy. What if your school finds out?"

"Yes, it *is* crazy. And that's exactly why we should do it." He sat down next to her, put his arm around her and gave her a little squeeze. "Look, you don't have to decide now. Have some coffee. We'll go for a walk around the lake and then have dinner. If you want to leave after that, we will. I found a map in that gift shop; we'll find our way back."

"I guess there's no harm in that and I would like to see the lake up close. It's really quite beautiful here."

"Great. Oh, and I got you a little snack to have with your coffee so you have enough energy for the walk," he said as he went to the kitchenette. When he returned, he carried two pieces of huckleberry pie with a scoop of vanilla ice cream on top. "See, the perfect meal with all food groups accounted for."

By the time their steaks came at dinner that night at the resort's restaurant Regan had agreed to one more night there. She had to admit she was having a good time and felt relaxed from all the fresh air and beauty that surrounded them. Her anger had dissipated some and she actually felt a little happy. She also had to admit she loved all the attention Brendan was showering on her. She also was enjoying their little ruse especially as she answered to Mrs. Gallagher when the desk clerk greeted them on their way into the restaurant. She hadn't seen this adventurous, slightly wild side of Brendan before and she liked it. A lot. Maybe she could love him.

"Let's stop in the bar for a nightcap," Brendan suggested as they passed it. Regan, having decided at dinner to be more impulsive, happily complied. While on their second drink, they were approached by a clean-cut man in his mid-thirties who asked if he could buy them a drink because they looked like they were having such a good time. They accepted and since he looked a little lonely, they invited him to drink with them.

After introductions they learned he was the minister who was supposed to marry the couple that was a no-show for the room they were in. It was supposed to be a pretty big affair. The bridal couple's families had rented out many of the cabins for themselves and their guests. The whole shebang was going to be at the resort from the rehearsal dinner on Friday through the wedding on Saturday plus a big brunch Sunday. Some of the bride's extended family had even planned to stay on the whole week following the wedding for a kind of family reunion.

"Pamela, the bride, chose this place," Reverend Chris Walker explained, "because her family had been coming here ever since she was a little girl. This resort, this lake was very special to the family and especially to Pamela. They'd had a number of family gatherings here. Pamela was an only child but her parents came from large families and she had dozens of cousins from Boise, Missoula, and Spokane. The families would all meet here every summer for a week or two. Pamela loved having *brothers and sisters*, if only for a couple of weeks each summer. She was so full of life."

Regan caught the past tense when Chris referred to the bride. "Was?" she asked.

"She's dead. I officiated at the funeral on Friday morning."

Brendan signaled another round.

"It's not often that you plan a wedding for two of the nicest people you know and end up doing a funeral for one of them instead," Chris continued.

"What happened?" Regan asked.

"She drowned last Monday. A boating accident. Such a tragedy. I'm surprised you didn't hear about it. It was all over the news."

Brendan and Regan shook their heads in unison at the sad news.

"We were busy planning a wedding last week too," Brendan said before all three of them fell silent again.

Chris broke the silence by raising his glass in the air. "To Pamela," he said. He took a long pull, finishing it. He signaled for another and continued, "After the week I had, gosh after the month I've had, I decided to stay up here. For the weekend anyway. Pamela's family had paid for my cabin in advance and I just couldn't bear any more sadness. And look at my good fortune. I met you two, another happy couple. You restore my faith in love, in goodness, and in marriage."

Regan let that slide trying to keep the conversation on him so she asked what other sadness happened this month and Chris told them his wife had left him three weeks ago. He said she didn't really understand what it would be like to be a preacher's wife in a small Idaho town. They'd met in college and fell in love while he was in divinity school. He thought she could handle it but she said she hated the feeling that everyone was watching her, waiting for her to mess up. Chris said he thought the real reason she left him, though, was they hadn't yet conceived a child.

"We'd been trying for five years. Marcie was devastated by it all. Each month she retreated from me more and more. I don't know who she blamed more, herself or me, but she finally couldn't take the disappointment anymore and she left." Chris was quiet for a moment. "I don't know why I'm telling you all this. You're just married and ready to start your life together. Do you plan to have children?"

In the look that flashed between Brendan and Regan, she let him know, *this was your idea, you deal with it.*

"Uh, well, the truth is, we're not married. The wedding we were busy planning was for my brother and her sister."

"Oh," said the minister apparently not drunk enough to hide his surprise.

"But you know, maybe we should be married. Life is unpredictable. Look at poor Pamela. One minute her future is shining brightly before her. Then, boom, the next minute she's gone." Brendan turned to Regan with tears in his eyes. "We've got to grab life now, Regan. We have to dare it to be different," he said before getting down on one knee in front of her. "We've had such a great time and not just today. Every date we've had. There's no reason we can't have what Jack and Quinn have. You're wonderful and I'm a good guy. I know I'm not as flashy as some guys, especially Jack, but maybe that's all about to change. No one would have suspected we'd do something crazy like we've done. Getting married would be even crazier, but great." He grabbed her hands in his and finished, "It would be so great. Really it would. Regan, I would be so honored if you would consent to be my wife. What do you say *Mrs. Gallagher?*"

"I say you're drunk," Regan answered.

"No, no I'm not . . . well, yes I am but that doesn't change how I feel. We deserve happiness too. Come on, Regan. Let's continue this adventure. Let's continue to act crazy and let the chips fall where they may. Let's do something we've never done before, something no one would expect us do to. Chris can marry us right now. Please . . ."

Regan turned to Chris. He shrugged his shoulders and smiled. "Alright, let's do it," she said, "but we can't do it right now. We don't have a license or anything."

"Congratulations," Chris said as Brendan rose up off his knee and gave Regan a quick peck on the cheek.

Chapter 5

Seattle Now | 2013

Monday   November 25   7:40 AM   Sean

"Mornin' doc. You're a little late today. The usual double Americano?" Jeremy said with his huge smile that softened the overall threatening look created by his dyed flat-black grunge hairstyle set off by eyebrow piercings and enough tattoos on his arms to tell an entire comic book story.

"Please . . . no wait. How about an extra shot?"

"Late night?"

"Yeah."

"A woman?" Jeremy said as he smirked and raised his left eyebrow so that it looked like his eye was doing mini-bench presses with a tiny barbell.

"I wish."

Sean began every morning in this coffee shop. The whir of the grinder and the distinct aroma of fresh ground beans got him salivating as easy as Pavlov's dog. He was such a coffee hound that Savannah bought him his own espresso machine to use at home the Christmas after she finished grad school. But after they broke up, he started coming back to this neighborhood shop every day to wait on a line that nearly runs out the door even at 6:15 am, his normal time to stop in. The banter with the barista beat drinking his first cup alone at home. And the overstuffed couch and chairs (always full even in the early morning) gave him a comfortable feeling. He imagined he would have experienced a similar feeling if he had ever gone to his grandmother's—the one he would have visited if Regan had only told him who she was. To hear Regan tell it, he was one of the unluckiest guys around since his parents, grandparents, and every other relation he had, were dead. No family whatsoever. But he never quite believed it. He could just *feel* that he had family somewhere.

"I saw you in the paper last week, Doc. You were awesome, dude!" Jeremy said as he began the ballet of movements that would produce the perfect cup of coffee with three shots of espresso to get Sean's brain in gear. "How's that kid doin'?"

"As well as can be expected," Sean answered. He looked down pretending he was deciding on a muffin or donut as a signal to stop the conversation. Jeremy missed, or ignored, that signal and plowed on.

"I hear the Dad tried to off the whole family . . . purposely tried to kill 'em all after he stabbed his wife before going over the guardrail," Jeremy said with an insider's knowledge.

"Don't believe everything you hear," Sean said wondering how Jeremy had gotten such accurate information.

"It's from a pretty good source, Doc. That *Times* reporter whose been looking for you. She came in here earlier, about your usual time, hoping to run into you. You should give her a call. She's quite a babe!" Jeremy said as he turned to the grinder.

"Man, that must have been one sick family. Hope the kid doesn't grow up to be a nut-job like his old man. Poor kid. He's all alone now." He shouted his final comments as he ground the beans, deftly pressed and tamped the coffee, and then pulled three shots from a machine that came all the way from Italy. The strong, comforting fragrance of perfectly roasted and pulled espresso began to fill Sean's brain just before that familiar sharp pain flashed just behind his eyes.

Sean usually enjoyed this idle morning chatter with the pierced and tattooed barista. But he hated gossip. He wondered how so much information was leaking out. He couldn't abide people taking bits of what they thought they knew and making up the rest as if someone else's troubles were nothing more than lurid entertainment. He had refused to speak with any of the reporters who kept hounding him. Talking to reporters was not part of his job. And in this new HIPAA-era of patient privacy, he knew administration wasn't releasing information on the family. So how did the reporter find out so much? He couldn't wait until people got bored with this story so the reporters—who reminded him of a pack of hungry wild dogs—would find other meat for their stories.

"Anything else this morning, sir?" the bouncy new girl behind the register asked Sean as Jeremy put the finishing touches on his drink.

The question didn't register. Sean was lost in thought. He hadn't had another fainting episode, but he'd come close. All weekend he'd willed himself not to pass out because he needed the distraction of work. He didn't want another visit from Michael's dead sister and he didn't want to have to report any other incidents to Kenji. There was also no reason to tell Ken about the nightmares that plagued his sleep again or the occasional blinding flashes of pain behind his eyes that cursed his days. He'd had tests before and nothing showed. Nothing would show now either so why mention it? The weekend hadn't been that restful after all.

It had been five years since he had the nightmares, though the pains that flashed through his head like lightning tortured him intermittently. He kept meaning to write down when they happened so he could see what kind of pattern they made, but he never got around to it. Nightmares and pain flashes were pretty constant right before Savannah left but in this last year they became so sporadic he thought maybe they were gone for good. Until last week. Until Michael. Lost in his thoughts, the bouncy girl had to say "Sir" three more times before Sean realized she was talking to him.

"No thanks, I'm good," he said absentmindedly handing her his credit card. But in reality, he was not very good at all right now and there wasn't enough coffee in the world to fix the particular version of not-good he felt descending on him.

This coffee house always provided an odd sense of belonging, of being part of a family even if most of the regulars like him only knew each other well enough for the occasional nod. They recognized each other's faces and knew each other's coffee habit or favorite place to sit, but not names. Still, that bit of familiarity and constancy was comforting. Public privacy. How very Seattle.

The regulars were very Seattle too. Since he didn't know their real names, he made some up. There was Pink-hair Granny who always sat on the deep burgundy chenille chair with her newspaper; she appeared so prim and proper like any other granny except for the tattoo that peaked over her collar and looked like some sort of prehistoric multicolored creature ready to devour her left ear. Then there was Bluetooth, the nerdy guy who always sat on the right side of the couch near the window overlooking the park. He sported an earpiece permanently embedded in his right ear, his iPod headphone attached to his left, and his laptop stuck to his thighs. Surely, he was an IT guy (or wannabe) for some high-tech start-up. There was also Scotty, the guy who dressed in kilts and Doc Martins and sat at the counter lining the north window. The other counter sitters were Thelma and Louise, the lesbian couple who always left their pug tied up outside. And finally, there was Jane, the girl in her twenties who just looked like an ordinary girl in her twenties, wearing huge black glasses as her only mask. For Sean, any one of them could be a long-lost cousin. But maybe that was just the silly childhood wish of an orphaned only child.

After Savannah left him, this little coffeehouse became his refuge. On his days off, he would come here to sit for hours just reading. Somehow the noise of other people kept him from feeling completely alone in the world. Of course, he wasn't completely alone. He still had his mother's sister Regan. She raised him but the warmth he got from these familiar faces in this little coffeehouse was a thousand degrees warmer than anything he ever got from her. In her company there is an ice that no coffee, no matter how scalding or how perfectly made, could ever melt. He'd guessed that she resented his intrusion into her life. But with no other family to take care of him after his parents died, even she wasn't cold enough to send him into foster care.

"Here ya go Doc. Triple Americano," Jeremy said. "Enjoy the mist and have a great day."

"Thanks Jeremy. See you tomorrow."

"You can count on it for sure," Jeremy said with a huge smile that was most pronounced in his eyes.

"I do," Sean smiled back. More than you know, he thought.

With his coffee in hand, Sean walked toward the door checking his cell phone as he went. He had twenty minutes to get his ass over to Ken Takano's office so he could get the all clear to return to work. No problem. It was only a ten-minute walk. He took a sip of his coffee, breathed in deeply and opened the door. A truck going down the hill backfired. Lightning flashed behind his eyes and in an instant, everything was black again.

∞

"Hi again Dr. Sean."

"Faith! Oh crap, not again. What's going on?"

"You called me," Faith said as the light around her widened a bit. She was bathed in a golden glow from head to foot and she seemed to sparkle with flashes of pink and purple around the edges. Sean could see that she was wearing shoes this time. He hadn't been able to see her whole form the first time. But shoes?

"You want to ask me something," she said matter-of-factly.

"How could I call you? I don't even know where you are. Where we are." She shrugged.

Apparently we don't get all our questions answered when we die, Sean thought. He had always hoped that in death he'd find the answers to all his questions since he had so many that Regan refused to answer. The priests certainly led him to believe that heaven was a place for answers. But Faith doesn't seem to know much more about wherever the hell she is, or how this all works, than he does.

As if listening to his thoughts again Faith answered, "I still don't know how everything works here but I do know that you called me because you wanted to ask me something. So go ahead. Ask." Her words were direct but her tone was kind. He had so many questions but he asked the one most urgent to him in this moment.

"Is Michael going to live?"

"That's up to him. I don't think he's decided yet. It's a big decision and not so easy to make when you're as young as he is. My guess is that he'll stay if he knows he can be safe. Anything else?"

"Did you try to save him?"

"I did. I knew we were in big trouble this time. My dad had gotten angry before. He hit my mom lots but not us. Not until that night when he hit Michael. I think everything kind of got out of control that night."

"What happened when he hit Michael?"

"Daddy punched him and Michael's head hit the car door. He didn't move after that. After we were driving for a while, Daddy let me go into the back with him. I tried to protect him as much as I could. I hope it helped."

"Yes, it helped very much."

They both were quiet for a moment realizing that neither of their efforts for Michael had been quite good enough so far.

"I like your lady friend," Faith said changing the subject. "I like her name too. It's pretty, like her."

"My lady friend?" he said as his right shoulder started to wiggle a bit.

"Uh-oh. They're calling you back again," Faith said as Sean could begin to hear Jeremy's voice. "Call me anytime," Faith said as she began to fade away. "I like talking to you." She smiled and was gone.

∞

Jeremy's face replaced Faith's and the shock of the difference made Sean jump. He was back in the coffeehouse on one of the couches.

"Whoa, Doc. Hang tight. You passed out as you went out the door. Mrs. B screamed call 911. We had quite a commotion. You were out cold and I didn't want you laying half out the door on the sidewalk like some bum so I picked you up and set you here to wait for the ambulance."

Sean looked beyond Jeremy's shoulder. All the regulars were staring at him. "Shit," he said.

"Totally. Right?" Jeremy agreed.

Kenji Takano sauntered into the room where Sean was lying on an exam table, staring at the ceiling. "So I said in my office first thing Monday, not emergency. What about that did you not understand, SPT? What'd you do now buddy?"

"Apparently I passed out again," Sean said as he sat up and hung his feet over one side.

"You're making quite a habit of that lately. Looks like you get a few more days off work and as an added bonus, you get a little spin in that big whining tube you talked me out of on Friday. Today we're going to take a peek at that empty space between your ears and see what's up that may be knocking you down." He smiled at his own cleverness and Sean had to join him. Ken was one of those guys who was always just one step away from laughter. The world was one huge cosmic joke and Ken thought that poking around in the brain just might give him the ultimate punchline.

Sean hoped the MRI would find something. He did not plan to tell Kenji about what was happening when he passed out no matter what the results of the MRI. But it would be so much simpler if they found something. Anything that would explain what was going on, other than that he was going crazy.

"How long before someone comes to get me?" Sean said.

"Why? You have an appointment?"

"Apparently only with the MRI but I have two small things I want to do before that. I've seen my patients wait for hours sometimes to get on the schedule. And I know my present condition isn't serious enough to keep me from getting bumped. So how about you bend the rules just a tiny bit, give me a time to be at radiology and I'll meet you there. I'd like to check on Michael Brennan plus I want to grab another cup of coffee. I'd only had one swig of my coffee when I passed out. I promise I won't leave the grounds."

"Oh no. No way I'm cutting you loose before you get that MRI this time. How would it look if you passed out again, this time with a coffee in your hand? People would be slipping all over the place breaking who knows what. Or worse, what if you conked out on that poor kid. We'd both be in real trouble then. And that kid already has enough problems," Kenji said in a sympathetic tone devoid of any hint of the big cosmic joke. "Nope. You stay put this time my friend. I don't know what is causing your untimely naps but I'm not letting you out of this room until transport comes to get you in a wheelchair to get that MRI."

After an affectionate chuff on the shoulder, Ken turned from Sean and picked up the in-house phone on the wall near the door. Sean overheard him saying he had a special rush request and making arrangements to bump him to the front of the queue (after any serious emergencies). When he was done, Kenji turned back to Sean and said, "I was able to get a slot for you in thirty minutes. In the meantime, you stay put and I'll have one of the volunteers grab you a coffee from the stand in the lobby. My treat. And just because I like you, I'll find Rose and have her come down here to give you a report on the kid."

"Thanks Ken. I owe you one."

"No worries buddy. I'm not keeping score." And Sean knew that was true.

Ten minutes later his coffee arrived carried by a college student with a flexible schedule who was hoping to get into med school. I'm sure getting coffee for doctors (or patients) wasn't on his list of things he yearned to learn. But every job in a hospital, even (or especially) volunteer ones, had its share of scutwork.

As a way to show his appreciation for the warm latte now in his hands, Sean asked the kid about his plans and hopes. Sean shared that he once had been a volunteer here too and what he learned had really helped him decide that medicine was for him. In truth, he always believed that medicine was for him, but at least as a volunteer he realized he didn't keel over at the sights, sounds, or smells that were all too common here. Now if he could only keep from keeling over at the drop of a hat, his life would be back on track.

Ten minutes after his coffee came, Rose walked in and said, "We have to stop meeting like this" before seeing the young volunteer. Sean could tell by the kid's face that he wasn't sure if Rose was serious or not. The young man quickly excused himself with a "thanks for everything" exit. Rose looked puzzled and asked, "What'd you do?"

"Nothing. He wants to be a doctor and I encouraged him. How's Michael?"

"Same. Nothing's really changed since you were in last Friday. No better but no worse either, knock on wood. His grandparents are there constantly, at least his grandmother is. The granddad goes to a hotel at night to sleep and then brings his wife fresh clothes and breakfast every morning. Then she naps on one of the fold-out chairs while he sits with Michael. If Michael doesn't show some signs of improvement today, I'm going to call the social workers to see if they can arrange an apartment close by. I have a feeling this is going to be a long haul."

"I'm guessing you're right about that."

"Now, what's going on with you? I heard you fainted again. Maybe next time you end up in an emergency room, you'll listen to your doctor and get an MRI before you saunter off saying you're fine, you just need some rest," she scolded with a motherly tone. "I swear, doctors make the worst patients."

"Let's hope there isn't a next time."

"Well, did you at least rest over the weekend like you said you would?"

"Yes and no. I tried. But the nightmares started again. Lots of violent stuff. No doubt from nearly getting run over and then hearing about Michael's mother's condition. His dad was one crazy bastard."

As he said this, buzzing began in his ears. He recognized it as the sound that kept preceding his fainting so he quickly changed the subject. "You'll never guess who I ran into in Michael's room on Friday."

Rose said, "Savannah."

"You knew she was here?"

"Not until I ran into her in too. She's a chaplain now. She looks great. The work must suit her."

"She does look great," Sean admitted. "It's funny, just before everything happened last week, I was thinking about her again, wondering how she was, wondering where she was. And now she's here."

"Does that scare you or give you hope?" Rose asked. Rose had known how much Sean loved Savannah. She was the only one he'd shown the ring he never gave Savannah. He didn't tell Rose why he didn't give it to Savannah. Just as he couldn't admit now what was happening to him.

"Both," Sean said falling silent. Rose sat on the exam table next to him and put her arm around his shoulder. He closed his eyes and leaned into her embrace thinking, *I bet this is what it feels like to have a mom.* This time there was no buzzing and he hadn't felt himself fainting or falling asleep. Yet everything was darkness again.

∞

"Hi Dr. Sean," Faith chirped. "I never got to tell you what happened so Mama decided to come with me this time."

"Hello Dr. Thomas," Lexi began. "Thank you for saving Michael."

Sean nodded.

"I know this must be very confusing for you."

Sean nodded again.

"I'm sure it will begin to make sense after a time. I don't quite know how all *this* works yet," Lexi said using a sweeping gesture with her hand that Sean presumed meant the place where they were meeting, but really he had no idea what she was talking about so he was unsure how any of it could make sense. Like Faith had done before, Lexi seemed to hear his thoughts.

"I know this doesn't make sense to you. But our families' paths are crossing through you so I can only assume that we have something in common. Since I don't know your story, I'd like to take a moment to explain what happened to us before my husband Richard nearly ran you over. I'm not certain why it is important that you know. I just know that it is," she said. She swept her hand in the other direction. Sean followed the movement and an image emerged that began moving. As Lexi spoke, Sean saw the images come to life as if he were in a movie theater.

"Going somewhere?" Richard sneered.

I jumped at the sound of his voice as he came up behind me while I secured the last of our things in the back of the Explorer.

"Richard . . . You scared me," I said but all I could think of was, Oh God, he's awake. What is he doing awake? He never wakes this early. I willed myself to stay calm and stick to the plan.

"You only need to be scared if you're planning on leaving me," he said in a voice so smooth it unnerved me. I had a back-up plan if he woke up. All I had to do was remember what it was. Stay calm, I told myself. Think.

"Of course I'm not leaving you. We are just getting ready to go to that little cabin near Leavenworth. Remember? We talked about it last week. For Thanksgiving. The kids were so excited, I figured I'd get an early start packing before waking you."

I said this with what I hoped sounded like breezy confidence. I didn't want him to sense my growing fear, though I could feel bile rising from the pit of my stomach. Sweat was dampening my armpits and my legs were twitching slightly, ready to run. I locked my eyes on Richard's, trying to read his mind. I had seen that look on his face too many times. But I willed my hands to remain steady and commanded my lungs to breathe normally.

I had planned so carefully, there was no way he could know. I didn't even tell the children anything until I put them to bed with their clothes on. By then Richard was already off at the bar he liked so much. He staggered in drunk sometime after 2:30 am and collapsed in bed to sleep it off. I pretended I was asleep when he got into bed and then I waited almost an hour until his breathing was slow and steady before beginning to pack the Explorer with everything I had hidden under the beds in the children's room. I'd been practicing for weeks, moving around in the middle of the night, seeing how much noise was too much. All these weeks I could count on him sleeping like a dead man until at least 7:00 am and if he woke up then it was just to pee before going back to sleep until at 9:00 or 10:00, long after other husbands were at work. That night had been like all the others so I had no idea why he was awake.

"Are you sure that's where you're going? I don't remember *us* making any plans to go away. But it appears you've been making all sorts of plans," Richard sneered again as he held up his phone. He played a snippet of a conversation I had had with my boss last week and another one I had just a few days ago with a domestic violence counselor who was explaining how to get a protection order.

"How did you . . ." I began to say. But the rest of my words suddenly were stuck in my throat. I don't know how he did it. All my preparation and he knew all along. But I still hoped I could save my children. That was my only goal now. Keep my children safe.

"You're not the only devious one in this family," he said as he slowly walked a circle around me. If he intended to make me feel like a cornered animal, it was working. He continued to cycle through weeks of recordings he'd made until I heard my sister's voice saying 'call me as soon as you're on your way' before Richard stopped.

"Sounds like the only thing you're planning on is leaving me," he said as he stopped circling and threw the phone at my face. I raised my hand just in time as the phone struck me with surprising force. Richard began to pace back and forth in front of me. He knew better than to yell and attract attention to us. He was a master at quiet intimidation. He started in on me again and the depth of his rage was evident in his curses.

"Do you think some fucking liberal-ass dikes are going to keep me from my family?" he said as he slowly moved closer to me. I could see the muscles in his arms jump as he clenched and unclenched his fists. "Do you think that some piece of paper from a judge can stop me from having what's mine?" he said as he grabbed my arms, lifting me slightly, just enough to keep me unbalanced. He put his face right in mine and I could smell the foulness of digesting whiskey and feel the heat of his anger. But I didn't turn away since I knew that would only make him more enraged.

"Did you really think your sister could hide you?" he said as he released me with a push as if being near me disgusted him. I stumbled but quickly regained my balance. He started circling me again and I could feel the energy around us popping and sparking. We had danced this dance before and I knew what was next. His rage had begun its slow and certain spiral out of control. I had feared this day for months. For years really.

This was my day to die.

That realization kept me from focusing on Richard's ranting as I looked for any means of escape. Every instinct told me to run but that was impossible. At almost fourteen, Faith could keep up, if she weren't too terrified to run. But Michael never could. He was only six. He was too big for me to carry and too small to run. My best hope was to calm Richard and stall as I tried to find a way to save my babies. I extended my arms in supplication and willed myself to move toward Richard. I put my arms around him and held him hoping he could not feel my heart racing or smell the fear leaking out of every pore of my body. I knew I had to calm him.

"Richard, I love you. I've always loved you," I said as I hugged him and stroked his back. I *had* loved him. Once. I did still love him when he was sober. But he was so seldom sober now. I had to protect the children. I would do or say anything to keep them safe.

"We weren't leaving. I planned a trip for us. All of us," I said as I reached for the paperwork I had in the back pocket of my jeans that showed a cabin reservation. I held it out to him but he refused to take it so I hugged him again and said, "I was going to surprise you. I got a bonus at work for all the extra time I put in. You've been so stressed lately I thought you could use a break. I was going to call you as soon as the car was packed."

"Looks packed to me," he said pushing me away from him as he walked to the back of the Explorer. I tried again, following him.

"I was just going to get the kids buckled in and then call you."

Richard lunged at me, grabbed my left wrist, twisted me around and wrenched my arm behind me lifting me completely off my feet as he slammed me against the side of the Explorer, pinning me.

"What cabin?" he quietly raged into my ear as he pressed his body against my back, wrenching my arm even more.

"Richard, you're hurting me," I whispered not because I wanted to be quiet but because I was barely able to breathe. His left hand held my wrist high on my back while his right arm pinned my shoulders to the car. I tried so hard not to sound pleading, not to sound submissive enough to add fuel to his rage.

"What's the name of the cabin we're staying at?" he hissed. I could see the children huddled together trying to become invisible. My heart was breaking for them. When my tears started to fall, he let go of his hold on me. "That's what I thought," he said as I fell to the ground. But he misunderstood. I remembered the plan. I remembered the name of the cabin. But the pain in my arm was so intense that I couldn't speak. And the pain in my heart was even greater when I looked at the fear in my babies' eyes. How could I not cry?

Richard turned to them and said, "So, kids, what should I do now? Your mother, this lying bitch, is trying to take you away from me." He started a slow swagger toward the children who had backed away from the SUV. I jumped up and ran between him and them.

"No, Richard. No. I wasn't taking them away. It's Meadow Creek Cabin and I was just about to get you."

"Shut up, bitch," Richard yelled as he backhanded me. I stumbled backward again falling a few feet from where the children cowered. As I fell he said to me, "I don't want to hear another fucking lie come out of your fucking mouth."

The children started to cry. Richard hissed at them to stop. He moved toward them again but I got in his way once more. I put my arms around him again, ignoring the searing pain in my left arm. I tried to slowly steer him away from the children as I held him, trying to soothe him. I pleaded with him, "Richard please. Please don't yell at them. They're just scared."

"What the fuck are they scared about? I'm their father," he said as he pulled my arms off him and shoved me away saying, "You've done this. You've turned them against me, you fucking, lying, whoring bitch." When I fell to the ground a third time, Michael ran toward Richard with his small arms flailing.

"Stop it!" he screamed. "Don't hit her."

As Michael reached his father, Richard wheeled around raising his arm in a swinging arc and hit our son with his full strength. I couldn't believe my eyes when Richard's backhanded punch landed on the side of Michael's face, lifting my baby backwards into the air and crashing him into the Explorer's side door with such force that his head left a dent. Michael fell in a crumpled heap.

He didn't cry. He didn't move. He looked as lifeless as a rag doll.

A primal, guttural "No" came from my depths as I crawled toward my little boy lying so quiet and still. Finally, neighbors' lights began to turn on and I could see someone peeking through their blinds. I prayed they would call 911, that someone could save my sweet little baby boy.

Richard also saw the lights come on just before a male voice called out from the darkness, "What is going on out there? Is everything alright?"

Richard silenced me with his look and answered back in a voice so calm, so normal that I thought he surely must be possessed by evil spirits to be able to change so fast.

"Sorry for the noise," he called in the direction of the voice. "Just a little accident here. Everyone's fine. We're on our way now." We both knew nothing was fine, and never would be again. And we also knew the police would arrive any minute.

Richard hissed under his breath to me and Faith, "Get in the damn car." He opened the back of the Explorer and quickly threw out some of the gear I had packed. Then he scooped Michael in his arms and wedged him into the space he had created. When Michael still did not move, I knew, and I'm certain Richard did too, that he had crossed a line that changed everything. Richard slammed the tailgate door before getting behind the wheel. "Fuck," he cursed as he hit the steering wheel and turned the key in the ignition.

"We have to get Michael to a hospital," I pleaded as Richard drove away. "Just drop him off with Faith. I'll stay with you. Faith won't say anything," I said as I turned to her, "Will you honey?" She looked back at me and I could see the terror in her expression. She said, "No Mama." But Richard wouldn't relent.

"Shut up." He said. "This is all your fault. When will you learn to keep your fucking mouth shut?"

"Richard . . ." I tried again but he cut me off.

"One more word and you get this," he said reaching into his jacket pocket and pulling out a switchblade. "One more word," he said again as he pressed a button and the knife jumped up and locked into place. "Now shut the fuck up and let me think."

Richard drove exactly at the speed limit, coming to a full stop at every sign, staying a few blocks off the main thoroughfare. He drove south in the direction of the police station. I knew what he was thinking. No cop would stop him if he didn't look panicked and no fool would drive *toward* the police instead of running away, unless he hadn't done anything wrong. I wondered if Richard had been doing as much planning for this night as I had. The difference between me and Richard: I was planning to get my kids to safety and I think he was planning all along to destroy us.

Sitting in that slow-moving car with my son possibly dead and certainly dying was surreal. The neighborhood was so quiet and peaceful; there wasn't a soul out walking a dog or delivering a paper. Small houses with their sleeping inhabitants stood dark behind the eerie glow of street lights burning halos into the night's fog. The fog would have been soothing if it hadn't hidden us so well. Less than a mile from our apartment, we saw a police car on the main arterial. Its siren was off, but its lights were flashing. It was heading in the direction from which we had come. It couldn't have been more than three minutes later than we needed. All hope of rescue faded when I saw the blue and red flashing lights get smaller and smaller behind us. I'm sure the police never saw us. Richard smiled. He stayed on the back streets moving slowly and steadily away from his latest abomination.

I couldn't help but think of how I got to this place, in this car, with this man. None of my friends from before would recognize me anymore. Hell, I couldn't recognize myself. It was only in finally deciding to leave that I had begun to remember who I was, what I could do. What I needed to do to find safety for my precious babies.

The shelter counselor had warned me that I had to plan carefully because the day I decided to leave would usher in the most dangerous time of my life. My planning had been patient, meticulous, and careful. I wrote nothing down. I gave no hint to Richard that life wouldn't continue exactly as it was. At least I didn't think that I had. I studied him for weeks noting how often he would go out to drink and how long he was gone every time he left. I memorized every detail of his habits.

Planning my escape, planning the life my children and I would live gave me a growing sense of power. But ultimately, I had to move more quickly than I wanted. Richard's rage was building again. The beatings were getting more frequent and becoming more violent. He wasn't even trying to hide the bruises anymore. And neither did I. With Kristen, my boss, I didn't need to. She understood completely. She too had once gotten away.

Driving around in that car, I realized that this moment, this horrible, horrible moment, was in a twisted way, my fault. I realized that it was the hope I felt that must have tipped-off Richard. My shelter counselor and all those women I'd seen on Oprah didn't warn me that hope itself could be the give-away.

Richard must have seen something was different about me so he started spying on me. I'm sure he thought he would catch me loving another man. Instead he caught me loving *me*. Restoring me. And in that renewed sense of power, I knew I had to leave before my tiny window of opportunity closed. So many women do make it out alive. I had desperately wanted to believe that I could be among them.

It had taken me a long time to admit that Richard used violence to control me and that I had lost myself bit-by-bit since I married him. My mother and sister tried to warn me but I believed for too long that Richard could change. He loved me and I loved him so nothing was impossible. We had made it through other rough patches and I thought we could do it again. But as his drinking got worse, his temper flared at the slightest provocation, and then, with no provocation at all. It was one thing when he went after me but then I began to fear that the kids were in his crosshairs too. He hadn't hit them yet but he didn't hit me at the beginning either. Finally, after his last relapse I had to get away. I didn't want Faith or Michael to become Richard's punching bags too. It was bad enough he yelled at them but I knew I couldn't bear it if he ever hit them.

As Richard drove aimlessly around Capitol Hill, I began to cry silent tears as I realized how badly I had failed my children. I turned around to see Faith sitting alone and perfectly still in the back seat, hands folded in her lap. I caught Faith's eye and my brave daughter gave me a small, sad smile. Michael, lying in the cargo area among the things I hoped to salvage from my life, made no movement or sound. I couldn't stand to look at what I had let happen. I turned to face forward and peered into the blackness of a neighborhood I didn't recognize now. I now had no idea where we were but I knew without a doubt where we were going. I could still feel Richard's rage and in that moment, I hated both him and me.

I longed for the days when I had been able to believe in Richard. The man I fell in love with, the one who never hurt me, who made me laugh. That Richard was long gone now, if he ever really existed at all. When we moved to Seattle, I had deeply wanted to believe that we'd have a fresh start but after Richard lost his job yet again, I knew nothing would change. He had promised me he would stay sober if I trusted him once more and gave him this chance. He said that in a new city with a new job, it would be like it was when we first fell in love and nothing could come between us. It was a not-so-subtle reference to what he saw as meddling by my family.

I didn't want to be the first one in my family who failed at marriage. Maybe in a different city without the pressure of having to live up to my family's standard, Richard could become the husband and father I knew he could be, the one I had seen when he was sober. I wanted that for him. For me. For the kids. And it worked for a few months. I thought he'd finally turned the corner. But then he relapsed.

First it was only a drink now and again after work, to bond with his team he said. Then it was a little something each night at home to help him relax after a long day. Then he was drinking at lunch to handle the stress of the job. But his boss didn't appreciate the many afternoons he returned to work drunk. His boss was more patient than most would have been and even offered a rehab program. At that suggestion, Richard told him he "didn't need that bullshit." He quit but in truth he was fired. After he lost his job, he drank almost all day long as he ranted about how unfair "they" all treated him. The only good thing that came from his job loss was that I convinced him I should get a part-time job. He only agreed because we needed the money.

When I started working, I realized just how controlling Richard had become. He controlled the money even though I earned it. My paycheck was directly deposited into a joint account but he had the only checkbook and only he knew the password for the online account. I had a credit card but he paid the bills and grilled me on every charge. I even had to ask permission to get a cup of coffee or have lunch out with people at work. Richard drove me to work and picked me up every day, but he couldn't control me while I was there.

Those few precious hours of freedom helped me remember who I once had been. I loved the challenge of my work and quickly took on more responsibility adding a few hours here and there or taking work home so I wouldn't have to leave the kids alone with Richard too often. Then one day, after I had been repeatedly late for work, my boss, Kristen, called me into her office. I thought she was going to fire me but instead she asked about the bruises that I couldn't hide anymore because Richard no longer had the control to carefully place them where they wouldn't be easily noticed. Who could have guessed that she had left a violent marriage too? She became the friend I desperately needed.

It wasn't long after that, Kristen asked me to come in early for what I thought was a budget meeting. A woman from the domestic violence shelter joined us and suddenly what had once been impossible began to seem plausible. After a few more *budget meetings*, I was committed to leaving Richard and starting over with my children to give them the life they deserved. With Kristen's help, I was able to siphon money from my paychecks to begin saving for my escape. I almost made it.

Richard's voice startled me back to the car. After what seemed like an eternity of driving in silence, Richard told Faith to jump into the back and check on Michael. I recognized where we were now. We were on First Hill. I couldn't see through the fog enough to see the lights that I knew illuminated the large white outline of a red cross marking the helicopter landing platform on top of Seattle Regional Hospital but I recognized the neighborhood. The hospital was only five or six blocks away. For a moment I hoped Richard would do the right thing.

Faith moved some things onto the seat where she sat to create a small space next to her brother. She climbed over the seat. I turned to watch her. Michael still made no movement or sound. The hospital was so close. Maybe Michael could survive this nightmare. Faith too.

If only I had seen things more clearly. If only I had acted more quickly. If only I'd made it. Silently, I mouthed "I'm sorry," but Faith didn't see. I wondered in that moment if Michael and Faith would remember how much I loved them.

I watched as Faith reached out to smooth Michael's hair but then pulled back before touching him. She reached again and carefully stroked his cheek. I could tell Faith was afraid she might hurt Michael. Faith had always been Michael's protector, always spiriting him away into their room when Richard would come home drunk, yelling and itching for a fight.

I mourned that I had allowed Faith to lose so much of her childhood so fast. I had convinced myself that I had protected my children from the worst of it, but I finally understood how much pain I had allowed my children to bear.

Faith reached out her hand and held it just below Michael's nose. I could see her relax slightly. She then placed her hand on Michael's chest and I could see that she was feeling for its feeble rise and fall.

"He's breathing and he's warm," Faith told her father. "I don't see any blood but there is a pink fluid coming out of his left ear."

As she spoke, I marveled at how adult Faith sounded. She had just witnessed her father attack his wife and child yet she reported her brother's condition as if she were a meteorologist giving the weather for the day. I hoped that it wasn't too late to teach Faith that love does not include getting beat up.

I wondered who would do it.

"Dad, he looks like he's asleep, but I can't wake him," Faith's voice rose slightly as her feelings leaked into her final report.

"He's hurt bad," I was sure I heard my daughter whisper as she laid down on her side next to her little brother and drew him close to her. I watched as she grabbed a blanket and wrapped Michael in it. She then put pillows all around him. Finally, I saw Faith cross herself and then make the sign of the cross next to Michael's left ear and then on his forehead before settling with her arms and legs around him, doing her best to shield him. I prayed silently with Faith that Michael wouldn't die. I prayed that Richard wouldn't take them too. I knew he would kill me but I still desperately hoped that he would not kill the children.

I saw Faith's hand catch her tears and I silently began to cry too. My tears were blurring the street lights so that they looked like shooting stars as we moved past them. It was a moment of sheer beauty. And in that beauty, I could no longer bear to watch my beautiful children. The next time I looked back, Faith was asleep.

Faith did not stir when I pleaded with Richard one last time to take Michael to the hospital. She blessedly did not stir when her father's angry voice said, "I warned you bitch" before that sickening sound of knife slicing flesh. She did not stir when bubbles of air briefly mixed with blood in the sound of my last breath. Faith did not hear the roar of the engine or the sound of fences crunching beneath the tires. Faith, to my everlasting regret, did not hear anything again in that life.

Sean moaned. Rose touched his arm and said, "It's okay Sean. You're safe."

Sean opened his eyes. He was again lying down on the exam table in the emergency room. "I fell asleep?"

"I suppose that is one way to frame it," Rose said. "When your coffee cup fell to the ground I realized you were having another one of your episodes so I laid you back down on the bed before you followed your coffee. It's been a few years since I had to muscle a full-grown man to the bed," she said with a smile.

"Sorry about that," Sean said without any further explanation. "How long was I out this time?"

"Maybe twenty minutes or so," she told him. "Kenji's been here and gone again. He's keeping you overnight for observation since you missed your MRI. He's rescheduled you for the morning."

"Great."

"Where did you go?" Rose asked.

He knew exactly what she was asking him and he could tell that her intuition told her that something more than passing out was occurring in Sean's episodes. But how could he tell her he was visiting a bizzaro world where he talked to dead people? So he simply shook his head and looked up at her with all the confusion he truly felt. She met his eyes with a sad smile, patted his hand, and told him she had to get back to work. She promised to come to his room later to check on him.

CHAPTER 6

SPOKANE THEN | 1992

TUESDAY   JANUARY 15   3:00 PM   BRENDAN

EVERY JANUARY SINCE IT HAPPENED, Brendan went to a bar to trying to forget. This was his first January back after a couple of years in the Peace Corps. Years he'd hoped would wash him clean. It didn't work. So here he sat six years later, as guilt-ridden as ever. Whiskey his one true friend.

This bartender had all the time in the world to hear Brendan's sad tale. The bar was empty except for the two of them. Even the weather was cursed on this day, so much so that the other alcoholics wouldn't venture out in the storm. Nope. It was just him and the bartender. And if he'd told this one his tale of woe before, the bartender didn't let on. He showed no impatience. He just let Brendan ramble on and on. Maybe, Brendan thought, if he confessed again, he could finally do something positive with his life. Go back to teaching. Be a coach. Be happy again.

Regan and I were both second choices. We were never in love really. We thought we were but looking back now I think it was more a desperation to be important to someone rather than love. And we did have one other quality that we shared so intensely that its familiarity seemed like love at the time. We each existed in the shadow of a sibling whose light was of a quality we could never match. We both should have known better than to reach beyond our measure.

I met Regan's sister Quinn first. We were attending the same teachers' workshop and I was immediately attracted to her. Quinn seemed like she was interested in me but experience proved me wrong. It's amazing how our desires color our perception of the world.

Quinn wanted a friend, a mentor even. She was a new teacher and I had a few years under my belt. We started meeting after school and mostly talked about teaching but then we started telling each other about more personal stuff too. I took it as a good sign. I invited her to a family dinner one weekend to celebrate my brother's impending return to civilian life. I introduced her as a friend and colleague. I had been hoping for more but we weren't there yet. I should have known better than to let Jack meet her. As soon as she met him it was all over for me. Dad said it was the uniform; girls are suckers for guys in uniform. But I knew better. She was not the first girl who left me after meeting Jack.

Jack was everything I wasn't. Adventurous. Wild. A little dangerous. And there was a part of him that would always remain untamed. Girls believed they could tame him after they enjoyed his dangerous side for a while. I was the guy who was tame from the start. Jack was animated; I was serious. He played football; I played with ideas. He would dream up mischievous pranks that I thought were juvenile and he would pretend to gag when he saw me carrying a book on philosophy, a subject that had smitten me when I was in high school. He loved action. I loved reading. He wasn't a guy who would ever work in an office and he certainly would never be satisfied being "just a teacher." *"Oh, don't get me wrong Brendan,"* he once said to me, *"teachers are great. I just could never be stuck in a classroom all day with a bunch of hooligans like I was."*

It was obvious he needed more. More excitement. More danger. More freedom. So, after two years of college, he signed up for the Marines be-cause he was afraid the conflict in Vietnam would be over before he finished school. He didn't see it as going to war; he saw it as defending democracy. I saw nothing but useless killing. I couldn't kill a bug, never mind a person. If the draft lottery had started in the '60s, I would have been a conscien-tious objector or maybe I would have even risked the short drive north to Canada. But those decisions weren't necessary then. I simply stayed in col-lege, became a high school teacher, and believed I could change the world through the spirited discourse of ideas without all the violence of a war that eventually killed far too many of my students.

Jack was the perfect Marine. Completely dedicated to God and country, he willingly put his life on the line for democracy and to, as he said, do his part to stop the red scourge of communism. It was so black and white for him; democracy was right, communism was wrong. End of story. After his tour in the Marines, Jack came home and joined the FBI to continue his mission to stamp out evil. The FBI was perfect for him; he loved being right, defending the law, and putting away the bad guys. But he didn't mind at all when his Marine Reserve Unit was called back to service before the Tet offensive in 1968. He was honored to do his duty. He spent another year heroically fighting communism before returning to the FBI once again.

After college, I went home to be a teacher while Jack kept the world safe. My parents were proud of me, but when folks asked about "the boys," it was always Jack's exploits that they recounted. I understood it, sort of. Jack's life was exciting. Mine was ordinary, although *I* thought teaching was damned exciting and back then I truly believed that mentoring a young life was the best job in the world. I loved seeing my students minds open up to new ideas. But I guess you had to be there to understand it. Quinn understood it. And looking to me as a more experienced teacher, Quinn wanted to know how I did it.

Even after she met Jack, Quinn and I remained friends. While I continued to yearn for more, she gave to Jack what I had longed for. Still, I figured a little bit of her was better than none at all. We continued to meet a couple of times a week for lunch when our schedules lined up and then about once a week after school to discuss teaching. Soon she started to play match maker for me. She told me that she took one look at Jack and it was love at first sight, and as my friend she wanted that for me too. I guess she never knew how I felt about her.

One Sunday, she brought her sister, Regan, over to the big weekly family dinner. Regan, Quinn said, would be perfect for me. Well, if Jack was everything I wasn't, Quinn was everything Regan wasn't. Regan was nice enough and she was almost as pretty as Quinn, but she wanted different things in her life than I did. I had always wanted a whole bunch of kids to mimic the life I had growing up but Regan wanted a career, not children. She liked competing with men and winning. She enjoyed strategy, not nursery rhymes. When we met, Regan was in law school, near the top of her class. After graduation, she planned to land the job that all her classmates wanted. But we started dating and then on impulse, we got married right after Jack and Quinn.

Years later, after Quinn had Daniel, Regan would sometimes wonder how Quinn's brain didn't turn to mush spending so much time with him. She had no need for the little parasites, as she called them when they annoyed her (which was most of the time). Regan enjoyed her success and liked all the attention it brought her. She was a professional woman, a lawyer in a specialty few women were allowed. She had no room for children in her finely attired life. I realized too late that we probably should have talked about children before we married. But of course, we never even talked about getting married. We just did it. Out of spite. Out of anger. Out of jealousy. Who knows? I think we both figured we'd learn to love each other. But it didn't quite work out that way.

If I had to choose the tipping point, the point of no return, it was when Jack went missing during an undercover operation. Jack and Quinn had been married for about ten years by then. Jack was on the fast track in his career with the agency. He had been chosen to be a part of a new undercover task force and his first assignment was to infiltrate a group of suspected drug runners in the North Idaho woods. While Jack was living his pretend life at the camp, I was living my pretend life at his house with his wife and kids. Regan had left me again and Quinn always felt a little guilty when Regan would take off because she was the one who introduced us. She knew I loved the kids so she would invite me over for dinner, for Daniel's soccer games, for tea parties with Colleen. I loved it all. Besides, Quinn needed the help. She was taking a couple of night courses to get ready to go back to teaching once Colleen started first grade in the fall. I became the de facto babysitter. On those nights, Quinn would get dinner made and I would show up right after soccer practice. She'd take off and I would feed the kids, read them stories, then put them to bed. It was a great routine that worked for all of us.

I always loved being with Quinn and the kids. I was even her Lamaze coach for Daniel because Jack was away at the FBI academy in Quantico.

She first asked Regan to stand in but Regan asked why she didn't just schedule a C-section and be done with it. Quinn was horrified and hurt that Regan didn't understand how important the whole natural childbirth thing was to her. So I stepped in with Regan's blessing. After Daniel was born, Quinn took time off from teaching and joyously embraced every aspect of motherhood. She was thrilled when she found out she was pregnant with another child after Daniel.

Jack didn't adjust to fatherhood so well. He liked the idea of having kids. It was the reality that irritated him. He loved them in his way but he was so focused on his career that he rarely spent much time with them. And he was so driven that he didn't know how to play without needing to win, even if he was playing with Daniel or Colleen. I thought at the time it would get better when they were older, but that never worked out either.

Regan and I had just passed our tenth anniversary too. Our marriage was on the rocks yet again and neither one of us marked our anniversary with even a phone call. In fact, I was surprised divorce papers hadn't shown up. We were barely speaking then. We were separated for the fifth time and Regan lived in San Francisco.

Just the week before, Quinn had told me that Regan was planning a pilgrimage to Tibet later that summer. She constantly searched for what was missing in her that was innate for Quinn. Leave it to Regan to do the most dramatic thing she could think of to find that missing piece. I was tired of all her drama. Another reconciliation just didn't seem possible that afternoon in early June 1979 when Quinn called me to say Jack was missing.

Quinn said Jack's commanding officer told her something was wrong in Jack's undercover operation; the activity around the encampment had changed and Jack had missed his last two updates. Even undercover, they had a system for updates. They tried to prepare her for the worst. Jack was either being held hostage or there was the possibility that Jack had been killed. Quinn was frantic.

I rushed over as soon as I could. By the time I arrived, my parents and three of my sisters, with attending children in tow, were there. My mother had already commandeered the kitchen and dad was outside playing a furious game of hide-and-seek with Daniel, Colleen, and their cousins.

The house was a zoo by dinner time, but at least the activity kept Quinn occupied. Since the day was unseasonably warm, my parents suggested a bar-b-que in the backyard to the delight of all the grandkids. A bar-b-que with cousins on a school night in June was an anomaly to be celebrated with gusto. Besides, it helped my mom too. My mother was someone who believed she could hold the world in its orbit if she just cooked the right thing. When Jack was in Vietnam, she sent enough cookies for the whole platoon almost weekly. The bar-b-que kept her busy; kept her from thinking what might be happening, or might have happened, to her baby boy.

Throughout that afternoon and into the early evening, one of my sisters (Kit, Sissy, or Brigid) was practically stapled at the hip to Quinn. Each time Quinn reached for the phone to call Jack's commander, they took it from her reminding her that he had promised to call as soon as he had any news and she shouldn't tie up the phone in case he was trying to reach her. As the day wore on, Quinn's face showed the strain. It was devoid of color and deep parentheses scored her brow and pointed to her reddened eyes. Her shoulders were so tight they looked like they were two inches closer to her ears. I reached for her once to rub her shoulders and she nearly jumped out of her skin before visibly relaxing as I massaged her neck. I then made the rounds easing the tension for everyone else too. Being a coach gave me good technique and my mother and sisters regularly took advantage.

After dinner was done, my parents suggested a sleep over at their place for Daniel and Colleen as my sisters collected their children to head home. It was a school night after all and who knew how long the waiting would go on.

"You'll stay with Quinn, right Brendan?" Dad said as my mother took the kids upstairs to gather some clothes for the next day.

I looked at Quinn who said, "Please Brendan. I don't want to be alone. I always have the guest room fixed up for when Regan is in town. You could sleep there. Please stay."

What could I do? No one knew I still loved Quinn and only a monster would take advantage of the situation. Besides, I could never refuse Quinn anything. It was one of the favorite topics for arguments between Regan and me before we split this last time. Since Jack was gone so often, Quinn would ask me to do many of the chores around the house a husband does. Regan would scream at me, '*you're not her husband*,' but I would go anyway. It wasn't just for Quinn though. I loved being around Daniel and Colleen too. I wished more than once that they were my family. Jack was a fool to spend so much time chasing bad guys and missing the smiles I regularly got when I tossed Colleen in the air or when I taught Daniel the intricacies of the perfect slide tackle.

After Mom and Dad left with Daniel and Colleen, Quinn turned to me and burst into tears. "I don't know what I'll do if he's dead," she said.

I wrapped her in my arms, reminding myself that she was my brother's wife. I held her until her sobs exhausted her. When she quieted, I saw that her eyes had become little slits and her tears mapped a red-streak path down her cheeks to her chin. I suggested she take a long hot bath. It was as much to relax her as to get her away from me. More than just feelings were stirring in me and I knew it wasn't right. I needed her away from me so I could pull myself together. I promised I would call her if the phone rang. After her bath, she came to say goodnight. It wasn't terribly late, but the day had been a nightmare of worry with no answers in sight. From the guestroom, I listened as sobs overtook her again until, mercifully, she went to sleep.

When there were no more sounds coming from her room, I tried to read but I couldn't concentrate. I kept thinking what an ass Jack was to cause Quinn such pain. Then I wondered if any woman would ever feel that kind of love for me. I doubt Regan had ever cried a tear of longing for me and I doubted she would once we were divorced, which I assumed was the foregone conclusion to our sham of a marriage. Celebration would be more her style.

I tossed and turned for hours but sleep would not come. Long after midnight, lying on the freshly made bed in the guest room, I tried not to imagine what might come next. I wanted to pray but couldn't quite figure out what to ask for. At least I couldn't admit what I wanted to ask for and I didn't think God would answer that kind of prayer anyway. Feeling frustrated and guilty, and in an effort to escape the endless what-if's that played in my mind, I went down to the living room to watch television. Even with the TV on, my mind kept running movies filled with possibilities that made me feel like the most horrible brother in the world.

"Anything good on this time of night?"

Quinn's voice made me nearly jump out of my skin.

"I have no idea what I'm watching," I admitted. Before she could ask anything else, I said, "I was hoping you'd sleep until morning."

"Me too. But I thought I heard the phone ring. I guess I dreamt it." She paused long enough for my heart to break open yet again. She looked so sad. So resigned. I think she was sure Jack was dead. Finally, she asked "Are you hungry?"

"Are you kidding? Mom made enough dinner for an army. She thinks that if she cooks enough, everything will turn out as she wants it to. I wasn't hungry then and I don't have much of an appetite now. Waiting for news is a real killer." As soon as the words left my lips, I realized how callous they were. I quickly added, "Sorry."

"It's OK. I know what you mean," Quinn said with a sad smile. "How about a little drink then? To take the edge off. I don't want to drink alone and I could really use a glass of wine."

Quinn was not a big drinker. She said she didn't like how it made her thoughts all cloudy. I guess cloudy thoughts would be a good thing now.

"Well, what kind of brother-in-law would I be if I let you drink alone," I said hoping a drink would take the edge off my thoughts too. Besides, how could I tell her no? If she wanted to drink, we would drink. As she went to the kitchen to get the wine and glasses she said, "Could you start a fire in the fireplace, I'm chilly."

When she returned she set the bottle on the coffee table. She gave me my glass and then wrapped herself in the couch blanket that Jack had bought her after Daniel was born. It was fraying just a little now since Daniel and Colleen continued to cuddle in it while they watched their single hour of television each evening. She told me she would wrap herself in it late at night when she was nursing so she wouldn't get cold. The image of her half naked, nursing a baby grew in my mind. I tried to block it out to keep other things from growing.

"I wish the commander would call. I'm not sure I can stand this much longer," Quinn said as she stared into the fireplace drinking her wine, speaking almost in a whisper as if there was no one in the room to hear her. She had the glass almost finished before she spoke again. "Jack and I used to sit in front of this fire every weekend after Colleen turned two. We had a rough patch after she was born. Jack was hardly home her first year. If it wasn't training, it was special assignments or extra duty to prove how committed he was. He's always been so driven. It was one of the things that attracted me to him. But after Colleen was born and Daniel was just barely three, I needed him to be committed to us too. He always chose his job first though. They apparently needed him more," she said with a sigh. Quinn was quiet again for a while, lost in her own thoughts. When she continued, she didn't look at me but stared into the fire as if she could see her memories in it.

"We had a really big fight after Colleen's second birthday party. I told him things had to change because if I was going to live the life of a single parent then I might as well become one. He asked what I wanted and I said I wanted just one night a week with him to myself so we could sit by the fire and talk like adults. I wanted to feel like I was as important as his job."

I refilled her glass. Quinn continued to stare into the fire. When she didn't say any more, I asked, "Did it work? The fireplace?"

"For a time. It was the one thing I looked forward to every weekend. Even if his job consumed him all week, I knew on Saturday night by nine o'clock he was mine. I would put the kids to bed and then dress in something really sexy. He would get the fire going and he even started getting special wines for us to try. I had one rule: we could talk about everything but his job and the kids. It was our time." She smiled remembering. She went quiet again, lost in her thoughts. By the time she spoke again, her wine was gone.

"About a year ago, he started to prepare for this undercover assignment. First it was only one weekend a month, then two. Then the assignment took over everything. Before he went to live out in the camp, he promised once it was finished he would ask for a transfer to another unit so we could have a more normal life. If that is even possible in the agency."

I reached out to wipe the silent tears that had begun to fall. She turned, put her head on my chest and began to sob. I held her tight. I hated myself for being glad to have her in my arms at a time like this, but it felt so right. It was all I ever wanted and I refused to think about why she was in my arms.

I began to stroke her hair which released a musky coconut aroma and I became lost in the salty-sweet heavy air between us. It seemed like an eternity before I lifted her chin and cupped her face in my hands. She did not pull away so I leaned down to kiss her swollen eyes. I then slowly mapped her face with kisses moving from her eyes to her cheeks, to her perfect nose, slowly making my way to her opened mouth. I tasted the wine mixed with her anxiety and her longing (or was it my longing?). Her breathing was ragged, uneven with the residual sobs that linger after a hard cry. I shifted her to cradle her in my arms. Her head lolled back revealing her neck. When she did not resist, I pulled her close. I kissed the milky white skin that had turned gold in the glow of the fire. I then kissed from under her chin to her collar bone and I could feel her body releasing the weight of her anxious waiting, falling almost limp in my arms.

I laid her down on the couch knowing I should have carried her to her bed and gone to my own. This was my brother's wife for God's sake! Instead, I knelt on the floor beside her. I noticed that her robe had opened just enough to expose the curve of her shoulder. Fingers of one hand traced this wondrous slope as my other hand sunk deep into her tresses. Her breathing became deep and regular. I stared at her closed eyes from which flowed a silent, continuous stream of tears. I wanted her more in that moment than I had ever desired anything before or since. But I couldn't bear it if I hurt her or if she came to hate me. I started to pull away from her but then she put her hand around mine and placed it on her breast. It was then that I locked my conscience in a box, placed it far behind my passion and abandoned myself to her invitation.

When the phone rang at 6:30 am, she startled awake. I had never gone to sleep for fear this moment would be gone forever. I reveled in the taste of her lingering on my tongue and the feel of her skin against mine. I breathed deeply the smell of her hair that reminded me of summer days at the beach. Making love to her was everything I imagined it would be. She turned to look at me and I smiled at her but her eyes opened wide in confusion. She looked at the empty bottle of wine and then at me.

"No," was all she said as she ran for the phone grabbing her silk kimono that was on the floor. I don't know if she meant me or the phone.

"Quinn, we found him," the commander said so loud that I could hear him. He spoke in a tone that offered no consolation.

"Alive?" She held her breath.

"Barely."

"But he is alive," she pleaded.

Knowing this would be the last time I would ever be privy to her nakedness, I tried to memorize every curve of her body, every graceful movement of her perfect limbs. I silently begged for her to turn toward me one last time so I could sear into my mind's eye the beautiful symmetry of the hollow in the center of her neck, the swell of her breasts with their pink nipples lifted ever so slightly upward, the triangle of strawberry blond fluff that stood guard over a place that, under cover of darkness, gave me ecstasy. A place I knew I would never again gain entry. My brother's life meant the death of my hope.

"They made him," the commander said. "He escaped but was shot. He's been in the woods a few days and he's lost a lot of blood. He's in pretty bad shape. The helicopter should get him to Sacred Heart in twenty minutes. Should I send a car for you?"

"No," she said her voice tinged with panic. "I have family here. They'll drive me. I'm on my way." With her back to me, she wrapped herself in her kimono. Without turning around, she spoke as if nothing had happened between us.

"They found him alive. He's on his way to the hospital. The helicopter should be there soon. Can you be ready to leave in ten minutes?"

"Quinn . . ." I began, but there were no words to bridge the chasm that was deepening between us.

"I will do whatever you need," I said finally even though I wanted to take her in my arms and beg her to run away with me. I loved her. How could I live now having experienced her? I needed her to survive. But the monotone of her voice and the countenance of her back told me that I was

75

not the Gallagher she loved. She loved Jack. We had a moment and that is all it would ever be. Pure ecstasy for me. Very likely a huge mistake for her. If I had only known how that mistake would reverberate through the years, I never would have touched her.

She was silent all the way to the hospital. I drove her to the entrance before parking the car. She turned to me before she got out and said, "I thought he was dead. I was so mad at him for leaving me . . ." She looked down and fidgeted with the clasp of her handbag. She continued without looking up, "The wine . . ." she said before her voice trailed off again as if she were searching for words she couldn't quite find. She looked up and I could see the pain in her eyes. "Please don't hate me," she said.

"I could never hate you."

"He's my husband. I love him."

"I know," I said and with that, she opened the door and left without a single backward glance.

When I found her in the emergency room waiting area, she was surrounded by men from Jack's unit. She reached her hand toward me, pulled me to her side (despite last night I was still her anchor in the storm) and introduced me to everyone. They all looked like Jack somehow; ramrod straight posture, close cropped hair, muscular bodies practically quivering with the anticipation of action at any moment. The restless energy was palpable and I swear I could smell the testosterone in the air as they paced back and forth like caged animals waiting for news that their "brother" would survive.

Jack and I were sons of the same father. Real brothers. And I loved him as much as any brother could. But it was obvious that he had more in common with all these men than he ever did with me.

Everyone expected Jack to be the risk taker of the two of us. No one would ever suspect that I had risked my very soul for just one moment with his wife. I wondered if this brotherhood of men, Jack's brothers in justice who were experts in observation, could pick up the traces of betrayal lingering on me. Would Jack?

Waiting there for news that Jack would live, I did not wish him dead. I just wished his wife was mine. And I didn't regret what I had done though I never could have guessed where it would lead.

So many years later, I would like to believe that if given the chance to do it all over again, I would have done something different. If I had, maybe Quinn would still be alive.

And Daniel and Colleen.

And my mother and my father.

The weight of their deaths makes it difficult to breathe sometimes.

The bartender looked at Brendan when he remained quiet after his long sigh. Reaching over the bar, he refilled Brendan's empty whiskey glass one more time.

CHAPTER 7

SPOKANE THEN | 1979

WHEN JACK WAS IN THE HOSPITAL recovering from his gunshot wounds, Quinn spent every day with him learning all the exercises he would need for his rehabilitation. She couldn't wait for the day he would come home. It wouldn't be long now. He was progressing so fast. Even with his fitness before his injuries, his healing was nothing short of remarkable. It wasn't just that he had been shot in the back; it was that he hid out in the North Idaho woods for three days and nights and was suffering from exposure and dehydration when they found him. Rescuers were amazed that he was coherent. Then he amazed the doctors with recovery that was progressing at a lightning pace. Even Quinn was surprised. But Jack simply reminded her that a disciplined body obeys a disciplined mind.

By his fourth day in the hospital, Jack was demanding to start physical therapy. He said lying in his bed was driving him crazy. He needed to get back to work and finish what he started and he couldn't get back to work until he was well. His doctors were urging caution reminding him that he could easily re-injure himself if he pushed too hard since they had decided to leave the bullet in Jack's back for now. The bullet was lodged dangerously close to his spine and removing it could potentially do more harm than good. After all the swelling was gone and his muscles healed, they would re-evaluate whether to remove it. Jack promised to start slowly if they would only let him start.

Jack was true to his word. He carefully followed all the doctors' and physical therapists' instructions. He made good progress, feeling his strength return with each passing day. By the end of the second week, the doctors agreed to let him go home as long as he continued his rehab and agreed to abide by a few restrictions—like no stairs or sex—until he had another x-ray to see if the bullet remained stable.

Quinn couldn't wait for Jack to come home. She cleaned the whole place from top to bottom even though Jack wouldn't be able to venture past the main floor of their vintage 1920s Craftsman. There wasn't a speck of dirt anywhere. Every surface in the kitchen shined bright and you could have eaten just as safely from the floor as from a plate. The living room was rearranged to make sure nothing could trip Jack up. There was no clutter visible anywhere.

Jack's trophies and citations that lined the top of the leaded-glass cabinets flanking the fireplace were dusted and polished, as were the andirons that held perfectly arranged logs. In the kid's rooms, the beds were made with military precision and all the clothes were neatly put in their assigned drawers or closet. Every toy in the playroom (which was really an extraordinarily large hallway almost the size of a room that connected the upstairs bedrooms) was in its assigned spot, just the way Jack liked it. Jack wouldn't climb the stairs to see this part of the house for weeks but that didn't enter Quinn's mind. She made sure everything was as Jack liked it on the day that he arrived home. Besides, she never could be sure that Jack wouldn't push himself once he was no longer under the watchful eyes of the doctors and she knew how much the kid's messes upset him, so it made sense to have all the rooms neat and tidy.

In fact, a break from all the cleaning was about the only reason Quinn was relieved when Jack was away on assignments. She had learned long ago to pretend he was on a business trip like anyone else's husband instead of on a stake-out or undercover operation with all its inherent danger. Ignoring danger was something she became accustomed to. When Jack was in the Corps, he always volunteered for the most dangerous missions. Jack thrived on danger and Quinn found that exciting. When he joined the FBI, she continued to put out of her mind the danger that Jack faced every day. Pretending all was well was a skill Quinn developed extraordinarily well.

The first few days Jack was home he followed the doctor's orders as carefully as he had while at the hospital. Quinn drove Jack to physical therapy after she dropped the kids off at day camp. After therapy, Jack napped (or at least rested in bed) until the kids got home in the afternoon. By Jack's second week home they added early evening walks around Manito Park for the whole family. Colleen showed off her new skills on a two-wheeler (no training wheels) and Daniel dribbled his soccer ball, running circles around his parents.

One night, Jack suggested to Daniel that they carry a football to toss instead of dribbling the soccer ball. Quinn recognized how desperately Daniel tried to enjoy his father's favorite sport, but invariably he would lose interest after misjudging his father's passes. One evening, Daniel missed three passes in a row and dropped a fourth. Jack yelled at Daniel in frustration so Daniel picked up the ball and kept his distance walking ahead of his parents far enough so he wouldn't have to talk to his dad, but not far enough to get in trouble for disrespect. He went to his room as soon as they got home. When Quinn went to kiss Daniel goodnight, she tried to soothe him.

"Daddy only yelled because his back still hurts. You know he loves you."

Daniel looked his mother squarely in the eyes as he processed this information. After a moment, he looked down and continued his thinking. Quinn waited. Rushing him would only make the silence complete. She wanted him to trust her, to be able to tell her anything.

Finally he asked, "Mom, how come Dad only likes to play the games he likes instead of the games I like?"

"He likes the games you like sweetie."

"Uh-uhhh. Whenever I do something really cool in soccer, he just says 'that's nice' but when I catch the football he calls me his boy and tells me how great I am. I don't really like catching the football but I play with Dad because he likes it. And even though I'm trying to catch it all the time, sometimes I don't. When I miss he gets so mad and yells like I did it on purpose. Then, when I ask him to kick the soccer ball with me because it is something I can do good, he's always too busy or too tired. How can I show him I'm good at something if he won't play what I like?"

"Do well, not do good," the ever-present schoolteacher in Quinn corrected. "He's hurt now, honey. The doctors wouldn't want him to kick the soccer ball."

"Before he was hurt he didn't want to play soccer and when he's better, he still won't want to play what I like."

"I'll talk to him," Quinn promised as she stood to tuck him in. She kissed him and said, "Only ten minutes of reading with the flashlight. I'll be back to check." But both she and Daniel knew he had at least a half hour of reading before his mom would remember to come back to check on him, if she remembered at all.

The older he got the less she remembered to come back and since Jack had been home from the hospital, she mostly forgot. But she was sure that was okay with Daniel who loved reading almost as much as he loved soccer. He read well beyond his grade level and his mother was so pleased when they went to the bookstore just before Jack got home and Daniel chose a classic books series - *Chronicles of Narnia*. They usually enjoyed reading together at least a chapter of whatever book Daniel chose each night after Colleen was in bed. But that changed too when Jack came home. She hoped she would be back to reading with him by the time he started the third book in the series. He kept telling her he was too big for her to read to him anymore, but Quinn said no one is ever too big to be read to. Daniel once told her that listening to her voice as she read to him was almost like watching a movie. He could close his eyes and her voice would be everything. Quinn was grateful he enjoyed the reading as much as she did.

When Quinn got downstairs, Jack was relaxing by the fire he had built while she was putting the children to bed. The lights were off, there were two glasses of wine on the coffee table next to the couch, and music was softly playing. She was startled by the scene that reminded her of the night when Brendan stayed over while they were waiting for word of Jack. The night she deliberately had not thought about since the phone call came saying that Jack was alive. She had kept herself so busy with Jack's recovery and homecoming that she couldn't possibly think about what would happen when he wanted to make love again. She felt a tiny part of her fracture off as she tried to close that memory in a box that she prayed would never have to be opened again.

She was not an adulteress. She loved Jack and always had. She was so scared that night. She just wanted to be held. When Brendan put his arms around her, she realized how angry she was with Jack. She thought he was dead. She thought he had left her alone to raise their children. She needed Brendan so much in that moment, who could blame her? She never intended it. It was a momentary lapse that would never happen again. No one ever needed to know.

"Are you allowed to have wine?" she asked. She guessed he probably thought she was concerned about the pain medication he was on but she was just trying to buy some time. She wasn't quite ready for this moment yet.

"I haven't taken any medication since this afternoon. I've been thinking about this for days now. I feel good. It's time."

"But I thought there was a restriction until you get that x-ray," now that she had thought about her night with Brendan she wanted a little more time to prepare herself, get her head on straight. It might be time for Jack, but not for her.

"I know what I can do. I'm fine. We've been walking every day for the last week. I'm strong. My back is fine and if you're that worried, you can go on top," he said as he smiled that all-knowing smile of a husband who knows what his wife likes.

"How generous of you," she said smiling back at him. She handed him his wine and sat next to him with hers. Their sex life had always been robust. She couldn't object any more without having Jack question her. Not that Jack would ever assume that she had been unfaithful. Especially never with his brother. She suddenly felt very guilty. And trapped.

They sat in silence for a while before Jack reached out to touch the tear falling down her cheek. He then began to stroke her hair. His touch opened the floodgates and her tears dampened her blouse. He pulled her into a protective embrace.

"Jack," she began.

"It's okay. Everything is going to be fine," he said after shushing her. He lifted her face up to his, kissed the tears off her cheeks and quickly made his way toward her mouth to silence her.

She relaxed into his touch as he whispered, "I'm so sorry Quinn. I know I put you through hell and I know you've been so scared. But I'm fine now.

Really." She did not resist when he began to kiss her neck, opening her blouse as he went.

A disciplined body obeys a disciplined mind, Jack's mantra, was her last thought as she abandoned herself to her body's sensations.

Jack pulled her to a stand and carefully undressed her while he continued to caress and kiss each part of her body that he uncovered. When she was naked, he stepped back to admire her. She loved the way he looked at her so directly, so longingly. He let his robe fall and then settled down on cushions he had set on the floor and pulled her on top of him.

When she climaxed, tears of shame . . . of guilt . . . of relief . . . of joy . . . of love covered Jack's reddish brown chest hair turning it a golden brown. If Jack noticed her tears he didn't say so. His breathing accelerated as she continued to move. When Quinn was on top, Jack's orgasm often followed hers. When he did come, he grunted heavily before going very still.

"Are you okay?" she asked. She could tell by his breathing that their workout, even with her on top, may have hurt him some.

"I'm fine."

She rolled off him and they rested in silence in each other's arms, each in their own thoughts and oblivious to the other's pain. She was glad he didn't ask her about her tears.

A shiver coursed through her naked body as the fire died down. "It's time for bed," Quinn said.

Jack took another deep breath. "You go on. I'll be right there."

"Don't be long, my love." She kissed him and went to their room, relieved.

When Quinn left Jack tried moving his legs. They were dead weight. He tried to wiggle his toes. Nothing. The lightening that convulsed through him after his orgasm faded into a tingling that buzzed his lower body. Pins and needles, the kind you get when you hit that spot on your elbow, covered him from the waist down. Maybe if he lay still for a bit, normal feeling and movement would return.

He could hear the clicking of the hands on the clock in the kitchen. Each tick reverberated in the stillness around and within him. Five ticks, breathe in. Five ticks, breathe out. Control your mind, control the situation.

The fire in the fireplace was nothing more than a few embers now. No light, no heat. Darkness enveloped the room. His robe had fallen to the floor near the fireplace out of reach. The only blanket in the room was on the couch. He couldn't reach that either. Cushions offered some protection from the cold floor, but his body began to shiver.

Was he shivering from the cold or from pain? He concentrated again breathing with the far-away ticks of the kitchen clock. He tensed the muscles in his arms and chest to generate a little heat. His shivering stopped. "A disciplined body obeys a disciplined mind," he said out loud to no one.

"Flex," he commanded his toes. They didn't respond.

Tick. Tick. Tick. Tick. Tick. Focus. Breathe. If his legs wouldn't move, maybe he could army crawl at least to his robe. Fire surged in his lower back as he tried to roll onto his side. *Tick. Tick. Tick. Tick. Tick.* Focus. Breathe. To his toes he said, "Flex, damn it." Nothing. *Tick. Tick. Tick. Tick. Tick.* Focus. Breathe. Over and over and over again.

Quinn, and the comfort and warmth of their bed, suddenly seemed a thousand miles away. He didn't want Quinn to see him like this. Especially after all he had just put her through. He prayed to God his legs would move after a bit of rest. But sleep refused to come.

Just before dawn, he heard Quinn calling to him in a quiet whisper. Her calls grew louder and raised in pitch as her steps grew faster with her frantic search of all the rooms from the back of the house where she'd set up their temporary bedroom to the front living spaces. She gasped when she found him in the living room exactly where she'd left him hours before.

"Call an ambulance," Jack said with no hint of emotion in his voice.

The bullet had shifted and was pressing on his spine. The doctors couldn't tell him if the paralysis he was experiencing was permanent or not. Jack told the doctors he was sure his chances of recovery would rise once the bullet was removed. He couldn't go through life with a constant worry about paralysis every time he wanted to make love to his wife. They reminded him that he could have had the surgery this week had it not been for this setback. They would now have to wait another week until the swelling subsided again. They also reminded him that surgery was risky. Even if they were able to remove the bullet, they would not guarantee that he would walk again.

Jack knew he would walk again. *A disciplined body obeys a disciplined mind.* It got him through football. It got him through the Marines. And it got him through three days and nights in the wilderness after being shot. He would walk by the end of the summer if they just got the damn bullet out. No doubt about it.

While the doctor said he liked Jack's enthusiasm and positive thinking, he wanted him to be realistic. Even if everything went perfectly in the surgery, all the traumas his body had suffered in the last month would challenge anyone. And now he was back to square one because of this most recent injury. His body would need time to build strength.

Jack listened and then marked the day on his calendar that he would walk. He then set about creating the plan to make it happen.

Chapter 8

Seattle Now | 2013

| Thanksgiving | November 28 | 1:15 PM | Savannah |

SAVANNAH SANTIAGO WAS IN HER THIRD WEEK of her new job as chaplain for Seattle Regional Medical Center so she was not surprised to have holiday duty as the newest member of the team. She fell into her groove her second week there when she began seeing patients and their families after an initial whirlwind of introductions and orientation to the facilities and departments of the enormous medical center. It was exciting and Savannah relished every bit of it. She realized how much she had missed working in a hospital in the five years she'd been gone. Five years had been a lifetime ago.

It wasn't just any job that could tempt her back. She had loved her job at the Northwest Center for Faith and Healing and had worked there for nearly three years, including her internship. The work and the setting (a sleepy hamlet on Bainbridge Island) had been perfect for her, especially during her year of grieving. But when she met SRMC's senior chaplain at a healing conference in San Francisco in September and he recruited her to work with him, she saw the opportunity as Providential. She was looking forward to the challenge of bringing some of the spiritual theories and practices that served her and her clients at The Center to this huge public institution. And it was time to move beyond the physical and metaphorical safety of her island and face life head-on.

The timing worked out perfectly for her to spend a week between jobs with her mother on the coast. Savannah had suggested they do something together to keep from letting the sadness of the second anniversary of her father's death overwhelm her as it had the previous year. Why couldn't she be more like her mother? Since her father's death, her mother had been both spiritually and emotionally composed. Savannah knew how strong her parents' bond was yet her mother was almost tranquil, as if she knew something no one else knew. Maybe Geneviève's tranquility came from her own brush with death. But for Savannah her father's death was a cruel twist of fate. When she went home five years ago, she had a broken heart after leaving the man she thought she would marry. And she thought she was going home to help her mother die. Her plan was to help her father care for her dying mother and hope that in doing so, she would forget at least some of her own pain.

During that time, Savannah and her parents discussed only important things. There was no room for trivialities. Watching how her parents cared for each other made her sad about the love she let go of with Sean, but it also convinced her that trust was essential in a marriage. When her mother survived, Savannah gratefully re-charted her life's course keeping a watchful gaze for the love she knew she deserved.

While her father took her mother's reprieve in stride, saying that every day with his beloved Geneviève was a treasured gift from God, Savannah wanted to make sense of the miracle she had witnessed. Her mother had less than a four percent chance of surviving her cancer. A cancer Geneviève was convinced came from the hurt she'd suffered from her own father's rejection. When her mother recovered completely and spontaneously after a religious experience that Savannah witnessed, she returned to school to study the intersection of healing and faith.

While in school, she often spent weeks at a time house-sitting for her parents while they traveled to places they had always dreamed about. It was an opportunity they'd assumed was lost to them when Geneviève got sick, but once she was well they gorged their travel bug. After visiting far-flung places on both their bucket lists, they travelled to her father's hometown. It was in a little village just outside of San Miguel Allende in Mexico. Her mother was instantly smitten. Before long, her parents were talking about buying a house there to escape Seattle's soggy winters. They'd found the perfect little spot in San Miguel and had signed the papers, planning to go for their first extended stay right after the Thanksgiving holiday. Then it happened.

One fall morning two years ago, her father kissed his wife goodbye, jumped on his bike for an errand downtown and never returned home.

Nothing in all her years of schooling in psychology, counseling, or spiritual direction prepared Savannah for the crushing weight of the grief she felt over her father's unexpected death. She struggled to forgive the drunk driver as her mother had. But even knowing that forgiveness was at the root of her mother's miraculous recovery, Savannah labored to grant pardon. Yielding to that forgiveness was the hardest thing she had ever had to do. It was only last month that she finally felt the last vestiges of resentment blow away with the October winds at Ocean Shores. She was glad to start her new job feeling peaceful, ready to be open and vulnerable to the pain of others.

With her own grief and peace still so fresh in her heart, she knew she was the right person to attend to the Brennan/Powell family, a case she took the lead on this past weekend. Before she went to Michael's room, she remembered that when she visited the day before, she had promised his grandmother she'd find a priest to anoint Michael, which was not a particularly easy task on Thanksgiving. But she knew if she called Father Charles Jablonsky (CJ) he would do it. CJ was a priest in the order of the Society of Jesus—a Jesuit—who taught at Seattle University. He did not have parish work, so with the holiday he'd likely have a little free time on his hands. She could have asked any one of the priests assigned to SRMC (though she didn't know any of them yet) but she had a special place in her heart for CJ and she was certain of the gentleness he would bring.

She'd met CJ ages ago through Sean; she always enjoyed their conversations when the three of them gathered for dinner. When she and Sean split, she didn't see CJ again until she returned to school. He was one of her instructors in the Spirituality and Healing master's program. He taught the ritual prayer and healing class. He was also her advisor while she was in school and then he became her spiritual director (a relationship she would be happy to resurrect in person now that she lived in Seattle). If it hadn't been for CJ, she may never have been strong enough to embrace the forgiveness she knew she needed to move on. He was her spiritual rock when nothing made sense after her father's death. And to top it all off, he was the one who orchestrated the internship for her at The Center that subsequently led to her job with them. The mission of that place and its location had been exactly what she needed as she grieved.

CJ was the kind of guy you could always count on and she knew he'd come to the hospital to minister to Anna and her grandson, even on Thanksgiving Day. "I'll be there in twenty minutes and then we can go for a cup of coffee to catch up," he said when she called him.

True to his word, CJ knocked on Michael's door exactly twenty minutes later. Savannah could see Anna Powell's shoulders drop a little as she relaxed into CJ's consoling presence and prayer-filled ritual. He not only anointed Michael, he anointed Anna too.

When she protested saying it was Michael who was hurt, CJ said, "Not all pain is physical. A broken heart is reason enough for a sacramental anointing. You grieve your daughter and granddaughter. And you suffer watching Michael, hoping for your miracle. Anointing reminds us that God cries with us. And that resurrection will follow every kind of death."

They were just finishing the prayers over Anna when the door to Michael's room opened. She looked at the door and before her eyes could readjust to the room's darkness, she heard a voice that caused stomach butterflies to take flight.

"Savannah! CJ! What are you two doing here?" Sean said.

"Sean . . . I mean, Dr. Thomas," Savannah corrected herself. She was surprised to see him again in Michael's room. When they bumped into each other there the previous week, she relaxed a bit when she heard he was on medical leave. She still needed time to figure out how to be in such close proximity to him.

When they broke up, he was finishing his final year as a resident at the University of Washington's Medical Center. Now he was at Seattle's flagship trauma center. She shouldn't have been surprised; she just never expected them to end up in the same hospital in a city with so many of them. It made sense when she thought about it though. He always said he wanted to be just like the doctor who saved his life and what better place to do that but at one of the few Level 1 trauma centers in the Northwest.

"How good to see you again," Savannah said quickly composing herself as she reached out to grasp his hand between both of hers. She held on to him longer than if he'd been a stranger but not long enough for Anna Powell to notice that he meant anything to her.

"I'm the chaplain on duty for the holiday. When Mrs. Powell wanted a priest to administer anointing of the sick, I immediately thought of CJ."

"Right," Sean said. He paused and Savannah wondered what he was thinking as an awkward silence grew. Finally he said, "Please . . . Don't let me interrupt."

"We just finished," CJ said as he approached Sean with his arms outstretched to give one of his famous, bone-crushing bear hugs. "So good to see you, son. It's been much too long."

"Work . . . you know," Sean said without any conviction. A slight blush of redness became visible in the V of his oxford shirt leaving splotches of color on his neck.

Savannah noticed Anna smiling at them. It was the first time she'd seen Anna smile and it was beautiful. It reminded her it was time to get back to work and exit the room gracefully so that Sean could visit Michael too. Turning away from Sean she said, "We'll pick up again tomorrow Anna. I'll stop by around the same time, if that is OK with you. We can just keep getting to know each other until Michael wakes up."

"Yes, I'd like that. Thank you," Anna said.

Savannah noticed how tired Michael's grandmother looked. She hadn't left Michael's side since the crash almost a week ago. She wouldn't even go to the cafeteria for a meal. Judge Powell brought all her meals in, not that she ate much. The only time she wasn't here was when the Judge insisted she go to their hotel for a shower or a nap. He promised to stay with Michael and call her if there was the slightest change, and so far, there had been nothing.

The Judge left Michael's room when CJ arrived. He usually left when Savannah came by too. He would be polite enough but then would say he had to take a walk, make a phone call, or get a cup of coffee. Any excuse not to be around when Anna wanted to talk about God, the meaning in suffering, or (least of all) forgiveness. Savannah felt sad for Anna. She seemed so alone even when the Judge was with her. Anna could have used the support of a husband like her father had been. The kind of husband she wanted in her life. The kind of husband she had once hoped Sean would be.

CJ also turned back to Anna before he left, approaching her with his arms outstretched. She reached for him and he hugged her, saying words only Anna could hear. It reminded Savannah of when she saw her mother similarly hug a priest she'd just met. The one whose touch and whose words, Savannah was certain, healed her mother. She wondered how it was that certain priests engendered such immediate trust. She felt it when she met CJ and obviously Anna felt it too. He was gifted; you were safe in his presence.

Savannah thought Sean looked a bit embarrassed watching CJ hug Anna. Perhaps it was the emotional intimacy Anna and CJ already shared. Or maybe it was being in her presence again. His presence certainly unsettled her. They hadn't spoken to each other since the day she left over five years ago yet seeing him now, it felt like only a moment had passed. Even though she was the one who left him, she felt a twinge of regret for what might have been. Much more than a twinge truthfully, but she was so used to deep sadness now that it was all relative.

When CJ was ready to leave, he put his arm around Savannah's shoulder and gave her an affectionate squeeze before leading her to the door. She enjoyed that he was always so full of love. He simply couldn't contain it and shared it often with hugs and squeezes. His joy, his love of life and people, was infectious. He was like a large Polish leprechaun who poured out compassion from such a deep well of holiness that it was hard to stay sad or confused or anxious in his presence. She was grateful he was with her now as she saw Sean again. CJ paused just as he was opening the door and turned back, "Sean, could you step outside with us for a moment?"

The door was almost closed when Sean slipped through. He was as attractive as Savannah remembered. Seeing him now, she realized in the years they've been apart, she'd measured the appearance of all the other men she'd dated against him. They all came up short. None had the dark curls that were so thick her fingers would get caught in them when she rubbed his head. None had his features that, with her artist's eye, she could see were perfectly proportioned; his deeply set golden-green eyes, a straight, elegant nose, and full lips that sat over a square chin with the most adorable, barely noticeable cleft. None had the long, lean body that exuded a restrained strength and dynamic energy. The grace of his movements allowed his body to effortlessly glide whether they were skiing, kayaking, running, or on the dance floor. But what she loved most were his hands. She called them piano hands because they were so long and slender. She always said they contained a healing magic that she knew came straight from his heart.

"Savannah's shift is over late this afternoon," CJ began. "When she's done we're going to find a nice restaurant and talk about what we're grateful for." As CJ began to speak, Savannah realized she had been staring at Sean and that everyone else had noticed too. Her cheeks became warm as she looked down, only half listening to what CJ said. When his words finally registered she stammered, "We are what? I thought we were going for coffee now?" Savannah knew where this was going and she was not sure she was ready for it.

"We can have coffee too. It's Thanksgiving and I'm guessing neither of you has dinner plans. Seeing both of you today has me feeling particularly grateful," CJ answered her then shifted his gaze back to Sean and continued, "Why don't you join us? My treat." CJ turned briefly back to Savannah, "You don't mind, do you? It could be like old times," he said with an impish smile. Sean waited for Savannah to nod her head. When she did, a smile lit up his face and he shrugged his shoulders as if to say, "he's got us where he wants us." He accepted CJ's invitation.

"Okay, then, CJ said. "I'll wait for both of you at the Jesuit residence on campus. I'll look online to see who's open and we'll go from there. I'll see you around 5:30ish."

CJ hugged both of them once more, then left. Sean looked at her and smiled again in a way that made her heart flutter more than she wanted it to. "See you later," he said before retreating into Michael's room.

For the rest of her shift Savannah felt distracted. Her thoughts would wander back to Sean after every patient she saw. Because of the holiday, the hospital was quieter than usual; no surgeries, no follow-ups, no deliveries (except in maternity), no administrative staff, and only a handful of volunteers with very little to do. There was just enough medical staff to handle emergencies and the patients too sick to be discharged.

The whole place seemed to have the same unsettled quiet she now felt. She did everything possible to keep busy. She visited with all the patients on her list, wandered through pediatrics, checked the waiting areas in emergency, cardiac, and ICU to see if there were distraught family members waiting on news (all were empty). She finished all her paperwork, re-read the new employee handbook, studied the campus maps, re-read the bios for the other chaplains on staff, set up files in her computer and on her desk, organized her small workspace, and she still had three-quarters of an hour left on her shift.

She called her brother to let him know she'd be going to dinner with CJ so she would stop by later than planned. Her mother, her sister, and all her nieces and nephews were gathered at her brother's house for a feast that, for the second time, did not include her father. Dinner was already done by the time she called (always at 3 pm sharp) and she could hear the happy chaos of children playing in the background. She felt a wave of sadness.

Savannah didn't tell her brother she was meeting Sean for dinner. She wasn't hiding it. She simply didn't know how to feel about it and she knew her brother would ask. Though she tried to convince herself that she was over Sean and would be fine seeing him both as a work colleague and socially, the unsettledness that followed her all day let her know her argument was weak. She couldn't help being both a little concerned and very curious about why he was on medical leave. She knew Sean wouldn't be on it forever. She knew she would have to work through her feelings sooner rather than later.

After she hung up with her brother, she grabbed her pager and went to the hospital chapel to discuss with God what kind of woman loved a man who didn't want her. No, that wasn't quite true. She knew he did love her and he did want her. She felt it every day they were together. The problem really had been that he didn't trust her with his heart. He had a wall that she couldn't get around no matter how hard she tried. She knew from watching her parents that trust was essential for the kind of marriage she wanted. Leaving Sean was the hardest thing she ever did—until she grieved her father.

CHAPTER 9

SPOKANE THEN | 1979

JACK'S MOM, MAGGIE, expected this year's annual Labor Day picnic at their ranch on Sunday to be the biggest gathering yet. So many folks were planning to stop by to see Jack. Stories about his escape and the shooting had been in the papers for weeks. None of us could go anywhere all summer without people asking about him. Friends we hadn't heard from in years seemed to materialize out of thin air. The Gallagher name hadn't been in the papers this much since Jack led his high school football team to the state championship in what seemed like a lifetime ago. I never expected the night to end with me in the hospital. But then, since Jack started drinking, I was never sure what to expect.

Jack's parents moved out to a small ranch north of town shortly after Jack and I married. Maggie had complained for years that their home had gotten too small for all the family gatherings and with Tim just a few years from retirement she wanted to get out of the city and back to the country. They purchased twenty acres and Maggie designed the house that she and Tim spent the next few years constructing. They moved into a camper on the property that first summer and hired out enough of the work to have a working stove and a toilet before the first snowfall. Tim built the fireplace so they would have heat and then they hunkered down in the shell of their new home and set about completing the rest of the work themselves. The ranch was their second greatest source of pride and pleasure—family was first. Colleen's christening almost six years ago was the first big event in *the house that love built*, as Maggie was fond of saying.

It was a beautiful house. From the front door, you had a clear view outside through the floor-to-ceiling windows that lined the back of the

95

house. The view of grazing meadows and rolling hills swallowed by woods to the north and leveled plains that fell off the bluffs to the south made me smile every time I went there. I have to admit to being slightly jealous for the huge kitchen that was truly the heart of that home. It stretched from just off the front entryway through the back patio. It was a kitchen that rivaled the size of many small restaurants with two sinks, two dishwashers, two refrigerators, two ovens plus a six-burner stovetop and a multitude of prep areas on yards of counters. Maggie designed it to accommodate a minimum of four cooks with lots of little helpers so that meals could come together in a joyous riot of activity involving everyone.

The kitchen area also had large comfy chairs and a window seat with cushions as comfortable as any couch because Maggie said, "we all live in the kitchen anyway." Eating happened at an enormous round kitchen table topped with a thirty-six-inch Lazy-Susan, the size of other people's tables. Many a toddler enjoyed a merry-go-round ride on it when it wasn't stuffed with food.

When there wasn't a crowd, Tim, Maggie, and the guests that would invariably show up at meal times, would sit either at the counter that surrounded the eight-foot island in the middle of the kitchen or at the rollaway table that snugged into the wall by the window seat. In the summer, the southwestern wall of the kitchen, a combination of French doors and sliding glass doors, made al fresco dining the favorite of all the grandchildren.

To the left of the entry, within view of the kitchen, a great room warmed by a huge stone fireplace that Tim built with rocks from the property invited all to gather on cold winter nights. The master suite to the south plus two guest bedrooms to the north flanked this central heart of the house, each with a bathroom that could be accessed from the back patio. Nestled on a terrace below the patio was a large pool and spa made to look like a natural lagoon; it included a slide hidden beneath a small water fall that provided endless entertainment for adults and children alike. It was the perfect party set-up.

The ranch was also home to four horses, two dogs, small flocks of sheep and chickens, and a variable population of barn cats. Maggie's garden took nearly an acre of land and supplied the whole clan with fresh produce all summer long. From July onward Maggie would share her garden's bounty. After Labor Day, she became a canning fiend.

With the animals, the garden, a pool, and the creek and forest beyond the pasture, the Gallagher ranch was a kid's paradise. Tim and Maggie's brood of grandchildren happily congregated there as often as possible.

Colleen and Daniel spent most of July and August at the ranch after Jack reinjured himself and ended up in a wheel chair. He had become very impatient with the noise the kids made so it was easier on everyone, especially me, when Maggie would come in the mornings to get them. After a few trips, Maggie suggested the kids stay at the ranch for a few days, which turned into nearly the whole summer. A few times a week when Jack was at physical therapy, I made the drive north to relax by the pool or putter in the garden alongside Maggie and Colleen.

Colleen, who Maggie dubbed a budding St. Francis because of her affinity with nature, split her time between the pool, the garden, and the animals depending on who was there; me or one of her many cousins. When I was there, Colleen would excitedly show off the produce she had nurtured and present it to me as if it were an offering to the gods. Then she started pestering me almost daily for a loom when Maggie promised that Colleen could help the next time they sheared the sheep.

Daniel spent most mornings with his grandfather doing chores and his afternoons in the woods alone. He would pack a lunch, saddle a horse and head out to explore on his own. Now and again, one of his tomboyish cousins would join him but most often he wanted a little distance from the overwhelming number of Gallagher girls who appeared at the ranch on a daily basis. By Labor Day, he was tanned to a golden bronze and his hair lightened from dark auburn to a flaming red. He knew every trail and creek bed, every rock outcropping, and every open field that would provide a good spot to eat and think. Daniel, it seemed, had a lot to think about since his father was shot.

School was to start the Wednesday after the Labor Day so I kept the children busy most of that final week of summer with back-to-school shopping while Maggie got the ranch ready for the big Labor Day bash. I had my share of shopping to do too for maternity clothes that would take me through the fall. I had gotten a long-term substitute position at Holy Rosary School filling in for a teacher who was having complications for a baby due in late December. I was guaranteed work through February, which would work out perfectly since our baby was due at the end of April.

That final week of summer, the house had been filled with happy expectancy and the smell of new clothes, shoes, backpacks, markers, and notebooks. That smell brought back wonderful memories of my early years teaching. I had forgotten how exciting getting myself ready for a new school year could be.

Jack ignored all the hoopla. As these final days of summer passed, he became increasingly angry with his limitations and withdrew from us more each day. It had been nearly eight weeks since the operation to remove the bullet from his back after our little Fourth of July whoopee moved it, paralyzing his legs. He had planned to be walking by September yet his legs still tingled and refused to support his body. He could feel sensations in his legs but they were far away and foreign. He said it reminded him of biting down on his lips when Novocain hasn't completely worn off after a trip to the dentist. You knew you were supposed to feel more than you could. He said feeling pain would be better than feeling numb.

Being in a wheelchair at the end of August was not part of his plan. His timetable for walking kept getting pushed further and further out and with it so did his prospects for returning to his job. In that final week of August, his unit commander started making noises about Jack taking permanent disability. Jack was furious about it. What kind of loyalty was that, he screamed at me one night after brooding over his third beer. I stood silent as he ranted about still being at the top of his game; he was tough, cunning, resourceful; they needed him. I knew it was true. He wasn't just good at his job, he was outstanding and he had the citations to prove it. Even while in the hospital, he was able to provide valuable information he'd gotten while undercover at the North Idaho encampment of a white supremacist group that he'd infiltrated. He didn't know what tipped them off or who shot him, but he was able to explain their operation and how they were funding it with drug money. He knew who they collaborated with and what they were planning. The group moved underground after Jack escaped but the Bureau had a good idea of where they'd show up next because of Jack's intelligence.

Jack reminded me every time he talked with his commander that nothing gets done without good intelligence and he risked his life to get it. He felt betrayed when anyone mentioned anything about retirement. I tried to reassure him that everything would work out. But he would get angry and ask no one in particular what was he supposed to do? How did they expect him to feed a wife and two kids? Oh yeah, three kids now; another thing for him to get angry about, the child we never planned on. He said more than once that this child may be the reason he never walks again. I felt hurt that he blamed me. During one argument he said to me, "how could you have been so careless?" like I was the one who initiated sex that night.

I really did understand though. The baby was more pressure and it was coming just as his whole sense of manhood was threatened by the possibility of losing his job with the Bureau. I, however, wouldn't be disappointed if he wasn't an agent anymore. I was tired of the anxiety. But if this sullen, angry man was how he would be without that job, I couldn't live with that either.

Daniel and Colleen being home all that last week of August didn't help Jack's mood and he took his anger out on them. He became increasingly critical of everything they did. He said their lack of discipline was driving him crazy. All that time they spent at the ranch was turning them into slobs he said. I told him they were just being kids. Good kids. My kids. But Jack couldn't help complaining. If he wasn't yelling about something blocking his way as he tried to maneuver his chair around packages, clothes, or books on the floor in the hallway or living room, he was criticizing how Daniel combed his hair or how Colleen ate her food. I tried to be a buffer, to be the one to notice anything that might be in his way, but it's hard getting used to life with someone in a wheelchair, and it was exhausting trying to keep Jack from exploding. Part of it was that he felt that the whole family was moving on and he was "stuck on his ass." That was another thing. His crass language in front of the children was really starting to burn me.

When the screen door slammed shut, I realized that all our happy noise in the kitchen was irritating Jack. The kids and I were in the kitchen making our share of the food for the huge picnic on Sunday at the ranch.

Jack threatened not to come. He had the audacity to accuse his mother of playing show-and-tell with her crippled son. He had expected to attend the picnic walking or at least on crutches. And he said he would have if the doctors would let him workout like he wanted but they were moving him at a snail's pace. They were being overly cautious since the surgery. He was stuck in that chair and, as he said, "turning into a freak of nature" as the muscles in his legs wasted away while the ones in his arms got huge. He was working out every day but the physical therapist wasn't allowing Jack to do weight bearing exercise with his legs. He rarely let me see him undressed anymore; he didn't want me to see his "spindly chicken legs."

"Jesus Christ, will someone get that fucking phone," he yelled from the porch where he'd maneuvered his chair to get away from us. The whir of the blender had masked the ringing phone. I heard it only a moment before Jack yelled. I motioned for Daniel to answer it.

"Dad, it's for you," Daniel called from the kitchen.

"Bring the goddamn phone here," Jack commanded. Daniel looked at me with fear in his eyes so I took the phone from him and stormed toward Jack ready to give him a piece of my mind for his language. But then I realized Daniel had said, "just a moment sir" to the caller. It must be Commander Swift again so I decided not to say anything, though I did give Jack a rebuke with my eyes. He grabbed the phone from me, refusing to look at me or acknowledge the boorishness that was becoming a fixture in his personality.

"Agent Jack Gallagher," he said. He had been answering the phone like that for the last few weeks as if he kept saying *agent* it would continue to be true. Jack knew this call was coming. He had a doctor's appointment on Thursday and was supposed to call Commander Swift on Friday with the results of his latest tests. When they showed no changes, he didn't call. He figured he at least had until after the holiday weekend. It was Saturday and I could tell from the way Jack stared straight ahead, as if he were standing at attention listening to a drill sergeant screaming in his ear, that his commander was not happy. Jack's face masked any emotion but I could see the tiniest twitch in his cheek. I knew that he was holding in both rage and disappointment. The bureau had been pressuring him to retire, as they called it, but the paperwork would say that he would be separated because of permanent disability. Jack would never stand for that. He simply couldn't.

I went back to the kitchen to give him privacy since he couldn't move his chair while holding the phone. He hated being weak and he hated even more that I would see him as weak. I didn't see his injury as weakness but that was not something I could communicate to him no matter how many times I said it. I was learning a whole new language filled with silences, downcast eyes, and sidelong glances. And I was learning about a side of Jack I never would have guessed existed. But then again, maybe it was always there and I just refused to see it before.

With Jack on the phone, I had the sudden urge to finish my bulletin boards in the classroom I would occupy next week. It was just down the hall from the one where Colleen would start first grade and directly below the classroom where Daniel would join the big kids upstairs in the fourth-to-eighth grade wing of the school. Enlisting the help of both Daniel and Colleen, we quickly cleaned up the kitchen, packed up construction paper, glue, glitter, and some snacks and headed to school. Finding out what Jack talked about with his commander could wait until later when, maybe, he would be in a better mood.

He did not mention the call from Commander Swift during our dinner conversation that evening, if you could call *"pass the salt"* conversation. Our dinners had always been a time for telling jokes, sharing the news of the day, and in summer, giving book reports (I always prepared summer reading lists for Daniel to keep him from getting rusty during his time off). But during the final week before school started, the kids were too intimidated to speak and Jack became increasingly silent. After dinner he would spend the rest of the evenings in the workout room I set up for him in the sunroom. I had hoped it would help him heal. Instead he used it to escape from me. The next morning, Jack was sullen as we readied to go out to the ranch after Mass—which he refused to attend.

"It's time to go," I said when I had the car packed with food and kids.

"I'm not going."

"But your parents, your sisters, everybody is expecting you. You haven't been anywhere in weeks. They all want to see you."

"I am not a goddamn freak show."

"No one said that. No one even thinks it. They want to see you because . . ." and as I paused he continued for me.

"To see how much better I am? Well, I'm not better. Any idiot can see that. I don't need to parade it around so the whole family—and God-knows how many of my mother's fucking biddy friends—can look at me with pity and tut-tut as I wheel by."

"Jack, they don't pity you. They love you. They want to help you." I ignored his cursing in the same way I was ignoring his angry tone. It was becoming a habit.

"Can they help me walk? Can they? Because that is all I need right now. I have one fucking month to get walking or I lose my job. If they can't help me with that, then screw them."

"Oh, honey," I said as I crouched down to hug him but he turned his chair away as I reached for him.

"Mom, we're going to be late," Daniel pleaded from the back door.

"Just go," he said so softly I could barely hear him. "I don't need your pity either."

"I'm coming baby," I called to Daniel, "Get back in the car, I'll be right there." I moved toward Jack and put my hand on his shoulder.

"Jack, it's going to work out. You'll see. I thought you were dead, but you're here. And we're having a baby. I know the timing is bad and we didn't expect it, but it's a reminder that life is good. Miraculous really. It will be with you too. You'll walk in time. And if you don't, I'm OK with that because you're here and you're alive and I love you. We'll be fine," I said as I kissed the back of his head.

In response, he moved his head forward as he gave his chair a push to get it out of my reach. Before I turned to leave, I said, "I love you." Jack only grunted.

"Where's Jack," Maggie asked when we arrived. I explained what happened and Maggie stomped inside to call Jack. I didn't think Jack would pick up the phone but then I heard Maggie say in her lilting Irish accent, "Son,

Gallaghers don't give up and we don't give in. Stop feeling sorry for yourself, boy. You're alive. Today is a day to celebrate that."

I couldn't hear Jack's response but I'm sure it had something to do with work because Maggie said next, "If the good Lord left you here on earth, then you still have work to do. Do not doubt our God. Get yourself together. I'm sending Brendan over to get you."

Brendan called when he got to the house saying he and Jack were planning to do a little male-bonding and would show up before the fireworks, but they never made it. When I got home with the kids, there wasn't a light on in the house. I sent the kids upstairs to get ready for bed and went looking for Jack. I found his empty wheelchair next to the back steps leading to the patio. Panicked, I called his name as I ran past the landing and down the stairs to the basement.

"We're out here," Jack called.

He and Brendan were in the backyard with at least a dozen empty cans of beer on the ground around them and a half empty bottle of Jack Daniels in Jack's lap

"Some brother you are," I said to Brendan. "Help him back into the house."

"Uh-oh. Quinny is pissed off. Did we do something bad, Brendan?" Jack laughed.

Brendan was wise enough to keep his mouth shut and made a hasty retreat after helping Jack back into the house and his chair. Jack locked the doors and made his way to the bedroom.

"How were the fireworks," he asked.

"Like you care."

"Come on, Quinn. Can't a man have a drink with his brother without you getting all bent out of shape?"

"It was a lot more than one."

"So we had a few. At least he understands what I'm going through."

"He understands? What about me, I'm the one who has been here all summer helping you to get from the chair to the bed, from the chair to the couch, from the chair to the toilet for God's sake. I wanted just one nice day with you this summer. One day that we could enjoy as a family before I go to work and the kids go back to school and you couldn't even show up."

"But I . . ."

"It's not just about you Jack," I cut him off. Tears started to well in my eyes so I turned from him and went to the bathroom to brush my hair that was growing like a weed since the pregnancy began. I heard a lamp crash and went running back into the room. I found Jack on the floor struggling to get on the bed after falling from his wheelchair.

"Get away," he hissed. "I can do this." When he fell for the second time, I moved toward him to help. His left arm swung out to keep me away. He pulled himself up again bracing himself on his wheelchair and flopped onto the bed face down pushing the wheelchair as he fell on the bed. As he struggled to turn over I approached him again.

"Jack, please," I pleaded, "Let me help you."

"God damn it," he yelled. "I can do it myself." He raised up on his side and he pushed me hard. The thrust of Jack's arm sent me reeling. I twisted and fell over the wheelchair knocking the wind out of me and sending a piercing pain through my abdomen.

For the second time that summer, an ambulance was called to our house. This time it was for me.

Chapter 10

Seattle Now | 2013

Thanksgiving   November 28   6:00 pm   Savannah

CJ WAS A MAN WHO ENJOYED his food and it showed. While he wasn't exactly portly, there was something about his rounded physique that reminded Savannah of Friar Tuck. As a Jesuit, CJ didn't shave his hair in friar's tonsure but his hair was thinning in front and balding in the back in such a way that it resembled the monastic cut. Of course, without his clerical garb, the effect wasn't as noticeable. In the civilian clothes he wore this evening—a crisp, starched white shirt, maroon sweater, a tailored sport coat, and dark wool pants—he looked like any other middle-aged man who paid meticulous attention to his grooming. The same attention to detail was also evident in his cooking, which Savannah had enjoyed with him on many occasions.

CJ was a dedicated foodie, an excellent cook who with a little more notice, she was sure, would have created his own feast for them instead of finding a restaurant for their Thanksgiving meal. When he said they were going to the Space Needle, Sean complained that the food was terrible (his Aunt Regan had taken him once as a kid). CJ simply said, "Memories can be unreliable and sometimes things change. Trust me son."

Savannah was excited. She'd lived in the shadow of the famed tower for most of her life but had never gone to the top. As the youngest in the family, the trip to the top had been made long before she was born. She didn't care if the food was good or not, she wanted to see the city from five hundred feet high.

When they reached the revolving restaurant portion of the needle, Savannah chose the side of the table that would allow her to move forward with the platform's rotation. The movement was slow enough not to be disorienting when you walked yet quick enough that the view shifted ever so slightly every time she looked up (the whole dining room made one revolution every forty-five minutes). CJ, Savannah, and Sean ordered their drinks and then studied the menu. Savannah made her decision quickly so she could watch out the windows while the others took their time making up their minds. A child-like excitement enveloped her as new sights came into view every few minutes. Savannah could see the cars whizzing by on the Aurora Bridge, whose streetlights hovered in the blackness high above the water. She chuckled as she imagined its famous troll lying in wait underneath, sleeping in the darkness. She could pick out the ferries as they buzzed back and forth through the Sound like giant moths being drawn to the lights of Bainbridge, Bremerton, Vashon, or the Seattle terminals lined up along the piers that jutted into the Sound from Alaskan Way. Her only disappointment was that it was too dark to see Mt. Rainer. But the festive holiday lights already adorning homes visible on far away islands and in the close-by neighborhoods so familiar to her made up for it. She was so engrossed in the sights that the server cleared her throat twice before Savannah realized it was her turn to order.

As soon as the server left, Savannah jumped in with a question for Sean, "How long have you been at Seattle Regional?"

"Three years. How about you, when did you become a chaplain?" Sean asked, shifting the focus right back to her.

"I graduated in 2010. I was working at the Northwest Center for Faith and Healing until last month when I was offered the chance to bring some of that unique perspective here."

"Faith and healing . . . really? Do you believe in that . . . ?" Sean seemed to hesitate looking for a word he couldn't find. Finally, he simply added, "What happened to art therapy?"

She ignored his art therapy question to answer his question on faith and healing. "I do believe in it. I watched my mother's cancer go into complete remission because of faith."

"Your mother has cancer? Why didn't you call me?"

"Had cancer," Savannah said emphasizing the first word. "I found out just after we broke up. We were going our separate ways and there wasn't anything you could have done. She had only been given a few months to live so she didn't do any chemo. But she recovered fully. It was truly a miracle. Now, after working at the Center, I know my mother's case was not unique. I think miracles happen all the time," she said with absolute certainty and absolutely no defensiveness. "I still use my art therapy and counseling skills in my work but now I start from a different place in my heart. And my soul. I have a different understanding of forgiveness and its power to heal."

"There is a scripture passage that might help your understanding," CJ interrupted.

"I knew there must be one somewhere in this discussion," Sean said smiling.

"It's from Exodus, in the Old Testament. The passage says that the sins of the father will be visited upon the sons to the third or fourth generation," CJ began. "It is not that God is cruel, but that people who are wounded and who manage their lives without any kind of faith or spiritual center, often cannot love completely. Without a spiritual center, these wounded souls rely on human teachers, most often their parents who were also wounded souls and who similarly lacked the skill to love completely. Such wounded parents are unable to fully meet the needs of their children and this, in turn, wounds those children. The incomplete or conditional love they give is the best they can do, but it is not enough. And so the cycle continues, sometimes through many generations."

"That sounds pretty hopeless," Sean said. "But how does that have anything to do with miracles or healing?"

"Ah, but the passage continues on to say that the love of God is poured out unto the thousandth generation. God can fill in where our human love is inadequate. God helps us to forgive the wounds that bind us. God's love empowers us to tap into energies within us to heal the kind of wounds that can make us sick. Forgiveness is often the key that opens the tap."

"Forgiveness is all well and good for when you get cut off when you're driving, or when you get the wrong change, or your steak isn't done right, or even when you want to forgive those you love who disappoint you," Sean said as he caught Savannah's eye briefly before continuing. "But how can you forgive someone like Michael's father? Aren't there some things that are just unforgivable?" Sean asked.

"Depends on how you want to live," CJ said.

"What do you mean?" Sean asked.

"Not forgiving, especially for the most horrendous assaults, is like drinking poison and hoping the other person will die. Forgiveness doesn't equate with condoning and it doesn't prevent the wounded from setting protective boundaries or seeking justice. Forgiveness is about recognizing in the offender our shared humanity. It is about letting go of resentment, hatred, or the desire for revenge because such emotions create toxins in the soul. And just maybe also in bodies. Forgiveness washes those toxins out of your soul and perhaps, sometimes, out of your body too," CJ answered.

"Are you saying people cause their own diseases? That's an awful assertion. I know of no patient who wants to be sick. I will agree that some folks could do more to stay healthy, but no one would choose cardiac disease or cancer or any of the other awful things we attempt to heal. And Michael certainly didn't do anything to end up where he is," Sean said.

Savannah detected more than a hint of anger in his voice. His resistance wasn't uncommon. Many people, especially doctors, assume that relating healing in the soul to healing in the body are factually baseless and unscientific. Savannah learned by experience and scientific literature that both assumptions are untrue. And when you approach healing with an open mind, some of the more unconventional ideas can be life changing. If she hadn't witnessed so many miracles already, she would still be a skeptic too.

"No, son, it's not like that at all. Some things that happen are just a natural consequence of living in the world. Like Michael. His body was injured through terrible violence perpetrated upon him. And that little body needs all that modern medicine can provide to help that precious boy heal. But when his body is well, he'll require other methods to make sure his spirit and psyche heal too so that he doesn't bring his family wounds into his own future," CJ said in a soothing tone. Savannah could see Sean relaxing as CJ continued.

"Imagine for a moment though, what potential there might be if you looked at some of the diseases that are presented to you as metaphors and approached their treatment plans holistically. You already know that heart attacks spike on Mondays and around holidays and that people who have experienced the death of a loved one are accident prone. Something in their spirit or mind, or emotions or psyche is at work and you see the effects in your emergency room. If the spirit or mind can contribute to making someone sick, then why couldn't they also contribute to making them well? And maybe physical healing is not the miracle itself but a by-product of a different miracle. Maybe it is forgiveness—as in living without resentment and continuing to love when you've been wronged—that is the miracle. And maybe restored health is a secondary benefit of the choice to love when love is the last thing someone seems to deserve."

"Well, yeah but that isn't what you're saying. You're saying people cause their diseases," Sean said.

"No, that isn't what I'm saying at all. What I am saying is that there are multiple ways that disease can begin. What I'm saying is that the body may be a resonance chamber for what is going on in the soul or in our emotions. What if the man with cardiac disease didn't just have triglycerides gone amok but really had a broken heart from a wife who divorced him or from the realization that he spent his most generative years trading financial success for success in the most important relationships in his life? Would knowing that make a difference to his medical protocols?"

They all stopped speaking for a moment as the server placed a dish of oysters Rockefeller in the middle of the table. Savannah continued the conversation as Sean and CJ enjoyed the succulent gift from the sea.

"In the beginning, I had a hard time with feeling like I was blaming people too, Sean," Savannah admitted. "It's not as simple as it sounds or as simplistic as some would like to make it. There isn't always a direct line between cause and effect. But take my mom as an example. She has always been a good and loving person, not the kind of person who should have anything eating her insides, if we use a metaphor as CJ suggests. But she had a cancer that had started in her gut somewhere and had already metastasized by the time she was diagnosed. She was not a person who harbored any apparent anger or hostility or resentment. But what she did hold deep inside was the pain of rejection by a father who disowned her when she married my dad. Her sadness from having to choose the love of my father over the love of her family literally ate away at her insides," she looked directly into his eyes.

"How can you link the two?" Sean demanded.

"I didn't. She did. After her diagnosis, she wanted to put her affairs in order before she died. She tried to reconcile with her father but he rejected her again. She went to a priest. A healer," Savannah's eyes darted momentarily toward CJ before she continued. "He helped her forgive in a way she hadn't experienced before. Then she made her peace and got ready to die. That's when the miracle happened. Her cancer disappeared. She'll be the first one to tell you it was from the forgiveness."

"Are you sure she was diagnosed correctly?"

"I'm sure she wouldn't mind if you looked at her records," Savannah offered. "She definitely had cancer but she also had hurts from long ago that she'll tell you were "eating her alive." She'll be the first one to say her cancer was a physical manifestation of her emotional pain."

"No one is saying that people earn their diseases, unless of course they smoke, drink, or otherwise abuse themselves," CJ said. "But there is a growing body of evidence from credible scientific researchers confirming a mind-body-spirit link for many people suffering with many illnesses, and for many others who heal by non-traditional means. Medicine can't explain miracles or spontaneous remissions like Geneviève's. But it is not hocus-pocus. It is real healing and, in my humble experience, it arises from a spiritual place."

"I wish I could believe in miracles," Sean sighed. "I'd start with one big one for Michael and then take a tiny one for myself."

"You need a miracle too?" CJ asked.

"I've had a fainting spell or two. And those nightmares again. They started up again after rescuing Michael. The fact is, I've been placed on medical leave until it all gets sorted out." Sean said. "I was in Michael's room today on my own time."

"I remember those nightmares," Savannah said remembering how hard she had tried to get Sean to confide in her. That he wouldn't, or couldn't, trust her was why she walked away. Apparently though, given how she felt right now, her love for Sean hadn't diminished much in the years that followed.

"Have you ever thought about seeking spiritual healing for them?" CJ asked.

"I haven't," Sean confessed. "But I may need something soon, spiritual or otherwise. First though, I'll see what Kenji says next week about my MRI. You remember him, Savannah. My old roommate from college. He's a neurologist now."

Savannah nodded thinking of all the times she'd begged Sean to see someone, anyone about the headaches and nightmares. She was sure Ken was a great doctor, but she guessed he wasn't going to find anything specific. If everything started again after rescuing Michael, her hunch was that Sean's problems had a source that wasn't necessarily physical. She'd heard him talking in his sleep and had seen his panic when he woke. Sean had something that needed healing but she was pretty sure it wasn't anything solid that a doctor like Kenji could see or touch.

Chapter 11

Spokane Then | 1979

"Mr. Gallagher?" The doctor couldn't tell which man in the group huddled at the far end of the waiting room was Quinn Gallagher's husband. The group parted and she realized that it had to be the man in the wheel chair since Mrs. Gallagher said she tripped over a wheel chair. The doctor wasn't convinced that was exactly how things had occurred, but the woman was adamant that she tripped; "It was my fault," she said. How many women had she heard that from this weekend? She hated being the on-call obstetrician on holidays. She hated men who drank. And she hated that women covered up for them.

"Agent Gallagher," Jack corrected. The doctor ignored his correction. Now she was sure of her dislike for the man.

"Your wife is in serious condition. She's lost a lot of blood. And unfortunately, she also lost one baby. We are going to keep her here on bed rest for a few days and hope the other one holds on. It will be touch and go for a while. When she is more stable, we will release her, but she will still need complete bedrest to ensure the survival of the other baby."

"Don't worry, Doctor," Maggie interrupted. "When Quinn gets home, we will give her round-the-clock care." The doctor nodded at Maggie then turned her stern gaze back on Jack.

"That was a nasty fall your wife took. You should be more careful with that thing."

"Excuse me?" Jack said confused.

"That chair. Your wife said she tripped over it."

"Oh. Yes. Of course."

"She must have fallen awfully hard. We usually only see her types of injuries in pregnant women who are in car accidents or when they're hit or pushed with great force." The doctor watched Jack's face for any hint of culpability. He was expressionless. But then, aren't they all.

She didn't care that her face showed her disgust. In fact, she hoped the rest of the family would take the hint. She couldn't say to her patient, *you're lying,* even though she knew it was true. And she certainly couldn't say anything more to the family. But she was so tired of seeing the women she cared for suffering from abuse. Pregnancy was supposed to be a sacred time, not the most common time for domestic violence to begin.

After glaring at him without response, she walked away. When she got to the doorway, she turned back and said, "The nurse will let you know when you can see your wife. I expect she'll sleep until morning. Don't wake her." And then she was gone before Jack or anyone else could ask any more questions.

❧

When the doctor left the room Kit and Clare, Jack's middle sisters, shrugged their shoulders at each other before older sister Sissy, a nurse, said, "Don't mind her Jack. Those on-call docs can get pretty grumpy this late on a holiday weekend."

Jack let out a big sigh. Maggie grabbed his hand, "Oh Jack, she lost a baby. Did you know there were twins? Thank God one is still there. Poor Quinn . . . I didn't see her drink at all at the party. I wonder why she tripped. That is so unlike her . . . I hope she's not having dizzy spells. I had them with Kit and they were awful. Just awful . . . She was having such a good time tonight and then this. It is just so sad . . ." Maggie prattled on and on.

Jack had tuned her out. Quinn didn't tell the doctors he had pushed her. That's good. But the way the doctor looked at him, he knew she didn't believe Quinn. What did she expect, that if there was enough accusation in her tone that Jack would confess? He had already told his family Quinn had tripped and almost convinced himself that was true. It all happened so fast.

He didn't mean to push her. He certainly never meant to hurt her. He loved her. He was just under so much pressure. She should have just kept her distance and left him alone. He didn't need her help. If only Quinn would learn when to stay back. He wondered if Quinn knew she lost a baby. But thank God they weren't going to have two. They hadn't known they were having twins and she still has one baby. She'll be fine. But still . . . he had to make it up to her. He wasn't sure how, but he promised himself that he would make it up to her.

"Jack!"

By the time he looked up, Maggie was on her haunches in front of her son demanding his attention.

"The nurse said two of us can go in now. I'll take you in." Before his mother could grab the handles of the wheelchair, Jack yanked one wheel to turn his chair. He quickly rolled away without a word to his parents or his sisters or their husbands who had gathered at the hospital.

Why does every Gallagher gathering remind him of a circus lately? But his sisters were good for something this night. One of them had called Quinn's parents at their lake house in Coeur d'Alene where Jane and the Colonel spent weekends. Quinn would need her mother if they had any hope of refusing his mother's plan to move all of them out to the ranch. It was obvious Jack couldn't care for Quinn. But with what they'd been through, he didn't need his mother's prying eyes watching their every move.

His mother had just caught up to him when Jane and the Colonel appeared in the hallway. Jane called out to Maggie who ran to her and hugged her.

"She's going to be fine, Jane. She took a nasty spill. She lost a baby, but still has one. She had twins, Janie. Wouldn't that have been wonderful! But thank God she's going to be alright. You go with Jack. She can only have two visitors. I'm sure she'll want you there. She's sleeping and the nurse said not to wake her. But she'll know you're there." Maggie did not give Jane a chance to say anything. She hustled Jane off with Jack and took the Colonel to the section of the waiting area they had made their own.

After ten minutes, Jack returned. He was sure that in his absence his mother had been orchestrating a care plan for them. He hated needing their help. He hated needing anyone's help. When he came through the doorway, the Colonel stared at him like he knew it was Jack's fault. Jesus! What was happening to his life? One moment, everything was fine and the next everything was in pieces all around him. He spoke first before his mother had the chance.

"Jane is going to stay the night here with Quinn, in case she wakes up. Mom, could you and dad take me home? The kids are still up with Brendan, I'm sure. I need to get them to bed."

"How is she?" Sissy asked.

"She's asleep," Jack barked, ensuring no one asked any more questions.

"Jack," Maggie scolded as if he were a child, "it's been a hard night on all of us but that is no reason to be rude. Just tell us how she is." Jack dutifully obeyed his mother.

"I'm sorry Sissy. But I don't know any more yet. I didn't wake her but I could tell she'd been crying." With that, his composure started to crack. His mother saw it and started toward him, but he held up an arm to let her know to stay back. Tim, understanding his son's discomfort said, "It's been a long night. Let's all go home, say a few prayers, get some rest. Everything will look better tomorrow."

The Colonel continued to glare at Jack until Jack turned his wheelchair away and pushed toward the exit door to escape the awful truth.

CHAPTER 12

SPOKANE THEN | 1981

Tuesday	March 17	10:00 PM	Quinn

WHEN SHE HEARD THE CAR PULL UP in the driveway, she had a brief moment of relief before anger set in. Daniel and Colleen had gone to bed hours ago. She was in the living room nursing Sean-Patrick and tried to get upstairs with him before Jack got inside. She really didn't want to speak to Jack at the moment for fear of the words that would come out of her. He should have been home more than six hours ago. She was embarrassed trying to make excuses when both his parents and hers asked where he was before they cut the cake. They had all made such a big deal of Daniel's and Colleen's first birthdays but Jack didn't bother to make it home for Sean-Patrick. He didn't even call.

This was their last baby. Jack had made sure of that. Even so, she wanted to let go of her sadness (both for the baby who died and because she couldn't have any more children) and experience the same joy she had felt with their first two. Was that too much to ask? All she wanted for Sean-Patrick is what Daniel and Colleen had—two parents who were over the moon about him. Two parents who cared. But after all that happened between them this year, she wasn't sure that was possible.

Jack surprised her by coming in the front door instead of through the garage. He blocked her way up the stairs. They looked at each other without blinking and she could smell the whiskey on his breath. Despite her best intentions, her voice cut the silence between them with words dripping in sarcasm.

"Ah, you've been celebrating. Too bad your celebration didn't include your son; it was only his first birthday," she said.

She really hadn't wanted a fight, but she couldn't contain herself when she smelled the whiskey again. Not a single argument they had this entire

117

past year made any difference, except to make things worse. In this one year, they created enough hurt to fill two lifetimes. And now she felt devastated by the realization of their failed future if they continued this way.

"I know exactly what day it is," he sneered back. "You never let me fucking forget."

No matter how much he drank, neither one of them could forget the fight they had on this day last year. He nearly killed Quinn that day. God, there was blood everywhere. It wasn't a big push. It really wasn't. Not nearly as hard as the first time. But she was so pregnant she lost her balance. She started hemorrhaging. The baby was taken prematurely by Caesarian section. Quinn needed a hysterectomy to stop the bleeding. Both Quinn and the baby almost died.

She could see the memory of that day in Jack's eyes every time she looked at him. She could tell it haunted him. He had promised he would never touch her again in anger and she knew he meant it. She also knew that she could push every button in him. It was almost like radar. It certainly wasn't intentional and her therapist had to keep reminding her that women and men grieve differently.

It also didn't help that she and Jack were grieving different things. The therapist had given her some tools to deal with her anger and grief. But when Jack drank, that was just too much. How could she not be angry when his drinking was ruining everything she was working so hard to rebuild?

Jack stopped drinking after the first push, the one that made her lose Sean-Patrick's twin. She gave him the middle name Thomas and planned to tell him about his twin when he was older. And Jack didn't drink again until this past Thanksgiving. Just one he said. In thanksgiving for his family. But after that one, it was just one to celebrate Christmas. Then he got drunk on New Year's Eve (*doesn't everybody*, he said when she got upset). After that it was just a couple with the guys after work. Or just a couple with Brendan and his dad. Didn't anyone else see how all that drinking was ruining their lives? And now this. Showing up drunk after leaving her to make excuses to their family. Ignoring their precious Sean-Patrick.

Her words came tumbling out.

"Damn it Jack, it is not the baby's fault. It never was the baby's fault but you blame him. And you blame me," she had been thinking these words ever since she found out she was pregnant but saying them out loud suddenly released a weight she had not realized she was carrying.

"I don't blame him," Jack said as his fists opened and closed. She saw he was taking deep breaths, trying to control himself even in his drunken state. She moved closer to the stairs after he closed the front door, trying to increase the distance between them. She knew she should leave this conversation until morning. She shook her head, turned away from him and took another step towards the stairs before he grabbed her.

"Don't you turn away from me. I said I didn't blame the kid. I just needed time alone today. I didn't feel like celebrating."

She shook free of his grip, yelling back, "I heard you once tell Brendan that if it weren't for this baby your whole life would be different. But that is not true. This baby was all your doing, Jack! The doctor told you to wait; he told you that sex could reinjure your back. But you knew better. You couldn't wait, you had to have what you wanted, when you wanted it and I let you. God forgive me, I let you. And now we have a child that you can't stand to look at and a life that you resent."

The words she had hardly dared to think for months were suddenly free and she couldn't stop.

"This baby did not cause your injury. He did not cause you to lose your job with the Bureau. He did not force you to take a job as a policeman. He did not take away your future. You did that all by yourself."

The flush that had started at her neck now spread to her chest and cheeks. Her eyes glistened as tears gathered but did not fall. "This baby is a miracle," she screamed at him. "He hung on when his twin died. Remember that night Jack? Remember? That was the first time you pushed me. I should have left you then but I knew you didn't mean it. The Jack I married would never do a thing like that."

She could see the stinging truth of her words land as Jack flinched. His fists stopped moving and his shoulders dropped. Despite his defeat, she continued as hot tears traced red lines down her cheeks.

"Then this precious child hung on for six more months with the doctor telling me every month that he might not survive. I got on my knees every day and prayed asking God to forgive me for whatever I had done to deserve this. And I prayed that God would forgive you for what we both know you did," she said, her tears baptizing the baby's head.

"God damn it, Quinn," Jack said, "Lower your voice or you'll wake the kids."

But she was enraged now and her voice could no longer contain her emotions.

"The kids know, Jack! They remember the night Sean-Patrick was born. Do you Jack? Do you remember that night? It shouldn't be too hard. It was last St. Patrick's Day, this very day last year. That was the second time you pushed me and the second time you nearly killed this precious child. He was born that day not yet ready for the world. He didn't do anything but live through hell and yet you blame him for your so-called fucked up life because you're a cop instead of an FBI agent. But *you* did that, not him. He should hate you, but he lights up every time you walk in the room because he's only a baby and he doesn't know how much you despise him." When she finished, she slumped down on the first step of the stairway landing, sobbing. The baby started to cry.

"Momma," a small voice called from the top of the steps.

"See what you've done now?" Jack said to her as he moved toward the steps. He called up, "Get back to bed, Colleen." But Colleen began to cry more, calling *momma, momma* and then the baby started to wail and though Quinn tried to soothe him, he refused to be comforted. Moments later, Daniel was at the top of the stairs calling to his mother too. The crying, calling, and wailing were swirling into an emotional tornado of pain, guilt, and fear. And Jack, with his drinking, his wounds, and his anger, stood in its center.

"Damn it. I told you to get back to bed," Jack screamed as he stormed toward the steps again. "Doesn't anyone listen to me anymore? Get back to your beds or I'll put you back in them."

"Don't you dare," Quinn said as she stood up on the landing blocking Jack from going up. He pushed past her and took the steps two at a time. Daniel screamed, "Mama, no" as Quinn fell forward, barely missing the baby's head on the newel post. The sudden quiet that followed stopped Jack midway up the stairs. He turned to see Quinn lying prone on her back on the floor with the baby hugged to her chest. No one cried. Not Quinn. Not Sean-Patrick. Not Daniel. Not even little Colleen.

When Jack reached her side, she looked at him and said, "You pushed me while I was holding the baby." He couldn't stop saying he was sorry but Quinn could hear nothing but her own thoughts. She let him help her sit up and she looked directly in his eyes and said in a voice so calm it felt like it belonged to someone else, "I can't do this anymore. I want a divorce."

Slowly, she got off the floor, went into the living room and called her parents. Her voice was hollow and held no emotion when she asked her mother to come right now to get her and the children. Without a single question, her mother said they'd be there in twenty minutes. Quinn then went upstairs and told Daniel and Colleen that they were going to spend the night with Grammie and Grampie. She asked Daniel to read a story to Colleen in his room while they waited. With Sean-Patrick in her arms, she packed a single bag with changes of clothes for each of them. Jack met her in Sean-Patrick's room as she packed diapers.

"Quinn, I'm so sorry," he said. She had heard the exact same apology with the exact same sincerity when she awoke in the hospital having lost one of the two babies she carried. She heard it again after her hysterectomy. But she refused to hear it now. His pain had no effect on her this time. She had to protect her kids. Their pain was the only pain that mattered.

"Please . . . please! Don't do this," he pleaded. "I'll change. I promise I will."

"Jack, the problem is that you did change. The Jack I married could never do what you've done. When that Jack comes back, then we'll talk," she said with no anger now.

All he could say was "But . . ." The rest of his thought hung in the air between them. She knew what he was thinking, *Catholics don't get divorced.*

With the bag complete, she turned to look at him and said, "I've already talked to Father Garibaldi. He knows everything . . . about when you were shot . . . the babies . . . the drinking . . . the violence."

"What violence?" Jack interrupted. "I never hit you," he said.

"You didn't hit me Jack; you pushed me," she said matter-of-factly. A wall had come up within her to keep her emotions at bay so that she could do what needed to be done. For this one moment, she could report on her life as if it had happened to someone else. "You pushed me so hard you killed one baby and then you did it again and nearly killed me and this baby. I made excuses for you before; you were recovering, you hated that wheelchair, you were betrayed when the FBI put you on disability. I tried to understand, I tried to help. But I can't make excuses for you anymore. I won't let you hurt Sean-Patrick again. And I won't let you hurt me again. Father Garibaldi said I can probably get an annulment."

She had been considering leaving Jack for some time, though she hadn't admitted it to anyone in the family. Would anyone in his family believe that their favored son, their hero, had a dark side? She could hardly believe it herself. Her mother had suspicions, but Quinn told her mother the same lies she kept telling herself, making excuses for behavior that was inexcusable. When her mother asked not a single question tonight, Quinn realized that her mother knew all along. She was relieved to know her mother would understand. She was relieved that the nightmare was about to end.

It was well after midnight when the policeman knocked on their door more than an hour after Quinn's parents should have picked her up. Jack recognized the young cop standing there; he had seen him now and then at shift change. Jack was grateful he didn't have to start on nights. His years at the Bureau accounted for something giving him not only detective status but some seniority for assignments too. The young cop's expression was drawn tight against his youthful face and he fingered the hat he had removed immediately as the door was opened.

"Sir, there's been an accident," he said.

Chapter 13

Seattle Now | 2013

Savannah knocked quietly before opening the door to Michael's room. Anna was sitting by her grandson's side stroking his hair, singing. The door hadn't fully closed before the Judge stood, greeted her gruffly and then, as he'd done the last half-dozen or so times, said he needed a little fresh air and left.

Anna smiled when she saw Savannah. She was pleased to announce that Michael had had a peaceful night and so had she. She thanked Savannah for bringing CJ to see them.

"It was my pleasure, and his I'm sure," Savannah said. "You two seemed to have an instant connection."

"Yes, he is a holy man. Quite special," Anna said. "Speaking of special," she continued with a wry smile, "how long have you and Dr. Thomas been in love?" Savannah was taken aback by the question. As she tried to think of a way to answer, Anna continued, "I saw how you looked at each other, how you held his hand just a bit longer than friends would. There is definitely something between you two."

"Well, there once was," Savannah said. "We broke up almost five years ago. There's nothing between us anymore."

"That's not what I saw," Anna said with a little chuckle. She turned back to Michael and stroked his hair again. "Given what my daughter just suffered, and with the behavior you've seen from my husband lately, you'd think I'd have soured on love. But I haven't. My husband is a very good man, but he doesn't do well in situations where he's not in control. That he could not keep our daughter safe is haunting him." She stopped speaking but Savannah knew to wait. Anna was not done and she would not need any prompting to continue. She only needed space, holy space created by unhurried listening, to honor her thoughts.

"Our daughter, Lexie, paid a terrible price but I can't blame her for loving her husband, for trying to make her marriage work, or even for going back to him." She paused again and Savannah could see the pain in her eyes before she looked down at Michael. When she looked back at Savannah, Anna continued, "There was a time when Richard Brennan was a good man. A man worth loving. My daughter hoped for too long that the good Richard would reappear but his failures and his drinking changed him. He became violent and controlling. Though the violence shocked Lexie, she was used to men who were controlling so she didn't fully understand the danger until it was too late. It is hard to know when it is time to leave a relationship," she said with the tone of certainty of a woman who's been there. "Lexie loved a man whose disintegration destroyed her and her family. But we still have Michael. There was a lot that was good in that family once. And if Michael survives this, I'll teach him about all those good things."

"I'm sure you will," Savannah said.

"You know love isn't like in the movies or books," Anna continued. "Fear so often gets in the way. Fear got in Richard's way; in Lexie's way. It gets in my husband's way and it has gotten in my way. But I'm going to change that and be more like CJ. CJ loves fearlessly. That kind of fearless love is worth taking chances for. To have it, it's worth facing your biggest fear."

Savannah felt like Anna was looking directly into her heart. Yes, she was afraid of her feelings for Sean. Look where those feelings had already gotten her. Could she open herself up to that kind of pain again? Anna reached out and took Savannah's hand and spoke again with urgency.

"If you have a chance at love, real life-giving love, take it. There are no guarantees and sometimes you lose, but when love is good, when love is reciprocal, when love is true, it can heal wounds as deep as Michael's. Terrible, awful things happened, but good can come from it. Looking for that good, and holding on for dear life to its promise and potential to heal, is one of the few things giving me hope right now."

Light and sound spilled into the room as the door opened slowly. Savannah saw Sean carefully pushing the door open with his rear-end while holding a take-out tray with three cups of coffee. When he finally turned to enter the room, she could tell he was startled by her presence.

"Shoot," he said.

"What?"

"I only have three coffees and none of them are how you like it. I didn't realize you'd be here this early," Sean said. Savannah could tell he was clearly pleased that she was.

Anna jumped in, "How sweet that you brought us coffee again. Savannah can just have James's. He went for a walk."

"It's fine," Savannah said. "I'm sure he'll want it when he gets back. I have to run anyway. I haven't even checked-in yet."

"Let me make it up to you," Sean said quickly. "Have coffee with me tomorrow morning at the BuzzStop. Just like we used to do on Saturday mornings. I'll buy and you can tell me more about your mother's case."

When Savannah looked back to Anna, Anna whispered to her, "Fortune favors the brave."

Savannah accepted Sean's invitation. They would meet at 9:30am. As she walked to her office, she questioned her sanity but her intuition was telling her that opening her heart again to Sean was the right thing to do. She sincerely hoped her intuition was right.

CHAPTER 14

SPOKANE THEN | 1981

JACK RELAYED WHAT THE YOUNG COP had told him. Her father was killed instantly when a drunk driver crossed the center line. She stared at him as if he hadn't spoken. He asked her if she heard him and she nodded and then asked if her mother was in the car too. When he told her that her mother was still alive but seriously injured, she said, "Take me to the hospital." Jack tried to convince Quinn that his mother, Maggie, should come to stay with the children while they went to the hospital but she refused. Quinn said the children had already been through enough tonight and they needed her. But it was Quinn who needed the kids near her. Jack called Brendan to have him track down Regan so that they could all meet at the hospital. Quinn would need her sister.

At the hospital Brendan told Quinn that Regan was on her way from Seattle. He didn't know if she would drive or fly but she'd be there in just a few hours. For the briefest moment Quinn's eyes welled with tears before she regained her composure. Brendan reached to comfort her but Daniel moved in quickly to put his arms around her first. "Hey, Danny-boy, I'm surprised you're still awake," Brendan said as he smiled at his nephew and gently cuffed the back of his head.

"I'm not your boy and don't call me Danny." Daniel said. Quinn, always a stickler for politeness, didn't even shush him. Brendan asked where Jack was and Quinn, who held her sleeping baby with one arm and her oldest child with the other, cocked her head to point to the other side of the room where Jack sat with Colleen curled up asleep on his lap. Brendan offered to take the kids home but Quinn again insisted they stay with her. When Jack's mother arrived and offered to hold the baby for a while, Quinn refused that too. Quinn overheard Maggie comment that Quinn was behaving strangely but Brendan answered back that he would be acting strangely too if his father had just died. Jack stared straight ahead without saying a word.

As the sun rose on a clear, cold spring morning, the surgeon walked into the waiting room which by then was filled with Gallaghers. A nurse had shuttled between the operating room and the waiting room giving updates. The news throughout the night wasn't encouraging. When the doctor arrived, the set of his face telegraphed the outcome. He said, "Jane Kelly's family?" Quinn rushed toward him. Damn it, where was Regan?

The doctor shook his head as he said, "We did everything we could, but . . ." He got no further before Quinn whispered "No" as her legs gave out. The doctor caught her, careful not to hurt the baby in her arms. He gently placed them on the nearest bench. Jack put the sleeping Colleen in his mother's lap and Quinn allowed him to put his arm around her shoulder. She flinched the tiniest bit. She hadn't forgiven him but the comfort of his arms helped.

Before the doctor could say more, Regan arrived. She sat next to Quinn and held her hand while the doctor explained that the extent of their mother's injuries had been too great. Her heart finally gave out.

A tearless Quinn said, "I know how she felt."

TUESDAY	MARCH 24	NOON	QUINN

Snow fell out of gray clouds that seemed to hover just above their heads on the day of the funeral for Colonel Seamus and Jane Kelly. Regan and Quinn were not surprised when the Chapel at Fairchild Air Force Base was filled to capacity. Current officers and men from the unit her father led until his retirement came decked out in their formal winter blues bringing a brief smile to Quinn's face. She always had a special place in her heart for a man in uniform. His golfing buddies and their wives filled almost three rows. Representatives and fellow volunteers from all the charitable organizations for which her mother lent her many talents filled another two rows on both sides of the chapel. "The Snow Bunnies," a group of women who skied together whenever there was enough snow—were her mother's favorite friends. They all sat together filling another row looking shocked to be attending Janie's funeral instead of hearing her deep, lusty laughter as they raced with her on their favorite runs at Schweitzer or Silver or 49° North.

When the service was over, Colleen held Regan's hand and Daniel held Quinn's while the sisters walked arm-in-arm following their parents' caskets. Tim Gallagher followed behind the sisters holding Sean-Patrick as they slowly walked past the honor guard that stood at attention while the lone bagpiper led the procession out the door.

Regan had taken charge of all the arrangements. Since the Chapel was small, she requested that only in-laws involved in the service attend. If all the Gallaghers had shown up, there would not have been enough room for their parent's friends. So only Tim, Jack, and Brendan plus their brothers-in-law came. All but Tim were pall bearers. It takes a lot of men to carry two caskets.

The rest of the in-laws, Maggie and her six daughters, prepared food at the Kelly's home for the reception that followed the burial. At the house, Regan was visibly annoyed by all the children, but Quinn was glad to have them. The cousins kept Daniel and Colleen occupied and the older girls kept Sean-Patrick happy with their endless singing of nursery rhymes and patient games of peek-a-boo so that Quinn could tend to her parent's friends. It was nearly 10pm by the time the last guest went home.

The Snow Bunnies had the hardest time leaving since Janie always had them to her house for an après ski bowl of chili and glass of wine. Seamus, uncharacteristically mellow in retirement, always had everything prepared and waiting for them. To a person, the Snow Bunnies told Quinn that they couldn't bear to imagine some stranger living in Janie's house. Each one wanted just one more minute to remember everything just like it had been while Janie was here. Quinn decided each woman should have something of her mother's and promised herself that she would find just the right gift to give them when she went through her mother's things. She hoped Regan would stay in Spokane at least another week to help her with all that.

When Regan and Quinn went into the kitchen, they found it spotless. The dishwasher was running with its final load and Maggie was sitting alone at the kitchen table with a mug of tea.

129

"Would you like some?" Maggie asked. "It will help you settle down." Both women nodded and Maggie signaled them to sit while she prepared their tea.

"The baby is asleep in the guest room and Tim took Daniel, Colleen, and Jack out to the ranch," Maggie told Quinn. "I hope you don't mind. We all thought you could stay the night here with Regan so that you girls can relax before you have to take the next steps."

"Thank you," Quinn said. It had been an exhausting day. An exhausting week. And there was still more to come. She was dreading going through all their parents' things, selling their furniture and then the house. Burying your parents was hard enough without having to settle their estate too.

"You're welcome to spend the night too, Maggie," Regan suggested. "There's plenty of room and you've been working hard since dawn. It's so late. Don't drive out to the ranch now."

"Yeah, look what happened when our parents were out driving late," Quinn said without revealing that she was the reason they were out. "I don't think I could go through this again. Please. Stay."

"I'll stay under one condition," Maggie said. "You let me make you breakfast in the morning and you eat it. I don't think I saw either of you eat more than two bites all day."

At breakfast, Regan came into the room holding some papers in her hand. Maggie gave her a cup of coffee which she accepted with a smile as she breathed in the aroma. She sat in *her chair* at the table before she noticed that Quinn was already sitting in *her chair* nursing Sean-Patrick.

"Geeze, when are you going to wean that kid. He's a year old already," Regan said. "Don't you want your body back?"

"This is my last baby and I hope he nurses for another year," Quinn said hurt by her sister's callousness.

"I'm sorry, I didn't mean it like that," Regan said before quickly changing the subject. "I have the will. Dad sent me a copy last year after they updated it when Sean-Patrick was born."

"Oh?" Quinn knew that Regan would be the executor of their parent's estate. She was the oldest and even though she and their father had a prickly relationship, he trusted her. Quinn knew her father adored Regan but the two of them were so alike, they got into constant arguments. She just thought it was their way of showing affection. And besides being the oldest, Regan was a lawyer.

"The house is paid off and they left it to both of us. I don't want it. I'll sign my half over to you," Regan said matter-of-factly. "I'll take care of all the paperwork. I don't really need the furniture either. Take what you want, sell the rest and keep the money."

Quinn was still processing the crash, the deaths, the funeral. She knew they had to take care of all this, but first thing in the morning? Before breakfast? No small talk at all? Regan was a lawyer but she was also her sister. Plus, Quinn was unprepared for such an officious tone. This house and its contents were filled with memories of their parents and Regan acted as if she were a stranger doing her lawyering job and this was all just meaningless *stuff*.

"Quinn, pay attention. This is important," Regan scolded, ever the elder sister. Regan then continued, "Dad set up trusts for each of your kids, for college. They have a sizeable sum in them already. I'll manage them, if you like. When they turn thirty, the kids will get whatever is left over after college. You and I will split the rest of Mom and Dad's investments. Dad invested wisely and well. Congratulations, sis, you are now a wealthy woman."

Regan passed some documents across the table. The numbers on them were outrageous. Quinn was speechless. She knew her father tinkered in the market but she had no idea he had done so well. She couldn't quite figure out what to feel. She already felt guilty enough that her call to her parents caused their deaths. Now she was going to profit from it? Quinn burst into tears. Maggie went over to Quinn, took the baby and gave him to Regan, and then held Quinn while she cried.

"Oh, sweet dear. Shush. Shush. All will be well. All will be well. All matter of things shall be well," Maggie said quoting one of her favorite saints, Hildegard of Bingen.

Quinn cried until her tears ran dry. She was completely numb. She could never tell Regan that she was responsible for their parents' deaths. Regan might never forgive her and she didn't know how she could go on if that happened. Maybe Maggie was right. Maybe all could be well.

Jack had been perfect since that night. He was the Jack she had married. The kind one. The thoughtful one. The one who could read her mind and give her what she needed. He even took time to play with Sean-Patrick. Maybe things could work out. With all the support Quinn knew she could count on from Jack's family, she wasn't sure if she was strong enough to leave him now that she had no family of her own other than Regan. And if she left Jack now, Regan would want to know why. No. She couldn't leave Jack now. She couldn't be alone.

Regan's offer to give Quinn the house was so generous. Under the circumstances, it was kind of understandable too. Even though Regan and Brendan were still married and he lived here, Regan lived mostly in Seattle, where she made more money than she needed. She only came to Spokane if she HAD to. Like now.

Regan didn't seem to need people the way that Quinn did. When they were kids, Quinn often wondered if that was a brave facade or if Regan really didn't care that they moved away from family and friends time after time. She never cried the way Quinn did. The sisters long ago lost touch with their Texas cousins after their grandparents died. So now Jack's family was all Quinn had. Would they, could they, believe her if she confided what had been happening? Maybe she wouldn't have to confide in anyone if Jack stayed the Jack he'd been this week.

Money had been one of the big stressors between them. Maybe with the house and her inheritance, that would change. Counseling was definitely in their future. Jack would have to agree to go with her now. And with a house that was big enough for them and a little extra money, perhaps they could work things out. She could relax and be a full-time mom and they could pay off the rest of the medical bills that still hung over them. With those gone, maybe the guilt and anger would be gone too. She really wanted to believe it could work out. It had to. For the children's sake.

CHAPTER 15

SEATTLE/SPOKANE THEN | 1986

| WEDNESDAY | JANUARY 15 | 11:40 PM | BRENDAN |

"MR. AND MRS. GALLAGHER, your son is in critical condition. He has lost a great deal of blood from two gunshot wounds," the doctor rattled off. The doctor's white coat didn't hide the blood splashed all over the front of his blue scrubs. Brendan's thoughts went back to the house. God, there had been so much blood. He'd never seen that much blood in his life. Brendan hadn't told Regan the details but no matter how hard he tried, he couldn't stop going over them himself.

Quinn had called Brendan in a panic saying she was afraid. But by the time he got to their house, it was too late. Jack had shot Quinn in the chest. She was alive when Brendan found her but she didn't last long. She whispered her last words to him, "Jack shot my babies." Daniel, just on the cusp of manhood, died apparently trying to protect his mom. Brendan found him face up on the stairs near the kitchen, the baseball bat still clutched in his hand. A center-mass shot killed Daniel, in mid-swing no doubt. Colleen, sweet Colleen, died trying to shield little Sean-Patrick with her body. They were both upstairs in Daniel's room, slumped against the wall furthest from the door. Brendan saw blood all over Colleen, front and back. Sean-Patrick, still in Colleen's embrace, was covered in Colleen's blood plus his own but he was still breathing. Sean-Patrick had to survive. Maybe he could raise him, be the father he always wanted to be. That thought gave Brendan hope that some good could come from this nightmare.

"He needs surgery," the doctor continued. "We have to find all the bleeders but we're worried he won't make it through the surgery without more of his type than we have on hand right now. We are hoping that someone in your family is a match and could donate."

"He's our nephew," Regan's monotoned voice interrupted.

"What?"

"He's my sister's child."

"Is your sister here?"

"No."

"Can you call her; this is very serious," the doctor said, his voice edged with impatience.

"She's dead," Regan said without emotion.

The doctor looked at Brendan who had been silently watching the exchange, then back at Regan. He continued with a bit more compassion, "I'm sorry. But we need a donor or your nephew could die too. His blood type is not common. We don't have enough on hand. We could give him another type but after what he's been through, it would be so much safer for him if we could get blood from a family member with the same blood type. Does anyone in the family share his blood type?"

"What is it?" Brendan asked, certain that he already knew the answer.

"AB negative."

Brendan hesitated for a split second wondering now if his brother found out. How he wished that this would not be the way that his wife would find out too. With a wistful glance toward Regan he turned to the doctor and said, "I can donate."

Regan let out a moan as she sank down into the chair. Confused, the doctor asked, "Are you alright, Mrs. Gallagher?"

"No! I'm not alright," she shouted at the doctor. Her brittle voice rose bit by bit as she said, "My sister was just murdered by her lunatic husband. He also killed her other children. Everyone is dead except for Sean-Patrick, who you're telling me still may die. And his blood . . . Oh God, his blood . . . his blood." Sobs overtook her words. Brendan watched as the realization took root in her.

Regan looked at Brendan as if she were about to say something but no words formed. She doubled over as her sobs turned into keening. The mournful sound emanated from deep within her as she wrapped her arms around her body and rocked back and forth.

Brendan wanted to reach for her but he remained frozen in place just watching, and wondering if her arms were attempting to hold in the last vestiges of a world that was disintegrating into total chaos.

The doctor told Brendan that he'd given Regan a mild sedative to help settle her. Brendan nodded and ignored the unspoken questions he could see in the doctor's eyes. Finally, the doctor spoke again giving Brendan instructions for where to find the lab. Brendan walked as far as the elevator with the doctor hoping to get more assurances that with his blood Sean-Patrick would pull through. But both men were silent and the doctor didn't look back when Brendan stopped to push the elevator call button. Brendan found the lab, gave his blood, and prayed that it would save Sean-Patrick's life—and thus grant him some small measure of absolution.

He was desperate for Sean-Patrick to pull through. He could not bear another death on his conscience, especially now that he was sure Sean was his son, not Jack's. A son whose life was held by the most tenuous thread. If that thread breaks, Brendan would never get the chance to see his son grow up. The only hope the doctor offered about Sean-Patrick's chances was that if Brendan's blood was a good match, it could possibly stabilize the boy enough to allow them to do surgery without incident. Then if Sean-Patrick survived until morning, it would be a positive sign.

When Brendan returned from the lab he found Regan asleep on the couch in the empty waiting area closest to the ICU. Her breath had the ragged catches of someone who had cried long and hard. He didn't have the courage to wake her. He sat down on a chair next to her hoping to think of a way to explain. At 6 am he startled awake when someone came in to fix coffee. Regan was gone.

As the fog in his brain lifted, he remembered the nightmare events of the previous day. Quinn calling to say she was afraid. Brendan rushing to Quinn's house finding everyone shot. Sean-Patrick airlifted to Seattle. Regan figuring out Sean-Patrick was his.

The only thing that could make everything worse would be the boy's death. Brendan rushed to Sean-Patrick's bed in the ICU to see if he had made it through the night. Regan was already there, her head leaning on the window, her eyes trained on Sean-Patrick whose little body had so many tubes sticking out of it that he looked like Medusa.

Without looking at Brendan she said, "How dare you come here."

"Regan, please . . ."

"Don't! Don't say another word. I don't want to hear it. For god's sake Brendan, my sister?" Regan turned to look at him but before he could answer she spit out, "Quinn was my sister. Jack was your brother. How could you?" she asked before quickly saying, "Don't answer that. I don't want to know."

"It wasn't what you think. You had already left me. Jack was missing. Neither one of us ever meant it to happen."

"When did you know?" Regan said looking again toward Sean.

"I was never certain. At least not until last night."

Regan stood, turned her back to him and stared out the window. She wrapped her arms around her midsection as she had done the night before and Brendan thought she looked as if she was trying to keep her body from exploding from all the pain he'd created.

"I hate you," she said turning back toward him. "Your brother was the monster who pulled the trigger, but you were the one that killed them. All of them. Jack must have found out. And he's been so crazy lately, Quinn told me she was scared of him."

Brendan had the exact same thoughts while he was giving blood last night. He shook his head and whispered, "No. Regan, no."

"I want a divorce. You weren't worth the effort before but now, after this, I don't ever want to see you again. When Sean-Patrick is well, he will stay here with me in Seattle. You will never, NEVER, contact us. I don't ever want to hear the Gallagher name again, so keep your parents away from us too."

"How will I do that? He is all my parents have left."

"I don't care how you do it. But if I ever see anyone in your fucked-up family, I will tell them the truth about you. And I won't stop there. I'll tell your boss at that stupid Catholic school where you work, where they all think you are a saint. Hell, I'll even call the newspaper and give them a real scoop. I can just see the headlines now; adulterous history teacher and soccer coach fired after it's revealed that his love child is the only survivor of his murderous brother's rampage."

"Regan, please . . . ," Brendan begged.

"You get off easy, you coward. My sister and her children are dead."

"But Sean-Patrick needs his family even more now. He'll want to see us."

"I'm all the family he needs now. And I'll make sure he won't ever want to see any of you again. Hell, I'll make sure he won't even remember you. He's not even six goddamn years old yet. He got shot in the head. We'll be lucky if he lives. And if he does, I'll make sure he never knows you exist. Not even as his uncle. I'll help him forget everything that could hurt him."

"Regan . . ."

She turned away from him and he knew that was the end of this conversation.

But there would be more. There *had* to be. Sean-Patrick would need a father. And the boy was his son. The child he'd longed for.

When the shock of everything wore off, and when Sean-Patrick was getting better, he'd have another chance, he consoled himself. The way things looked now, even if he survived, Sean-Patrick would be in the hospital for some time after he woke up from the coma. And with his head wound, who knew what the damage would be. Regan never wanted a healthy child, never mind one who would need a lot of care. She would need Brendan's help to care for Sean-Patrick. She'd relent once she realized how hard being a parent was. He'd bide his time. Then he'd talk to her again. He would see his son again. He was sure of it.

Brendan was near the nurse's station when Regan called to him. "One last thing, don't you dare bury Quinn or the kids with that murderer. Bury them with my parents. At least my parents truly loved Quinn."

"I will," Brendan said. "I promise."

CHAPTER 16

SPOKANE THEN | 1986

TUESDAY   FEBRUARY 4   4:30 PM   BRENDAN

THE PHONE WAS RINGING when they walked in the door. Maggie Gallagher looked at her husband, shook her head and went to their room. There were no tears. She had cried them all out days ago. Only resigned exhaustion remained.

"Get that, Brendan," Tim said. Tim didn't even look at Brendan before shuffling into the kitchen to make tea. Media calls had been hounding the family since "the incident."

In the phone's insistent ring, Brendan heard a line from *The Bells,* an Edgar Allan Poe poem he'd memorized in grade school: *Brazen bells. What a tale of terror, now, their turbulency tells!*

Brendan walked to the living room to silence those brazen bells but unlike his dad, Brendan was hoping for a reporter because if it was Regan, he knew he was about to be kicked deeper into the living hell within his own tale of terror that he was already suffering.

It wasn't enough that his perfect baby brother killed his wife and two of their three children, but the only child to survive was the one who shared his rare blood type. The evidence of his complicity. His sin.

The idea that Jack found out and that's why he killed everyone haunted Brendan. But Jack's life had been on a downward spiral since he injured his back. His physical pain, Brendan thought, mirrored the pain of his disappointment from being retired from the FBI. Jack pretended that being "just a cop" was fine with him. But there were many times when good old Jack Daniels loosened his brother's tongue enough to break through his façade. Then he would complain bitterly to Brendan that the FBI betrayed

139

him when they forced him on disability. Brendan knew that sense of betrayal fed a smoldering rage deep within Jack.

There were times Brendan suspected (and times when he was sure) that Jack was self-medicating and not just with legal stuff like whiskey. Then with the allegations of being a dirty cop, Jack was at a breaking point. Were those allegations another betrayal? Or was it possible they were true? Quinn confided to Brendan that she was afraid of Jack, especially when he was drinking, which was often.

Jack was not a nice drunk. He was an angry drunk. But Brendan never thought he would hurt Quinn or the kids. She never said he had. But then why was she afraid of him? Brendan could tell Quinn's fear was real. Quinn told him she suspected that the allegations about the drugs were true; Jack was becoming someone she didn't recognize. She even floated the idea of leaving Jack. Brendan never knew if Quinn told Jack of her plans to leave but if she did, Jack would see that as another betrayal. Is that what made him snap? Still, Brendan couldn't help but wonder if Jack found out about the affair after all these years. His own brother's betrayal would definitely be one betrayal more than Jack could bear.

Quinn never told Brendan that Sean-Patrick was his. She always said he was premature but Brendan had done the math. It was only that one time but the blood thing confirmed it . . . right? As he reached for the phone, he knew it was Regan. He wondered how he would face his parents when they found out the truth. Regan was in such a state before, he was certain she would tell everyone now. His hand shook as he reached for the phone.

"Did you bury Quinn and the kids next to my parents?" Regan demanded as soon as she heard Brendan's hello. They were so beyond courtesies at this point. He knew she wanted only one answer from him. The one word that would prove he had, for once, chosen her over his family.

When Brendan told his mother that Regan wanted her sister and the kids buried with her parents at Fort George Wright cemetery, his mom broke down. Maggie conceded that Regan was right, Jack shouldn't be buried in the same plot with his family. But she pleaded with Brendan to get Regan's permission for all of them be in a Catholic cemetery near her. In consecrated ground, his mother had said. Holy ground.

Regan never agreed but Brendan didn't tell his mother that. Avoidance was only part of it. Reporters dogged the family's every move; they left the house as seldom as possible. Plus, they all were in the middle of the circus of the police investigation with the indignity of the autopsies. Even though it was obvious what happened, they had to suffer damning, detailed autopsies before the bodies were released for burial. In the weeks of waiting, Brendan was terrified that his parents would want to go to Seattle to see Sean-Patrick. Planning the funerals was the only way to keep them in Spokane. Brendan called the hospital daily pretending he was getting updates from Regan but he never got further than the ICU nurses. And the news there was always dishearteningly the same. No change.

Brendan's Irish-Catholic mother was beside herself with the funeral planning. She bounced back and forth between fear for her son's eternal damnation and fear about her grandchildren's souls if they were buried in unconsecrated ground. None of her logic, spiritual or otherwise, made any sense. But neither did it make sense that her son killed his family.

One priest, and only one (a guy Tim Gallagher went to high school with) was willing to give Maggie the solace of a Mass and Catholic burial for Jack. With that concession, and the countless Rosaries she prayed, Maggie felt hope for Jack's eternal salvation. Brendan's job, he reasoned, was to give his mother solace for her grandchildren too. And with all she was going through, she said she didn't know if she could do multiple services.

Regan couldn't possibly understand what all this was doing to his parents. But after hearing his mother's sobs night after night, Brendan knew. Regan's demands would force him to knowingly hurt his mother even more. Jack had made her feel a pain no mother should ever have to feel. Brendan knew he couldn't add to that. So, ignoring his promise to Regan, he told his mother to do what she thought best about Quinn and the kids. He hoped he could make Regan understand.

"I couldn't arrange it," Brendan said praying for compassion he knew he didn't deserve.

"Where are they?" Regan demanded.

"Not with Jack," Brendan said as if that would make a difference.

"Where are they?" she demanded again.

"Please understand . . ." Brendan begged. "My mother . . ."

"You bastard! You buried my sister and her babies with that fucking murderer, didn't you?"

Brendan inhaled in to speak, but she cut him off.

"Don't say another word!" she screamed.

In the silence that followed, Brendan imagined Regan was holding herself again like he'd seen her do in the hospital. He really had loved her once and the thought of her pain broke his heart—what little there was left of it. Most of it had already shattered into a million pieces when he found Quinn barely alive on her kitchen floor and knelt in the thick burgundy pool of her blood spreading over the white tile.

When Regan's breathing began to pulse in rapid bursts Brendan realized she was fighting to regain her composure. Brendan knew that the time for his sentence had come.

"Never . . . ever . . . come near . . . me again," her voice hiccupped. "I never want to see any of you again." She took a deep breath. "Sign the divorce paper as soon as you get them," she hissed.

"What about Sean-Patrick?" Brendan pleaded. "What will I tell my parents?"

"Tell them he's dead for all I care."

"But he's my son."

"How dare you!" she screamed again. "How dare you say that!"

Brendan had never said those words out loud but he had often thought them since Sean-Patrick was born. It was only one night so it wasn't like he could ever be sure. Quinn certainly never let on but it was a family joke that Sean-Patrick, with his thick black curly hair, looked more like Brendan than Jack. The Gallaghers were a family of blondes and redheads, except for Brendan and Sean-Patrick and some great grandmother way back in Ireland. Brendan wondered if Regan always suspected it and he begged God's forgiveness if Jack did too.

"Sean-Patrick is my sister's son. Not yours . . . My sister's!" Regan's voice seethed with hatred. Brendan could feel the heat of her rage burning through the phone lines. She took several deep breaths before continuing with an eerie calm in her voice, "Sean-Patrick is mine now. Stay away from us or I will destroy you like you've destroyed me. If I ever see any of you, you will live to regret it. I will tell everyone that you couldn't keep your hands off your brother's wife. Jack pulled the trigger, but you killed them. You killed them all. How many sins is that? You liar. You hypocrite. You adulterer. You murderer!"

She was saying exactly what Brendan said to himself a thousand times since that bloody day. Regan took another deep breath before finishing, "You are as dead to me as my sister, you bastard. I hate you."

Then she was gone. In the emptiness of the dial tone, Brendan heard the echo of his empty soul. *To the throbbing of the bells . . . Of the bells, bells, bells . . . To the sobbing of the bells . . .*

He sat back and closed his eyes. Before he could think of any way out, Tim was back with the tea.

"You look like you could use this," Tim said as he placed the cup next to Brendan. "Was that another damned reporter?"

"No, it was Regan," Brendan said truthfully. Then he lied.

"Sean-Patrick's dead," he said. He looked into his lap refusing to meet his father's gaze. Regan's words reverberated in him. Liar. Hypocrite. Adulterer. Murderer. Now, he thought, he could add coward too.

His parents had been through enough. He couldn't let them know that he was as awful as Jack. That maybe he was even worse because it was his sin that made Jack snap. What good would come from knowing the truth? Brendan reasoned that Sean-Patrick likely wouldn't live anyway, so why make them suffer more knowing that both their sons were responsible for this horror. This way at least he could somehow make it up to them in time.

Tim Gallagher let out a huge sigh and collapsed into his chair. He didn't flinch when his tea spilled over his hand before he set it on the table next to him. He sat as if made of stone and stared into space. Brendan watched the blood drain from his father's face. Silence grew between them. His father suddenly looked very old. Slowly Tim began to shake his head from side to side as if he were trying to remove Brendan's words. Without looking at his son again, Tim placed both hands on the arms of his chair and with a throaty groan he pushed himself to stand.

"Dad, wait . . ." Brendan said, wanting to tell him the truth, but Tim put his hand up to silence his son. It was already too late.

"How could Jack do this to us? All of them now," Tim said as he began the walk back to the bedroom he shared with Maggie. He made it as far as the foyer before he collapsed. Maggie came running when she heard the crash of the coat-tree Tim grabbed as he was falling.

Maggie called 911. Brendan started CPR. But Tim's heart was irrevocably broken.

To the tolling of the bells,
Of the bells, bells, bells, bells,
Bells, bells, bells...
To the moaning and the groaning of the bells.

PART 2

THE TRUTH WILL SET YOU FREE

*One does not become enlightened by imagining figures of light,
but by making the darkness conscious.*
—Carl Jung

CHAPTER 17

SEATTLE NOW | 2013

SATURDAY   NOVEMBER 30   9:30 AM   SAVANNAH/SEAN

SAVANNAH WAS HALF A BLOCK AWAY when she saw Sean pacing outside the BuzzStop, attempting to appear nonchalant. He was early and so was she.

When they went to dinner with CJ on Thanksgiving night, they fell into an easy rhythm again. CJ made sure to steer the conversation so that both Sean and Savannah admitted that there was no one special for either of them. When Sean saw her in Michael's room again yesterday, he asked her if she would meet him this morning for coffee. For old time's sake, he'd said. Plus, he wanted to hear more about her mother's spontaneous remission. He beamed with honest surprise when she said yes.

Once he left, Anna remarked again on the chemistry between them. Since Anna seemed able to see right through her, Savannah admitted that she still felt something for Sean. She thanked Anna for the advice from the previous day but said she was still planning on being cautious. Too much had happened between them not to be. Savannah was surprised by Anna's take on love given all she was going through but Anna assured her that caution was only necessary with some people. Other people deserve your whole heart. The problem was, Savannah *had* given Sean her whole heart. It was Sean who couldn't give her his.

Jeremy jumped out from behind the counter when he saw Savannah and gave her a huge hug. "Long time no see. Where have you been hiding? Oh, no matter. It's just good to have you back," he gushed with his familiar smile. His left eyebrow flexed its little barbell as he stage-whispered while tilting his head toward Sean, "And with him, eh???"

Savannah returned small talk with Jeremy and ordered her drink before she sat down at their old spot while Sean waited by the counter for their order. She couldn't believe it had been five years since they had done this together. In one way, it seemed like a whole lifetime ago yet in another way it seemed like yesterday. She knew she still loved him, but everything she'd experienced these last few years confirmed that love just isn't enough.

Sean set their coffees down and slid into the booth, sitting across from her.

"I went to your apartment once after we broke up. The manager said you had moved out but left no forwarding address. I supposed I could have tried harder to track you down, but I have to admit, I was still licking my wounds. I figured if you wanted me in your life at all, you would have let me know where you'd gone."

"I was hurting too," she said not wanting to rub salt in the wound, just wanting to be honest. She continued, "Then my mother called to say she had cancer and I just dropped everything. Literally. I quit my job, put all my things in storage and went home." Savannah remembered how horrible that week was. She'd set off an emotional bomb by leaving Sean and then it appeared as if her mom would leave her. "Since Mom had decided not to do chemo, we thought we would just have the six months her doctors had given her. She was feeling fine at the time, which made her diagnosis all the more shocking. We tried to convince her to do the chemo, but she said she would rather have six good months than a year of misery that the chemo would create. *'I've had a good life . . . no use messing it up just for a few extra months,'* mom said. Once I heard what the chemo would do to her, it seemed like the right thing."

"I wish I had known," Sean said.

"There wasn't anything you could have done"

"I could have been there for you"

"Ummm . . ." she replied with no hint of anger. But it did seem to sum up what their relationship had been. She had wanted a commitment from him that allowed her emotional entre, not just an indefinite comfortable arrangement that served his needs more than hers. And she hadn't moved in with him, not because she was a prude but because she didn't want to get stuck to a man who couldn't fully engage in a relationship with her.

"I always loved your mother," Sean said. "Did I ever tell you I sometimes fantasized that my mother had been beautiful, loving, and kind just like Geneviève?" Savannah could hear the pain and sadness in him. Family was something he'd craved. She knew he longed for the connection that she'd tried to give him. She wondered if either of them could love as fearlessly as Anna urged.

Savannah smiled, "Mom loved you. She still does. She was so disappointed when we broke up. She had hoped you would be the one to give her a curly-haired grandchild," Savannah smiled as she remembered the not so subtle way her mother would hint that it was time her baby girl settled down to make her some more grandbabies. She wasn't pushy about it but you always knew just what she was thinking.

"Yeah, she even said it to me once," Sean said. Savannah shook her head and mouthed *sorry* before continuing her mother's story.

"When she got her diagnosis, she decided to live right up to the moment she died. She said it was a gift that not everybody gets, knowing that your time is coming to an end. She made a list of all the things she needed to get done—to put her affairs in order she said—and we set about doing them. She planned to die without any unfinished business or a single regret. Who could have known what would come instead," Savannah paused as tears began well in her eyes. She couldn't recount this story without the pain of her father's absence coloring it. Sean reached out and placed his hand over hers and she did not pull away.

Savannah took a deep breath and continued, "We started out with a trip to Greece. It was tops on her list. She had always wanted to go with Pop. The Christmas after I graduated from college, they had given themselves a Mediterranean holiday to celebrate their new life as empty nesters. They had planned a month in Greece. My father had retired just before Thanksgiving that year and the holidays were wonderful, until Pop's heart attack. Luckily it all turned out fine that time but they never got back around to planning that trip to Greece. So, after her diagnosis we all went. Every single one of us. My parents paid for everything. A whole month in a Greek villa, though my brother and brother-in-law only came the last two weeks. My parents were up every morning before dawn to watch the sunrise and we toasted the sunset every night with Ouzo. Mom said she didn't want to miss a minute of the beauty of this world.

"At the end of that month, she gave me letters she had written for each grandchild about the gifts she thought they possessed. I am to give them the letters on their sixteenth birthdays. She said every child deserves to know how special they are, especially in their teen years. She was so happy that month it was hard to believe she was sick at all. Just before we left Greece she said that she had one last thing to tie up before she died and I was the only one who could help her."

"What did she need to do?" Sean asked when Savannah paused to sip her coffee.

"My mother wanted me to take her back to Georgia to try one last time to reconcile with her father. When we got there he refused to see her but she forgave him anyway, for her own sake she said. I think that is what ultimately saved her life. Her doctors were amazed. We were amazed. And my parents had a couple of really good years before my dad died. Sometimes life just isn't fair when a good man like my dad dies too young in a freak accident and a horrible man like my grandfather survives forever."

Jeremy appeared out of nowhere after Savannah landed her bombshell. Sean often wondered if Jeremy had a bit of a crush on Savannah. Her drinks always had a little something extra in them. And though the barista was great with everyone, Savannah seemed to make his eyes twinkle just a little brighter. Jeremy interrupted to say he was off for the day and hoped he'd see Savannah again "real soon." It gave Sean the moment he needed to compose himself.

Sitting so close to her again, he realized he still loved her. But then, he had always loved her from the moment he set eyes on her. He had wanted so much to give her the commitment she needed and deserved. He had even bought the ring. Then the nightmares started. She tried to get him to tell her what they were, but he shut her out. He spent more and more time at work and then somehow never found the right moment to give her the ring. So she moved on. When he went to her apartment and she was gone, he never imagined it was because her mother was sick.

He was dumbstruck by the revelation that Savannah's father was dead. He felt like such a selfish prick, not just for letting her leave but because he could have been there for her through all of it. He could have given her what he always craved: the comfort of someone who really knew you and accepted you. He could have loved her through her grief. It was impossible to believe she would forgive him such selfishness.

Sean could see so much of Geneviève in Savannah now, though when he first met Savannah's mother they appeared to be complete opposites. Savannah's coloring was nothing like that of Geneviève LaFontaine Whitcomb Santiago who, though she left her Georgia roots nearly forty years before Sean met her, continued to exude wealthy Southern aristocracy in her posture, her manners, her genteel understated appearance, in everything except snobbishness. Her insistence on the French pronunciation of her name, "zshan-vee-ev" instead of "jen-a-veev," never struck Sean as pretentious. Rather it was as elegant as the woman herself.

Geneviève had rosy-white skin that, even in her late sixties, rested agreeably over a nearly perfect, classic bone structure. Comfortable with her looks, Geneviève never used her beauty as a weapon to control others; her face beamed an openness that constantly invited both stranger and loved ones close. A towhead as a child, her thick straight hair darkened into her twenties, then turned completely white before her thirtieth birthday. As she aged, she kept it in the casual, elegant cut of a woman who was effortlessly at home in her body. Joy and love animated her and radiated from her like light.

Savannah's appearance, in contrast, bore the marks of her father's ancestry with a golden-brown skin that tanned into a deep mocha at the first hint of sunshine. Her face, slightly broader than her mother's but no less perfectly balanced, was surrounded by hair that was almost blue-black and fell in thick waves down her back when she didn't wear it tied back for work. Savannah's hair was the first thing that caught Sean's eye. In grad school Savannah always wore it loose until she started her internship. Sean was grateful that she only tied it back rather than cutting it as so many other professional women do.

When they were a couple, she used to purr like a kitten when he would run his hands through its silky mass before dinner. It had been one of their favorite rituals. They would meet at his apartment or hers for a quiet dinner after work. They both saw patients every day and liked the tranquility of home cooked meals rather than excitement of sushi bars or trendy restaurants that assaulted their budgets and their senses. On days when it was his turn to cook, he would have a drink waiting for her when she arrived. She would come in, hug him and then rub his back as she asked about his day. In her embrace, he would untie her braid and put his hands through her hair. He loved that something so simple could make her melt. Some nights, they would skip dinner altogether, getting lost in each other.

After Jeremy left, they sat in silence. But it was a comfortable silence. Savannah continued to let Sean hold her hand. He finally said, "Grief sucks."

Savannah let out a little laugh, "Yes it does. And no one knows that better right now than my mom, though you'd never know it from observing her. She has a seemingly endless well-spring of forgiveness that took me years to develop. For the entire first year after my father died, I hated God for the dirty trick of threatening my mother but then taking my father so suddenly. It was all such a shock. But there isn't a hint of hatred in my mother. Not for God. Not for losing the man who loved her almost perfectly. Not even for the driver who ran into him." Savannah sighed.

Sean looked at her but said nothing. He'd experienced Geneviève's love and missed it when he and Savannah split. And he remembered Geneviève's compassion for her own father despite the rift between them. He could understand, at least intellectually, forgiving her father but he had no idea how someone develops the depth of compassion that forgives a driver whose selfishness kills the love of your life. He knew he didn't have either kind in him. All you had to do was look at his relationship with Regan to see that.

"It's kind of amazing that your mother's cancer didn't return after the stress of your father's death," Sean said. "She must have been completely healed," he added realizing that the notion of emotions and sickness were not as foreign a concept to him as he made out during Thanksgiving dinner.

"Initially I did worry about that," Savannah admitted. "But something profound happened to her when we went to Georgia. The peace she found there, the peace that healed her, became intrinsic to her."

"What do you mean?" Sean asked, truly intrigued.

"After our month in Greece, my mother wanted to go home to Georgia and she wanted me and my father to take her. She said I should at least lay eyes on the city that gave me my name. We flew back to Seattle, bought tickets to Savannah and spent the better part of two weeks contacting her old friends and more cousins than you can imagine. Momma might have been an only child, but she did not grow up alone. She was so excited to head back home. The first week was a whirlwind of visits but her father was never far from her mind. She would ask everyone we met, *'Have you seen my daddy lately? How's he doing?'* The answers were always evasive. After meeting my cousins, I realized that my mother had always kept in touch with her mother. The cousins all had photographs of us and said my grandmother would constantly brag about us, as long as my grandfather wasn't around. Everyone knew not to even say my mother's name in his presence. Sight unseen, I despised this man."

"Where was your dad through all this?" Sean asked.

"Right where he'd been all my life, at my mother's side and comforting her as only he could," Savannah said as she looked up at Sean. She sighed and began again, "Finally, it was the day she had blocked out to see him. She didn't contact him in advance knowing he'd never agree to meet her. That morning, for the first time in my life, I saw my mother unsure of herself. Next thing I knew, I was standing on the porch of an old southern mansion asking to see a man who, as far as I knew, was as cruel a bastard as had ever been born."

"She sent you?"

"Yes. She knew she couldn't bear the rejection again if he turned her away. She sent me to ask him to meet with her."

"Did he agree?"

"No," she said barely audible. "He was too proud and too bitter." She paused again lost in her memories and Sean waited. He wondered what kind of shock it must have been for the old man to see Savannah. Except for the coloring, Savannah looked so much like her mom. And even if the coloring threw you off for a moment, looking at Savannah's eyes were like looking at Geneviève's. It was their eyes that Sean first noticed were the same. They were an exotic almond shape with tight lids that defied any application of artificial hues that would only detract from the natural, Caribbean azure blue of their irises. The only difference in the eyes between mother and daughter was the addition of little flecks of gold scattered in Savannah's eyes while Geneviève's color was pure ocean. Geneviève's eyes, though striking, seemed so natural with her light hair and milky white skin. Savannah's dark hair and complexion made her eyes stand out like lighthouse beacons in a storm. They were eyes that drew you in and wouldn't let you go. And filled with tears right now, they caused Sean to sincerely wonder at the sanity of a man who could let those eyes go. And he didn't just mean Savannah's grandfather.

Savannah's athletic body was also the mirror image of her mother's, though it looked more delicate and fragile on Geneviève. Savannah had defined muscles that enabled her to whip his butt every time they had skied together and served to add strength to the graceful gestures that were clones of her mother's. The movement of both women's bodies conveyed a purposeful confidence and self-assured composure that could diffuse the most difficult situations. That composure must have been sorely tested when Savannah met her grandfather, Sean thought.

Savannah continued, "His maid answered the door and I asked to speak with Gaylord Whitcomb. The woman asked if I had an appointment. I said no, I was his granddaughter. The woman eyed me suspiciously and said that there were no photos of any grandchildren in the house and that his only child died when she was 22. Then she said, '*Sir keeps the last photo of her—the one taken the day she graduated from college—on his desk.*' When she said '*poor dear*' I didn't know if she meant my mother or my grandfather but I felt like strangling her. Instead I just said please tell him I am here. The maid was visibly annoyed. She huffed, '*wait here*' and closed the door."

"She didn't even invite you in? So much for Southern hospitality."

When she began again, Sean noticed that Savannah's voice seemed far away, almost disembodied. He knew the conversation did not go as she had hoped.

"When my grandfather came to the door, I introduced myself, 'Mr. Whitcomb, I am Savannah Whitcomb Santiago. Your granddaughter.' I could tell he recognized me but he stared right through me and said, 'you must be mistaken miss, my daughter died before she had any children.' My mother had tried to prepare me for how he would be, but. . ." her voice trailed off again. Sean waited again knowing there was nothing he could say that could rationalize such cruelty.

"I told him my mother was dying and she wanted to see him. He stared at me for what seemed like an eternity. Then he said, '*wait here.*' He turned and left me alone on the porch again. Moments later he returned with a box. He handed it to me and said, 'I found this after my wife died. I am sorry that your mother is dying but *my* daughter died when she was 22. She made her choice. Good day young lady.' And that was it. He closed the door."

"What did you do?"

"I sat down on the steps of his grand porch. I knew my presence would annoy him and I also knew I couldn't face my mother so soon. So, I opened the box. In it were letters from my mother to her mother and photographs of all of us as we were growing up. There were even a couple of photos of my mom and grandmother with me and my brother and sister at a beach house when I was about two. I put the photos and letters back in the box and went back to the hotel where my mother was waiting with my dad. When I handed her the box, she knew what his answer had been. I didn't have to say anything, which was good because I couldn't bear to tell her he refused to see her or that he tells people she's dead. She sat for a moment on the bed looking through the box and came to the picture of us at the beach when I was two. She studied it for a moment and sighed. Then she looked at me and my dad and said, '*There is a priest I need to see and then I'd like to go to noon Mass.*' I knew then that my mother was expecting this all along."

Their coffee was long gone and Sean could tell there was so much more to Savannah's story. He offered more coffee or a walk in the park to finish her story. It was unseasonably warm and sunny out so Sean was delighted when

Savannah chose a walk. He told her he knew the perfect spot in Boren Park.

Sean took Savannah to his thinking tree deep in a ravine of an old growth forest that was an oasis of natural beauty, an unexpected jewel in such an urban area. He told Savannah he'd found this spot when he was a teenager but hadn't been back in years. Body memory helped him find the exact tree that had comforted him so often as a boy. It was a massive cedar that had fallen ages ago. Even in its brokenness, it still exuded grace and power. Sean felt a kindred spirit in the tree.

When he found it again, the sun was shining down on them as they settled together with their backs against the tree. It felt like a good omen to Sean. They sat in silence for a bit just absorbing the warmth of the sun and the beauty that surrounded them. Finally, Sean said, "When we were in the coffee shop, your mother had said she wanted to see a priest. Is this the priest you mentioned at dinner on Thanksgiving night?"

Savannah nodded. Tears glistened again in her eyes but didn't fall.

"My mother wanted us to pray for her father at Mass. I said, you've got to be kidding me! After what he just did? But mom said, please do this with me. And so, I did. How could I not help her finish what she had to do even if I thought her father deserved to rot in hell for what he'd just done."

"He really told people she was dead?" Sean asked. "Just because she married your dad?"

Savannah nodded again and Sean shook his head in disbelief. He couldn't understand how someone could knowingly give up his flesh and blood child. He reached for her hand and was pleased when she let him hold it again. Savannah continued her story.

"We arrived at the church quite early. My father went into the main part of the church, knelt by a statue of the Virgin Mary and began saying the Rosary. Mom found the priest. I watched from a respectable distance as the man went from stranger to confidant in an instant. I found out later that they had corresponded in letters before she arrived, but this was the first time they met in person. The priest listened to what my mother was saying with a grave look on his face. He nodded, saying nothing until she stopped speaking. At the end of her confession a single tear slipped out and traveled un-accosted down her cheek."

Sean noticed a tear fall from Savannah's eye as she remembered her mother's pain. Sean wanted to take Savannah in his arms but he hadn't earned that right. Instead he gave her hand a gentle squeeze. After another moment, Savannah continued.

"When my mother didn't say any more, the priest put both hands on her shoulders while he spoke looking directly into her eyes. As I watched them I felt a twinge of embarrassment as if I were a voyeur. At least I was far enough away that I couldn't hear the exchange between them because it was obviously very personal. The priest then put his right hand on my mother's head and continued to speak as he traced the sign of the cross on her forehead. This last touch opened the floodgates for her. The priest put his arms around my mother as her tears gave way to sobs; he held her until her broken heart poured out all the hurt it held. Nothing in the priest's demeanor rushed my mother as his presence gave witness to pain that flowed from years of her father's rejection. As I watched, it seemed as if the old priest was actually absorbing some of my mother's pain."

"Did she ever tell you what the priest said?" Sean asked after Savannah fell silent again.

"Not directly but I think what we did after Mass had something to do with what he'd said to her and I think it was essential to my mother's miracle. But even before that part, when she came over to me in church, there was a peacefulness in her that was palpable and I wished I had access to it. We found my father and sat with him and Mass began. When my mother squeezed my hand during the line in the *Our Father* that says forgive us our sins as we forgive those who sin against us, I felt a pang of guilt because I wasn't anywhere near ready to forgive. After Mass, my mother wanted to go to the beach for a picnic, but first she said we needed to stop back at the hotel to get the box my grandfather had given me."

"And you think it was what the priest did or said that caused her miraculous recovery?" Sean asked.

"That was a big part of it. But what *we* did next, the ritual, was also a big part of it. I didn't understand that fully until I went to school following my mother's miracle, but I really understand it now."

"Why? What happened? What did you do?"

"We went to the beach near the Whitcomb family summer house and burned photos," Savannah replied. "I know it sounds a little crazy. There was more to it than just burning photos, but there were two particular photos of my mother with her father. One was when she was a little girl and one was when she graduated college. She had the same brightness in her in each photo but her father looked so different. In one, he exuded joy as he reached to embrace the little girl running to him. In the other one, his expression was stiff and angry like life was a terrible burden. My mother had already refused to marry the man my grandfather wanted her to because she loved my father. Her father couldn't accept that. The happy man in the first photo looked nothing like the stern man in the other one. There was no joy in him anymore. Burning those two photos on the little altar my mother made in the sand released something. Not just for my mother, but for me and my father too."

Savannah fell silent for a moment. The sun was high in the sky, still warming them through the naked trees as they sat on a carpet of orange and gold leaves. Sean saw some clouds building to the west. Occasionally, the light breeze gusted enough to rustle the few leaves that clung to the trees. The warmth wouldn't last much longer.

Savannah sighed.

"You know, our lives could have been so different if my grandfather had been able to love my mother enough to accept my father."

"That must have been a difficult day for all of you," Sean said, not knowing the right words to comfort Savannah.

"It was, and it wasn't. It was terrible seeing the pain my grandfather caused my mother. And seeing that old beach house boarded up and decaying in such a gorgeous environment was also really sad. In one of the photos in that box my grandfather had, I was on that same beach as a toddler and the beach house was grand. The differences in the house then and now were almost as stark as the differences in my grandfather."

"It's kind of amazing," Sean said filling the space when Savannah fell silent again, "how places not only hold but also reflect the experiences and memories of the people who occupy them." He thought about the house he grew up in with Regan, how it held so much of his sadness. Then he shifted his thoughts back to Savannah's story. "You said that it wasn't difficult. How so?"

"Before we burned the photos, we sat on a blanket sharing cheeses, fresh bread, and wine while my mother and father told stories from their childhoods. It was so serene and joyful. And I learned things about both my parents that I hadn't known before. We had a wonderful time. Before sunset, my mother smoothed out a place in the sand in the shelter of a nearby dune, lit candles, and placed those two photos near the candles. She became very serious again and told me that hoping a person will change to suit your desire is nothing more than predestined disappointment. She said to allow people to be who they are and forgive them for being neither perfect or who you need them to be."

"Sounds like very sage advice," Sean chimed in.

"It is. She said forgiveness is a sign of mature love and is the one true gift we can give each other."

"She sounds like CJ now," Sean said hoping he didn't sound rude.

"I know. But they both have a point I think. She told me that my grandfather drank a poison of resentment and is so alone because of it. She said he needed our compassion, not our anger."

Sean let out a low whistle. "Wow, she's really something. After everything her father did to her all those years and then refusing her dying wish to reconcile and she wanted to forgive him? To show him compassion? Geneviève is one tough—and loving—cookie."

Savannah nodded and continued. "My mother took each photo, kissed it, and then held each one over the candle flame, turning until the edges glowed red and then curled back. When the heat became too intense, she dropped them onto the sand and we all watched as the images melted into ash. Then she dug a small hole, scooped in the ashes, patted sand over them, and whispered, 'I will always love you Daddy.'

"Three weeks later, when my mother's oncologist insisted she stop by for a check-up, they found no cancer in her. The doctors did tests for the next two weeks and every test confirmed her cancer was gone. When they asked what she'd done, she told them she was simply living and loving her way to the end. I asked her why she didn't tell them about her father, or the priest, or the forgiveness ritual. She said that doctors have faith in science. She told them that love healed her, but they didn't probe so she knew they didn't want to know the particulars."

Savannah took a deep breath and then shivered just a bit when a cloud shrouded the sunshine. Sean felt her shiver and moved a bit closer to her but didn't put his arm around her. Savannah pulled up her knees and hugged them.

"Maybe we should go," Sean said. He was glad when she didn't make any move to get up. In her presence, the world made more sense. He would be pleased if they could just wrap themselves in the cocoon of this sunny ravine forever.

"Faith and science aren't mutually exclusive," Savannah said as the sun came out again from behind the cloud and she stretched out in its warmth. She looked directly at him as she continued, "but it's hard to credit faith when you need science's proof." He smiled at her wondering how he could have been so stupid five years ago. She let him take her hand as he breathed in to admit his stupidity and then stopped short. He felt so close to her in this moment. He didn't want to ruin it by bringing up their past. Her story was about her mother, not him.

"What?" she asked.

"Nothing," he said.

"What?" she said again. "I know that look." She knew him so well. He placed both his hands around hers before he continued. "It just makes me wonder."

"Wonder about what?"

"About forgiveness . . . and resentment," he admitted.

"What about them?"

"I don't know yet," he said. "It's just that I worry about Michael and . . ." He stopped again. Was Faith a miracle of some sort? He really wanted a few miracles. For Michael. For himself. His past. The headaches. The passing out. It was all so confusing.

"And?" she asked as another cloud covered the sun.

"Brrrr," he said. "Let's head back before the clouds close in." He stood and then reached for her hand to help her to her feet.

They walked in silence among the towering trees for a while, lost in their own thoughts. At the top of the trail, they stopped to admire the view of Lake Washington and Husky stadium on its shore. When they were students at the University, they used to sit near the banks looking up this way. She chuckled out loud.

"What?" Sean asked.

"I was just remembering how we used to sit down there," she said as she pointed to the grassy area just east of the stadium, "and look up this way. I never knew there was a park here. It made me realize how things can look so different when you change your perspective."

He smiled at her. "More to think about," he said. "Over dinner?"

Chapter 18

Seattle Now | 2013

Sunday   December 1   4:00 PM   Sean

MICHAEL'S ROOM WAS THE PLACE Sean most wanted to be since being placed on medical leave. It wasn't just that he kept running into Savannah who visited Michael's room every morning and again when her shift ended, though that alone would be enough of a draw. It was something about Michael himself. It seemed crazy, but Sean knew Michael was the key to his own past.

Sean could tell Michael's grandparents didn't mind his presence. And they seemed to appreciate the extra attention from both Savannah and him. They asked him questions they'd already asked the other doctors who were now in charge of Michael's care. They knew he gave them more detailed information to make sure they could fully understand what was happening (or so far, not happening). These experiences observing the interactions of the doctors with the family were causing him to rethink how he listens to, and deals with, the families that come to his emergency department. He always felt he was a good listener, but seeing his colleagues miss cues that are so obvious to him made him wonder. Because of his time in Michael's room with the Powells, Sean was becoming a more fully present listener—a skill he could use when he returned to work—because not returning to work wasn't an option.

As the days dragged on with Michael still unconscious, Sean wondered about his Aunt Regan's vigil over him all those years ago. She was alone. At least that's how he always pictured it since she insisted they had no other family.

There was so much that Regan wouldn't speak about. Secrets hung between them like mines in a harbor. One misplaced word, memory, or question and boom! The emotional fallout would resurrect a wall of stony silence, disrupting the emotional détente Sean always worked so hard to build between them. Once childhood was past, it was easier to let physical distance protect them both so he was surprised when she left him a few messages last week saying she wanted to see him. He assumed she must have seen his picture in the paper after Michael's rescue. He had been meaning to call her back but time slipped by, as it often did between them. They had drifted so far apart it was like having no family at all. They sent cards for holidays, but rarely saw each other. It was just so much work to be around her.

That Regan steadfastly refused to talk about the accident that killed his parents made Sean feel somehow responsible for it. Why else would she refuse to discuss it? He must have done something, everyone died, and then she had to give up her life to raise him. He could tell when she looked at him that she blamed him. He tried to ask her about it, he wanted to understand. But she would say, *Everyone's dead, Sean. Talking about it won't bring them back. Remember the good parts.* That only served to frustrate him more since any memory he had she declared untrue (*Of course you don't remember right. You were only a child; children confuse fantasy and reality*). Now he couldn't remember anything, either good or bad, from his life before his accident. There were only the dreams and nightmares and they made no sense at all. As a kid, when he tried to talk to Regan about them, she'd shut him down. Fast.

Nonsensical nightmares have been the singular constant in Sean's life; nightmares that awaken him but leave no substance or understanding behind. Now, the nightmares have debilitated him; he's sure they're causing the headaches and blackouts—with unusual characters like Faith now added to the mix. Sean hopes Michael won't share a similar fate when he awakens. Michael will have good reason to have nightmares but his grandparents will make such a difference. They really love Michael. They truly want him to survive.

Listening to the stories Michael's grandparents tell has made Sean more curious than ever about what happened to his family. Could the crash that killed his family also have been some monstrous intentional act? He had barely gotten that thought formed when he could feel the darkness closing in on him again. He was about to stand and excuse himself. Then everything went black.

∞

Sean spoke first this time. "This is becoming quite a habit for me. Please tell me you have some idea why this is happening," Sean said to Faith as she appeared to him.

Faith shrugged and said, "Maybe you're fighting too hard."

"Fighting? I'm not fighting anything."

"The way I hear it you've been fighting it all your life. At least your life since you were five. Life is so much easier when you live in truth even when the truth is hard. And it's much easier when you let others help you. Mom says she wishes she'd learned *that* lesson sooner."

"Well, you seemed to have learned quite a few things since you got to wherever you are. If you know something about my truth and what *this* is, about what's happening to me, please just tell me."

"I have learned a few things and I'm learning more all the time. One thing I've learned is that everything you need to know about all this, about your truth, you already know. It's just buried deep. I think you want to unbury it. That's why you've decided to keep coming here. So we can help you."

"I have no idea where here is so how can I decide to come?"

"You know so much more than you acknowledge. You've wanted the truth all your life and your body is reminding you of that now. You're ready. And your friend CJ has been preparing to help you since you almost confided in him when you were in high school. He's ready now too. Plus, Savannah is still willing to help. If you'll let her."

"Savannah? It's too late with Savannah. I hurt her so much already."

"It is never too late to trust love. You love her. If you let her, she will love you."

"I do still love Savannah. I will always love Savannah."

"You're on your way back again. Until next time . . . Please tell Nana and Granddad I love them."

∞

"I'm right here," Savannah said as Sean opened his eyes reorienting himself to Michael's room. He was sitting in the chair next to Anna.

"Were you dreaming?" Savannah continued. "Anna said you've had your eyes closed for a while now. When I came in, she shushed me so we wouldn't disturb you. When you said my name, I turned to answer you but your eyes were still closed. Were you asleep? Are you OK? Should I call Kenji?"

"No. I don't need Kenji. I must have dozed off. I'm fine. It was just a dream."

"Your dreams aren't always just dreams as I recall. Let me take you home. With what you've been through lately, I don't want you walking up and down these hills alone. Who knows when another dream will come. I get off in an hour. Will you wait for me?"

"I'll agree under one condition. You have dinner with me first. It'll be an early dinner like the old folks do," he said before realizing his faux pas. "Oh, excuse me, I didn't mean you," he said as he looked at Anna.

"No offense taken," Anna said as she smiled. "You're welcome to wait here with us. Michael always seems to relax a bit when you're here." Then Anna looked at Savannah and said, "I'll take good care of him until you get back."

When Savannah left the room, Sean asked Anna if he said anything other than Savannah's name when he spoke. Anna smiled at him, patted his hand, and said, "Only that you'd always love her. And in the broken world we live in, that is a very good thing."

CHAPTER 19

SEATTLE NOW | 2013

SEAN ARRIVED FIFTEEN MINUTES EARLY for his appointment with CJ. A young woman who sat at a desk in the right corner of the room gave him a standard four-page intake form before returning to work on her laptop. Graduate student no doubt. He guessed it was a plumb job. The form took him less than three minutes to fill out and that included using two of the three minutes to decide how to answer why he was there: *headaches* he wrote. When you don't have any family history to speak of, intake forms are a breeze. He looked over the nearly empty pages, took a deep breath, got up and handed his paperwork back to the girl who barely looked up from her computer as she said, "Have a seat please. The doctor will be with you shortly." Huh. It had never occurred to Sean that CJ was a *doctor*. How many degrees must that man have?

Sean scanned the reception area. It was small but deliberately appointed: four petite but comfortable chairs lined two walls; each set of chairs was separated by side tables that held lamps for adequate (but not overbearing) light and real blooming plants—for a homey touch. Classical music played quietly but loud enough to cover any sounds coming from the room behind the other door. The artwork on the walls consisted of an Andrew Wyeth reproduction and framed diplomas—lots of them.

Sean never realized CJ had a real office somewhere off the high school grounds where they first met. At the time, Sean was the typically self-absorbed high schooler, and CJ—the cool priest who also coached the girls' varsity soccer team—was a guidance counselor and the Superior for the Jesuit community of priests who taught at the school. CJ had this idea to gather a group of young men together to talk about their futures. Sean and

167

the rest of the boys guessed that CJ was hoping that at least one of them would consider a religious vocation but Sean always knew his future meant becoming a doctor. However, these lunchtime meetings included food and no self-respecting, hungry teenaged boy refused free pizza. Especially when it came with friendship and great discussions.

Through the years Sean was so focused on the support that CJ offered him, that it didn't occur to him that CJ might have a variety of interests of his own. He'd always known that some of the letters that followed CJ's name related to therapy stuff but he never gave it much thought. Now, there seemed to be even more letters that followed CJ's name than Sean remembered. Another overachiever, he laughed to himself.

Sean picked through the eclectic selection of magazines on the table next to him but couldn't concentrate enough to make a choice. Next to the door, he spotted a narrow table that held a few coffee mugs, packets of tea, instant coffee, sugar, and instant cocoa. Beside the goodie table was a water cooler—the kind with the blue spigot for cold and red spigot for hot. He chose a packet of chai tea and a red mug with the flaming sun logo of the Jesuits emblazoned in gold. The smell of the spices and warmth of the mug was surprisingly soothing. He remained standing and closed his eyes.

He had been reluctant to go to therapy. It wasn't that he was opposed to it on principle. He just wasn't a therapy kind of guy. As a doctor, he'd seen patients manifest all sorts of illness when the only real problem resided in the gray matter between their ears. He hated to think he was that kind of guy. But he knew he couldn't be the doctor he wanted to be, or the man he needed to be, if he didn't find out what his mind was working so hard to hide (an idea Kenji suggested). Plus, now that he added regular encounters with a comatose Michael's dead sister, he was beginning to have serious concerns about his sanity.

It was such an inconvenient time to go crazy. Seeing Savannah every day in Michael's room reminded him of what he'd let go. Would it be too much to hope she might give him another chance? But he can't offer up a crazy man who can't work and who hears and sees things no one else does. It was time to swallow his pride and see a shrink. Not the MD kind, he told Savannah when he asked her for a recommendation. He didn't want drugs to make him feel even less like himself. He thought perhaps a trauma specialist was what he needed. And he knew he needed someone he could trust.

Savannah wholeheartedly agreed with that and wondered if CJ would be willing. Without admitting his fear about being crazy, Sean said he didn't want a spiritual director. He needed a real therapist. Savannah said CJ was a real therapist. One of the best, as far as she was concerned. He was her teacher and advisor during her master's program. And he was the one who taught her to address the whole person, body-mind-spirit. He was also a certified hypnotherapy master.

Sean wasn't surprised in the "whole person" approach CJ had; it was so Jesuit. But he didn't put much store in the kind of hocus-pocus he associated with hypnotherapy. What good could come of something like that? Despite that, CJ seemed like a very safe choice. CJ had known Sean since he was a kid. He knew Regan too. Just those two things would save hours of time. Sean almost opened up to him once on retreat in high school, but with all the guys there, his friends, he just couldn't admit how much he hurt. He couldn't let them see his weakness.

Now everyone could see his weakness. He couldn't hide it anymore. If he was ever going to get back to work, he had to trust someone. Sean trusted CJ's wisdom and ethics. Now he was determined to trust him, man-to-man as his friend. That trust was going to be vital because ever since meeting Michael something shifted in him.

He realized they shared a profoundly traumatic event and not just when Sean rescued Michael. Sean wondered what life would have been like if he'd had a grandmother like Anna Powell to care for him instead of Regan. What might have been different if he'd trusted CJ more when he was in high school? Now he hoped it wasn't too late to put all the crazies back into their boxes and silence the nightmares once and for all.

The voice of the grad student startled him. "The doctor will see you now," she said. When he turned to look at her, she was walking toward an interior door with a folder in her hand. CJ opened the door just as she arrived. He took the folder from her and smiled while gesturing for Sean to come in. They walked into a room double the size of the reception area with a small couch opposite an antique desk accompanied by a padded leather chair on wheels. A plush chair perpendicular to the couch faced a floor-to-ceiling window looking out on boats in the waters of Lake Union, a tranquil scene to calm the nerves.

"Do I lie down on the couch?" Sean asked. He wondered how many times CJ had heard that with someone new. But Sean didn't know the rules for this kind of thing; maybe he was supposed to lie down. He'd seen it in movies.

"Only if you want to. Do whatever makes you most comfortable," CJ said as he sat in the chair next to his desk. Sean took the chair facing the window. After an uncomfortably long silence simply looking at each other, CJ spoke first. "Well, this is a whole new ballgame in our relationship. When you were young, you were one of my greatest challenges. You were full of promise yet burdened by a sadness that was so corporeal I almost set an extra place at the table for it. There were times I tried to draw you out but you so seldom let your guard down then," he began. "In fact, you were a catalyst for me. When I met you as a freshman and saw that none of my skills could touch that pain in you, I decided to head back to school to figure out how to help you. Spiritual direction, my focus then, was fine but sometimes, for some people, it's not enough."

"Don't blame me that you like hanging out with crazies," Sean said in a feeble attempt at humor.

"Ah, the wall is still there," CJ said with a smile.

"It's a hard habit to break."

"You said you wanted to come to me because you would be able to trust me. But we can only find that trust on the other side of the wall where you're completely honest with yourself and with me."

"I know," Sean said. "Savannah was the first one to mention the wall. I hadn't known it was there but when I thought about it, I realized I had put it up to protect myself from my aunt. Unfortunately, it worked to keep everyone else at a distance too. But maybe if I can learn to live on the other side of it, Savannah will take me back."

CJ smiled, "Ah you both enjoyed our little Thanksgiving dinner then."

"Very much. We've met outside of work a few times and I see her every day in Michael's room. I realized what a self-centered jerk I've been when it comes to Savannah. She has been through so much in these last five years and she's still so full of love that she made it her job to share it. She didn't put up a wall to keep her safe from pain. Instead, her pain made her more open."

"She is quite special."

"But there's one more thing. If I don't get on the other side of that wall, I may never get to practice medicine again."

"Why is that?"

"I'm still on stress-related medical leave. You'd think a trauma doc like me would be immune to seeing the kind of tragedy that hurt Michael. Did you know I was first on the scene?"

CJ nodded.

"Since then I've gotten to know something about the family from the grandparents. After our discussion at dinner the other night, I'm wondering if what's happening to me physically has a deeper cause. Especially the passing out."

Sean left out what happens when he passes out and continued, "Neuro can't find any cause for the fainting or the headaches. Everyone said it must be stress. But see this scar right here," he said as he pointed to the scar that started at his collar bone, ran up towards his ear, and ended at an indentation in his occipital bone at the back of his skull.

"I got this when I was just about Michael's age. I was in a car accident that killed my parents, just like Michael. After hearing about the violence in Michael's family and knowing how Regan always shut me down when I asked about my family, I'm wondering . . ."

"Wondering what?"

"Ages ago, when Rose—you've met her, the nurse who always works with me—suggested a sleep clinic because of my nightmares, I was reading stuff about dream interpretation and found out that each person in a dream is a fragment of yourself. My dreams were—my dreams are—so violent, and I started wondering if some fragmented part of me was capable of doing the things that the man in my dreams did. I don't know anything about my father. What if the accident I was in was intentional like Michael's? What if my father was violent like Michael's father? And what if the nightmares are warning me that I am like that too? Could I hurt Savannah?"

"Ah, I see," CJ nodded. "Did you ever tell Savannah your worry?"

"No," Sean said. "I wanted to but I knew she would tell me that she knows I could never do that. I would like to believe that but . . ." his voice trailed off. CJ waited patiently. Sean thought about the times Savannah had pleaded with him to trust her, to let her in.

Finally, he said, "It's that trust thing. How could I trust Savannah to know me if I couldn't even trust that I know myself?" He took a deep breath hoping to stop the buzzing that had started in his ears. He was determined to not let anything get in the way of his resolve to be open and honest.

"The thing is," he continued, "if I could figure out what's causing all of this—the headaches, the fainting, the nightmares—not only could I work again but maybe I could even win Savannah back. I still love her. But there's no way I could win her back now. Not like this. Not if I'm crazy."

"What makes you think you're crazy?" CJ asked without a hint of judgment or sarcasm.

"In med school we covered just enough about mental illness to be able to recognize the most obvious kinds. Some have a genetic link and I have no idea if I inherited some mental disease that's showing up in these headaches and nightmares and . . ." Sean stopped.

"And?" CJ prompted but Sean didn't answer.

Sean hadn't told anyone about seeing Faith. He knew that would certainly prove he was crazy. Voices and visions are as good as an engraved invitation to a padded cell. They both looked at each other in silence and Sean began to squirm ever so slightly under a gaze that was both warm and somehow all-knowing. Finally, CJ spoke.

"Sometimes our reactions to trauma can make us feel crazy but often they are completely normal. Sorting through those reactions, listening to what they are telling us usually helps resolve them. Trauma can come out in dreams but it also can come out in our bodies. Our bodies, it seems, have a memory all their own and a way of communicating what they remember."

Sean squirmed a bit as that idea resonated somewhere deep inside him. CJ continued, "To heal, we need to listen. When we refuse to listen to our inner voice, that part of us that knows our essential truth, then our psyche ratchets up the ante, using whatever it can—dreams, physical pains, illnesses—to get our attention. Your headaches and nightmares have a long history but so far have revealed little about your essential truth."

Sean looked out the window, unable to meet CJ's gaze. Sean had always wanted the truth. He sighed.

"Our bodies, minds, and spirits are finely tuned toward healing," CJ spoke again when Sean remained quiet. "First though we may experience the pain necessary to get our attention to move us toward that healing. Once acknowledged, pain can be the catalyst for growth toward wholeness. In your case, your psyche has upped the ante by adding fainting. But nothing you've told me so far would make me believe that you are, as you say, crazy. Perhaps everything you're going through is simply your inner voice—your soul—trying to speak to you. If you were to guess, what do you think that inner voice wants to say?"

"Hah! If it were only *my* inner voice," Sean blurted out without thinking. He hoped CJ didn't see his neck turning red under the collar of the perfectly pressed oxford shirt he always wore. He shifted uncomfortably in his chair trying to figure out the words that would make him sound less crazy than he felt. CJ noticed and broke the silence.

"You've come this far. You don't have much more to lose by laying it all out now."

"Only my freedom. When you hear the rest of it, you'll be ready to sign the commitment papers." Sean reached for his now-lukewarm tea and took a big swig hoping to wet the cotton that had suddenly coated his tongue. He gazed at the boats outside the window realizing that none of the small things that comforted him when he walked in comforted him now. He could get up right now and leave. His legs twitched with the anticipation of it. He stood. But rather than going for the door, he went to the window. He knew if he bolted now nothing would change. Savannah, and his job, would remain out of reach.

Staring out the window, he said in a barely audible voice, "I hear voices and I see people who aren't here."

"When did this begin?" CJ asked as he turned his chair to face Sean's back. Again there was no judgment in CJ's tone. Sean wondered if they taught that in therapist school or if CJ really didn't think he was crazy after all.

"The day after the crash. A policeman and Michael's grandfather were questioning me. My head started to buzz and I blacked out. While I was unconscious, Faith came to thank me."

"Who is Faith and what was she thanking you for?"

"Saving Michael. Faith is his sister. Initially I thought I sort of dreamed it but she told me her name and when I regained consciousness, I asked her grandfather her name. It was Faith. I had no idea what to think. Since then, the blackouts have continued and when they happen, I go to some kind of different dimension where I talk to Faith, and sometimes her mother. I know other people are there too. I can sense them but I haven't seen them yet. Then, sometimes when I visit Michael, I hear his thoughts. But he's still unconscious. He can't say anything. Crazy, right?"

"I suppose that all depends on your definition of crazy," CJ said. "Do you believe that there is any part of us that survives physical death?"

Sean turned around but remained standing by the window. "I used to hope that was true. When I was a little boy, I used to have dreams about my mother especially in the first year after my parents died. But not just dreams. Honestly there were times when I was awake and thought I heard her voice, or smelled her perfume, or even saw her face. Whenever I told my aunt, she would get angry with me, saying *stop that nonsense, Sean*."

"Sounds like she was having a hard time with her grief too," CJ said.

"I used that excuse for her for years and maybe that could explain some of her cruelty. But one thing's for sure, she didn't want me to ever ask questions or mention anything about our family. *They're dead, Sean. The past is dead. Leave it be*, she'd say."

"How did that make you feel?"

"Alone."

"Did the dreams or experiences with your mother continue?"

"For a while. I don't really remember now. I just know that as I got older I didn't dream as often. When I was about sixteen, the nightmares began."

"Do you remember the contents your dreams or nightmares?"

"Some. When I was in grade school, it was standard kid stuff with monsters chasing me. As I got older they were more realistic, more violent. I was always in mortal danger from a man with dark red hair. Sometimes it was just me, other times I was a part of a family with a sister and brother I had to keep safe. The man with red hair was always trying to kill us. Sometimes he caught me and beat me with his fists. Once it was a baseball bat. Other times he chased me down with a gun or a knife and he'd corner me. Sometimes he'd kill me, other times I'd wake just before he did."

"Did you ever notice any correlation to the dreams with anything else going on in your life?" CJ asked when Sean grew quiet again.

"When I was ready to ask Savannah to marry me, I bought a ring. I wanted to find the perfect moment to give it to her but the nightmares started immediately and then came almost every night. This time the man wasn't after me but after a woman I needed to protect. So even though I was a little boy in the dream, I was trying to stop him. I was never successful. I saw the woman die over and over again. I'd wake up in a panic, sweat drenching me. Savannah kept asking me what the dreams were, but I couldn't tell her. Instead, I kept pushing her away. When she finally left me, I was devastated but at least I knew she was safe. If that man who was haunting my sleep was an aspect of me, then Savannah would never be safe with me."

Sean looked up at CJ, exhausted. He sat back down in the chair and said, "That's what you do for someone you love. You keep them safe no matter the cost."

"Did you ever think there might be an explanation for the dreams other than they were aspects of you?" CJ asked.

"I didn't go to an expert if that's what you mean."

"Ah, but you're with one now," CJ said smiling. "It is true that some dreams help us understand aspects of ourselves. And many times, dreams do give us insight into our shadow but it's not a straight line from a dream to our behaviors. There are many types of dreams and they come to us for many reasons. Some are memories, some are mind-junk, some are prescient, and some reveal the hidden parts of ourselves, our shadow. No matter the source though, dreams speak in the language of metaphor and every person has a unique metaphorical dictionary based on his or her unique life circumstances. Sometimes books and websites can offer insight to the meaning of the metaphors, but not always."

Sean breathed an audible sigh of relief.

CJ continued, "I also think there are some rational, even scientific, explanations for your blackout experiences that don't point to mental illness. You've made a huge trust leap today and that shows a real willingness to get to the bottom of all this. I think together we can help you get some clarity on the nature of your nightmares, and your headaches, and some resolution for fainting and all that goes with it."

"You're not ready to have me committed to the psych ward?" Sean asked only half joking.

"I don't think that's necessary at this point," CJ said with a smile. "But I do have to warn you, things may feel worse before they get better. Sometimes the dark secrets we hold inside will resist revelation," CJ said with grave seriousness. Then his impish smile returned as he rubbed his hands together and used a throwaway movie line with a silly accent, "But ve have our vays."

"What's next then?"

"Let's set up another time to meet to unpack some of your past and begin hunting for some of the secrets underneath."

"Tomorrow? I've got lots of time and the quicker I get to the bottom of this the quicker I get my life back," Sean said.

CJ opened a large black appointment book, the kind that you fill in by hand. He smiled when he saw Sean's expression and said, "I know, this is ancient but writing things down helps me remember. Emily, my assistant, puts everything into the calendar on the computer so she knows my schedule but I do all my notes and appointments the old-fashioned way with pen and paper."

Sean stood as CJ handed him a card with his appointment time on it. He had a good feeling about this. CJ didn't think he was crazy and that was huge. Sean let CJ know that he'd like to work together every day if possible. He wanted to get back to normal. When Sean started toward the door he came in, CJ pointed to a door on the opposite wall that led directly into the hallway—to protect client privacy he said. Sean was grateful.

As he reached for the doorknob, CJ said, "One more thing, Sean. How do you feel about hypnosis?"

"As long as you don't make me bark like a dog, I'm up for anything that will work. I trust you, remember."

"Okay, then. We'll dive in tomorrow."

CHAPTER 20

SEATTLE NOW | 2013

AFTER MORE THAN TWO WEEKS of her leaving messages, Sean finally called his aunt back. When she said she needed to see him, he invited her to dinner. He assumed she wanted to be able to gloat to her friends that she had inside information. She knew he couldn't tell her anything substantive about Michael's situation but she insisted that she needed to see him. That it was urgent. Something in her voice made him acquiesce. Besides, Michael's family's story was bringing up all sorts of questions for him, as were his sessions with CJ. Regan might have something urgent she needed to say to him but he also planned to confront her about the man in his dreams that he was guessing was his father. He wasn't sure whether the dream was a memory but he knew Regan knew. And his continued status on medical leave until he was back to normal (whatever that might be) made him more determined to get her to tell him the truth.

The idea of confronting his aunt unnerved Sean. Especially after what he'd been through with Michael. She always got under his skin so he was grateful Savannah would be there. Sean had thought of inviting CJ too but decided against it. He didn't want his aunt to feel threatened even though the thought of ganging up on her thrilled him just a little. What he wanted from Regan was going to be difficult enough for her and she never particularly liked CJ. She told Sean that CJ was a meddler; since he didn't have children of his own, he meddled in the lives of the students he counseled. Sean didn't see it that way at all. CJ was his mentor, a father figure, a man he could look up to, a man who would answer any question Sean asked. Sean felt accepted by CJ, not judged, especially now that he was helping him remember. But as usual, Regan took offense at anything that made Sean feel the tiniest bit secure. She was kinder to his other mentor, Dr. Kovac, but that was because she saw a doctor as much more useful than a priest.

When CJ kept showing up at Sean's graduations, Regan was visibly irritated. High school was one thing, she said, because CJ worked there but she thought college and medical school were over the top. Even after Sean told her that he invited CJ and always appreciated that he took the time to come, Regan continued to call CJ "the meddler." After med school graduation, CJ invited Sean and Regan out to dinner to celebrate. Regan and CJ tussled over who would pay the bill. CJ said he would; it was his invitation. Regan said she would, Sean was her son—though it was a term Sean never heard her use before or since. The closest she came was when she gave an interview to a reporter after Sean rescued Michael. She told the reporter that she raised him and he was "like a son" as if to take some credit.

He wasn't surprised when Regan contacted him after the story hit the papers. He put off their meeting as long as possible but, true to form, Regan wanted what she wanted. She didn't know that this dinner was going to be about what Sean wanted. He wanted information and he wanted it now. Tonight.

Only a part of him felt bad that he was going to blindside her. His conversation with Savannah about forgiveness and resentment resonated with him. But truth be told, he had more work to do on the part of him that was taking some joy in knowing how Regan would squirm. He wanted to be more loving and more forgiving, like Savanah and Geneviève. He could see the peace it gave them. And over these last weeks, he felt a real transformation occurring in his life, in his spirit. But it was a work in progress. He truly desired to forgive his aunt for the life they had lived together. He wanted to hear her story and understand why she had lied to him all these years because he was surer than ever that she had lied. But the more human, less spiritual part of him couldn't help wanting her to suffer just a little bit for her complete lack of love for him, for the loneliness it caused, and for all those lies. He couldn't help but want his aunt to feel a bit of what she always made him feel—confused and alone.

"Hey, you okay?" Savannah asked as she came up behind him and snaked her arms around him resting her cheek against his back. Sean's thoughts had interrupted him mid-task and Savannah's embrace brought him back into the moment. He continued to open the bottle of wine.

"After all those sessions with CJ and all our conversations about love and forgiveness, I thought I was ready for this, but now I'm not sure," he said.

"What are you unsure about?" she asked still holding him.

"I don't know," he said as the wine bottle opened with a resonant pop. "I don't know if I'm worried about her or about me. What if the memories I had under hypnosis aren't true? What if I didn't have a brother or sister and they are only the hopes of a hurt little boy, as Regan always told me? And if I did have them, what really happened to everyone? What if it's something truly awful? Maybe the past really should stay in the past."

"You can let the past stay put as long as it doesn't hurt your present. But *your* past, even though you didn't remember any of the details until now, was with you every day keeping you from what you wanted," Savannah said as she slipped around to look into his eyes before she continued, "Keeping us from what we wanted." She kissed him softly in a way that reminded him of his med school days when her kisses could relieve stress he didn't even know he was carrying. He couldn't imagine what he had done to deserve a second chance with her, but he was determined not to mess it up this time. She hugged him, sighed and moved back to her sauce on the stove and said, "Besides, what can she say that would be worse than what you already know?"

"I don't know," he said. "But I have this nagging feeling that the other shoe is about to drop."

The ringing phone interrupted Sean before he could say anymore. He pressed the code to buzz Regan in reminding her he was on the top floor, last apartment on the right.

"You never gave her the code to get in?" Savannah asked.

He looked at her and shrugged, "Would you?"

"I suppose not," she smiled. Savannah did a last-minute cleanup of the coffee table near the couch and returned to the kitchen to set the appetizers on a tray. She was in the kitchen when Sean opened the apartment door.

The years had not been kind to Regan Kelly. She looked a good ten years older than her sixty-nine years. Her closely cropped white hair had a dull yellow caste to it that accentuated the bluish-gray pallor of her skin. Without soft edges now, her face had completely lost the beauty he saw in her when he was a child. Her skin hung like loose crepe over her cheeks and pooled a bit at her jowls before cascading down her neck. Her nose was more prominent than Sean remembered, jutting out beyond cheeks that had sunken inward. Even the blue of her eyes looked dull. Despite his surprise at how she had aged, he told her she looked lovely knowing how she craved such compliments. And in fact, he could tell she dressed specifically for the occasions. She wore a red business suit (though it looked at least a size too large), diamond studs on her ears, and a collection of diamond and gold bracelets on her wrists. The only accommodation she had made to aging was a pair of low-heeled pumps that straddled the line between sophisticated and sensible. Sean couldn't help smiling that she had worn her power outfit to visit him.

When she smiled back, he noticed her large tobacco-stained teeth. He also noticed her eyebrows turned downward near her nose in a look of anger that seemed permanently etched on her face. The incongruence of her smiling mouth and angry eyes unsettled him and he realized that it was something that had caused him confusion his entire life. But as he looked at her now, he felt a twinge of compassion. Her smile could not hide the fear he saw lurking in her eyes. She couldn't possibly know what he wanted to ask her, so he wondered if fear always had been there. Was it only now that he was able to recognize it? Or was that look really hatred rather than fear? Did she hate him? Growing up he was never quite sure. And he wasn't even sure now.

As usual, their greetings felt forced, stilted. Sean finally said, "It's been a long time." She nodded as he swept his arm and said, "Please come in."

"You look well," Regan said as she walked in with a slight limp he hadn't seen before. Her voice quality was huskier than he remembered and she had a slight, stale aroma of burnt tobacco that ambled in with her. He was grateful it was not the overpowering stench of his youth. Perhaps she had at least cut back.

"You look like you've lost a little weight," Sean said knowing how vain she had always been about being thin. He meant it as a compliment but he could have sworn she winced slightly when he said it. Before she could respond, Savannah appeared with appetizers and set them on the coffee table next to the bottle of wine. In movements as fluid as a dancer, she continued on to embrace Regan with opened arms and a genuine song of greeting. Sean was surprised when his aunt did not pull back but stiffly tried to return the gesture.

The two women, Sean thought, always had an odd relationship, mostly because they had one at all. They never vied for Sean's affections but then Sean always said Regan didn't know the first thing about affection so why would she ever compete for it? Savannah could never make much headway convincing Sean to have more compassion for his aunt. When they dated before, Savannah had tried to mediate his relationship with Regan. He appreciated the effort but said it was hopeless. Savannah told him nobody has their guard up as high as Regan's without cause. Savannah was certain Regan's heart had been broken but Sean scoffed at that idea saying Regan had no heart to break.

Sean watched as Savannah put Regan at ease. He'd spent his whole life trying unsuccessfully to do that and given their discomfort moments before at the door, he remained unsuccessful. Yet Savannah, in an instant, was able to get Regan settled on the couch, wine in hand, making small talk about the travel that took so much of her time since she retired. He was surprised to hear her say there were no upcoming cruises or safaris or archaeological digs on her calendar as she nibbled and sipped yet seemed to consume nothing.

The evening progressed smoothly, thanks mostly to Savannah. Sean even good-naturedly autographed all the newspapers with his face plastered across the front page his aunt had brought along—for her girlfriends she said. He had assumed this was the reason for her visit and he figured it was the least he could do since his agenda included demanding information from her that she spent a lifetime keeping secret.

At dinner, Regan raved about how delicious the food was though she hardly touched a thing. The conversation turned to names at one point with Savannah confirming that she indeed was named after the city in Georgia, her mother's hometown. Savannah wondered if Sean shared his father's name.

"Oh, heavens no," Regan said. "Only my father was vain enough to name his kids after himself. Regan was my father's middle name, and Quinn was dad's mother's maiden name. My mother, it seems, didn't even get a voice in the naming. No, my sister and I both thought everyone should have their very own name. Quinn liked the name Sean, Sean-Patrick actually. A good Irish name for a boy born on St. Patrick's Day she said." Regan looked down and said in a barely audible sigh, "I miss Quinn."

Sean was surprised that his aunt had used his full name. But he was shocked that she mentioned his mother, even in passing. She spent a lifetime avoiding speaking about her whenever Sean asked. But now *she* brought it up. Sean was determined to seize the opportunity to ask about his family. He took a deep breath to ready himself to speak when Regan began to cough. Though it started small, the cough quickly took control over her body. She held up one finger as if she knew she had interrupted him and covered her mouth with the other hand. Sean noticed that her hands were barely more than skeletons covered in mottled, paper-thin skin. In between coughs, she gasped for air. She grabbed for her purse, struggled with a pill bottle that Sean finally opened for her. She downed a pill with a big gulp of water to drown out the spasms that were wracking her small frame. Sean thought she would spray the table with water when the cough attacked again mid-swallow but she kept her composure and swallowed anyway—an obviously practiced maneuver. Her chest rattled as she doubled over trying to regain control, sucking in air that seemed to refuse to inflate her lungs.

Finally, she calmed the storm, sat up with tears falling from the outside corners of each eye, dabbed her mouth with her napkin, looked at him with an unblinking gaze and said, "I'm dying."

Sean was momentarily stunned. Her frail appearance, her sickly coloring, her clubbed fingertips, her history of smoking. Of course. If he hadn't been so focused on what he wanted tonight, he might have noticed as soon as she arrived. All the signs were there.

"When?" he asked.

"A few weeks . . . perhaps a month if I'm lucky," she said matter-of-factly. "It's why I kept calling you. There is so much I need to tell you. So much you have a right to know," she croaked before another fit of coughing seized her. Savannah went to Regan and placed a hand on her back—another move that Sean was surprised his aunt did not reject—and waited until Regan was calm again. Savannah then gently placed one arm around Regan to help her rise as she suggested they go to the living room. Sean was again surprised when Regan allowed Savannah to assist her. The two of them walked away from him arm-in-arm like old friends.

As he watched them walk away, Sean momentarily wondered if Regan was faking but listening to her cough, Sean knew she was dying. And he didn't think his aunt had a month. She would be lucky to live another two weeks. But, if sheer force of will could stave off death, it was anyone's guess how long Regan Kelly might live. She might turn a deaf ear to the grim reaper and refuse to hear death's siren call.

Savannah settled Regan on the couch, gave her another glass of water, then went to the kitchen to make some "soothing tea." Sean sat in a chair across the room leaving the spot on the couch next to his aunt for Savannah.

Regan looked at him and said, "I wish I had done things differently. I am sorry."

Sean had no idea how to react. Regan was a mere shadow of herself now. He didn't know if it was what he'd been through or what she'd been through but the woman he'd feared, the woman he sometimes hated for what she'd done—and for what she refused to do—was nowhere in sight. And the woman who sat in her place was an enigma. This was not what he expected tonight. Not what he planned for in the conversations he'd imagined over and over in his mind. He had no desire to blindside her now. He couldn't purposefully hurt her. Confused about how to proceed, he asked her about the cancer to bide time and collect his thoughts.

Regan explained that she picked up a bug on her last cruise about six months ago. It turned into pneumonia that left her with a cough that burned in her chest and wouldn't go away. Her doctor wanted to do a CT scan, but she refused until after a second round of pneumonia. A little over a month ago, she got the diagnosis. By the time Savannah returned with their tea, Sean had gotten the briefing on his aunt's oncologist (one of the best in town of course); her treatment protocols (she had chosen Hospice care over chemotherapy); and her prognosis (three to six weeks). He also decided he would care for her until she died.

When he spoke the words out loud, he was almost as shocked as everyone else but listening to her as her voice faded and watching exhaustion overtake her, he had lost the will to hate her and hoped that time together would answer some questions for him. It took a bit of work to convince Regan he was serious. Savannah jumped right on-board telling Regan with Sean's help Regan could stay out of the hospital—a place she had steadfastly avoided since taking Sean home over twenty years ago. With Sean there, Regan could stay in her home.

Finally, Regan acquiesced. They settled on Sean moving back into his old bedroom on Friday, only two days away.

Regan would let Sean help her die.

CHAPTER 21

SEATTLE NOW | 2013

SEAN STOOD ON THE SIDEWALK, duffle bag in hand, wondering if he had the strength to really do this. This house reeked of loneliness and loss. Regan didn't ask for his help and a part of him knew she deserved to die alone. But if he allowed that to happen, he'd never learn the truth about his past. Living in this house once more for a few weeks was a small price to pay for the truth.

CJ said that being in this space could fill in parts of his memory that remained stubbornly blank. But Sean didn't need memories from this house. He needed the ones that caused him to be here. And he hoped that Regan's approaching death might finally be the catalyst for her to tell him. Besides all that, despite how badly their relationship had been, he believed he owed her. She took him in when she didn't want to and now it was his turn. They were all either one had. He simply couldn't let her die alone. He got as far as the porch when the door opened, startling him.

"Oh, hello," said the woman as she gently closed the door behind her. "Can I help you?"

"Do I know you?" Sean asked feeling an immediate sense of recognition.

"I don't think so. I'm a recent transplant from Eastern Washington. I don't know too many folks here yet."

When Sean didn't respond, the woman continued, "Ms. Kelly is resting so if you're here for a visit, later would be a better time for her."

Sean still didn't respond, so the woman said, "I'm Cate, a nurse and caregiver Ms. Kelly hired." Extending her hand, she asked, "Are you a relative?"

Sean was so startled by the woman's looks that he continued to stare at her for an uncomfortably long moment before extending his hand too. "I'm her nephew," Sean said before falling silent again. When he shook her hand, he'd felt something like an electrical current tickle his palm. His brain was churning trying to figure out how he knew this woman.

Cate continued, "I come by each day to help Ms. Kelly with nursing care, personal care, meal prep, and I even do a bit of housekeeping for her. She's so particular about everything, as I'm sure you know. Are you here for a few days?" she asked pointing to his duffle bag.

"Moving back in, actually, until . . . ah . . . you know . . ."

"Well then tell me what you like to eat and I'll be happy to fix extra food for you too, ah . . ." Cate's pause prompted Sean to introduced himself.

"Sorry. I'm Dr. Thomas," he stammered before correcting himself. "Sean Thomas."

"Great to meet you, Dr. Thomas," Cate said enthusiastically. "Your aunt is lucky to have a doctor in the house, someone familiar with what will happen."

"Please just call me Sean. I'm not here as a doctor. Just a nephew."

Sean looked down, finally realizing he'd been staring at Cate this whole time. It wasn't that she was beautiful, although she definitely was that. It was that he had such a strong feeling in his gut that he knew her. There was something even about her voice that was so familiar. But before he could question her anymore she casually moved past him bounding down the steps with a quick wave and a "*see you tomorrow*" farewell. Cate was out on the sidewalk before the faint scent of her registered in his brain; a smell that made his chest ache. He attributed the feeling to what was coming next.

Needing just a moment more, he sat down on the top step. It was a familiar perch on this grand old porch that looked out over a neighborhood of vintage houses from the early twentieth century, most of which also boasted big porches. His porch sat regally above five broad concrete steps attached to the flagstone walkway connected to the sidewalk beyond. The porch was the length of the whole house and about ten feet deep; deep enough to prevent the setting sun from baking the living room in the summer. The floor was wide-plank dark hardwood finished in a clear varnish to protect it from the elements; it reminded Sean of the beautiful wooden boats that cruised Lake Washington. Tongue-in-groove panels painted gloss white covered the porch ceiling.

The antique wicker settee and a matching chair that he never sat in as a child still looked almost brand new (*Sean, for God's sake sit still before you break that!*). Regan must have had them painted because the swing (which hung perpendicular to the north side to the house and was fully his territory) looked sad by comparison. It also brought sad memories. He would swing on that swing every day as a boy, the smooth rhythms and creaking chains soothed him while he waited for his aunt to return from work. He wasn't allowed outside nor was he allowed to have anyone inside. But technically, since the porch was a part of the house, he figured it was neutral territory.

Not one to give much thought to the needs of a child, Regan didn't seem to notice Sean's loneliness as a latch-key kid. And she never realized that the porch was Sean's ally in his quest for human connection. It became his way to have friends over. By third grade, the porch was both his refuge and his hang out.

From the porch he could watch for her car on the rare occasions she arrived home before seven. And from the porch he could quickly answer the phone when she called randomly to check on him. By high school, sports kept him at school until long after she got home and by then she didn't much care where he was so the porch swing went still. But it was so important in those early years when he had no one to talk to, no one who would listen to his fears, and no one to distract him from the ache of being so different from the kids who had parents who loved them, parents who waited for them to get home.

Sean sighed and stood feeling the weight of his memories. He shook them off and took a deep breath before moving to the huge oak door. His instinct was to knock and wait to be let in. But when he volunteered two days ago to move back in to help, Regan gave him a key and told him to simply walk in since she slept so often anymore.

Only two days ago. A lifetime ago.

Everything was quiet when he entered. Other than a faint antiseptic smell, not much had changed since he had last opened this door. To the right of the grand foyer, the main living area occupied the whole right side of the first floor. Three enormous oriental rugs still marked the music, living, and dining areas. The grand piano, always off-limits (*Sean, stop! You're leaving prints.*), still sat in the expansive space created by the floor-to-ceiling bay window that faced the street. Two white velvet sofas (also off-limits unless invited in on special occasions) still flanked the fireplace in the center of the room. And the dining table still sat in front of the French doors that opened onto the deck for summer parties (*Make yourself scarce tonight, Sean. I'm having people from work over*).

He didn't enter that empty room but turned left, as was his custom, walked past the main staircase and Regan's home office to the end of the hallway. He stopped on the landing of the back staircase.

Perturbed by what he felt, he hesitated. He thought to himself, *For God's sake, you're a grown man and an accomplished doctor. You tend broken bones sticking through the skin, knives sticking out of skulls, and bodies broken sometimes beyond recognition without the slightest bit of anxiety. Going up to your childhood room couldn't be worse than what you experience at work.* "Get a grip, Thomas" he said out loud. "It's just a room." Taking another breath, he began to walk up the stairs but before he made two steps, he heard her call.

"Sean, is that you?" Regan said in a hoarse straining voice.

"Yes" he said, dropping his bag on the landing and going to the main stairway where she approached with careful, slow, measured steps. Steps that signaled a journey that he didn't feel prepared for and wondered if she felt the same way.

As he made his way to her side, the thought occurred to him that the house looked the same and the furniture was the same but everything else was different. And he was pretty sure that neither of them fully understood how much more things were about to change.

CHAPTER 22

SEATTLE NOW | 2013

FRIDAY   DECEMBER 13   4:20 PM   SEAN

SEAN RACED TO MEET HIS FRAIL AUNT before she began to descend the stairs.

"I met the hospice nurse on the porch. She said you were sleeping. I'm sorry if I woke you," Sean said, supporting one arm as her other hand held the railing.

"Yes, Cate. She's not with Seattle Hospice. She's the private duty nurse I hired. I was just resting before the Hospice social worker arrives. When I mentioned you were moving in this afternoon, she wanted to meet you."

As Sean settled his aunt on the velvet sofa in the living room, he could have sworn she'd lost weight since she'd come to his apartment two nights ago. But before they had time for any conversation, there was a knock on the door. After the social worker settled herself on the couch facing him and his aunt, she took command of the conversation.

"Your aunt tells me you're a doctor," the social worker said.

"Yes, emergency."

"Ahh . . . a take charge kind of doctor," the social worker said with a knowing smile. "Many traditional doctors have a little difficulty with Hospice's approach. They're so used to saving lives that it's hard for them to stand down as nature takes its course."

Sean noticed the way the social worker emphasized the word traditional, like there was something wrong with it. He wasn't sure he liked the implication, and he wasn't sure he liked the social worker either.

"I am not here as a doctor. I'm here as a nephew," Sean said. "My aunt wants to be at home. I'm here to support her." Regan reached out to put her hand over Sean's. He startled and nearly drew his hand away. Small offerings of affection from Regan would take some getting used to. He could feel the

189

heat from his flushing cheeks when he realized the social worker saw their exchange. She was smiling yet Sean wondered if she was judging him too. An unfit caregiver? A caregiver who desperately needed something from the dying person? A caregiver more interested in his needs than the needs of the person he was supposed to care for?

"You won't be alone in your support," the social worker continued. "We have a whole team assigned; I stop by whenever I'm needed, our nurse will stop by once a week, and Dr. Sanchez is a quick phone call away. Your aunt has chosen to hire additional private duty nurses who are not part of our team, but we're acquainted with them. Cate Webb is excellent. Starting tomorrow, Cate's schedule will increase and she'll be here every day from 10 am until 7 pm. Then a team of overnight nurses also hired by Ms. Kelly will arrive at 11 pm and stay until 7 am. Most of them have worked for us before choosing private duty so you'll be well covered day and night. If you need it, we can arrange for a chaplain, a certified nurse assistant, or volunteers to help in any way you need. Feel free to ask questions of any member of the care team or call our main number twenty-four hours a day, any day of the week. Everything you need is in this binder and we leave it next to Ms. Kelly's bed with phone numbers for all of us."

Listening to the social worker, the reality of it all sank in. His aunt was dying and it would happen sooner rather than later. Sitting back and waiting for it to happen went against everything he believed about medicine. He had heard about hospice but never quite knew what they did, how they did it, or why. He couldn't understand how any doctor or patient would willingly sit back and let the disease win.

Rather than debate the philosophy of it, he simply asked, "Won't she suffer?"

"Not if we do our jobs right. Your aunt is a remarkable woman . . . determined . . . strong-willed . . ."

"You noticed," Sean interrupted, with a little chuckle.

"I did indeed," the social worker said smiling at Regan. "Suffering is not inevitable, even with such advanced cancer. Palliative medicine has made great strides in these last decades. As she lets us know, we will adjust her pain medications. And we have learned that a good deal of the suffering one experiences leading up to death comes from emotional or spiritual issues. That's why we have counselors and chaplains on staff to offer support as you request it, either one of you. Dying, when faced head on, can be a graced experience, an honor to participate in. And from what I know of Regan so far, she plans to live fully until the moment she dies."

Sean was startled by how openly this social worker was talking about death with Regan sitting right there. Sure, death happens. He'd seen it many times. But he never liked it or accepted it without a fight. And with the often catastrophic nature of the cases he saw, he wasn't used to talking about it with the patient.

"We can't keep the cancer from completing its course," the social worker continued, "but we can ensure that Regan has the journey she chooses with as much comfort and dignity as possible." She paused a moment, looked at both of them and said, "Questions?" Regan shook her head. Sean shrugged.

The social worker gave Sean a booklet on hospice care and said, "This might help you understand a bit better how and why we do what we do. Feel free to call me whenever you have any questions." With that she stood, gave Sean her card, and gathered her belongings. She said her farewell to Regan then turned to Sean, "Regan tells me there is so much the two of you have to do, so I'll get out of your way and let you do it. Call me anytime, Dr. Thomas. We're here for you as much as we are for Regan." Then she was out the door leaving Sean and Regan alone.

Two days ago, moving in seemed like a great idea but now Sean was not sure how the reality would work out. His discomfort wasn't just from the potential of finally learning the truth. He realized now that he wasn't sure if he had what he needed to walk this final path with Regan. He met with CJ this morning in an effort to prepare but now he couldn't remember a single piece of CJ's advice. Sean glanced at the table of contents in the booklet that the social worker left but couldn't concentrate on it. Finally, he looked at his aunt and asked, "We have a lot to do?"

Regan nodded. She struggled to stand, steadied herself on her cane, and motioned him to follow her as she limped slowly toward her office. Sean wondered if the cancer had spread to her bones. In his mind's eye he saw an army of nasty black cells devouring her piece by piece. He shook his head to get the image out of his mind. When they got to the office he smiled when he saw everything exactly as he remembered it from the day that he had mapped it when he was nine years old. With that surreptitious success, he eventually rummaged through Regan's desk, finding the photo of his mother that he took and hid in his room. He still keeps that photo on his dresser in his bedroom.

Regan grabbed a key out of the desk drawer and opened a locked door on her credenza. She pointed to a box and asked Sean to remove it. She sat on the leather couch and motioned for him to sit next to her. "I should have shown you these years ago. I'm sorry. And I'm sorry for all those times you remembered something about a brother and sister that I told you were not real." She opened the box and handed him a stack of photos.

"They were real," she said. "Daniel, that's your brother, adored you. And so did your sister, Colleen. They both tried to protect you and that's all I was trying to do too."

Stunned, the buzzing started in Sean's ears. Regan jumped right into the deep end with no warning. He took slow deep breaths to calm himself. He wanted to remain fully present to this moment. He was almost afraid to touch the photos, as if they would suddenly disappear from him, taking his family away again. Then he noticed it. Colleen, his sister! He'd seen her with Faith during a visit he made to the other realm while he was in a session with CJ. He was about to ask her a question when CJ said something that roused him; CJ hadn't realized that Sean was on one of his other-world visits. It was all beginning to make sense now. His sister was with him in those visits. And if Faith is any indication, Colleen has likely been with him all along. He hasn't been alone.

As Sean sorted through the photos, Regan told him about simple things like birthday parties when his mother made elaborately decorated cakes and how on his fourth birthday his cake was so top heavy with a dinosaur scene Quinn had designed herself that the cake slipped off the plate as she was showing everyone and Sean jumped onto the floor to eat the sugary dinosaurs. She told him his sister liked to dress him up and pretend he was her baby; she would paint his nails and put bows and barrettes in his long curls (which Jack hated). Then as he got older, she would read to him endlessly.

Regan said Sean worshiped Daniel and would mimic everything Daniel did, which never annoyed Daniel but seemed to endear Sean to him all the more. He learned that Daniel was very protective of Sean and Sean would often go to Daniel's room in the middle of the night when he had a bad dream—which, he suddenly remembered, was often even back then. Daniel liked to carry Sean on his shoulders and even put a kiddie seat on his bike and took Sean for long rides, just the two of them. At family gatherings in the last few years before *it* happened, Regan said, Daniel seemed sullen if Jack was around. But even then, Sean could always bring a smile to his face. Quinn used to say that she was amazed at how both Colleen and Daniel cherished their baby brother as if he was a special gift just for them.

Regan gave Sean so many details about Colleen and Daniel that they started to become real to him again. She also told him about his mother, how much she loved all her children, how they completed her, how she struggled through her pregnancy with him and how she treasured him all the more because he would be the last child she was able to have. She explained to him the special meaning of his name and confessed that his name wasn't just Sean Patrick Thomas but Sean-Patrick Thomas Gallagher. When Regan said his full name, that pain like a lightning bolt made him gasp.

"It wasn't an accident was it," Sean said with dread as he touched the scar at the back of his head. He knew the other shoe was about to drop.

"No," Regan said softly. "Jack Gallagher, your father, shot my sister, then Daniel, and then you and Colleen before killing himself. You survived but just barely. You were airlifted here. It was weeks before you regained consciousness. When you did, you were so confused. You didn't seem to know how you were injured so I made up a story. I couldn't bring myself to tell you the truth."

She gave him the newspaper article she'd saved. After he read it, he sat staring into space. All those nightmares weren't unexpressed bits of him. They were memories. Of real events. He opened his mouth to speak, but words didn't come so Regan continued with other stories from happier days that made it seem as if he inhabited two opposing worlds in his first five years of life: one full of love and the other full of violence. He was in two opposing worlds now too: one that made so much sense and the other that made no sense at all.

He listened to story after story as they sorted through the photos. Sean saw not just siblings but aunts-uncles-cousins and a part of him wanted to be angry. Very angry. This truth, this family is what he'd longed for his whole life. He hadn't been alone; he had been a part of a family in which he was loved. And that family still existed yet Regan had kept it from him. But he didn't want to say or do anything that would make her stop talking. At this moment, he wished more than anything that she would never stop talking.

At the very bottom of the box was a small jewelry box. Regan handed the box to him. He opened it and saw his mother's engagement and wedding rings. He gingerly lifted the rings from the silk pillow in the box and set them in the palm of one hand, afraid that if he held on too tightly he would break the spell cast over them. These rings once touched his mother. She wore them for years. She lived with them. Died with them.

Gently placing his other hand over the rings as if in prayer, he closed his eyes, hoping if he shut out the world he might feel his mother's presence in them. He brought his hands to his face knowing that there would be no scent on the rings but unable to resist the urge to place them near his nose. Finally, he put the rings back in their box. He then put his head in his hands and cried for the woman who had given him life.

He could sense Regan's discomfort with his emotional display. Anger again began to gnaw at the fringes of his thoughts as he remembered all the nights he stifled his childhood cries because it would upset his aunt. As if she were reading his mind, she placed her knobby hand on his shoulder and said, "I could never really face the truth of my sister's life . . . or her death. It was an anger that ate away at me every day. And even if I could put it away for a few moments at work, I'd come home and see your face and I would remember all over again."

Did she really blame him just for existing? Before he could say anything, she continued, "I am so sorry. You were a child who had lost your mother . . . your siblings . . . everything you knew and loved. I wanted to be what you needed but I let my hatred get in my way."

"It must have been hard to lose your sister," Sean said as a conscious decision to choose compassion as a way to mitigate his own growing irritation. He could see Regan was getting tired and he didn't want his anger to give her a reason to leave now. He was grateful when she continued.

"If it were only that, I think I could have gotten past it," she said. Regan looked out the window. It seemed to Sean as if she were watching a movie of memories flow across it. Sean had learned from watching Savannah with Anna Powell to give someone the space they needed when there were hard things to say. He could tell she wasn't finished yet so he waited in silence. He continued to pick up photos until he picked up a photo of Regan and Brendan. Sean recognized him as a Gallagher. It was hard not to since Brendan was simply a darker version of his father, Jack (the red-haired man of his dreams). In fact, if it weren't for the old styles of hair and clothing, Sean might have guessed the photo was of him. He had always thought he looked like his mother, but now seeing photos of Jack and Brendan, he realized he bore many of the qualities of a Gallagher.

"You knew my dad's brother?" Sean asked.

She nodded. "I married him. His name is Brendan." She took a deep breath, ready to say more but instead started to cough. Although a thousand questions immediately popped into Sean's mind, he didn't say a thing. He noticed that when Regan had something very emotional to reveal, the cough started as a prelude to the revelation. He waited. He trusted that her insistence in getting a hold of him meant she wanted to tell him the whole truth. He needed to be patient and let the story unfold in Regan's time, not his. Taking another cue from Savannah, he reached out to rub Regan's back. The physical contact seemed to help and slowly Regan's cough subsided and she continued her story.

"I'd like to say that everything I did—dropping your last name, keeping you from that family, telling you that you were an only child—I did to protect you but that isn't the whole truth. I did it to protect me too. And I did it because I was so angry with Jack *and* Brendan." As she spoke, Sean started to hear that familiar buzzing in his head that signaled what he now knew as emotional overload. He stood up to shake the feeling off. Regan reached her hand out to him but he ignored it. He wished Savannah or CJ were here.

Regan continued. "I was married to Brendan Gallagher though I'm sure he always loved your mother more," she said. "When I realized that you were Brendan's son after Jack murdered everyone, I just couldn't take it."

"I'm Brendan's son?" The buzzing stopped as if shocked by the ridiculousness of this revelation. "What in the world makes you say that?"

"When you were in the hospital after Jack shot everyone, you needed blood. Brendan was the only one who could give it to you. You and he share the same blood type. I guess it's kind of rare."

"Having the same blood type doesn't mean he's my father," Sean said with the certainty of a medical man.

"But it was rare and you both had it," Regan said.

"We were from the same family."

"Anyway, that night in the hospital he confessed that he had had an affair with your mother. That was one reason I told him never to contact us again. It was horrible enough that his brother had killed my sister and her children but knowing that my husband had an affair that may have caused all the murders . . . Was I that much of a shrew that he could never love me?" Regan paused and Sean waited hoping she would continue but she was lost once again in her memories.

"You think Jack killed everyone because he found out about the affair?" Sean finally prompted.

"I don't know," she said. She looked directly at him. "I always suspected that you were Brendan's son. I don't know if Jack did too. It was Brendan who was in love with Quinn; I could always see that plainly. But Quinn was madly in love with Jack so he might not have been as aware as I was. I don't know how the affair happened, but I always knew it was Brendan's fault. He betrayed me and I hated him." She looked out the window once more and then leaned back. It was obvious to Sean that her confession, and the power the hurt still had over her, left her completely spent.

With her eyes closed and almost no energy in her voice she continued. "I don't really know what set Jack off that day. It might have been the affair but maybe not. Jack's life was falling apart by then. He was under investigation at work. He was drinking heavily and Quinn had told me she was afraid of him. He had hit her. In fact, he hit her when she was pregnant with you.

She told me he once threatened to kill her. Towards the end, despite the fact that they lived in my parent's old house that was paid for, money was a problem again. Quinn suspected that Jack had added drugs to his very obvious alcohol problem."

Sean always said he knew his aunt was lying about his life but he never could have imagined how hard the truth would be. He realized now that he was either the son of a murderer or an adulterer and that he was raised by a liar. Why couldn't the lies have ended with the stories of Colleen and Daniel?

Determined, he pressed on. He asked quietly and gently, "You said the affair was one reason you told him not to contact us. What was the other?"

She kept her head back on the couch but opened her eyes. "Brendan buried your mother in the same cemetery as your father. I wanted her buried next to my parents but Brendan never cared what I wanted," she said with the tone of a whining child. Sean was surprised by the smallness, the childishness, of her voice. His aunt had always been an all-powerful presence in his life. She had control over information he'd always wanted and the affection he needed as a child. This needy side of her was a whole new animal.

"I lost it," she continued closing her eyes again. "Brendan betrayed me. Jack betrayed my sister, and he tried to kill you. As far as I was concerned, Gallagher was just another word for betrayal. I wanted to save you from them . . . I wanted to save me from them . . . I told Brendan to stay away from you and to make sure no one else in the family ever contacted you or me. If they did I would reveal the affair. I didn't care if he told everyone you were dead, I just wanted them all to stay away. I don't know what he said or did but I never heard from any of them again. When I returned to get some of your things packed up while you were in the hospital, I made sure he would not be around. I couldn't stand to look at him, though when I looked at you as you were growing up it was like looking at him."

Sean wasn't sure if that was an apology of sorts but understanding her pain helped him see why she was always so distant. He had wanted to understand her story and now he had a big chunk of it, but the story she was telling created as many questions as answers.

What if she died before giving them? Was she hoping for some kind of absolution from him? Was he up to giving it to her? Could he forgive his father, whoever that might be? And his mother, who he'd remembered in flashes as his aunt spoke . . . why did she stay in such an unsafe situation with children? With him? Her decision to stay cost him everything short of his life.

He was shell-shocked from all the revelations. It was as if his aunt was talking about someone else's life. But he had an intuitive sense that she was really, finally, telling him the truth Not the whole truth. But the truth as she knew it. Listening to Michael's grandparents, and even talking with Savannah about her family's struggles, Sean realized there wasn't a single truth that encompassed all the complexities in a marriage or a family. And he also knew that memories accurately stored the pain of an event but not necessarily all the facts. There was plenty of pain to go around and Sean hoped there was time to get more facts. Even if Regan died, now that he knew his full name, he could find out more from the family he always believed existed. They couldn't really be as monstrous as Regan made them out to be. Could they?

Seeing her so exhausted, so frail, it was hard for him to continue to hate her or be angry with her. Yet could he really forgive her? Then again, could he be so callous to let her die without it?

Forgiveness. Just what was that going to look like, feel like? After all he'd learned today—and all he surmised was left to learn—forgiveness was something he was going to have many opportunities to practice. But how do you forgive those who are dead? Like his mother. If Regan was telling the truth and her suspicion that Jack was also culpable in her own parents' deaths long before he turned a gun on his wife and children, how in the world could his mother stay with him? Who was Jack really? Who was Quinn? How had she allowed herself to become Jack's victim? Didn't anybody notice there was a problem? Quinn paid dearly for not leaving Jack. It cost her everything. Just as it had cost Michael's mother everything. Sean needed to talk to Anna again. He must be missing something.

He wanted to ask Regan more questions, but when he looked at her he knew he had gotten all the answers she could manage today. As soon as she finished speaking, she had instantly fallen asleep. He wondered why they had not been able to be like this before with each other—talking truthfully, caring openly. He picked her up and wondered if she could have lost even more weight by confessing, she was so light.

He carried her to her room and placed her on her bed. By the time he pulled a blanket over her, she was snoring lightly. Her strength was waning quickly. There would not be much time to get all the answers he wanted but he was grateful for this beginning. He watched Regan for a few moments unable to name any of the feelings jumbled inside him. Shock had covered his emotions in a haze that he'd hoped Savannah could shine a light through. He was determined not to shut Savannah out this time. He would not shut out the memories either. Not if he ever wanted to return to work.

Returning to the photos in the office, he stared at them scanning his brain for memories that would connect him to all these strangers who were his family. Their smiling faces provoked a profound sadness in him.

Then he called Savannah. Just to hear her voice.

CHAPTER 23

SEATTLE NOW | 2013

SATURDAY   DECEMBER 14   1:30 PM   SEAN

REGAN SLEPT FOR THE REST of the day following her confession to Sean. He was grateful because it gave him time to begin to process what she'd told him. He checked on her a half-dozen times since putting her in her bed. She never stirred. When the night nurse came, he asked that she awaken him if Regan woke. The nurse reported that Regan had been restless numerous times but she slept through the night.

On Saturday morning, Sean called CJ to see if they could meet after Cate arrived to watch over Regan. While out, he'd also take the opportunity to visit Savannah and Michael. Savannah had stopped by after work the previous day and her presence calmed him as he related what he'd learned. He felt the need to see her again this afternoon, to hold her hand, hear her voice, feel her loving energy. And after all he'd learned yesterday, Sean also needed to tell Michael that he didn't regret deciding to live. His life was good, despite all its losses and complications. And if he could finally love Savannah the way he'd always wanted, and if she was truly willing to let him, then life would become very very good indeed. Michael needed to know that he'd be safe and that there was still enough love in his world to make his life good too.

It was early afternoon when Sean arrived carrying his usual gift of coffee for all, this time from Vivacci's. Savannah had been listening to Anna reminisce about the happier times in her daughter's life. The women were smiling and animated. The Judge, who remained in the room sitting close to the barely audible television, was sullen. Sean could see that he was trying to mask his emotions but a simmering rage was evident in the set of his mouth; his upper lip drawn in so tight that it looked like a hash mark

201

scored under his nose. His eyes glared under furrowed brows. Even though he wasn't a father himself, Sean understood Judge Powell's anger. Any man would.

Sean greeted everyone, handed out the coffees and sat near the women to listen to Anna's reminiscences. Listening to stories of Lexie and her accomplishments in a life that had once seemed so full of promise didn't quite square with what he knew of the final days of her life—not just from the autopsy but from his meetings with her and Faith too. Finally, Sean asked a question that plagued him all the years he worked in the emergency department. Sean had seen it so many times. Women coming in beat up saying they fell or walked into a door and hurt themselves. Protecting the scum who did it to them.

"Why didn't she leave him?"

"She did leave him. Twice. Well, three times if you count this last time." Anna said. "But he would always come crying and begging and saying how sorry he was. He promised her over and over that it wouldn't happen again. You know, the first time he hit her was when she was pregnant with Faith. She came home right away that time."

"I should have . . ." the Judge began to say before a look from his wife silenced him.

Anna continued, "Richard tried for most of that pregnancy to reconcile. Lexie went back to him just before the baby was born believing he had changed and that it was just the pressure of becoming a parent that made him snap. She wanted the happily ever after. They named the baby Faith—because they had faith in their relationship. They told each other it would work."

"He never fooled me," the Judge piped in. "I knew he was a con from the moment I laid eyes on him. All his *trying* was just an act."

Anna shot him another silencing look and continued, "Richard was good for a while. He joined Gambler's Anonymous and AA. He even went to counseling with Lexie before she would let him back. But after a couple of years, he hit her again. She left him for almost three years that time. But they reconciled once more. Then she found she was pregnant with Michael and she felt she had to make it work. She had two children now and Richard was good again for a while. When he was good, he was so charming that there wasn't a nicer guy in the world. Lexie loved the good Richard. I loved the good Richard. I wish they had stayed close by. We could have helped when he lost his job again," Anna said, remembering. Her vacant eyes stared into a past whose outcome now was so obvious.

The Judge took the moment of silence to say what he'd wanted to say for so long now, "I knew he would kill her. He started life as a controlling bastard and he died that way, murdering my daughter and granddaughter in the process."

Anna had heard this all before, "James, please. Your anger isn't going to . . ."

"Don't you think I know my anger can't bring her back," the Judge whisper-shouted under his breath, barely controlling his rage. "But what else am I supposed to feel now? That son-of-a-bitch took everything from me. Lexie was a smart, beautiful girl. Why the hell did she pick him? I never should have let her marry him and after she did, I should have taken control and gotten her out of there."

"*She* took control and she *was* getting out, James," Anna's soft voice was sharp. Though Sean didn't know them well, he sensed a shift in their relationship.

Turning her attention back to Sean and Savannah she continued, "And this time I am sure she would have stayed out. Richard knew it too. That's why he killed her. Lexie had called her sister to say she was planning her escape. That is what it had come to; my daughter feeling like a prisoner in her own home, in her life. Richard had isolated her when they moved to Seattle. She had no friends, no family. He even kept the key to their mailbox so that we couldn't send her money. He allowed her one credit card that he monitored like a hawk. She didn't have access to the checkbook. He controlled all their money and with that, he controlled her. And that was just the way he wanted it." Anna fell silent again. Sean could see the pain in her face and hear the fear in her remembering.

"After fourteen years of being married to him, he had eroded so much of her away. It took real courage to decide to leave him," she said. Sean heard in Anna's tone both pride and resignation.

The Judge got up and left the room saying he needed a walk. A palpable energy departed with him. Sadness and defeat lingered in the space he vacated. Michael moaned. Anna jumped to Michael's bedside, stroked his hair, and began that little song she was always singing to him. Sean could see it comforted Michael. He wished he could tell Anna about his encounters with Faith and how she said Michael likes it when his Nana sings to him. But Anna would think he was crazy. Hell, even with CJ's assurances he still was unsure if it might in fact be true.

The nurse on duty came to check on Michael in her regular rounds while Anna was soothing him. No change. Not yet. Anna sat down again near Sean and Savannah after the nurse left the room.

Savannah asked Anna, "Have you ever felt like a prisoner?"

Sean was surprised as Anna nodded her head and mumbled, "Ummm . . ." Anna chose her next words carefully. "You might have noticed that my husband can be a little intimidating. I don't think he means it; it's just who he is. He is a good man, a good provider, a loving and protective husband and father. But everything must be his way, he doesn't like dissent and he's never quite understood how overpowering he can be. Both at home and on the bench. Before he became a judge, the chatter for years at Bar Association events was about James' fearlessness. Then when he became a judge, the mantra for new attorneys who hoped to keep their heads became "don't cross JP."

"His courtroom ran like clock-work and he wanted the same precision at home. Sometimes he forgot that I was his wife, not his assistant or his clerk. I was aware of James' intensity from the beginning and it was even one of the things that attracted me to him. He was always so sure, so confident. He made me feel safe. I didn't notice the downside of it until I decided to go to graduate school when our girls were in high school shortly after James was appointed to the bench. I figured I had helped him achieve his career goal and now it was my turn. But James didn't like the changes. I wasn't at his beck and call arranging parties, having his dinner on the table at 7:30 sharp, dressing his arm at important functions. He finally bullied me enough that I just quit. He was never overtly threatening and certainly never violent in any way. He simply wore me down. Doing things his way was just easier.

But now I wonder if I had held my own more if Lexie would have . . ." Anna's voice trailed off and her eyes welled with tears.

Sean hadn't known Anna long but from everything he could see she was an intelligent, completely put-together woman. How could a woman like that feel controlled?

Savannah said softly, "I've noticed you don't seem so willing to indulge him now."

"We are both struggling with blaming ourselves. I know James thinks he should have been able to keep Lexie safe. That was his job so he feels her death as his own failure. I blame myself for not giving Lexie a better example of how to not lose herself in a relationship with a man. But blaming won't do either of us any good. Now, we have to think of Michael and what kind of example we set for him. God knows that boy has seen enough of controlling men, and violence. If we want any hope of raising him into a man who does not use anger to intimidate others, we have to change. Me *and* James."

"What if the judge can't change?" Savannah pressed.

"He will," Anna said with a note of confidence. "We both have felt enough loss, enough pain to make the shift. And if he can't, then Michael and I will have to go it alone. None of us can undo what's been done but I will move heaven and earth to make sure Michael . . ."

Just then, Michael moaned. Anna rushed back to his side and began stroking his hair saying, "It's alright baby. Nana's here. Nana's here." She started singing the song once more. Sean and Savannah took that as their cue to leave. They waved to Anna as they silently made their way out.

CHAPTER 24

SEATTLE NOW | 2013

SATURDAY/SUNDAY DECEMBER 14/15 SEAN/SAVANNAH

AFTER LEAVING THE HOUSE, Sean called Cate nearly every hour to check in. At his 4:30 check-in, Regan was asleep so he and Savannah shared a quick dinner. Savannah followed him home afterwards to visit with Regan but Regan was still asleep on the living room sofa when they arrived and she didn't stir. Cate reported that Regan had awakened once but had stayed awake for less than an hour. She'd come downstairs and ate the tiniest bit and that small effort had exhausted her. Afterwards she made the short trek from the dining table to the living room sofa and promptly fell asleep in the time it took for Cate to move the dishes to the kitchen. Cate was sitting on the sofa facing the one on which Regan slept when Sean and Savannah arrived.

Sean carefully picked up Regan after Cate's report, carried her upstairs, and placed her back in her bed. None of them said it, but Sean was sure they were in agreement that Regan didn't have two or three weeks to live, as her doctors had predicted. She would be lucky to last another week.

After Cate left, Savannah and Sean shared the cozy oversized chair and ottoman in the reading nook in Regan's room looking again at the photos of his family. Each time he looked through them, Sean remembered more. CJ warned him when they met earlier that since his memories were those of a small child who was apparently often in great danger, the more Sean remembered the more his anxiety might grow. That was fine with Sean because perhaps then he would visit Faith again and maybe he'd get the opportunity to talk with his own sister. But rather than feeling the kind of overwhelming emotion that preceded a visit, he just felt numb. He worried that no one would come. As much as these ethereal visits had disturbed him, he suddenly had an urgent desire for one.

When he told Savannah this, she suggested that perhaps doing a guided meditation would open the door to the realm Faith inhabited. She knew the technique but when she tried to walk him through one, Sean was frustrated that nothing happened. Was he thinking too much? Was he too emotionally exhausted? Did he not trust Savannah enough? Savannah suggested they go to another room since they had to whisper and be so careful with Regan sleeping only a few feet away. And not just sleeping, but most likely actively dying as well. Sean didn't want to leave Regan alone and the night nurse wasn't due for a couple of hours yet. Savannah understood. So, after Sean checked Regan's vitals yet again, they settled once more on the chair to look through the photos.

Just past 10 pm, Savannah went to the kitchen to fix Sean some tea that she told him would settle him. After giving it to him, she prepared to head home; she had an early shift the next morning. Sean walked her as far as Regan's bedroom door and Savannah looked at him with such compassion he almost broke down. When she embraced him, resting her head on his chest, he could no longer hold back the tears. He hated looking so vulnerable and weak to her. She must have read his thoughts because she held him tighter and after he sighed deeply, she looked up at him and said, "Thank you for trusting me," and kissed him lightly on the lips. "Call me if anything changes," she whispered.

When Savannah left, Sean checked Regan again. He was there as her nephew but he couldn't help being a doctor too. And being a doctor, even for a few moments an hour, was a solid piece of him that didn't change with his name. It kept him from feeling that his identity was completely wiped out.

Though he was exhausted, Sean would not leave Regan until the night nurse came. He read through the hospice materials again noting that many of the markers for death were already present in Regan. It seemed like over these last twenty-four hours since her confession, Regan was simply losing her vital force.

As a doctor, Sean had not witnessed a dying process like Regan's. Most of the time if his patients died, they did so on their way to the emergency department or in a sudden burst once they arrived because their injuries were too severe. For critical, yet potentially survivable injuries, he'd stabilize a patient and send them on for surgery but he always had a sixth sense about the ones who would survive and the ones who would not. That sense was telling him that Regan's death was close. He could just feel it.

He scribbled a note telling the night nurse to come in when she arrived and ran downstairs to tape it on the unlocked front door. Then he pulled Regan's reading chair to the side of her bed and sat, holding her hand while she slept.

∞

Faith appeared before him smiling. Next to Faith was Colleen, who was also smiling. Faith spoke first.

"You've been through quite a lot these last couple of days."

Sean nodded.

Colleen spoke next, "You know who I am now, don't you?" Sean nodded again. "Do you realize now that I've always been close to you? Mom and Daniel too."

"I knew you were there when I was small," Sean replied. "I wish I'd been strong enough and brave enough to know you never left."

"You always did know. At least a part of you did. We're here to help you remember that part of yourself so you can believe in it, you can trust it."

Faith, who had faded into the background, came forward and said, "You can help make sure Michael never forgets. I know you've thought you were crazy because of all these visits, but now you know we're real. We're not just your imagination." Sean nodded again. "Will you please tell Nana, Granddad, and Michael now?" When Sean promised he would, Faith faded again and Colleen was before him. He and Colleen began reminiscing about the good things they had experienced together as children.

As they went through the memories, Sean realized that his sister seemed to look older and older. She now possessed the form and visage he was sure she would have had as an adult. Her face not only looked like photographs of his mother, it looked vaguely like someone else too. Sean wasn't disturbed by the age progression as they spoke. He'd come to accept that things worked differently in this realm. Maybe he could bring some of that acceptance into the world he inhabited with Regan.

Colleen must have read his thoughts because she said, "Regan tried so hard in her life and she did love you. But she was so broken and was never able to trust that she was loved. She misunderstood so much, got so many things wrong. I tried to help her a few times since I arrived here but she refused to acknowledge me. She even refused to hear or see mom. We did what we could but eventually everyone needs to decide on their own to open their hearts, be vulnerable, and love. There is only so much anyone else can do for them."

"There are so many things I still need to know from Regan and I'm not sure she will be able to tell me before she dies," Sean said with an urgency he couldn't hide.

"All you need to know, you already know. It may take a little time for you to allow it all to surface, but don't worry. It will come. Simply act out of love. Every choice you make, make it in love. Don't fear being vulnerable. And then trust the love being offered to you. All will be well. Especially once you bring your love back to the house."

"What house?" Sean asked but as he did, he could hear someone calling his name from somewhere very far away. He turned to look in the direction of the sound. When he turned back to his sister, she was fading from his sight.

∞

He opened his eyes and realized he had fallen asleep in the chair with his head resting on Regan's bed. He was still holding her hand. The night nurse was next to him with her hand on his shoulder.

The night nurse said, "Dr. Thomas, why don't you go to bed for a little while? I'll stay here with Regan now."

"I think she's close," Sean said.

"She may be but I don't think she'll die tonight," the nurse said with the confidence of someone who had experienced death many times.

"But when I checked her an hour ago, her pulse seemed so weak," Sean said.

As they stood together watching Regan sleep, Sean realized how exhausted he felt. In yet another effort to trust, he told the nurse, "I *am* exhausted." She nodded and he continued, "I'll be in the room right across the hall. Please get me if her breathing slows at all." The nurse nodded again, saying "*of course*" as Sean checked Regan's pulse once last time before he left the room. It was not strong but it was steady. The nurse was probably right. There was likely a little time still.

The nurse stood on the opposite side of Regan's bed while Sean checked Regan's pulse. When Sean looked at her, she smiled at him and said, "Don't worry, I'll stay right next to her. If anything changes, anything at all, I'll come get you. Get some rest while you can. It likely won't be tonight but it might be very soon."

Sean thanked her, went to the guest room across the hall and slept soundly for the first time in days. Nothing disturbed him. Not a nightmare. Not a dream. Not a visit to another realm. When the morning sun streamed in the window, he looked at the clock and realized he'd slept the whole night through. He jumped up and ran across the hall. The night nurse was holding two fingers on Regan's neck as she studied her wristwatch. When she finished, she looked at him and smiled. "No change," she said.

By the time Cate arrived Sunday morning, Regan's pulse hadn't changed discernibly yet her skin seemed to be embracing the pallor of death. She hadn't awakened (other than that single hour yesterday) since she fell asleep following her confession on Sean's first day there. After Cate read through Regan's chart and made her own notes, Sean filled her in on what he'd seen through the morning hours since the night nurse left. With Cate by Regan's side, Sean took the opportunity to fix himself something to eat. He checked in with Cate when he was done and she whispered, "no change" so he went to the guest room across the hall for a quick call to Savannah. He wanted to tell her about his visit to the other realm after she left him last night. He'd been thinking about it while he sat vigil over Regan this morning. There were so many more questions he had for Regan. He'd just finished telling Savannah that he didn't think he was going to get the opportunity to ask them when Cate came to the doorway. Her face startled him but before he could think about why, she spoke.

"She's awake, sort of. Her eyes are open and she's calling for you. She's agitated and there is something different about her energy. I sense we're close."

Savannah heard Cate and said to Sean, "I'll get someone to cover the rest of my shift. I'm on my way." Sean was grateful because as nice as Cate was, he knew he needed Savannah right now. When he woke that morning, he'd had the same feeling about Regan's energy. Physically, Regan should have had some time left but after her confession to him, she quickly began to fade away as if she couldn't face him now that he knew what she'd done. They hadn't spoken again since that first day he was there and he hadn't had enough time to . . .

Before he finished that thought, he heard a whisper of his sister's voice. "Act with love. Trust me. All will be well."

When Sean entered Regan's room, her tiny form was weakly thrashing about. She was moving both her arms and legs as if she were trying to escape. Her eyes were closed again and between mournful moans she was calling his name as if she was lost—and maybe she was. He could tell speaking was a great effort, her voice was nothing more than a croaky whisper. Once at her side, he took her hand and she opened her eyes but they were unfocused. Sean spoke, assuring her he was there. At the sound of his voice, her eyes focused on him and filled with tears.

"I'm so sorry. I'm so sorry. I'm so sorry," she choked out before her tears spilled down. She raised her hand, still grasping his and kissed his hand over and over. With his other hand he began stroking her hair, trying to soothe her.

"It's alright," he said twice before she caught his gaze again.

"I'm so scared."

"I'm right here."

"I'm *so* scared," she said again. Sean shushed her gently, continuing to stroke her hair. He could feel her trembling. She told him she was cold. When he asked if he could pick her up to hold her, her *please* spoke volumes about the depth of her fear.

Sean picked Regan up and carried her downstairs to the sofa in the living room. Could she be even lighter now than when he carried her up those same stairs last night? She was literally disappearing. He held her skeletal body to him in a protective embrace, like you'd hold a small scared child—which in that moment, she was. He settled onto one of her beautiful white velvet sofas, holding her head against his chest, using his own body to warm her. He could feel her trembling subside and her breathing slow. After a while, Sean noticed that the weak winter light was fading from the sky and the room was turning dark. He also noticed that the moments between Regan's breaths were getting longer and longer.

"I'm cold," Regan rasped once more. Sean asked Cate to flip the switch next to the fireplace to ignite the gas logs. The light from the fire cast a golden glow on Regan's ashen face. Cate wrapped a blanket around Regan, draping and tucking at her legs and shoulders being careful not to disturb her body's contact with Sean's. When Savannah arrived, the room was lit only by the fireplace and all was quiet except for some harp music playing in the background. Sean was holding Regan almost like an infant and rocking ever so slightly.

Seeing Savannah, he silently mouthed, "Soon" and she kissed the top of his head, then sat on the floor next to them. Regan's breathing was very shallow by then. Sean realized that his breathing had slowed also. Finally, he took a deep breath, both to restore his lungs and relax his body. He'd been rocking for so long and holding Regan so tight to reassure her, that his muscles felt stiff (though he knew it was more from emotion than exertion). When he slowly let that deep breath go, Regan turned her face up to him and with what seemed to be her last ounce of strength asked, "Can you forgive me?"

"Yes. I forgive you," Sean said as he stroked Regan's hollowed out cheek, holding her gaze with a steady gaze of his own. "I understand what you did and why you did it. I forgive you." And in that moment he knew it was true. He didn't get all the answers he wanted but he knew enough to understand Regan's pain. And he couldn't add to that pain now by not giving her the absolution she asked for.

Regan put her head back on Sean's chest and closed her eyes. Sean hugged her just a bit tighter, a physical reassurance of his words. Then he embraced her head with his free hand to hold it next to his heart. Kissing the top of it, he said, "And I love you too. Thank you for everything you could do. It was enough." One more tear fell from Regan's closed eyes and Sean could feel a slight shudder go through her body.

When Savannah asked her if she'd like to be anointed (as a chaplain, Savannah had brought her anointing oils just in case) Regan managed the slightest nod of assent.

Sean too had closed his eyes, perhaps in prayer, as Savannah anointed Regan while speaking words of comfort that came directly from her heart rather than any prayer book. When she finished, Savannah could tell that Regan's spirit was gone, leaving only the husk of a broken woman. Savannah was unsure if Sean realized that Regan was gone. Not wanting to break the spell that engulfed them, Savannah remained silent and still. Time seemed to have stopped with Regan's heart.

After Savannah put her anointing oils back in her satchel she sat again on the floor next to Sean without making a sound. The music continued its soothing background vibrations. Cate sat on the facing sofa, her head bowed, her hands folded as if in prayer. Savannah had no idea if Cate was a prayer kind of person, but she did know that everyone she'd met who worked in hospice had a profound sense of the sacred. Cate, it appeared, was no exception. When Savannah saw Sean reach for Regan's eyes to ensure they were closed, she touched his knee and asked if he was okay.

He nodded and said, "What should I do now?"

After Sean moved "back home," everything had happened so quickly, Savannah knew that Sean hadn't had time to discuss with Regan plans for after her death. Previously they'd been so estranged, Savannah knew that Sean had no idea whether Regan wanted a service, whether she wanted cremation or a coffin, or where she'd want to be buried. But his question was more than that. When someone dies in your arms, it's hard to know exactly what to do next. Savannah looked at Cate, who took that as her cue.

"I'll get a hold of the funeral home to let them know," Cate said. "It's after hours so it may take a little while before the hearse arrives. Would you prefer to lay your aunt on the couch or in her bed?"

"I'd better put her back to bed," Sean said. "Regan would die if her sofa got soiled." He chuckled and said it just slipped out before asking their forgiveness for being so crass. In the next moment Sean tenderly unwrapped the blanket that helped him keep Regan warm. He stood and readjusted Regan in his arms and Savannah saw him wince as Regan's limp arm fell away and her head draped back over the crook at his elbow. As he walked up the stairs, he was careful not to let her head or toes bump the wall or railings.

No one spoke as Sean placed Regan on her bed and pulled up the blankets as if he were tucking in a little child. He sat on the bed next to her, finger combing her hair. Savannah gave him Regan's brush remembering how fussy she'd always been about her appearance. Savannah smiled at the tenderness Sean was displaying, knowing that his aunt wouldn't want the funeral people to see her unkempt.

His vigil over her through these last two days was so all-consuming and it confirmed for Savannah that acting with love is intrinsic to who Sean is. She'd always sensed it, but that damn *wall* had gotten in their way. Well, Regan blew that wall to hell and back. Sean's emotions were ravaged and raw. And his journey through the hell of truth wasn't over. Watching him brush Regan's hair, Savannah realized that Sean was not quite ready yet to end his vigil, to leave Regan alone. So, Savannah now stood vigil over Sean, offering silent witness to his pain since there were no words that could soothe him in this moment.

What a whirlwind it had been since Regan joined Savannah and Sean for dinner less than a week ago to tell Sean she was dying. And in that time, before Sean could begin to process the reality of his last known relative leaving him, he found out he belonged to a big clan filled with aunts and uncles and cousins that Regan had kept from him all these years.

Savannah was so grateful, for Sean's sake, that he'd had some time with CJ before all this happened. She was also grateful for the conversations she and Sean had had about forgiveness. Michael and his family, and her own experiences in her family were plenty of fodder for forgiveness discussions and they'd had many of them since bumping into each other in Michael's room—yet one more thing to be grateful for. But she was most grateful that finally he was trusting her. Regan's confession put so much of her past experience with Sean into context. And she could only imagine what he'd gone through all these years. That he could love as well as he did was a miracle. Yet he was going to need just a few more miracles in the coming months.

From her own experience, Savannah knew that the choice to forgive was only the beginning of the healing process. Integrating that forgiveness would take a bit more work. But watching him now, Savannah knew Sean was well up to the task. He could have understandably chosen anger after Regan's confession, but he didn't. He chose love. Savannah knew that Sean had the benefit of some help from the other realm, including help from his own sister. Who could have imagined such fantastical experiences? Savannah was slightly jealous. Sean also had CJ in his life again. And he had her. In these next few weeks, he was going to need all the help he could get.

Savannah understood grief's pain and pitfalls. She experienced them with the shock of her dad's unexpected death and then seen them on many occasions with other families who experienced death. No matter how ready you are intellectually, the reality of death is always such a shock. And Sean's grief was going to be so much more complicated after finally learning the truth about his own family. Now he would not only grieve Regan, but his mother, his brother, his sister, and his twin (and who knows, maybe even his father) too. What toll would all that take on him?

Savannah knew one thing for sure. She would stand by him through it all because he was finally able to let her love him the way she'd always wanted to. If Sean was brave enough to risk trusting her with his heart, she was brave enough to risk loving him again. She was brave enough to surrender to love.

CHAPTER 25

SEATTLE NOW | 2013

SUNDAY   DECEMBER 15   6:30 PM   SAVANNAH/SEAN

WHEN SAVANNAH LOOKED UP, she saw Cate standing in the doorway of Regan's room.

"I've called the funeral home. They couldn't give me an exact time when they'll arrive but they thought it shouldn't be more than an hour or two," Cate said as she moved closer to the bed where Regan's body lay with her hair so meticulously styled now (perhaps not as Regan herself would have done it but done with Sean's love).

"When you're ready, I've got some special coffee downstairs," Cate said. "An old family recipe that Regan taught me for just this moment. Regan said every good Irish wake in Seattle must include the perfect cup of Irish coffee." Cate smiled with her eyes as well as her mouth, Savannah noticed. She also noticed that everything Cate did for them and for Regan seemed to be perfectly timed. She'd say it was thought out, but Savannah knew it was more than that. Savannah smiled back and nodded before Cate returned to the kitchen.

Sean told Savannah he needed a few minutes alone with Regan but assured her he would join them soon. When Savannah met Cate in the living room, she was greeted again with Cate's warm smile and an even warmer Irish coffee, including the whipped cream and chocolate shavings, all dolled up in a special mug.

"Wow, do you travel with the ingredients?"

Cate laughed and explained that she and Regan had spoken of this moment many times, the moment following Regan's death. Cate told Savannah that Regan had kept the ingredients on hand since the day she hired Cate. She'd even made Cate practice that first week she was with

Regan so that tonight, everything would be perfect. She'd prepared all the ingredients earlier so all she had to do was flip a few switches, grab the Bailey's, and make the whipped cream, which she did after calling the funeral home. Regan had left explicit written instructions for Cate to follow after her death.

"Sean won't have to do a thing," Cate said. "I have all the necessary contacts and instructions for the services and burial. Everything was paid in advance, including me for the work I will do now. Regan was very generous."

Savannah noticed Cate's eyes filling with tears so she silently raised her glass to Cate's as they wordlessly toasted Regan. In their silence, Savannah realized that the music playing in the background had changed from the ethereal harp music to Gregorian chant.

"Do you always play music when someone is dying?" Savannah asked.

"Not always," Cate began. "But sometimes it can help a person relieve some of their anxiety about the unknown. Regan and I had been talking about the dying process since she hired me right after her diagnosis. She was very afraid of dying. She said she'd done so many bad things. She talked almost exclusively about Sean so I think she meant regarding him. I was relieved when she finally connected with him last week. She was incredibly nervous when I drove her over to his place for dinner. And given what she'd shared about their relationship, I was surprised when he moved in. But it was good to see how he was able to comfort her. The music helped a little, but it was Sean who gave her peace."

Savannah chuckled, "No one was more surprised than Sean himself when he moved in. He acted on an impulse, something he's been learning to trust again. He'd been estranged from Regan for so long. But it seems that fate, or Providence, was giving both of them an opportunity for healing before her death."

"I've seen that often before. There is so much more out there than many people acknowledge. I feel grateful for my front row seat at this final intersection where out there and right here meet," Cate said using sweeping gestures with her arms to indicate out there and right here. "It is sacred work."

"How long have you been a hospice nurse?" Savannah asked. She had met other hospice workers and even considered it for herself when she was deciding on her path within chaplaincy. But circumstances brought her to the Faith & Healing Center, and she never looked back.

"I became a volunteer when I was in high school. Then in nursing school, I knew it would be my specialty. I'd known it since childhood really."

Savannah was visibly surprised so Cate continued.

"There was a lot of death in my family in the year I turned four. My uncle's whole family was lost; the parents and all three children died. My grandfather died on the day of the funeral and my grandmother lasted only a few years more."

"Wow, so much tragedy in such a sort time. How awful," Savannah said. Cate nodded and continued.

"As I grew older, I watched how all those deaths affected the different members of the family. And as the youngest in a huge family, grandchild number twenty-two, everyone thought I was too young to understand what was going on so nobody wanted to talk to me about it. I later wondered if the adults talked about it with each other at all since no one ever wanted to discuss it even as I grew older."

"I was the youngest too, I know what you mean," Savannah said.

"Right? Being youngest has its benefits but it also has its downside," Cate agreed. "And I learned that talking about death is taboo in my family so I stopped asking."

"Talking about death is taboo in many families," Savannah said.

"But I still needed to understand why some people fared well and others fared so poorly following a death, or as in our family, multiple deaths," Cate said. "Hospice workers came to talk to my religion class when I was a junior in high school. They talked more openly about death than anyone I knew. It was refreshing. Soon I became a hospice volunteer and that was the beginning of the understanding I craved. Then I realized I loved the work. There aren't many jobs that allow you to be really present to the challenges of life in all its glory and mystery quite the way hospice does."

Savannah and Cate both noticed Sean in the doorway of the living room at the same time. Savannah stood to give Sean a comforting hug and Cate ran to the kitchen for his mug of coffee. By the time Cate returned,

Savannah had already explained that this was Regan's idea. Cate handed Sean his mug, gave Savannah a fresh one, then raised her own mug as she spoke an impromptu blessing for the dead before the three of them clinked their glasses to toast Regan. Cate then also toasted Sean for his kindness and compassion. She shared how frightened Regan was that she would die without saying her piece (or was it peace) to Sean.

"You gave her a gift no one else could," Cate said as she reached for a book on the glass table beside the sofa. "If I were Jewish, I'd say what you did was a *mitzvah*. But since I'm Catholic, I'll just say you were a blessing. Regan thought so too. In fact, she told me to read a special blessing for you from a book she kept in her library. Once she knew you would be with her in these last days, she marked for me. She was uncharacteristically firm with me about reading it to you. She said it was very important." Cate emphasized *very* to add weight to Regan's request.

Then Cate held up her nearly empty glass toward Sean as she read:

May you live a long life full of gladness and health,
With a pocket full of gold as the least of your wealth.
May the dreams you hold dearest be those which come true.
And may the kindness you spread, keep returning to you."

"That was just lovely," Savannah said after they all clinked glasses once more. "Regan was more sentimental than I realized. She was so complex."

Sean added with a heavy sigh, "She was, and continues to be, an enigma."

After the three sat again on the sofas, Savannah continued with what she believed were innocuous questions for Cate about her background and where she was from. Then, knowing how much Sean was fascinated with stories about big families, Savannah turned the conversation to Cate's family, retelling Sean about Cate's position as the youngest of twenty-two grandchildren.

"You don't hear about families like that every day," Sean said smiling. Cate shrugged, blaming it on that Irish-Catholic thing, especially since her grandmother was right off the boat. She told them her grandparents had six daughters before having two sons. Only the older of the two sons was childless, the rest of them could have populated their own small village, Cate said as she laughed. The younger son had two sons and a daughter, and all the daughters had three daughters except her mom who had four. Cate was the youngest of the whole brood.

Sean laughed, "Eight kids and twenty-two grandkids? How in the world do you keep all the names straight with that many?"

Cate laughed too and said, "At least all of my cousins got their very own names. I did not; I'm another Catherine, after one of my aunts, but at least I'm not a "Mary" Catherine. My mother and all her sisters were named in the old Irish tradition of naming girls after the Virgin Mary so they're all *Mary-Something*, like Mary Elizabeth, Mary Ann, Mary Catherine. Other than the oldest Aunt Mary, and my Aunt Sissy, the rest of them use the second part of their name so it's not that hard to tell them apart."

"Sean, what is it," Savannah said noticing how the color suddenly drained out of his face.

Sean didn't answer Savannah. Instead he looked at Cate and asked what the family name was.

"Gallagher."

❧

Sean's head began to swim. He had a vague notion that Savannah was by his side, perhaps even touching his arm, but his senses seemed to have stopped working properly. It was as if he was floating weightlessly deep underwater in a muffled ocean with no way to tell up from down. His sister's grown-up face flashed in his mind—as a memory, not an invitation to another realm. He concentrated on his breath the way CJ taught him, trying to settle himself, to stay present. Shaking his head and calling his senses back into his body, he willed his eyes to focus on Cate.

Recognition.

This woman sitting across from him on one of his aunt's white sofas was his cousin. Something in him had known it all along. When they first met, he *knew* she was familiar. He couldn't place it but he definitely felt something when they met on the steps that day. And since then, he'd been so comfortable with her but he'd assumed that was because she was good at her job and because he was working so hard on being more trusting.

Suddenly another flash of memory came to him from a very long time ago. He saw himself as a child and there was a girl just slightly younger with him. They were playing at the river's edge, his mother and hers at a distance that was close enough to be safe but far enough away that they could explore the riverbed like big kids. He must have been about five, she couldn't have been more than four. That little girl had the same eyes as the young woman sitting in front of him now.

"You had blonde curls as a baby," he said as if everyone else could see his memory.

"What?" Cate answered, obviously confused.

"You had blonde curls," he said again. "I remember you. We were playing at a river's edge, maybe it was on our grandmother's property. I don't know. But we were the youngest of all the cousins. So many cousins. All girls. And so many aunts named Mary. I remember it. Our moms were friends. Don't you remember? My mom was Quinn and I called your mom Auntie B. I can't remember what the B stands for, but I remember everything else about that day," Sean said, his words pouring out. He stared straight into her eyes and said once more, "I remember you," as if willing Cate to remember too. But by the confused look on Cate's face, Sean could tell she still had no idea what he was talking about. She had no reason to suspect that Sean was a Gallagher; the cousin closest to her in age. The one that she thought was dead all these years.

Sean had heard the conversation Cate and Savannah had about why Cate became a hospice nurse. He realized that *he* was the cousin from the family that no one would talk about. The cousin whose lost family inspired her to become a hospice nurse. Regan's nurse. Regan wouldn't have had any reason to suspect Cate Webb was a Gallagher either. Why would she? What are the odds that she would hire a Gallagher from Spokane to care for her in her dying days in Seattle? And Regan obviously didn't share enough details about her life story for Cate to make any connection. Until now.

"B is for Brigid," Cate said. "My mom is Mary Brigid," she said adding that many of her cousins called her 'Auntie B.' Sean could tell that Cate was still confused though. She gestured for him to stand as she moved closer to him staring, studying everything about his face. Sean could see the light of recognition switch on in her before she seemed to lose her balance, "Oh my God. You're Sean-Patrick. You're not dead," she said. Cate reached for his face and began to cry. Sean put his arm around her and guided her to sit on the sofa where Regan had died less than an hour before. He now held Cate to his chest as she cried, just as he'd recently done for Regan. Instantly, Cate went from a trusted acquaintance to family so he enfolded her into a protective embrace with her head resting on his heart. The two of them then cried together as they both released decades of sorrow in the midst of the residual emotional charge created by Regan's death.

Sean was always cognizant of the sorrow and loss that weighed on him and he wondered if Cate had been consciously aware that she carried a similar weight. She was younger than he, not yet five when his family was killed, so what could she have remembered on her own? Her tears and sobs revealed that, conscious or not, she'd also carried the pain of loss. And most likely it was, like his, divorced from memories that would give it context.

Sean realized that he wasn't the only one affected by all these secrets that had been kept hidden underneath the veneer of normal. He wasn't the only victim in this story. Those who kept the secrets suffered and those who needed to know the truth suffered. Each in their own private hell separating them from what they truly needed. He wondered how deep Cate's pain was. And Regan's pain. And all the other Gallaghers he'd surely meet soon.

Sean was too emotionally exhausted to be embarrassed that he was openly crying not only in front of Savannah, whom he loved so deeply, but also in front of Cate. His cousin. His family.

That invincible wall he'd once used to protect himself from Regan couldn't be rebuilt in the light of the truth he now knew or in the wake of all these tears. And Sean knew not having that wall was a good thing.

CJ assured him that tears were a good thing too. Cleansing. He wondered, a parting gift from Regan? Yet his tears challenged his sensibilities about what it meant to be a man. He wasn't quite clear yet how all these tears could be signs of vulnerability (good) instead of weakness (bad, at least in his eyes). But he also figured he better get used to crying because he was an emotional wreck. He hadn't the strength to hold back the tears that were likely to come at the wake and funeral. Yet instinct told him it was better to let the tears flow than try to rebuild the wall to stop them.

As Sean comforted Cate, he was comforted by the knowledge that Colleen was right. All his questions would be answered in time. Regan wasn't the only one who could tell him the truth about his past. The Gallaghers must know his story too.

It was a shock to find out that he was a Gallagher and then to meet his first Gallagher cousin right here in Regan's living room. From Cate's reaction, he realized he was going to be as big a shock to the rest of the Gallagher clan as they were to him. He had no idea what secrets they had that Regan didn't know. Or how his presence would disturb those secrets.

But there was one thing he was sure of: someone there must know the answer to the one secret whose truth he *had* to know. Which Gallagher brother was his father? Colleen told him Regan misunderstood so much. Perhaps her belief—her fear—that Sean was Brendan's son was unfounded. If he was going to rebuild his identity, his understanding of exactly who he was, his idea of what it meant to be a man, then knowing the truth about his father seemed as good a place as any to start.

CHAPTER 26

SEATTLE NOW | 2013

SEAN HADN'T BEEN TO HIS AUNT'S downtown law offices since high school but the outer reception area looked just like he remembered it. Kingsley Strickland's office, which he'd never been in before, looked sophisticated and feminine with its glass furniture and artwork. Regan's office, with its mahogany furniture and paneling, made hers feel like a stogy aristocrat's library. Classic lawyer décor, she'd said. The way the two lawyers dressed was also as different as their offices. The lawyer sitting in front of him looked elegant, not severe. She wasn't as intimidating as his aunt, but she did seem to share Regan's seriousness. When she greeted him, she smiled with her mouth but not her eyes. Was that a lawyer thing or was it a signal that some bad news was in the offing?

"Thank you for coming in so quickly to see me before the holidays, Dr. Thomas," said the woman sitting behind a huge glass desk. When his aunt retired a few years ago, her law partner kept the practice going on her own. Sean guessed it wouldn't be too many years until she retired too.

"Or should I say Dr. Gallagher?" she continued as she motioned him to take the seat across the desk from her. "Dr. Thomas is fine," Sean said. He'd only been (as far as he knew) *Sean-Patrick Thomas Gallagher* for fewer than six years but *Sean Thomas* for nearly a quarter of a century. He hadn't had time to consider his name or the consequences of Regan's revelations about it. That past was quickly overshadowed by the present realities of Regan's death.

True to her word, Regan had made all the arrangements following her death. With Cate as the point person, Sean didn't have to do much but show up at the wake and then the funeral. He was surprised at the numbers

225

of people who came to both and by the stories they shared with him about his aunt which cast her in a completely different light. He was also surprised by all the people who knew about him. Regan, apparently, had spoken often and proudly of him.

It was evident that he had never seen her clearly or completely.

These last few weeks had been emotionally exhausting. Talking to CJ and Savannah helped, as did spending time in Michael's room (which included more visits to the other realm with Colleen and Faith when he dozed there, as he regularly seemed to do).

Michael. His little buddy who was the catalyst for all of this. Thankfully he was showing hopeful signs of real healing. Maybe he'll wake soon. Sean spent hours each day researching rehabilitation options for him. Having that little guy to focus on gave at least some structure to his upended life.

Sean had no idea what to do with all that he was learning about his past, which it turns out was more similar to Michael's than he could have imagined. His name was such a small part of the whole equation yet it was emblematic of his new dilemma: Who exactly was he? He hadn't yet given much thought to what would come next. Though sitting in the office of his aunt's attorney, he assumed he was about to get some clue.

"Dr. Thomas it is for now then. Your name is one of the topics on our agenda today. The other is the reading of Regan's will."

Sean nodded but said nothing.

Kingsley Strickland continued, "Regan and I have been law partners for nearly twenty years but we were friends before that. Our unusual masculine names first attracted us to each other at a bar association function not long after she settled in Seattle with you. Then we discovered we had similar passions about the law and different enough skills to make a good team. She finally convinced me to leave my large firm and join her here when you were about ten. She confided in me then about your origins and told me how she'd dropped your last name when she first registered you in school. She had wanted to legally change your name completely but you simply refused. She actually was proud of you for that, even though it did frustrate some of what she saw as necessary measures to protect you from your father's family. By the time we discussed the legalities, you had simply assumed the name Sean Thomas in school. You were so young that it wasn't a problem not having other school records. With Regan as your legal guardian, and a trusted lawyer, no one really questioned her."

Sean said, "I remember the argument we had on the way to school that first day. She wanted to call me Sam. She said it was almost like Sean. When I cried saying my name is Sean-Patrick, she relented because I think she was afraid I would make a scene once we got inside the school. When the teacher introduced me as just Sean, I didn't correct her. I don't remember her saying my last name. I think I was too young to worry about my last name. But after losing my whole family, I knew I couldn't lose my first name too. I'm glad I stood my ground then, but it sure makes things more confusing now."

"Quite," Kingsley said in agreement before quickly adding, "though not in a legal sense. Just an emotional one, I imagine. Legally, you've always been Sean-Patrick Thomas Gallagher," she said as she handed him one of the envelopes that were laid out on her desk. Sean opened the flap and found a social security card and a folded piece of paper. The card was old and yellowed. Regan must have sent for it when he was child. She'd made him memorize the number when he was applying for college but he'd never seen the card. She said memorizing the number was safer than carrying the card. *Safer for her*, Sean thought as he turned the memory over. He set the card down and unfolded the paper.

Kingsley continued, "All of your accounts and the house are in the name matching the one on your social security card, so Regan had me draw up that affidavit years ago saying that you, Sean Patrick Thomas MD, in fact are Sean-Patrick Thomas *Gallagher*. You can use this affidavit to claim all your possessions listed with your legal identity."

Ignoring the information about the affidavit and his legal name, Sean asked, "What accounts? What house?"

"Yes. That's next," Kingsley said looking down at the next envelope in her stack. She collected it and before continuing she leaned back in her plush red leather chair that bespoke both feminine sophistication and power.

"Before Regan's father—your grandfather, Seamus Kelly—died, he set up trust accounts for you and your brother and sister. When Colonel Kelly died with his wife, your mother inherited her parent's house. When your mother and siblings died, you were the sole heir of your family's wealth, including your siblings' trust accounts and the house you lived in before . . . ah, before . . . the event that orphaned you. Over the years, Regan managed that money very wisely and it has grown considerably. She could have used it for your schooling, since that was your grandfather's intent. But she never touched it. She paid for your Catholic grade school and high school, university, and medical school out of her own funds. She also made sizeable annual contributions of her own to the trust account on your mother's, brother's, and sister's birthdays plus another contribution on the anniversary of their deaths. She always felt guilty about what she kept from you. The payments were a form of repentance in her eyes. She had planned to give it all to you on many occasions; first it was when you graduated college; then medical school; then when you turned thirty. But she would always lose her nerve knowing she would have to explain the whole truth to you. She couldn't bear that you would hate her for what she'd done."

"She told me my grandfather had set up a trust for my education. I always assumed my aunt used it. I never thought to ask about it again after medical school. I was so busy with my residency, nothing else really mattered. When Regan heard I was buying an apartment, she gave me the purchase price saying it was from the trust account. I'd always assumed that was the rest of the money in the trust."

"Regan never used the money from the trust, even for your apartment. She was as giddy as a schoolgirl when she told me how she was able to give you that lovely apartment and you never knew. She knew you'd never accept the money if you'd known it was from her."

"Her guilt again?"

"Yes, partly," Kingsley said lowering her voice and her head, momentarily inspecting her perfect manicure through the two-inch thick beveled glass of her desk. When she looked up at Sean, she continued, "She really did want to love you the way she knew you needed. She knew her secrets and lies kept her separated from you. She hated herself for telling you that your memories were only dreams. She struggled with her own emotional demons and knew she was creating others for you. I think it was one of the things that fueled her work. Her anger at herself, at the circumstances that brought you to live with her, at her ex-husband. I counseled her many times to find a therapist or someone who could help her do what she knew she needed to do. Tell you the truth. She simply couldn't do it. She said she couldn't risk it. So she made your life as comfortable as she could manage. And she set about amassing a fortune for you for when she knew she'd be gone."

Kingsley Strickland opened an envelope containing bank statements for a trust account in Sean's name. She slid them across the desk to him. As he read them, beads of sweat formed on his brow. He felt the buzzing start in his ears and his head began to pound along his scar. Thoughts refused to form; they simply fell out of his head. He could see the numbers on the pages (so many pages) but he couldn't make sense of them. He massaged his scar as he sat back in his chair.

Kingsley quickly walked to the credenza that held a selection of fine liquors, a coffee maker with those tiny self-contained plastic cups for single-servings of espresso or other fancy coffee, and a pitcher of water. She poured Sean a glass of water, set it before him and asked if he'd like something stronger.

"Just water," he said in a feeble voice. Why hadn't he waited to see his aunt's lawyer until late this afternoon when Savannah or CJ could come? He hadn't given much thought to this whole process. He'd barely registered that Regan was sick before she was dead. Then at the wake and the funeral, he learned that Regan was an engaging woman so different than the one he'd known. She was funny and kind. She could hold her own with the powerful and she had an intense sense of justice—plus she worked pro bono for scores of women with domestic violence matters. And now her best friend was telling him (and showing him proof) of how she loved him, and how generous and thoughtful about him she was. For decades, Regan had been committed to his future.

Can you feel the loss for a love you never realized you had? Sean could see how much the secrets had hurt Regan too. He took a few deep breaths trying to will those damn tears not to fall for if he let his grief loose, who knew when he could corral it again. Finally, he looked up at Kingsley but no words formed.

"It is quite a sizable sum, Dr. Thomas. I can understand your shock. As the trust grew over the years, Regan hired an accountant to ensure that you would not be penalized with any tax consequences once you began managing it yourself. The name of the accountant is included among those papers. I've told him of our planned meeting today. He will be out of town for the holidays but he'll be happy to meet with you in the new year. He's assured me that all tax liabilities are current and that everything associated with this trust continues to be in order so there is no rush. He also informed me that Regan paid a generous retainer for his services to you for the next five years, out of her own funds. Of course, you can choose any accountant you like as well, but Damon Courtney is at your service, not only regarding the trust but for any business, investment, or tax matters that interest you as well."

"You said something about a house?" Sean said in a stronger voice, changing the subject.

"Yes. The house," Kingsley said taking a deep breath. She walked back to her credenza, placed one of those tiny cups in the coffee machine, pressed the button, and filled the room with the soothing aroma of coffee. She offered Sean a cup but he refused knowing water was the only thing his stomach could handle. Her discomfort unnerved him but he waited quietly while she prepared her coffee. Once in hand, she sat on the chair next to him instead of returning to her red leather chair across the desk.

"The house," she took another deep breath while again inspecting her impeccable manicure. "In Spokane," another breath. "Regan agonized over it for years. After she got a few of your things while you were in the hospital, she never returned to it. She couldn't bear it." Kingsley paused again and Sean guessed she was remembering conversations she and Regan must have had. Sean could see that his family's secrets even affected Regan's friend. Kingsley continued, "After the deaths, she hired a company to clean up and make the house presentable. She had planned to sell it but no buyer wanted to have a house where murders happened."

Sean winced when she said *murders*. She placed a hand on his arm, apologized, and continued, "Finally, she hired a caretaker who lives in a small cottage on the property. He has kept the grounds in order and the main house painted and maintained. Regan had hoped that after time passed and memories faded, the house might sell. It is a large, well-designed house on quite a few acres of property just outside of town. Under any other circumstances, it would have easily sold. Periodically she would list it again with a real estate agent. At one point in the 90s, she had a few interested buyers but as soon as the murders were disclosed, as the law had once required, the deals fell through. She gave up. That house haunted her even from hundreds of miles away," Kingsley paused again and Sean could see Regan's pain in Kingsley's eyes when she looked up at him and said, "She'd always hoped to put the proceeds of the sale into your trust account."

"When Regan bought our house here," Sean remembered, "I asked when I could go home. Regan said I'd never go to that house again. After that, I blocked it out, along with everything else eventually. It hurt too much to think about it. It never occurred to me that the house was mine."

"She didn't want you to have to ever go back to that house. She said she could only imagine what you'd remember if you went there. Her thoughts, her memories, haunted her and she didn't want anything to haunt you. She said to tell you she's sorry for what this house might do to you. But as your mother's only surviving heir, the property is yours," Kingsley said reaching for another large manila envelope on her desk. Sean opened it and saw real estate flyers that had been used over the years with photos of the house that had once been his home. There was also a piece of paper with the caretaker's photo and information on it, and a smaller white envelope with a set of keys.

"All your family's belongings are still in the house," Kingsley said. "The caretaker keeps all the furniture covered with sheets, except when the house was on the market. I have contacted him and he will have everything clean and tidy for you when, and if, you want to see it."

Sean sat wordlessly looking at the flyers with the photos of his home and memories washed over him. One flyer had multiple photos of the outbuildings, the wooded property, the cliff that his mother was afraid he'd fall from, and the main house with its various rooms. The house was large enough that all the kids had their own rooms. When he saw the photo of his bedroom, a memory flashed of playing Army on the rug next to his bed with Daniel's old collection of soldiers. He remembered his dad insisting that the little green plastic men posed with rifles pointing outward were the Marines, not Army (*Marines were the bravest of all soldiers,* his dad would declare). Sean was grateful for a good first memory of that house.

When he saw the photo of Colleen's room, he remembered hearing her yell for their mother's help when Daniel was taking too long in the bathroom they shared. Then he saw the wooden play set his grandfather had built for him in the back yard. In the photo, it still looked as massive as it felt when he was five. It was his club house, his private kingdom. He marveled at the workmanship of it, especially the large room built on top of a tall platform that he could climb up to with either the knotted rope or the wooden ladder. The room was big enough for even Daniel to stand up in. It had a shingled peaked roof, a Dutch door, and two windows (no glass). Sean remembered the time he and three friends camped overnight in it. Daniel slept in a tent on the ground nearby, just in case. It was a place where Sean could take refuge on days he was alone with his parents and they would start arguing. On those days, he pretended he was a brave Marine and fantasized that he would one day rescue his mother.

A single tear slid down his cheek.

Kingsley put her hand on his arm again and said, "I know this is a lot to take in, but we're not finished quite yet."

"What else could there be?"

"Regan's will. All that I've shown you so far is what was yours all along. But you are Regan's sole heir as well. And though she's made some charitable bequests, the bulk of her estate will go to you. Regan did very well professionally and she also did well in her personal investments. She would often comment that her father would have been so proud of her. From her descriptions and stories of him, I think they were very alike in temperament and interests. And they both were interested in making money, and lots of it, in the stock market," Kingsley said as she reached for the final large manila envelope left on her desk.

She pulled out a document that Sean could see was only a few paragraphs long and other papers he recognized as an automobile title and property deeds. As Kingsley began to read Regan's will, Sean felt overwhelmed by death, memories, and money. It took all of his self-control to stay present when the buzzing began again in his ears. His limbs felt like lead and the room had closed down so completely that when he looked up, all he could really see was Kingsley's head. There he saw her lips moving and knew she was reading all the particulars of Regan's will, but the words wouldn't register. He heard them as if she was talking to him under water.

Shit. Shit. Shit. He felt like he was going crazy again. What kind of weak son-of-a-bitch was he? If this was what it was like to be a Gallagher, he'd prefer to stay who he'd been.

Finally, Kingsley's body's movement and a tinkling sound shook him out of his fugue state. She had shaken out four sets of keys from the envelope she held. Sean heard her say that two sets belonged to Regan's new car (she traded in every year), one set was for her vacation home in Hawaii, and the final set was for her house in Seattle.

That morning when Sean awoke he was a doctor who still went by the name of Sean Patrick Thomas. He owned a small, but tasteful apartment in walking distance from his work and so had no need for a car.

By lunchtime he was a wealthy man with one more legal name, three more houses (all furnished), a fancy foreign car, a hefty trust account, a large inheritance, and (of all things) an accountant on retainer. It was enough to make anyone feel at least a little crazy.

Sean-Patrick Thomas *Gallagher* was a man who didn't know his own identity, who didn't know the true nature of the woman who'd raised him, and who didn't yet know where he fit into the family he'd always fantasized about. But this Gallagher guy . . . he sure had a lot of stuff.

Kingsley broke into his reverie by touching his arm again. "This is all so much to take in. I know you will have many questions in the days to come. Let's plan to meet again in a few days. I will call you."

Sean nodded, gathered everything she'd given him, and walked out of Kingsley Strickland's office feeling like he'd been run over by a Mack truck. He texted *when can we meet?* to both Savannah and CJ as he walked toward the stairs. By the time he was on the sidewalk, texts confirmed their plans for dinner. Sean's treat. He breathed in the cold foggy air, walked up the hill to the hospital, and slipped into Michael's room. His favorite place for a trip to the other realm.

CHAPTER 27

SEATTLE NOW | 2013

WHEN SEAN ARRIVED IN MICHAEL'S ROOM with his regular offering of coffee he was surprised to see Anna alone. "Good morning," he said as he scanned the room looking for the Judge in his usual place.

Anna sighed before saying, "He's gone back to Spokane to spend some time with our other daughter and her children. Waiting for Michael to wake up, it seems, has become too great a burden for him. It reminds him of his biggest failure."

"I'm sorry," Sean said as he gave Anna her coffee.

"I understand it," Anna said even though the sadness in her tone revealed her hurt. "I really do," she continued. "It's been weeks now and while Michael's tests show that his brain swelling is gone, he still hasn't awakened. We just don't know if he ever will," she said with a tone of resignation in her voice as she reached out to touch Michael's hand.

Sean wished he could do more to give Anna hope. Michael was breathing on his own since the second week of December and his brain scans didn't reveal a reason for his continued unconsciousness. But there was so much they didn't know about how the brain works. It wasn't the first time doctors couldn't explain what was happening. Even with a month's worth of healing, it was hard to know what more Michael would need to awaken. Sean's visits to the other realm hadn't revealed anything about Michael's choice. And it had been more than a week since Sean told Michael he was glad he had chosen to live, but still nothing. Sean wondered if Michael still didn't feel safe. Yet he didn't know what it would take to give that to Michael.

Sean pulled up a chair and sat next to the bed on Michael's left with Anna sitting in her usual chair to his right. Sean no longer checked the boy's vitals because they had been stable since he was extubated. All Sean had to go on now was his intuition and that was telling him Michael would not die.

"I've been doing a little research about Michael's rehabilitation prospects," Sean began.

"Do you really think he'll wake up?" Anna said with that same haunted look Sean remembered from the first time they met.

"I do Anna. I don't know why it hasn't happened yet but my gut tells me it *will* happen," Sean said before explaining more about his experience with waking up when he was Michael's age, a memory he'd just recovered the day before in a marathon session with CJ. He also shared more about what was going on for him when he would visit the other realm. He'd finally had the courage to tell Anna about it the day after Regan died. Much to his relief, Anna didn't act like Sean was crazy at all. In fact, she said she was jealous and hoped she would be able to access that realm too since it would be such a blessing to see her daughter and granddaughter again.

"Is Michael there, in the other realm?" Anna asked as she reached out to smooth away the hair that had grown so long that it was brushing against Michael's closed eyes

"Faith said he is, though I haven't seen him," Sean said as he took Michael's hand and cradled it between his. When he did, he thought he felt a twitch in Michael's fingers. Sean bolted upright.

"What is it?" Anna asked.

"I think he moved his fingers."

Anna leaned over Michael, picked up his other hand and held it to her heart. She stroked his face and pleaded with him, "Wake up my sweet boy. Please wake up. I will protect you."

Michael let out a little moan as his head lolled from side to side. Anna reached behind him, putting her arms around his shoulders to hold him in a protective embrace. She said, "Nana's here baby. Nana's here," as she began to sing the song that by now had become so familiar to Sean. He watched Michael's body relax into his grandmother's arms. There was something in that song. Faith had told him ages ago that Michael liked it when Anna sang it to him. Now that melody was calling Michael fully back into his little body and into the loving arms that held him. Anna's eyes were closed. It was as if she needed all her energy to project her love and protection into the melody she sang. She didn't notice when Michael opened his eyes, which were now looking directly into Sean's eyes, the hint of a smile on Michael's face.

"Anna," Sean whispered, afraid that the sound of his voice might break the spell and send Michael back into his closed shell. Anna opened her eyes to look at Sean and he nodded toward Michael just as Michael moved to put one arm around his grandmother to embrace her in return. Sean thought for a moment that Anna might faint, but instead she sat on Michael's bed, pulled his whole body onto her lap, buried her face into his hair and cried.

"Don't cry Nana. I'm ok," were Michael's first words. Then he looked at Sean and said, "Hello, Dr. Sean."

"Hey Buddy. Good to see you awake now," Sean said. He sat perfectly still, not wanting to do or say anything that could frighten Michael. "You were there with Faith when I visited, weren't you?"

Michael nodded. Anna squeezed Michael again and said, "It's a Christmas miracle."

Michael looked at his grandmother and said, "I'm hungry."

"Do you like ice cream?" Sean asked remembering how comforting it had been for him as a child. When Michael nodded, Sean asked what flavor before leaving the room with a promise of finding the best ice cream in Seattle.

On his way out, he stopped by the nurses' station to report what was going on so they could call the doctor. Then he texted Savannah and CJ. They'd all been waiting for this moment for so long. Now that it was here, it felt surreal. And unsettling. He hoped the cold air outside would help him think.

✑

When Savannah and CJ arrived, Sean was alone in Michael's room. He told them Michael was in the bowels of the cavernous hospital having one test after another, no doubt a little excitement for a Christmas Eve crew. And Anna, after promising to keep Michael safe, would not let him out of her sight. Wherever he was taken, she would be with him. No doctor or anyone else would prevent that.

Sean explained to them what he knew so far. He seemed especially pleased that, after his nasogastric feeding tube was removed, Michael enjoyed a few bites of the ice cream Sean found. Savannah knew how much Sean loved ice cream and she wondered if that was what he wanted when he awoke here in this same hospital when he was a child.

Sean had told them that the Judge missed all the excitement. Savannah wondered if Judge Powell even knew yet since he was hundreds of miles away. Noting the timing of everything, she was curious about what might happen when the Judge returned. But that was a worry for another day. Today was all about the miracle of awakening.

It had taken her and CJ nearly forty minutes to get to the hospital with all the holiday traffic. She had the day off because she would work a double on Christmas day and CJ had been with her at Geneviève's house. They had all planned to have dinner together there with the rest of Savannah's family. CJ insisted that he would do the shopping and cooking as his gift. It was going to be an early dinner so that Savannah's nieces and nephews could open presents before Sean and Savannah returned to Michael's room that evening with small gifts for Michael and the Powells.

Sean offered to go to the hospital alone after dinner since Savannah would be working a double shift on Christmas but she insisted on coming too. Anna Powell wasn't work because she was more than a client. She didn't presume friendship with Anna but she was drawn to her. If she'd met her outside of the hospital, they could have easily become friends. Savannah also wanted to come for Michael. She recognized that Michael was the catalyst for Sean's healing and she was so grateful. She felt the least she could do was be there, especially knowing now that Anna was alone in Seattle. Savannah had just finished that thought when the door opened. A beaming Anna pushed a wheelchair holding Michael. Savannah smiled. Anna wouldn't even let anyone else push Michael's wheelchair; hospital protocols be damned.

When Michael was settled again in his bed Anna introduced Savannah and CJ, who both stood at what Savannah thought was a safe distance. As strangers, Savannah was surprised that Michael was smiling at them. He looked back and forth between Savannah and CJ and said, "I know you." Then he looked at his grandmother and whispered loudly in that sweet way that children do, "They've been here with you a lot Nana. Faith told me it was okay to like them because they were nice to you."

Savannah stepped just a bit closer before sitting on a chair next to the bed. She now was at Michael's eye level. She was careful not to move too close to him before she asked, "Is Faith here with you now?"

Michael nodded and pointed to a spot just to the right of his grandmother. "She promised to stay with me if I wanted to come back," Michael said. Then he turned to his grandmother and said, "Nana, I'm tired."

"Of course you are baby. It's been a big day," she said. As Savannah watched Anna put Michael's bed down and tuck him in, she mused that Anna's beaming smile might be so bright that Michael would have trouble sleeping. Anna sat next to the boy, held his hand and told him she would be right there when he woke. Savannah wasn't surprised at all when Michael nodded off almost instantly.

Anna told them that so far all of the tests were coming back as normal. Even his weakness was normal after lying in bed for a month. She couldn't stop saying what a miracle it was.

"It is indeed a miracle," CJ agreed. "God knows we've been praying for one. And what better way to celebrate it than with the food we were preparing at your mother's house, Savannah."

"Oh, right. Dinner. I almost forgot," Savannah said.

Patting his hands on his midsection, CJ said with a smile, "This tummy never forgets. Let's do this. I will stay here with Anna to pray in thanksgiving and you two skedaddle back to Geneviève's to finish cooking. Then when dinner is done and the presents are opened, you come back here just as you'd planned before with enough food for me, Anna, and Michael to have a proper celebration."

When Sean objected saying he'd stay, CJ insisted. Michael needed the rest and Anna needed the prayer. Savannah knew he was right so she put her arm around Sean and said her mother was so excited to have him again for Christmas Eve dinner. When she promised they would return by 7pm, Sean agreed to leave.

Once in the car, Sean confessed that he wasn't sure how much more of this emotional rollercoaster he could take. He was thrilled that Michael was back he said, but then he worried about what would happen next?

"If Michael goes home to Spokane, what will I do? I'm still on medical leave and he has been the one constant for me in all this craziness."

Savannah tried to hide her irritation at that comment. Michael was the constant? Really? Just Michael? Savannah decided not to say anything but Sean must have felt her energy.

"What?" he said.

"Nothing."

"*What?*"

"It's nothing," Savannah said again. Tension grew in the silence. She didn't want to ruin this moment or the holiday. The only way past it was through it. She pulled the car over, turned off the engine and looked at him.

"You're right. There is something," she began. "I once loved you with every bit of my being and you shut me out."

"I know. I'm so sorry," Sean interrupted.

Savannah held up her hand and said, "Let me finish." She continued, "I have felt a real connection between us in these last few weeks. I haven't wanted to because I was scared that you would shut me out again. And I didn't know, I still don't know, if I could survive that a second time. Yet the truth is, when I left I didn't stop loving you. Anna challenged me to give in to that love for you if I thought we had a chance. But you give me mixed messages. I want to love you Sean. But I also need to know that you can trust me enough to love me back. I can't be the only one trying in this relationship."

Tears welled in Savannah's eyes. She knew that Sean was on shaky emotional ground and adding her fears to the mix might push him—and the potential for them—into oblivion. But she had to be honest with him. She couldn't push aside her feelings. She had to trust that he was making enough headway in his healing to hear her truth too.

"I do love you Savannah. I have always loved you."

"If that is true, then why would you say Michael has been the one constant for you over this last month?"

"I didn't mean he was the only constant. It's just that he's been the one thing I can hold on to that reminds me of what I have always been. A doctor. A man who knows what he knows."

"What *do* you know Sean?"

"Honestly Savannah, the only thing I know at this point is that I love you. Everything, everything else about my life is a mess. What kind of life can I give you when I don't know who I am or what I'm supposed to do? I'm still on medical leave and I don't know when that will end so am I really a doctor? My name isn't Sean Thomas yet I don't know who Sean-Patrick Thomas Gallagher is. I never really knew the woman who raised me. I don't know my family. I don't even know who my father really is." Sean's voice was rising with each thing he didn't know and Savannah could see the panic behind his eyes that he was working so hard to control.

"I don't need you to give me anything," she said with her voice matching the intensity of his. Then she softened, "The only thing I want from you is that you don't shut me out so that we can figure out all the rest together. If you love me, don't shut me out." All her anger had dissipated and she reached for his hand.

Sean took her hand and pulled her into a full embrace. He kissed her with a passion that made her shudder. Then he pulled back from her just enough to look into her eyes. She could see so many emotions in his gaze— his confusion, his fear, his love—as he said, "I have loved you from the moment I saw you, Savannah Santiago. And I loved you so much that I couldn't bear it if I hurt you. I never hit you but I hurt you in other ways and I will be sorry forever for that. I have never stopped loving you. And I promise you with my life that I won't ever shut you out again."

CHAPTER 28

SEATTLE NOW | 2013

"**HOW DID THE REST OF THE HOLIDAY** go for you," CJ asked once Sean was settled in his chair.

Sean wondered if all of CJ's other clients preferred the same chair; the one that gave a clear view of Lake Union. Sean guessed that looking out that window had a calming effect on just about everyone. Even on a gray day like this, there were boats on the water and every now and then, a seaplane landed. When the sun broke through the clouds, the way it shimmered on the water was mesmerizing.

"I went to Cate's for dinner on Christmas Day. I met her husband, Karl. He's a graduate assistant at UW. For his PhD, he's studying the effects of trauma on the brain. He wondered if you knew about the different energy therapies they're studying like somatic experiencing or EFT. When he watched me meet Cate's mother, he thought I might benefit from them."

"I do know those therapies, and yes, they could be helpful in your situation. Now that you have more information and more context about your family, it could be very helpful," CJ said as he scribbled a note to himself. When he looked back at Sean he asked, "What happened when you met your Aunt Brigid?"

"Nothing extraordinary. At least not for me anymore. Seeing her again, I began to remember more of my past and I just shut down. I excused myself, went to the bathroom and did the breathing exercises you taught me. But I suddenly felt exhausted. I stayed about a half hour more and then had to go home. My aunt asked for my phone number so she could be in touch. I gave it to her but now I'm terrified she will actually call me sometime. What am I supposed to say? How am I supposed to get to know these people when

243

being near them brings up confused emotions? I texted Savannah when I got to my place. She called to reassure me and even stopped by on her way home. But Jesus, CJ. Michael seems to be doing better than I am and he's only six. How do I make this stop? How do I become a normal person who can work, and be strong enough to be in a real relationship? I don't want to be a burden to Savannah. And I really do want to meet the rest of my family. But right now, everything, even getting up in the morning, feels like exhausting work."

"You have grief upon grief you're dealing with Sean. Your exhaustion is normal."

"Is feeling completely overwhelmed all the time normal? Cause if it is, then fuck normal. Fuck it all."

"Have you noticed that you're not shutting down now? It sounds like you're very angry and that is understandable. Anger used to shut you down but you're not shutting down now. That's progress," CJ assured.

"I get the connection. It's because I trust you. But that's not enough. It's not fast enough. I want a life again. I want to work again. I want to be a strong partner to the woman I love and I want to feel everything that goes with that. I can't stand this weakness. I hate it. I would say that I hate me except that I have no idea now who I am so there is no *me* to hate. I have no center. If I didn't have you and Savannah, I think I would just float away and disappear."

"How would that feel, do you think, to just disappear?"

"Like complete failure. When I let Savannah go before, I felt so isolated. Not being able to love her like I wanted has been my biggest failure so far. I can't fail at that again CJ. I want to love Savannah. I want a family of my own with children and the white picket fence and the soccer games and all the domestic trappings I can grab. I'm so close I can actually feel it in my bones sometimes. And then I hear that Michael will be sent home to Spokane in a couple of days because he's making such quick progress, or my aunt says she'd like to call me so she can get to know me better and I just shut down. I promised Savannah I wouldn't shut her out again. But that won't matter if life itself shuts me down. There has to be something in here," Sean said pointing to his head and then his heart, "to keep me right here, right now, where her love is."

"Ah, Michael's going home," CJ repeated. "What about that do you think makes you shut down?"

"Visiting him is the only thing that makes me feel competent. I know I'm not his doctor, but even as Regan was dying, I would find some time to research rehabilitation options for him. It turns out that he's doing great physically so there won't be too much there to worry about; a few balance issues and strengthening. Nothing out of the ordinary. He's making a remarkable recovery, miraculous really. I know Anna will do everything necessary to get him what he needs. But I worry. When the Judge came back yesterday, Michael seemed off. A little scared maybe. What if Anna can't be what Michael needs? What if . . ." Sean stopped talking mid-sentence. He began to rub his throat trying to release the huge lump that prevented any more words from coming and forced his breath to make a rasping sound. His hands started to buzz and his arms felt like lead.

CJ rolled his chair closer to Sean, put his hand on Sean's arm. "Look at me Sean," he said. When Sean complied, CJ continued. "Breathe with me," he said as he took a long deep breath in, held it for a moment, and then slowly let it exhale. They did this together until Sean felt his body and his mind calm. Sean turned his gaze out to the water.

"What were you feeling just then," CJ asked gently.

"Panic."

"For Michael or for yourself?"

"I'm not sure."

"What if you were to guess," CJ probed.

"Me, I guess," Sean said as he looked back at CJ. "Me as a kid. And me now."

"Can you locate on your body where you're feeling this feeling?"

"In my chest."

"Good," CJ reassured. "Now what would happen if you focused your attention right in that spot in your chest?"

Sean looked at CJ as if he'd just said, you have two heads. Which would have made about as much sense as focusing his attention on his panic. But he had promised CJ that he'd trust him. He knew logically he was safe in this room with this wise and gentle priest. But that isn't how his body felt. A part of him wondered if he would implode if he focused on his panic. Trusting CJ had worked before so Sean closed his eyes and turned his attention to the black hole in his chest, for that is how he imagined it. A black hole that was sucking his very existence into itself. In the far distance, beyond the buzzing that had suspended most of his hearing, he could make out CJ's deep breathing and he tried to mirror it. As he did, the black hole became smaller and smaller. The buzzing in his ears quieted. He felt his heart rhythm slow. He consciously continued to breathe in and out. A sense of peace washed over him.

Sean opened his eyes and said, "I'm still here."

"Indeed you are," CJ said with the familiar smile that lit his eyes. "How do you feel now?"

"Honestly, just a bit triumphant," Sean said, embarrassed to admit that such a simple thing as focusing on an emotion that had settled in his body could cause him to be proud of himself.

"Good. What you just did was no small feat. It took a great deal of courage and it showed how much you're willing to be in a true relationship. Many folks never achieve that in this life because it demands vulnerability. You trusted me. And you trusted yourself," CJ said with a tone that Sean assumed a father would use when he was proud of his son.

"I know the progress feels slow, Sean," CJ continued. "But look what you've already accomplished. You're remembering new information on your own, and yes, sometimes you shut down but you don't faint now. You have allowed yourself to be vulnerable with me, with Savannah, and with Regan. You opened your heart and forgave Regan when you recognized her pain and understood how much she needed you. You have true empathy and compassion for Michael and Anna, and even for the Judge. You are honestly grieving for the losses you have suffered, and that's not even the whole list of accomplishments in the last month," CJ said as he ticked off each item on his fingers.

"Those caring ways of being are the essence of who you are," he continued. "They didn't change because you now remember the horrific deaths of your family or your full name. The compassionate, caring, connected boy I remember from when you were in high school is the same man you are now. Only now you are also a human being who has the courage to feel fully. In opening yourself up, old hurts and memories surfaced at the same time you're grieving. All your pain is coming at once. But I guarantee that your good feelings are there too and will now be able to soar to heights you could not have even imagined before. The wall you removed protecting you from your hurt feelings is the same wall that kept you separate from the love you wanted. With that wall down, anything is possible now."

Sean smiled. CJ was right. He had accomplished a great deal. But he knew he still had a long way to go. "How long?"

"What?"

"How long before I get the good stuff?"

"That all depends on how you choose to look at things," CJ said. "We will add some other therapies. These can help ease and integrate the traumatic memories of the truly awful things you suffered as a child which are so present now because of Michael. That should help with the feelings of panic. For the love, you just need to be fearless enough to accept it from all those who are offering it."

Sean was ready to have some of those good feelings, especially with Savannah. "When can we start with the other therapies?"

CJ took a moment to answer, obviously thinking. "How would you feel about going to a retreat house in Idaho? It's an old cabin on a lake that was donated to us years ago. We go there when we need a bit of time away in the healing embrace of God's natural beauty. We could leave on Sunday and spend up to a week there. It is very rustic up there and it will be cold this time of year. But we could move through this work together without any distractions."

"I'm game," Sean said. "I want this over as soon as possible. I want my life back."

CHAPTER 29

SEATTLE NOW | 2013

FRIDAY DECEMBER 27 5:15 PM SEAN/SAVANNAH

THE KNOCK AT THE DOOR startled Sean. He didn't expect Savannah for nearly an hour. She didn't text saying she'd gotten off early but he was glad for the extra time with her. He'd invited her to dinner to tell her that he would be away for the New Year with CJ for a week of intensive therapy. He was both excited and terrified about it, but he needed it. Even with the information he'd learned from Regan and Colleen, and from his Aunt Brigid, there was still a nagging hole that he wanted filled. He had the outlines of his story, but he guessed that the hole contained *his* memories of that fateful day. He was sure it was his anticipation of climbing in with both feet that made him jumpy.

"You're early," he said as he opened the door expecting to see Savannah. Instead, it was a ragged old man who reeked of alcohol.

"You recognize me," the man said with certainty. Sean nodded and the man pushed forward into the room, uninvited. Sean wasn't nearly ready to do this now. But the words to object simply wouldn't form. His heart was beating so loud that Sean was sure his uncle could hear it.

"I heard my wife was dead," Brendan slurred after he sat down. "It figures she'd find one more way to hurt me before flying off to hell."

"Why are you here?"

"Why not? I'm your father, right?" Brendan answered. "Besides, I needed to know what lies Regan told so I can set you straight. I have suffered my whole life because of the lies that bitch forced on me. And now it's all for nothing. Who the hell do you think you are? All my sisters can do now is talk about when they will meet you. And I want to know if you're going to tell them I knew you were alive all along. You can't do that to me. Don't you think I've suffered enough?"

249

Sean's head was spinning; his thoughts unfocused. He stared at this angry, drunken man unable to speak. Brendan stood and grabbed Sean's shirt.

"Goddamn it, answer me."

Sean could smell the whiskey. It smelled like danger.

"What the fuck is wrong with you," Brendan demanded. "What kind of sissy are you? What did she do to you that you can't even talk to your old man?"

Sean saw darkness close in around Brendan's head as his body began to collapse in slow motion. When he hit the floor, he felt no impact. By the time the last vestiges of light turned off, Sean heard his uncle say "Fuck!" before the door to his apartment slammed. Then the darkness was complete.

"Oh my God. Sean! What happened?"

Sean could hear Savannah's voice and could feel her touch, but everything was an impenetrable blackness. He let Savannah help him up to the couch.

"Call CJ," he said. "Tell him I can't see."

"You can't see? What happened Sean? I should call 911. Maybe you had a stroke or something."

"No," Sean practically shouted. "Just call CJ. I need him. Only him."

"Sean, please."

"Just do it."

❧

When CJ arrived, Savannah was grateful that he was able to convince Sean to get checked out. Sean refused to go to emergency because he said he knew why this had all happened, although he wouldn't tell either of them what it was. He let CJ call Kenji who wanted to see Sean right away but Sean insisted on waiting for the morning. He said maybe it would all blow over by then. Kenji reminded Sean that it was Friday; he and his wife had a weekend getaway planned. If he didn't see Sean tonight, someone else would have to see him tomorrow or he'd have to wait until Tuesday.

Savannah knew Sean was stubborn enough to wait until Tuesday. He had gotten so used to fainting and headaches and panic attacks that she wasn't sure he was considering all the real possibilities. His body was definitely screaming out for help and while Savannah understood all the emotional causes stressing him, she couldn't be sure there wasn't something physical going on too.

Savannah could tell Sean was angry. Everything about him, his voice, his posture, his silence spoke of the anger—and the fear— he was so obviously trying to keep in check. But Savannah was angry too. And worried. What if it was a stroke? Or something worse. By refusing to see a doctor tonight, Sean could be throwing away their future together. If there even was one. When Sean refused to talk to her before CJ arrived she felt that same old feeling of being shut out that caused her to walk away before. She thought they were making progress, that they had a chance. But now this.

When CJ arrived, he told Savannah about the intensive therapy he and Sean were planning. But this set-back tonight convinced him that they were going too fast. CJ told Sean he wouldn't take him out to the lake house in North Idaho, so far from medical treatment, until he knew for sure that Sean's blindness was solely a traumatic reaction. CJ said he could deal with that, but if a medical reason was behind it, they all needed to know what it was. CJ would reschedule their time away after Kenji's assurances of no underlying illness. Until then, they would wait.

Savannah was relieved that CJ was being cautious. She wanted to confide her worries and hurts to CJ too. But she set that aside for the immediate concerns about Sean's health tonight—and through the rest of the weekend. CJ told her he'd stay with Sean to watch over him. He would call her first thing in the morning to let her know how Sean was doing and then they could work out the rest of the weekend as it unfolded. CJ said that perhaps Sean would be better in the morning. He suggested they plan to have brunch together and Savannah was relieved when Sean agreed to it.

When she went to kiss Sean goodbye, she felt how tense his body was. He didn't relax when she held him and he only grunted when she said she'd see him tomorrow. Savannah immediately realized that maybe Sean wouldn't be able to *see* her, or anyone else, in the morning.

When Savannah hugged CJ goodbye, it reminded her of her father. Her father could always read her mind when she was upset. Could CJ too? Could he read her worry that she and Sean were back at square one again? Or that Sean would never be well enough for them to have a future together? Or the thoughts telling her she was a fool for trusting Sean again? When CJ released her, they locked eyes. She didn't bother to wipe the tears that had begun to fall as he held her. CJ reached out once more and put his hand on Savannah's head to pray over her, to bless her, to let her know that she wasn't alone in all this.

"Sleep well, Savannah dear," he told her. "All will be well. All will be well."

Savannah suddenly had the urge to see Anna. Then she would go stay the night at her mother's house. With that thought, compassion immediately replaced her anger. Sean never had a place to be safe, to gather broken pieces and put them back together. Something awful happened before she arrived and shutting down was his only way to cope with it. He wasn't shutting her out; he was protecting himself in the only way he knew how. If he was brave enough to find a new way with CJ's help, she was brave enough to love him through it. Only then would she really be able to expect more from him. He was determined to move beyond his past. And she was determined to be there when he found his way out.

She said a silent prayer promising herself, and Sean, that she would fearlessly love him. She would become that safe space where he could always put the pieces back together. How can anyone who has been wounded as deeply as Sean fully heal without that? She knew from her own experience that healing from trauma or grief was not a straight road. Or an easy one. Especially when you had to heal both at the same time. Sean's road at this moment was so dark, literally and figuratively. The constancy of her love would be the light she could give him to pierce the darkness. She knew he would reach for it again. And again. And again. She would be there no matter how many times he needed it. She told him the other day that she didn't need him to give her anything, she just needed him not to shut her out. Now she would have to prove her love didn't come with any conditions.

She turned away from the door and went back to Sean. She sat next to him, held his hand and said, "I love you, Sean . . . Nothing today changes that. I will always be here for you. Always." She leaned over and kissed him. He kissed her back, at first tentatively and then with what she felt was gratitude. He put his arms around her and held her tight, as if he were holding on to life itself. "Thank you," was all he said before letting her go.

When she got to the door, she looked back at CJ. He nodded and blew her a kiss. He was making the sign of the cross in the air as she turned to walk out the door.

Chapter 30

Spokane Now | 2014

"Welcome my sons," the elderly Jesuit said as he warmly embraced first CJ and then Sean. CJ knew how Stephen struggled to move. He must have been waiting near the door for them since it opened almost immediately.

Father Stephen had been CJ's mentor when he entered the order. Now, at ninety-four he was finally "retired" though he spent his mornings in prayer and his afternoons dictating his nineteenth and twentieth books to one of the novices. He used to do all his own writing but when his eyesight deteriorated so that even with a large screen on his computer, he couldn't see what he was doing, he accepted help. The last CJ heard, book nineteen would be published in the spring so CJ was sure book twenty was not far behind.

Stephen was anxious to get them done. He'd once said God told him when he was a young man that he would author twenty books. At his ninety-second birthday party, he was already anxious to "go home" but said since he was still alive, God must be waiting for him to finish the books. Back then, CJ had assisted Stephen with drafting the outlines for a trilogy of books with the underlying theme of wholeness. Book one on truth was completed within a year and sold well. CJ had no doubt that book two on forgiveness and book three on healing would also do well.

Insights from the first two books of the trilogy had helped CJ help Sean so he was grateful to have been able to read an advance copy of the book on forgiveness. CJ was sure that the book on healing would be just as useful and hoped some of its wisdom would be available during this short visit.

CJ had a dual purpose in bringing Sean to Ignatius House in Spokane before heading out to the lake. One was to have Sean spend a little time with Stephen—who was always a balm for any soul. The other was to ask his brother Jesuits to participate in a healing ritual for Sean, led (of course) by Stephen. CJ wasn't taking any chances with Sean's healing. Kenji found no medical cause for Sean's continuing blindness so healing would require every measure, both spiritual and psychological, that CJ could throw at it.

Despite being legally blind, Stephen knew every inch of the home he'd lived in for the last twenty-seven years. He looped his arm through Sean's and led him toward the dining room chatting with the kind of small-talk reserved for new acquaintances: the weather on the pass, the weather reports for the cabin, and whether Sean had packed an extra pair of socks to wear in bed at night. CJ watched with bemused awe as Stephen's kindly welcome visibly relaxed Sean and steadied his unsure gait in unfamiliar surroundings.

Luscious smells of soup and bread filled the house and CJ was pleased that lunch had been held for them. The dining room was, as usual, simple yet elegant (beauty, to Jesuits, was an essential moral good). A linen cloth graced the long table, the one used when guests were expected and CJ smiled when he saw that the table was not set just for him and Sean. Everyone had waited to dine with them. Stephen led Sean to a chair, then sat next to him and began expounding on the rewards and challenges of the cabin in winter as other Jesuits appeared, each one hugging CJ in greeting.

Once they had been served, CJ appreciated how his brother Jesuits were consistently able to take simple ingredients to create a meal that satisfied all the senses. The bread was crusty and warm, filling the room with a sweet yeasty aroma. The soup was hearty with complex flavors, and felt like silk on the tongue. Even the presentation of the dark soup paired with the golden yellow bread and three different colored cheeses on simple white porcelain dishes created a peaceful tableau worthy of a fine watercolor painting. CJ was disappointed that Sean couldn't see how lovely everything looked, so he casually described the scene during his thank-you to their hosts.

CJ could see by the tentativeness in Sean's movements that he was self-conscious about how he would look while eating. Stephen, though he couldn't see an eagle if it landed on his nose, must have noticed it too. CJ wondered if Stephen could actually feel Sean's energy with his whole being. He watched as Stephen leaned close, touched Sean's arm and whispered something in his ear that made Sean chuckle. Sean's shoulders dropped and his arms and hands relaxed. Stephen placed his arm right next to Sean's nudging ever so slightly until Sean's hand grazed his silverware. CJ knew that this tiny bit of physical contact would further soothe Sean as it unobtrusively helped him find his tableware. Stephen then cleared his throat and everyone quieted.

"God within us, around us, and through us: we give thanks for the gracious gift of this food," Stephen began the blessing. "We pray that you bestow your grace and mercy upon all those whose hands toiled to bring it to our table this day. We are grateful for our brother CJ who has traveled so far to be in our company and for our guest, Sean, whose heart holds all the wisdom and all the love he seeks. May this food nourish us all as we prepare to nourish the Spirit of our brother Sean. Amen." With a smile, he then said, "Dig in boys."

The conversation over lunch was lively. CJ kept the mood light by asking for updates from each of the men. At the end of the meal, CJ thanked them for their hospitality before turning to Stephen saying, "Is everything prepared?" Stephen nodded and said, "In the chapel." CJ then said, "For all of you who will join us in a healing ritual prepared by Stephen for my dear friend Sean, please meet us in the chapel in ten minutes." The men rose, taking dishes from the table as they left and in less than a minute, the table was cleared. Stephen, CJ, and Sean remained seated, quiet throughout the bustle. When everyone was gone, Stephen placed his hand on Sean's and asked, "Are you ready son?"

Sean nodded. He had told CJ on the drive to Spokane that he would be open to anything if it meant his sight would return but he confessed misgivings about a healing ritual. CJ assured Sean that a healing ritual couldn't be any stranger for him than the visits he took to the other realm. And who knew, maybe some of what he experienced in those other realms would connect to what they were about to do. CJ was certain that the more Sean opened himself to mysteries that had no bases in the familiar—not in science nor in the world as we think we know it—the more Sean would heal. Sean had agreed that the ritual was unlikely to deepen his darkness so he had nothing to lose.

෴

After the ritual was complete, CJ decided it would be best to wait until morning to get up to the lake. They would stay overnight at Ignatius House since, as CJ said, the overcast sky was already giving up the scant light it held and darkness was settling on them. And from all he'd heard so far, the darkness in Spokane was nothing compared to the wild darkness that would envelop the lake. Not that it mattered to Sean, but it did matter to CJ. Stephen was thrilled. He said he could experiment on Sean (with his permission, of course) with a new ritual he was writing about for his book.

Sean had taken an instant liking to Stephen (as he insisted on being called saying that whole *Father* thing was a bit too clerical for him). The old man was an irreverent radical of sorts whom Sean could tell, even without the benefit of eyesight, was eternally young. He could feel Stephen's impish smile and twinkling eyes that were almost as sightless as his own.

Stephen took Sean to the in-home library of Ignatius House while CJ and the other Jesuits readied two guest rooms for them. During their time alone, Sean had asked Stephen if he missed his sight, especially since he needed so much help writing his books. Sean was surprised when Stephen emphatically said no. His blindness, he said, was a gift to be savored. It helped him experience the world with other senses that he'd never fully developed while sighted.

"Of course, I miss a bit of my independence," Stephen admitted. "But at 94, I've gone everywhere I wanted to go and done all the things I wanted to do out there," he said. Sean could hear the swish of his shirt as he moved his arm. Stephen continued, "And inside my home here, I get around fine so my independent movement is more or less intact. The loss was gradual so I had time to get used to it. And what I've gotten in return is so precious that it was worth the trade. I had to become humble enough to accept help for simple things like preparing food and maintaining shelter. Plus, I think my journey into darkness has brought a whole new—and necessary—level of understanding and insight to my writing."

"How do you mean?"

"Well, for one thing, my physical blindness eliminates distractions," Stephen began. "Those distractions kept me blind to so many other things. Not just the insights that arise only in darkness, but the workings of my other senses as well. For example, I'd like you to tell me what room we're in right now."

"But I've never been here before and you know I can't see anything," Sean protested. "How can I know what room we are in?"

"Your mind is so focused on what you can't see that you haven't noticed what you can," Stephen said with such gentleness that Sean didn't take it as a rebuke. It was a simple truth.

"How can I learn then to see again?"

"It is a simple process of letting go. Let go of what you think you know and reach for the Light that is always there. In that Light, you will always find your answers."

Both men were silent and Sean noticed that it was not an uncomfortable silence. He thought about the *letting go* that he'd experienced lately. Letting go of his anger and resentment of Regan, letting go of his job, letting go of his fear of hurting Savannah, of his fear of being fully known. It was hard to do. Risky even. But in many ways, he was better for it, even if he didn't have control over any of the circumstances that had him here, blind now. He couldn't imagine living the remainder of his life without his eyesight but perhaps the only way to get it back was to let go of his *need* to see. Maybe there was a gift in the darkness for him, as there had been for Stephen. With his visits to the other realm, Sean knew there was so much he didn't yet understand. Not just about his life but about the Light that Stephen sees.

"Can you help me see the Light you see?"

"You already know how. All I can help you learn is how to pay attention."

"Teach me," Sean said with an urgency that he didn't mean to betray. "Please."

"Let's start with something easy," Stephen said placing his hand over Sean's. Stephen's hand was alive with warmth and Sean felt a slight electrical current in it. Stephen spoke again saying, "Close your eyes and breathe deliberately." Sean mimicked Stephen's breathing and closed his eyes even though leaving them open would have meant nothing. Sean relaxed into the moment and felt quite peaceful. Stephen's voice was low and inviting when he spoke again.

"Tell me what you hear."

Sean focused his attention and then said, "I hear the ticking of a clock, perhaps a very old clock," Sean began. "And distant sounds; the murmur of conversations in another part of the house, the low rumble of a train outside, music playing somewhere."

"Excellent," Stephen praised. "Now what do you smell?"

Sean concentrated hard, breathing deeply again only this time paying attention. He rose from the chair. He walked toward the musty smell that drew him to shelves behind him. He reached his hand out to touch what he knew would be there. "Books. I smell books." He slid his fingers across shelves above and below him. "Lots of books."

"Ah, good. Then tell me, what room are we in?"

"The library, of course."

"Of course," Stephen repeated. "And you knew it when we arrived, you simply hadn't paid attention. Did you notice that you needed no assistance finding your way to the books behind you? When you pay attention, you can navigate even without the help of your eyes."

Sean stood still *feeling* the space he was in. He listened again and walked to the clock. He felt the massive wood carvings on its sides and could hear the slight hum of the moving gears. He stood still once more, listening. He walked to a window feeling the cold glass. The distant rumble of the train registered a minute vibration on the glass, making him smile. With his hand still on the glass, he went over his movements in his mind. He turned toward where he believed was the center of the room. He couldn't locate it on his body but he sensed what he could only describe as energy. It was just strong enough to register something in him. He focused on it, put a hand out ahead of him and walked straight to the chair next to Stephen. When he sat down back in the place he'd started, Stephen said, "You felt me, didn't you?"

"I did." Sean said with a twinge of amazement. He was getting used to not understanding these woo-woo experiences that were becoming a new normal for him. At least this time, he was awake, conscious, and focused. But feeling someone's energy? The scientist in him called it whack-a-doodle-world. Yet as he and Stephen talked about it, Sean realized he'd been feeling energy for years. He hadn't put those words to it, but it was what made him a good doctor. Rose called him intuitive. But it was all the same stuff. As Regan died, he could feel her hurt, loneliness, and sadness. Maybe he could since he was a child but he'd let his anger cloud it for so long. He felt Michael's indecision; it wasn't just buried memories of his own experience. It was Michael's thoughts, his being. He realized today, in talking to Stephen that he'd been afraid to really pay attention. Afraid of what would happen when he did. But now he knew the price of not paying attention.

Being with Stephen felt like coming home to himself. The self that would have developed naturally had his life been different. The hours Sean spent with Stephen felt as if they'd passed in the blink of an eye but also lasted into eternity. He was not uncomfortable with that sensation but curious about the contradiction it posed.

As he reflected on it, he realized his life was full of many similar contradictions. For a man so desirous of certainty, so intent on having his questions answered, contradiction had never fit comfortably within him. Perhaps if he could use this time in darkness to reflect on contradiction and mystery, some light might appear. He had spent so much time in his life afraid of what he didn't know.

Before he met Stephen, his biggest fear was not knowing if his physical sight would ever return. But being with Stephen helped him accept that the loss of his outer sight could not compare to the loss of his inner sight. Sean was determined to use this time in darkness to cultivate and nurture the inner sight that came so naturally to Stephen and gave him such great peace.

Stephen believed his blindness was a gift that opened him to seeing in better, truer ways. Given the circumstances, Sean had every reason to explore that territory now.

CHAPTER 31

NORTH IDAHO NOW | 2014

SEAN HAD TAKEN HIS TIME this morning reflecting on his nighttime experiences and had just begun to share them with CJ when the phone rang. Sean hadn't had the chance to tell CJ about the nightmare he had or about the odd experience that had preceded it around 3:00am. When he first awoke, Sean thought the timing of his dream and his other-worldly experience had to do with the fact that it was the anniversary of his family's deaths. As the phone rang, his intuition told it may have more to do with a more recent one.

CJ immediately passed the phone to Sean. It was Cate calling to tell Sean she'd found Brendan dead on the porch swing at Regan's house early that morning. She said a neighbor had called her concerned because it was so cold out and the neighbor was sure she saw someone sleeping on the porch. It was an occasional problem in a neighborhood so close to downtown. Homeless folks sometimes wandered onto porches to find a safe place to sleep—though usually not in the dead of winter.

When Cate went to investigate, she found their uncle dead, holding an empty whisky bottle to his chest almost the same way their grandfather had held his rosary beads in the coffin after his death when Cate was small. Cate said she wasn't terribly surprised. No one had heard from Brendan since just after he'd visited Sean, the visit that plunged Sean into darkness. Soon after, Brendan went to Cate's mother's house drunk and ranting about what Regan had done to him. And then he was gone.

He'd been on benders before but they could see he was unravelling fast. And they all knew that one day it would end as it had this morning. Cate apologized for interrupting Sean's retreat, but since he now owned the house, she figured she'd call him before the police did. She wanted him to hear it first from family. Despite all the other news, Sean smiled at that word. He was glad to have Cate as family.

When the phone call ended, Sean sat in a stunned silence. CJ put a hand on Sean's shoulder and asked Sean what he wanted to do. Sean said he didn't know. By the time the police called, Sean had decided he should go back to Seattle. The sergeant said his statement over the phone was fine but Sean wanted to go back. It was time. Brendan's death made Sean realize that he couldn't avoid the realities, or the difficulties, of his life. He couldn't, he wouldn't, throw away the precious gift of his life.

As of today, he'd had twenty-eight years of life that his mother, his brother, and his sister didn't get. His father took those lives and threw away his own. His uncle took all those twenty-eight years to finish throwing away his life. And for all those years Regan rejected love, so in essence threw away her life too. That was enough destruction for any family. Sean was determined to live his life fully with all the love he could give and get. Sight or no sight, his life was worth living. It didn't escape his notice that his life transformed more than once in the shadow of death. But death wasn't the enemy. The enemy was refusing to live life, no matter how broken or wounded it might be.

CJ spent the morning cleaning-up the cabin before contacting the local caretaker to winterize it knowing no one else would visit again until spring. Sean was relieved that he had a few hours alone to put his thoughts in order before attempting to articulate them. He and CJ were mostly silent on the drive to Spokane to get a flight to Seattle (CJ would leave his car at the Jesuit house). Finally, on the plane, CJ said to Sean, "You've been so quiet all the way here. Is there anything you want to talk about?"

"I had a dream about Brendan last night," Sean said. "More like a nightmare really. Both the man with the red hair, who I now know is Jack Gallagher, and Brendan were there. They were having a vicious argument about who was my father. Jack, who always had a gun in all my dreams, pointed the gun at Brendan and then he pointed it at me. He kept going back and forth threating to shoot us both. Brendan kept antagonizing him, making him angrier and angrier. It reminded me of the screaming I heard as a little boy on this very same day."

"Were you a boy in the dream?"

"No, I was as I am now."

"Were you blind?"

Sean shook his head. He was about to add that he did have his sight momentarily last night but decided against it. He was blind now, just like he'd been the day before and the day before that and for so many weeks now.

"What happened then?" CJ asked.

"I noticed my mother and Regan huddled in a corner. They were clinging to each other and then began screaming *NO* at my uncle who had pulled out a knife. I couldn't tell if he was threatening me or my father; if he was going to save me or kill me. I knew I couldn't wait any longer to find out because one of them would surely kill me. I figured the gun was more dangerous than the knife so I rushed Jack and fought him for the gun. When it went off, I woke up. I don't know who, if anyone was hit. Then we got the call this morning that Brendan was dead." In telling CJ this dream, Sean realized that this time when the gun went off, the muzzle flash was different. He had forgotten until now that the flash didn't terrify him like it always had before. It seared him. It had energy in it and it made him feel strong.

"Is that the first time you ever fought for your life in these dreams?"

"It was. But there's more," Sean said.

"In the dream, I wasn't blind. I could see everything clearly. But before I had the dream, I awoke somewhere around 3:00am and I could see then too, even in the darkness of my room. I could also smell something burning, something smoky-sweet. The smell was familiar, but I couldn't place it and I had no idea where it was coming from. I was so focused on the origin of the smell that I forgot that I'd been blind for weeks now. Seeing had been so normal that in the disorientation of awakening to this beautiful smell, I forgot about my sight."

"But it didn't stay? You can't see now?"

"It stayed for a time. Long enough for me to search my room and then walk down the hall towards the living room. The smell became less strong there but the sight of the living room bathed in moonlight jarred me. It was then I remembered I hadn't been able to see. I needed to see if it was real so I went out the front door and looked up to see a million pinpoints of light piercing the black sky. I saw the shadows of lodge-pole pines making a jagged edge between heaven and earth. A comet streaked across the sky." Sean fell silent remembering the wonderful sights.

"I had forgotten how beautiful the sky could be. How wonderful seeing could be," he began again. "It felt as if I'd been lost all this time in a desert and seeing the sky was like taking a long, cool drink of water. I was so grateful. I savored every point of light and felt what I can only describe as ecstasy at seeing the moon's reflection shimmering on the lake that I had only been able to smell since arriving. I could see the ice forming at the edges of the lake and it sparkled like diamonds. I have no idea how long the moment lasted. It was kind of like being with Stephen when time sort of stands still but is simultaneously eternal."

CJ laughed and said, "I know exactly what you mean." He let silence sit between them for a few moments before asking Sean to continue his story.

"I thought I caught a whiff of the strange smell coming from behind me, back toward the cabin. As I looked over my shoulder, I could see the edges of my sight turning dark again. Funny thing is, I didn't feel desperate. I felt grateful so I whispered a "thank you" to whomever or whatever put all those stars in that endless sky. The dark edges expanded slowly, closing over my eyes again like the shutter of a camera as I slipped back into the house. Once inside, the fragrance that apparently had no physical cause became stronger with each step I took. It guided me back to my room."

"You never found a source for the fragrance?"

Sean shook his head and said even after reflecting on it for hours, he couldn't quite place what the fragrance reminded him of. But it comforted him. It made him feel at peace.

"What a lovely gift," CJ said. "Stephen would surely enjoy hearing that story."

"I'll tell him when I come back to Spokane for Brendan's funeral." The tone of CJ's *oh* spoke volumes. Sean shrugged and continued. "I promised myself this morning I would live my life fully. That means getting to know this family I've longed for. These aren't the perfect circumstances to do it, but I've learned those only exist in our idea of life, not in life itself."

Sean closed his eyes. He needed a few moments of quiet to prepare to meet Savannah who was picking them up at the airport. When he told her why they were coming home, she didn't ask about his sight. He knew she would stand by him blind or not, but their lives together would be so different than he'd dreamed about before. Yet he was at peace with it. This whole time away, both with Stephen and at the cabin with CJ, hadn't restored his sight but it had restored something Sean hadn't even known was missing. He could now understand why men became monks. Without the distractions of the outside world, there was time for reflection. For understanding. For letting go. For peace.

CJ had created an even rhythm for their hours together, starting and ending their days with prayer that was nothing like any prayer he'd ever experienced before. It wasn't rote words but expansive feelings, ideas, silences, and music all taking turns to connect him to something at once beyond and within him.

CJ's wise nonjudgmental counsel and his probing questions made Sean simultaneously uncomfortable and grateful as they dredged up old hurts and angers that found a voice and often forgiveness (more often than he could have imagined before). Their shared meals and woodland walks were sensory experiences that made Sean feel a part of something mysterious with power that could heal in ways he knew all his medical training could not touch. He felt a sense of belonging within a profoundly wonderful universe and that had given him access to a well of courage. He was amazed that he could accept the return of his blindness without anxiety.

He still hoped that he would not remain blind forever but for the present moment, his blindness was a gift to be savored and cherished. It was giving him the time he needed to reach back into the past and recover the little boy that existed before the events of this day in 1986.

Sean settled into the quiet within himself, remembering the last bit of his nighttime wanderings. He had returned to his bed and just before sleep embraced him once again, he heard a voice say "I am here." He startled, sat up, opened his eyes and saw nothing. "CJ?" he softly called, listening in the intense way he'd learned from Stephen. He heard the rustle of a breeze through the pines outside, the faint ticking of a clock in the living room, and the gentle rumble of CJ's snore in a room down the hall.

The source of the sound was as mysterious as the source of the smoky-sweet fragrance that he had originally awakened to; it was still present, but much less intense. Sean remembered the overwhelming sense of joy he felt in experiencing these things and wondered what context to give them now. Was the fragrance and the voice evidence of spiritual movement in him? Just prior to falling asleep again last night, Sean remembered a scripture passage about the call of Samuel that CJ recently read to him and Sean whispered into the darkness, "Speak Lord, your servant is listening." Then he fell into a deep sleep and dreamt his searing dream. And now, both men in the dream were dead. What was he to make of it? And what was he to make of the peace he felt? Was it a coincidence that he felt such peace both before and after he knew Brendan died?

This morning, before Cate's call, Sean believed he could meet with Brendan again and be okay. He thought it would be a way to complete his healing and maybe then his eyes would see again. As he reflected on all this, he hoped he could hold onto the peace he felt right now. And he was willing, perhaps even eager, to accept his new situation and experience what would come to him as he opened himself to listen with his whole being.

"Do you smell that?" Sean asked CJ. That smoky-sweet fragrance was in the air, ever so faintly. But when CJ said *smell what?* Sean responded, "Nothing. It's nothing."

He leaned back, closed his eyes and smiled. The fragrance was his and his alone. Then he waited. Something good was going to happen.

∞

"Hello son," Quinn said.

"Mom! I've been waiting for you. Why has it taken so long for you to come?"

"I have been with you always. You haven't seen me because you weren't ready. But please know my love is with you eternally. I'm so happy you've forgiven me enough to recognize me now."

"Forgiven you? Why did I need to forgive *you*? It was Jack and Brendan and Regan who were responsible."

"We were all responsible for the tragedy that you lived until now. But it was my choices, or lack thereof, that set into motion everything that happened to you and for that I am so very sorry. It is so much easier to see everything clearly from my perspective now. My weaknesses in life turned into tragedy because I couldn't see them. Since I couldn't, or wouldn't, see them or accept them, I couldn't prevent them from defining my life. Or more tragically, defining yours and Daniel's and Colleen's and Amie's." As she said each of their names, his siblings came into view.

"Amie? My twin?"

"Yes. Her death was the warning I didn't heed. I still wanted, and needed, the fairytale life. The one that didn't actually exist. And I also let my guilt about how you two were conceived get in way. I knew I had sinned—at least as I understood it then—and I was willing to be punished. I didn't understand that the Creator, who is only love, doesn't work that way."

Sean could feel his mother's pain. Did the pain of our mistakes last forever, he wondered? And as if on cue, his mother answered his unspoken question.

"Love is the only thing that is eternal. Neither our pain nor guilt last forever. It is only in telling you that I experience it again in this now. It is an experience I am willing to relive a thousand times if it helps you. I long ago forgave Jack and myself for our parts in our tragic dance. And now with Regan and Brendan here, I have offered forgiveness to them since they are able now to hear me."

"Help me understand so I can forgive completely too."

"It's not all that hard to understand really. When your father was missing, I was afraid and angry and hurt. I let those emotions, fueled by way too much wine, draw me into a liaison with your uncle. Then out of guilt, I made love to my husband before he was healed. The consequences of those two decisions—or the non-decision in falling into in a tryst with Brendan—laid the foundation for all the tragedy that followed. In the aftermath, the stress of Jack's paralysis and another pregnancy, caused your father's anger to mount. He pushed me the day your sister died and he pushed me again on the day you were born. I made excuses because I needed to believe it was out of character. I was vulnerable and scared. But then he pushed me again on your first birthday. That was too much and I knew I had to leave him. I'd called my parents but they were killed coming to rescue us. Guilt and fear overwhelmed me again. I stayed and I hid what was happening. I didn't trust those who could have helped me. I tried to go it alone and I lost all that was precious as a result."

Sean took all this in and sighed. "My father *was* Jack?"

"Yes. He was such a good man once but he let his demons own him. When I tried to leave him that last time, his demons and mine destroyed us all and for that I am eternally sorry."

Sean could feel the depth of his mother's sorrow and pain just like he had felt Regan's pain before she died. And in feeling it, he knew he had to forgive even if he didn't understand all the whys of his mother's actions. Actions that had affected everything about his life. But he could also feel the depth of his mother's love and there was no way he could block that by withholding forgiveness from her. He already remembered too much of her goodness and maybe it was her goodness residing all this time in his unconscious self that led him to Savannah.

In all his visits to the other realm, he could see and hear Faith, Colleen, and Lexi. And he could sense Michael there and sometimes hear his thoughts. The fragrance that awoke him must have come also from the other realm. And now, visiting with his mother, he added yet another sense. He could touch her, hold her, and feel her touch in return. She was as present and real to him as she'd once been. He held her and they both cried.

In her embrace, he recognized that only by fully waking up to the power of his unconscious self would allow him to change how he reacts to life. And he knew that his courage came from the love he was able to accept from Savannah and CJ.

What if that kind of love was never offered? What if it was offered but never accepted? He understood now how broken everyone could be and how that brokenness defined actions. How could he expect forgiveness in his brokenness unless he was willing to forgive the brokenness of others? And how could he remain angry with those who didn't experience the kind of love that gave the courage to face, and embrace, the demons that are calmed only in the Light of unconditional love. As he finished his thought, his mother stepped back slightly and continued.

"Facing our demons, facing our fears, as you have done, is life giving. Forgiving those of us who couldn't, is life affirming. I wish we could have been as strong as you have been. I wish I had awakened sooner, while I was still physically alive. You have chosen life, my son. And with that choice, you can heal not only yourself but so many who will cross your path." With that, his mother embraced him again and as she did he felt a surge go through him. He felt her love and so much more. He felt her story, her wisdom, her sorrow, and her truth. And he knew all of it had always been, and would always be, a part of him.

∞

CJ nudged Sean's shoulder after the plane touched down. Sean had fallen asleep. It took him a moment to remember where he was and why. He rubbed his face with both hands and turned toward CJ as he opened his eyes.

Sean gasped, "Oh my God, it's you!"

EPILOGUE

SPOKANE | 2050

MY CHILDREN ARE PLANNING a surprise retirement party for me at the annual Labor Day picnic but Savannah warned me about it. She knows I hate surprises. I won't let on though. I'll let the kids think they pulled one over on their dad. But I'm glad to know in advance. Even after all these years, I still need to prepare my soul for big gatherings. Besides, I'm not really retiring. I'll still be coming in a few times a week when Savannah and I aren't travelling. It took so much work getting this center off the ground and it still gives me such joy to be a part of real healing. And staying involved in it will keep me young.

When I opened the healing center here in Spokane more than thirty-five years ago, my colleagues in Seattle thought I was crazy and maybe I was a little. But after what I went through I knew I had to do it. All that money (and all those houses!) that came my way after Regan died had to be put to good use. What better way to honor my mother, brother, and sisters than to help others find the healing I had found. As a doctor I'd always wanted to relieve suffering. In this center, we do that using every medical, spiritual, and psychological tool available, whether ancient or new. Every part of our work is a sacred calling. We offer space—physically, emotionally, spiritually—to facilitate healing the whole person. We hope that our approach is an invitation to forgiveness and love. We also hope it is a catalyst for transformation, like the transformation I experienced.

And who could have imagined that the home that was witness to so much death and so much pain could also be transformed? But we didn't take any chances restoring this desecrated house. CJ and Stephen invited a sha-man from the Coeur d'Alene tribe and together they performed a whole set of traditional Catholic and ancient indigenous healing and cleansing rituals to re-sanctify the house and the land around it. We then hired an architect, Sandra Colfax, who was a friend of Stephen's. Stephen was Sandra's spiritual advisor and guided her through her own personal crisis, so Sandra immediately got it when we told her what we needed. She designed spaces that were perfect. We have small cozy rooms for therapy, medical consultation, and spiritual direction; large rooms for workshops and group gatherings; rooms designed specifically for working with traumatized children (our special focus) including rooms for art, music, theatre, and dance; and we included staff spaces that echo the comforts of home (self-care being critical to our work). Of course, there are work spaces to keep track of all that we are doing but there are also quiet spaces for rest, prayer and reflection, and a kitchen. Plus, there dining spaces for gatherings large and small.

Sandra also designed the stables for the horses, the riding ring and paths, and the home for Savannah, me, and our wonderful children. Savanah and I could have chosen any of the houses Regan had left me but after Brendan's funeral, I knew it would be Spokane. My family was in Spokane, my past was in Spokane; and my gut told me my future was there as well. The adjustment to being a part of this raucous clan (and this conservative city) challenged everything I'd learned from Stephen and CJ about forgiveness, love, and letting go. But if I was going to be able to heal in the way I knew I wanted, living love and forgiveness myself was the only way I could light the journey for others. I had to integrate all of my life, the darkness and the light, to complete my transformation. Once I'd unearthed all the horrors of my past, neither places nor people could trigger me any longer.

When we got the healing center functioning, CJ came onboard and brought the therapies that had helped me so much; the ones I never would have considered at the start of my medical career, the ones that became the foundation for the work we do here. Cate came after Savannah became pregnant with the triplets. This raised my esteem in my Aunt Brigid's eyes. She was thrilled that her baby came back to Spokane. Plus, Karl was part of that deal too and he became our research program director. Karl was the one who insisted on the horses; he and Cate were part of the planning even before joining us formally.

Savannah and I wasted no time getting married after my eyesight returned. We chose her name, Santiago, as our surname. Her dad was the man I wanted to emulate as a husband. I was a Gallagher, but I wanted to be different than the Gallagher men who had come before me. I wasn't embarrassed to be called a Gallagher, but since my past was forcing me to choose not just how I wanted to be named but how I wanted to *be*, I chose Santiago. I probably have the longest name in the medical register, Sean-Patrick Thomas Gallagher Santiago, but I like it. For me Santiago is synonymous with steadfast love. Bernardo gave it to Savannah. Savannah gave it to me. And I wanted to give it to my children and all my patients. Looking back, it was a great choice. Sean Santiago—husband, father, doctor, cousin, nephew. Everything I'd always wanted.

It's good to know that the practice will continue on with my children taking over. We never planned to make this a family business but I'm glad it worked out that way. Our eldest daughter, Aimee Catherine, oversees the whole operation. As the oldest, she's used to being in charge. Each one of the triplets (Dan, Gen, and Charlotte) went into a different facet of the healing work we do here. And our youngest, Stephanie Regan, has a head for numbers like nobody's business. She is absolutely amazing as our CFO.

The triplets run the clinic and most of its programs. Our son (Daniel Bernardo) and his wife Ella have practiced with me for five years. Dan is working as both a clinician and as a researcher with Karl to continue to quantify our successes with research that proves our methods work. Gen (Geneviève Colleen-triplet two) joined us three years ago following her residency in a sub-specialty that didn't even exist when Kenji or I were in school—a Medical Doctor/Doctor of Divinity in Reconciliation Medicine. I'd like to say that my experiences and the work Savannah and I did together at the beginning of our healing center had something to do with the growth of that specialty. I think it did in a small way. And Charlotte Quinn followed her mother into the more spiritual aspects of our work. From the very beginning, we could see she was an old soul. And maybe naming her in honor of CJ and my mother had something to do with that. As the youngest and the smallest of the triplets, she was also the most calm, patient, and serene. All qualities which make her an excellent chaplain and therapist.

Savannah and I were blessed with five children as living evidence of love, mercy, forgiveness, and hope. They have healed the "sins of the fathers" both medically and spiritually.

Before Michael, I was resigned to enduring my loneliness. Those years in Seattle—with Regan, in medical school and working in the emergency department, and in love with Savannah even as I pushed her away—seem like another life all together. It all began to change that day I saved Michael. And even though that act ushered in a time of intense pain, on the other side of that pain was joy I would have never thought possible. For me or for Michael. We saved each other.

The intersection of our lives became the catalyst for everything good that happened to me since then. If it weren't for him, Savannah might never have come back into my life and this healing work I've done for thirty-five years wouldn't have been born. And Michael, the first recipient of what this healing center could offer, remained close to us throughout his life. When Judge Powell died of heart failure (a broken heart?) just two years after Michael went to live with his grandparents, Anna bought three more horses for our program in honor of her daughter, Lexie, granddaughter, Faith, and husband, James. Michael had been coming to the horse-therapy summer camp since it first opened; he came first as a camper and then as a counselor as he got older. Once he was in high school, he added working in the stables after school. During college, and throughout veterinary school, he returned each summer to work with the horses. When he got his DVM, he told me I had to hire him full-time as our in-house vet and director of the horse therapy program. I agreed, of course.

But Michael didn't simply remain a patient, an employee, or even a close family friend. He is now my son-in-law and the father of two of my grandchildren. And if my instincts are correct, one of my surprises this weekend will be an announcement of another Brennan-Santiago grandchild coming my way. Michael and Aimee are seven years apart but they were best buddies when they were children. Aimee always loved working with the horses too, so she and Michael spent a lot of time together in the stables.

When Aimee was sixteen, Michael told me he would marry her one day. I laughed it off then because it seemed so implausible. By then Michael was a man and Aimee was still a child. And there was no romantic attraction from Aimee that I could see.

But when Aimee was eighteen, she confided in Savannah she would marry Michael one day. When she was twenty, they started dating. They became engaged during Aimee's senior year of college and they married the summer she graduated. Savannah and I had worried that Aimee was too young and inexperienced but Geneviève reminded us that she married Bernardo when she was that young and she never regretted it. Not for a moment.

Anna and Geneviève became fast friends when Geneviève moved into the cottage we built for her shortly after the triplets were born. They each volunteered for the Healing Center mostly by hosting parties, luncheons, and other events that got the word out about our work. Those events always resulted in donations to the *Lexie & Faith Foundation*, which provides grants to women or children recovering from domestic violence. It also hosts educational workshops for judges, prosecutors, and law enforcement officers who interact with families mired in domestic violence. Anna continued to lead her foundation and volunteer with us until she was eighty-five when she shifted her focus to her first greatgrandchild. When Geneviève died, Anna moved into her cottage to be closer to Michael, Aimee, and the kids. She's still going strong at ninety-five.

Anna's friendship and example were reminders of the life-giving power of forgiveness, hope, love, and conscious action. She and Geneviève anchored Savannah and me with emotional and spiritual support to face life head-on with all the joys and sorrows, routines and surprises, and challenges and triumphs it has to offer.

To remind us of the inherent brokenness and sacredness (the darkness and light) that is in all of us, we decided to use an acre of the property to create a family cemetery. That acre is away from all the activity and homes that make up our compound. It sits on the farthest southwest bluff overlooking a creek that flows hundreds of feet below. In the fall, the grasses are tall and golden and dance in the breezes that kick up just before the most spectacular sunsets. There are no headstones but there are benches for contemplation scattered among life-size sculptures done by a local artist. My parents, my siblings, Regan and Brendan are all here.

Everything and everyone is out in the open on that sacred field overlooking the bluff. Nothing is secret anymore.

Book Club Questions

1. Part 1 of the book is called "Sins of the Fathers" and contains the epigraph quote by William Faulkner "The past is never dead. It's not even the past." Do you agree with that idea? How does your past affect your present? Can your parent's mistakes haunt you?

2. Throughout Part 1 we get to know the characters from Sean's past. Who do you feel most compassion for and who do you blame the most (and why) —Jack, Quinn, Brendan, or Regan—for the tragedies that befell Sean?

3. The interplay between husbands and wives, fathers and daughters, and sibling rivalry each add some fuel to the ultimate tragedies. What is most toxic in each of those relationships and how does each contribute to the violence in the Gallagher and Brennan families?

4. Addiction also contributes to the eventual tragedies in both families. When is the right time, and what is the most effective way, to forgive an addict? When is it time to leave an addict?

5. Domestic violence affects all of the families in this book, except in Savannah's parents' marriage. What do you think is the most dangerous and damaging part of family violence?

6. Until Sean uncovers the whole truth about his family, he fears he will hurt Savannah and therefore can't open himself fully to her. Have you ever experienced a fear so strong that it prevented you from loving as you wanted?

7. Sean has mystical encounters with people who have died. Do you think such encounters are possible? Have you ever had an experience or encounter with someone who has died?

8. Do you think consciousness, or the soul, exists after we die?

9. Sean and Faith have discussions about Michael, who is hovering between life and death. Do you think people in the in-between state, like Michael was, have a choice and can decide to live or die?

10. Is death a fearsome event?

11. Part 2 of the book begins with a quote from the famous psychologist, Carl Jung: "One does not become enlightened by imagining figures of light, but by making the darkness conscious." Why is it important to make the darkness conscious? Do you know many people who are fully conscious and/or enlightened?

12. Forgiveness and love take centerstage in Part 2 of the book. Sean's decision to care for his aunt until she died was a surprise, given their history. What motivated him more, selfishness or compassion? Were you surprised he was able to give her the absolution she desperately wanted?

13. Sean realizes after Regan died that he never saw her as a complete human being, that his assessment of her was only relative to him. Do you think it's possible to see our parents (or parent figures) in their fullness?

14. When Sean encounters his Uncle Brendan, all his healing progress seems to be undone with the physical problem of blindness added in for good measure. Was the blindness a fear response or an invitation to deeper, fuller healing?

15. Savannah had a moment of clarity about the meaning of unconditional love, deciding to stick by Sean even as he seemed to be shutting her out again following Brendan's visit. How do you know when its right to stay in a relationship? Savannah stayed. Quinn stayed. Lexie stayed. But Savannah was the only one who made the correct decision. What made the difference?

16. When Sean had his mystical moment of clarity in the cabin in the woods and his eyesight momentarily returned, he seemed ready to accept all that had happened to him, even the return of his blindness. What do you think was the meaning of that moment of clarity? Why did his blindness return?

17. Sean's body seemed determined to raise all the issues from his past that he had to understand and/or forgive. Do you believe that the body holds memory from past events? Has your body's ache or pain triggered a memory for you or made you conscious of something that you were hiding from yourself?

18. Do we as individuals—and traditional medicine as a whole—miss opportunities to heal when we ignore the emotional or spiritual connections to dis-ease?

19. After Sean's mystical encounter with his mother, he is able to fully understand his past. As she speaks to him, he is also able to feel her emotions and experiences. Do you think it is possible to do something similar with those we love; to be able to be so compassionate that we feel as they feel from their interior space rather than through our own point-of-view?

20. Are there things that someone you love can do that are unforgivable? Is there a difference between forgiveness and setting a healthy boundary in a toxic relationship? What would each look like? How are each accomplished?

ACKNOWLEDGEMENTS

THANK YOU TO THE MANY FOLKS whose love and encouragement enabled me to write this story. Thanks especially to my husband Keene who encouraged me every step of the way, reading and commenting on every version and iteration of this story. He endlessly listened to my fears and triumphs. His love has lighted my way for decades and given me more joy than I knew was possible.

Thank you to my mother-in-law (and former schoolteacher), Dorothy Little whose edits and comments were so instructive. Her wisdom, calm, and love have been welcomed support throughout my adulthood.

A simple thank you is inadequate for my friend and superlative editor Judi Heidel, whose encouragement meant the world to me; her suggestions were spot on, as were those of my writer friends, Bill Ramshaw and Mindy S. Halleck. Thanks also to the group of early readers who helped me discern if the story hung together: Hannah Thomsen, Linda Grille, Valarie Groves, Cheri Tilford, and Mandy Collins.

Thanks also to my family: my parents Edward and Manuela, and my sisters Veronica, Valori, and Melissa; I began this life journey with you and have learned so much from you.

Special thanks also to my children and grandchildren: you inspire me, teach me, make me laugh, and give my life meaning.

Finally, thanks to all my in-laws who have exemplified so many varied good ways of being, some so very different from my own. Your love and lives are intertwined with mine in bonds of love that may stretch but will never break.

Familial love, like all love, is eternal.

ABOUT THE AUTHOR

BARBARA MULVEY LITTLE is a writer, editor, and certified spiritual director who volunteered with hospice volunteer for nearly a decade. This is her first novel.

Her other books include: *Scripture & Meditations for the Rosary*; *Opening Hearts: A Cardiovascular Surgeon Reflects on Faith, Healing, Love & the Meaning of Life* with Lester R. Sauvage, MD; and a contribution to the anthology *Three Minus One: Stories of Parent's Love & Loss*.

Her children's book, *The Hermit Crab Shuffle*, is currently in production.